The shini…
of this bo…
Look for…
romance. …
quality an…

PRAISE FOR LINDA CAJIO'S *COLORADO GOLD*:

COLORADO GOLD GLITTERS WITH HUMOR, RICH CHARACTERIZATION AND MAGIC. THIS STORY WILL GRAB YOUR HEART AND WON'T LET GO. A STUNNING DEBUT!

—Constance O'Day-Flannery

MAGICAL, FUNNY, WARM AND WITTY . . . *COLORADO GOLD* IS A DAZZLING HISTORICAL DEBUT FROM A BEST-LOVED CONTEMPORARY AUTHOR. RUN, DON'T WALK FOR THIS ONE.

—Colleen Quinn, author of *Unveiled*

LINDA [CAJIO] SKILLFULLY CAPTURES YOUR ATTENTION IN THIS DEBUT WESTERN WITH A STORY FILLED WITH HUMOR, ADVENTURE AND ROMANCE. HER MEMORABLE HEROINE WILL KEEP THE PAGES TURNING. I HOPE IT IS THE FIRST IN A LONG LINE TO COME.

—Judy Spagnola
Area Manager, Reader's Market

LINDA CAJIO

COLORADO GOLD

ZEBRA BOOKS
KENSINGTON PUBLISHING CORP.

ZEBRA BOOKS are published by

Kensington Publishing Corp.
475 Park Avenue South
New York, NY 10016

First Printing: August, 1993

Printed in the United States of America

My heartfelt gratitude goes to Ann LaFarge, my editor, who said so many encouraging things about this first venture into bigger books, and to Adele Leone, my agent, who had tremendous faith and who still gets requests for manuscripts "like the Cajio book."

This book is dedicated to my support group, sensational writers and from whom I learned so much. I've got the popcorn ready!

Prologue

1864

The gunshot came from nowhere, the report exploding like cannon fire on the Antietam battleground.

Otis Wainwright sawed on the reins as Noah the mule reared and bucked in complete panic. Behind him, Otis heard the crack of barrels smacking together inside the little wagon and cursed at the thought of his latest brew spilling open. He had a feeling he'd used too much turpentine in the mix, and it would rot through the wooden floor. His trade goods wouldn't be worth much, either. And his books!

Not the books, he prayed, as he finally brought Noah under control. A flash on his right, coming out of the copse of trees by the wagon-rut trail, caught his attention; he tensed, fearing Indians. The Cheyenne and Arapaho were raiding again, and the Santa Fe Trail in the Colorado Territory wasn't safe. If only the wagon train he'd been travelling with hadn't voted him out. He couldn't help it if the scout's best horse didn't take well to the Tincture of Wellington he'd brewed and had keeled over, hooves up.

The sun beat warm on him. The sky was a brilliant blue, the leaves a vivid green and the grasses stirred in the light breeze. This wasn't a good day to die, he decided.

But his heart stopped thumping when the threat turned out to be something less than Indians. He relaxed somewhat as he surveyed the dirty-looking creature before him. It was halfway between boy and man, no more than about thirteen years, Otis judged. A ragged hat was pulled low over the boy's eyes. However, the revolver in the lad's small hands stared back at Otis like a deadly eye. An older girl, her eyes seeming to stare at nothing, stood next to the desperado.

Otis had been to see the elephant and back again on several occasions as a "medicinal dispenser" in the territories, but in his fifty-two years he'd never seen a more unlikely pair of robbers—especially out in the middle of nowhere. He could smell the fear in the boy.

"Could you put that gun down, lad?" he asked, in his most persuasive voice. "I promise I won't hurt you."

Unfortunately, the boy held the damnable thing fairly steady, enough so he was bound to hit something. *More than likely me,* Otis thought.

"Nope," the boy replied. "Now git down offen that wagon, mister. Me and Harriet needs it."

The backwoods accent came through clearly. Otis was a connoisseur of accents. "You're a long way from home, lad. Where's your people?"

"My pa's dead." His voice was hard, and he jerked his head behind him toward the tree grove. "Cholera. It got everyone on the wagon train. 'Cept me and Harriet."

Otis sucked in his breath at the thought that he'd nearly blundered into the deadly disease. Cholera could flare up on the trail like a prairie wildfire. One minute all was calm and in the next the flames of death were consuming everything in sight. In the heat of summer, it spread even faster.

Looking at the scene before him, he had to admit his situation wasn't much improved. A child with a gun was like a rattlesnake with an extra set of fangs.

"We ain't got it, mister, if that's what you're worryin' about," the boy added disdainfully.

But they'd probably have it before the week was out, Otis thought, feeling sorry for the pair. They already had more sorrow than most, being orphaned like this. It wasn't the first time the Santa Fe Trail had revealed the horrors it could hold.

The boy went on. "My father made us go away from the camp . . . but he hasn't come for four days . . ." He let out a ragged gasp, the only sign of emotion, then straightened. "He was a captain with Jeb Stuart. He taught me to use this gun, and I will if you don't get down offen that wagon right now!"

"All right," Otis said soothingly, noticing the down-home accent wavered in and out. Wealthy, educated men had made up the confederate officer ranks, and he wondered how one of them got himself this hellfire issue. He decided he'd ask later—either of the child or of the Lord, depending on whether he managed to live through the next few minutes. He wound the reins around the brake handle, his movements slow and deliberate.

Out of the corner of his eye, he saw Noah trembling. The animal gave him an idea that might keep him from being left in the middle of Indian country. "Noah, there, is a really touchy mule. You have to handle him just right, otherwise he refuses to do anything for you and runs away. He can untie any knot known to man. Why, every morning it takes me three hours to catch him."

The boy's face fell. Otis smothered a smile.

"I tell you what," he said. "How about if I drive us to Fort Lyon, just to keep Noah under control for you. But you and the girl stay in the back of the wagon and don't touch anything. I don't want your cholera."

The boy was silent for a long moment.

"No tricks," he finally said, stretching out his arms and pointing the gun straight at Otis. "I'll be keeping this right on your back, mister."

"No tricks," Otis agreed, meaning it. "You and your sister can ride on the back board."

The boy nodded. Otis smothered another smile. It wasn't good for business to grin after a sucker took the bait. The boy had been easy to hoodwink, but Otis had to admit he'd had many years to perfect his techniques of persuasion, stock-in-trade for a medicinal dispenser.

Suddenly, the girl began to scream and struggle. "They're hurting Mama, Mary Alice! Make them stop! Make them stop! No! NO!"

Mary Alice?

The boy pulled the girl back against him, all the while saying in a soothing tone, "It's all right, Harriet. Mama's all right now. It's over."

"Who are you?" Otis leaned forward and peered intently, looking for signs of womanhood.

The gun was raised level with his eyes, the one hand wavering only slightly with the weight.

"Mary Alice Macaffee," the boy said. "And don't think I can't put a bullet between your eyes because I'm really a girl. I can shoot a squirrel at five hundred paces."

"I see." Otis was impressed with her masquerade. Mary Alice Macaffee was one fine actress. She'd completely fooled him, a professional in his own right, and he mentally tipped his hat to her. "I am a gentleman, Miss Mary Alice, and we have a gentlemen's agreement. I will hold to our bargain. What's wrong with the girl?"

"She watched Union soldiers kill our mother." Mary Alice Macaffee's voice was hard and cold. "And more."

Pity wasn't an emotion he felt often, but he felt it now as he watched her pat the still-frantic and gibbering Harriet on the back and say, "Harriet, Mama's with the beautiful angels, remember? And Papa's with her now. He wants us to go with the nice man. Remember, he said we should go on if he didn't come back. You wouldn't want Papa mad because you didn't listen?"

Harriet seemed to calm, although the vacant, unfocused expression in her eyes was somehow more frightening than her sudden outburst. The girl gave the other one a gentle push toward the wagon, then picked up a bundle from the ground.

"You can take some water from the water barrel on the right," Otis said. It was Noah's, and he supposed their using it wouldn't hurt the mule.

The girl nodded. "Thanks, mister."

This time he did tip his hat. "Otis Wainwright."

She smiled bitterly. "We'll use our own cups, Mr. Wainwright, so we don't have to touch any of yours."

"I appreciate that, Miss Mary Alice."

The sad pair walked to the back of the wagon, under the makeshift awning. Otis waited until they were settled before unwinding the reins. He slapped Noah on the back. "Giddup."

The wagon lurched forward, then settled into a slow pace, the wheels tracing the ruts made by thousands of wheels before them. Otis slapped the reins lightly again, trying to hurry Noah. If the girls were to be sick, he'd rather it be in Fort Lyon where they'd be out of his hands. They looked healthy enough—so far. Maybe they'd been lucky and missed catching the cholera. Their father had gotten them out of the camp when the disease started; it was possible that quick action would save them. Some just didn't get it, either. He supposed if they survived they'd go back east to family. If there was any.

Poor little ones, he thought. He'd had to do some harsh things in his life on the territories, but leaving children behind, even deadly sick ones, stuck in his craw.

"Miss Mary Alice," he called back. "That was the finest acting I've seen in a long time. I really thought you were a boy. I don't believe that's your normal talking voice, though."

"Maybe it's not," she replied cautiously. "My papa says I have a good ear for voices. He also said I spent too much time with the Perkinses. They were from Tennessee."

He could already hear the faint English tone of his own voice in hers. She was quick. Otis admitted a child like that would be a boon to a medicinal dispenser's business.

"I'm sorry about your father. And your mother. And your sister."

He could hear the smothering of tears.

"Have you people back home?" he asked over his shoulder, trying to distract her so she could regain her composure.

"No, they all . . . the war took them. It took everything." Mary Alice began to cry again, softly, and all the more painful to hear because it was so soft. Suddenly, she said, "Don't think I'm a baby, because I'm not. If you break our agreement, I'll shoot you before you can blink. No one and nothing is ever taking from me again!"

Otis sighed. She was something. Poor things, though. He knew what it was like to be alone; he had been since he was eleven and shipped to

America as a cabin boy. Bravado was the only way to keep safe. Still, the child had talent—talent that would be very advantageous to his business . . .

An idea formed in his mind. Otis grinned and flicked the reins a third time. "There's some brown bread back there in a tin. You two can have it."

Maybe he had another gentlemen's agreement for Mary Alice Macaffee.

If she survived to Fort Lyon.

Chapter One

1873

"Now then, Countess, how about my Molly's cookin'? Have ya ever tasted better?"

Countess Elizabeth Barrett Browning looked down at the pile of pale boiled ham and mustard greens and stifled a shudder. "It's lovely, Mayor Wilkens."

The entire town of Redback, Colorado, applauded boisterously. The Countess smiled and tried to ignore the wave of odor assaulting her nostrils. All one-hundred and thirty-two souls, even the Women's Christian Temperance Union, were jammed into the wooden saloon, the largest building in the town. Self-righteous matrons and immigrant miners lined the long, scarred bar and crowded against the dull brown plank walls, their faces alight with eager anticipation. They were all there to watch her eat.

Every town in the territories was the same and

yet it always amazed, the Countess thought. She had never understood the fascination with nobility, but it had served her extremely well for quite a while now.

The mayor's wife's chest puffed out with pride at the townspeople's reaction to her compliment. So did the mayor's. He looked like a prairie chicken in full mating season, his mayoral medal almost gleaming in the dim room. The man had the richest poke in Redback, and she'd better remember that. Even the smallest poke among the residents was huge, considering the town literally sat atop a gold mine. All that lovely money, and nowhere to take it. She would be happy to help them out with their little "problem."

The Countess drew in a deep breath and readied herself for yet another performance. One thing she did understand was a frontier town's starvation for respectability and entertainment. Her visit always provided both, and she was happy to do it. After all, she left towns richer in so many intangible ways and all she required was a little monetary assistance. Slowly, daintily, she cut several slices of the meat into bite-size pieces and forced herself to eat them with a studied deliberateness, laying her knife and fork properly on the upper edge of Mrs. Wilkens's "fine" china. She lightly patted her mouth with her napkin, then folded the square of yellowed linen and placed it back on her lap. She swallowed politely. The meat tasted worse than it looked.

"Look at them manners, Delbert Hasher!" one woman exclaimed. "Why, she could give lessons, and you ought to take 'em."

Everyone laughed nervously. The Countess smiled a gracious smile. "It's simply a matter of taking one's time with the meal. Savoring it, if you will."

People nodded in agreement. If they savored anything, it was probably a pious church service, followed by a hanging at high noon. The Countess turned her thoughts from the latter. It was never good to think about the consequences of her calling.

"It is very kind of you to take me in these few days, after I've lost my travelling party as I have," she said. "Have those men who went looking for them come back yet?"

Mayor Wilkens shook his head. "No. But don't you worry, they'll find them."

If they did, she was in big trouble, the Countess thought. "I'm sure they will."

"I'm just sorry we had to have supper here," Mrs. Wilkens said, sniffing disdainfully as she stared around the long room. "If people didn't insist on being nosey—"

"Now, Emily, the Countess don't mind." The mayor's voice carried loudly over the sudden undercurrent of grumblings. "Do you, Countess?"

The townspeople had insisted on having dinner with the guest, over Mrs. Wilkens's protestations. A fight had ensued, and Mrs. Wilkens lost the argument due to several guns being drawn on her.

The Countess smiled, thinking of the incident. Mrs. Wilkens's cooking would have improved greatly if they had shot her. "I have always enjoyed the pleasure of another's company with my evening meal."

Applause again burst out in the room. The Countess took it as her due.

"Sing something!" a voice cried.

The room went dead silent for one long, embarrassing moment. The mayor harrumphed and said, "She ain't no hurdy-gurdy girl, Billy. You ought to know better. I'm real sorry, Countess."

"It's quite all right," she assured him. The last town hadn't taken "no" for an answer, and she'd been forced to sing until midnight. Still, if they were entertained, they would be more amenable. She needed them to be very amenable.

Touching her black enamel and gold mourning ring, a fine plait of hair woven between the pearl beads, she paused long enough to bring tears welling in her eyes. Blotting at them with the napkin, she said, "Although I don't sing very well, I have written a poem . . . a tribute to my late husband. I did love him so, and the Lord took him and left me all alone in the world. I still grieve, you understand."

Everybody clucked understandingly.

"We would be honored if you would recite your poem, Countess," a voice said gently.

"After she's through eating," Mrs. Wilkens said forcefully.

Oh well, the Countess thought. She finished supper in record speed, knowing the faster she ate the less she tasted. She left a considerable portion on the plate, saying, "One does, you know." She rose from the chair. Being tall for a woman, she was able to see over a number of heads and felt in sufficient command of the situation. The moment she opened her mouth to begin, however, two men grabbed her by the arms and hoisted her onto the bar.

After a gasp of surprise, the Countess straightened the fashionable bird's nest hat perched atop her head and smoothed down the jacket and skirt of her grey wool travelling suit, the skirt pulled back fashionably in a swag over the bustle. She faced the crowd. They tensed in anticipation.

"How do I love thee," she intoned. *"Let me count the ways . . ."*

A chorus of ecstatic sighs rose to the rafters.

"I'm right sorry the boys couldn't find hide nor hair of your party, Countess," the mayor said the next morning at breakfast.

They weren't alone at the table. Joining them were the banker, the owner of the dry goods store, better known as the shebang, and the minister, all of them expansive and still eager to please. Mrs. Wilkens was better at eggs and bacon than supper, thank goodness.

"Oh, dear." The Countess made a moue of anxiety. "I wonder if they've gone to another town? Is there one close to here?"

"Blossom City, but it ain't near as fancy as Redback."

"Oh, dear." She paused for a moment, then

added, "Well, I see I have no choice but to go there. The stage arrives this morning, I believe?"

"Well . . . yes." The mayor was clearly reluctant to have their celebrity go, especially to a rival town.

"I hate to leave," she said, sighing unhappily. "But I do need to find my party. I have nothing but the clothes I'm wearing. Oh! How will I pay for the stage?"

Everyone spoke at once, offering to pay.

"All of you are knights in shining armor. But I couldn't allow it," the Countess said firmly.

They protested loudly.

"No. I couldn't possibly." She brightened and opened her reticule. "I do have a letter of credit from my bank . . . it is very vulgar of me to talk business, I know, but if I could write a bank draft . . . I would feel that I wasn't taking advantage of your generous hospitality. It's Bank of England, of course."

"Of course," the bank manager said, smiling. "You'll find us much more solvent than those back east. Why, soon, Jay Cooke'll be coming to Redback for money . . . and we won't be giving any to him!"

Everyone laughed at the reference to the post-war financial crash on Wall Street, spawned by railroad barons like Jay Cooke.

"Then, shall we say five hundred?" the Countess asked, taking out her papers. The banker faltered. She exuded regal expectation, as she added, "I do believe I ought to have enough funds with me, should my party not be in Blossom City and I must travel onward to Denver or even San Francisco . . ."

The banker just stared at her. She smiled understandingly and returned the little leather-bound book to her bag. "I suppose if it's difficult for you, Blossom City can accommodate me . . ."

"Oh, no," the banker said quickly. The others put away their murderous looks as he added, "Blossom City couldn't even fund our petty cash!"

She smiled widely. "Very good. Then after this wonderful breakfast, I will go with you to your bank."

The man brightened. "That'd be just fine, ma'am."

Two hours later, as the stage coach pulled out of town, the Countess Elizabeth Barrett Browning relaxed back in the cracked leather seats and mentally transformed herself into Mary Alice Macaffee.

She ignored the other couple, a squat, barrel-chested man and his tiny wife, seated across from her. They had been on the stage when it had come into Redback. Her work was already done, no need for more. Besides, they looked considerably poorer than the folks she'd just left—although she'd just helped them to catch up.

It had almost been too easy this time, she thought, her hands covering the reticule on her lap. The double eagles clinked satisfyingly inside the purse. The hidden coins felt heavy on her lap, and her fingers lovingly traced the bust of Lady Liberty through the cloth. She could feel the profile, the crown on Liberty's head and the tiny bumps of the stars edging the coin. Every one was nice and hard and golden. At the last minute, she had "changed" her mind and asked for a thousand, and the men had gone for it. She bet they never felt better about helping a damsel in distress, either.

Bless you, Otis, she thought, missing the old man who had taken her and her sister in and taught her so much. She had worked his medicine show as the "cured" patient, singing the man's praises to all who would hear. Then Otis had gone into the land-speculating business. That had been most profitable, although riskier. He'd died two years back—no miracle cure for a treacherous fall into a ravine.

Mary Alice squeezed her eyes tighter, holding back the moment of raw emotion. Her second family had been snatched from her in one misstep. The world took away everything she ever loved. She remembered the tea parties of her childhood, her mother beautiful and gracious and her father tall and proud. And an elder sister, laughing and mischievious . . . and sane. She had wanted for nothing, being gently spoiled and pampered and loved.

Then the war had come. Her father had gone in a blaze of glory and returned a broken man. He'd found only the burned and twisted spires of his home and his two half-starved children living in the only surviving outbuilding.

Memories pulled her deeper to the place of horror she kept secreted away. In her mind's eye, she could still see the men in blue uniforms holding her mother and Harriet down while one, then another, lay on top of them, pumping and hitting and laughing. There had only been time to hide her as the soldiers had ridden up the drive. She hadn't been hidden enough, Mary Alice thought. The visions and screams were burned into her brain. Her mother had been killed outright, and Harriet had been left for dead. It had been up to her to keep her and Harriet alive until her father returned. His attempt to give them a better life in New Mexico had died on a deserted prairie. Harriet's mind, damaged by a blow to the head that had nearly split her skull, had never recovered after that. And then Otis . . .

Mary Alice tightened her grip around the reticule. The world had taken everything from her. It always would. She had learned that lesson too well. Now she took from the world what it owed to her. Harriet was with nuns in St. Louis, receiving the best of care. Otis had found them years ago, when Harriet became more violent and could no longer be with them. It was costly, very costly, but it was all Mary Alice could give her sister now. She would wire the money from the next town and Harriet would be secure for ten months. She sent extra constantly so the nuns could set aside the money for Harriet's future.

The thought made her smile. "The Countess" had enabled her to provide ahead for several years worth of care for her sister. Just a little bit longer and she could "retire." The Countess had been scary at first, without Otis, but she almost enjoyed it now. And the towns she left behind had been happy—happy to have a visit from nobility to add to their prestige and satisfy their need for respectability; happy to have a break from the harsh living they endured and a reminder of the gentility to come; and happy to have been good samaritans. All in all, even they would have to admit it was a fair bargain.

Touching the pocket watch hidden on a chain under her jacket, she hoped her father would forgive her for what she was doing now and understand why she had to. Funny, she thought, remembering when he'd left them outside the wagon train camp. He'd told her the watch would bring her good luck. It didn't even work. Instead, she'd had to make her own luck in the world.

Exhaustion invaded her body, leaving her feeling limp and heavy-eyed. She sighed contentedly and promised herself that at the first rest stop she'd transfer the money to the waist belt she always wore. There hadn't been time before she'd left the town . . .

Mary Alice was jolted awake by two loud bangs. She realized she had actually dozed off, and then saw that the stage was slowing. She heard another bang and knew it for a rifle shot. A cry of pain immediately followed it. The coach stopped so abruptly she was almost thrown into the other couple. Fear was on their faces.

"What is it, Sam?" the woman whispered.

"It's all right," the man said, patting her hand.

Mary Alice wished someone would pat *her* hand. It might calm the sudden churning in her stomach. She pulled the shade over a little and peeked out.

"Hellfire," she said, shoving her reticule behind her back.

Masked men were riding up alongside the coach, guns and rifles trained on the driver seated above.

The stage was about to be robbed.

From his hunkered-down position in the rocks, U.S. Marshal Hudson "Hud" Jackson watched the scene unfolding below him.

The masked men surrounding the stage to Blossom City had effectively blocked it from escaping across the valley floor. He recognized Jimmy Winslow from his trademark bright-red bandana. The Winslows weren't a bad sort, but they had shot the lookout in the shoulder. Knowing the boys, that had been a stray shot not actually meant to hit someone. Now they were hustling the people out of the coach.

One man and two females. One of the women, clearly a wife, clung to the man. The other stood straight, all by herself. She was slim and tall, probably nearly to his eye-level, he bet. She was wearing some silly hat and a suit that didn't hide her curves. He admired them. Dark chestnut hair shone in the sunlight. There was something about her that struck deep inside him. He hoped none of the Winslow gang took a liking to her. That could be trouble.

Still, Hud made no move to stop the robbery.

There wasn't much one man could do—except get killed. The Territory didn't pay him enough for that. Neither would it do the law any good for bringing the Winslows to justice if he were dead. He'd come upon this holdup while on his mission to find who was selling guns to the Cheyenne, Pawnee, and Sioux. Guns were always being sold illegally, but he had a bad feeling about this one. He'd been hoping to get close enough to a town to get a posse together. If he showed himself now that was bound to start the shooting anyway. Instead, he was an eyewitness. Well worth the wait, he thought.

He hoped the people below would give the boys what they wanted with no fuss, then everyone would have a nice little robbery with no bloodshed. Well, just the lookout, but that was only a wound. The Winslows weren't above killing, but they preferred to leave scared witnesses who could talk them up with the newspapers. Every two-bit desperado wanted his name in the paper nowadays, or better still, to have a penny dreadful written about him. And nothing got written if there weren't people alive to tell the tale.

He made sure his revolver was loaded, then set it on the rock in front of him. He took out the last two bullets for his Winchester repeater and stared at them. He slipped them into the rifle chamber. He had no intention of using either, but cursed that he was low on ammunition. It was possible, though, for the Winslow boys to blunder right into him if they came this way after the robbery.

He touched the pocket watch hidden inside his

vest. He had another job to do, one charged to him from his brother long ago. He had to stay alive until he found the two men who'd left John for dead nine years ago, and deserted their mission to bring gold from California to further "The Cause."

Roger Ward and Cullen Macaffee. His job as a marshal had allowed him to track those men whose names were branded in his mind. And when he found them, he would kill them for John . . . and for the wife and children John had left behind.

Unfortunately, it was taking much longer than he'd thought. He'd find a bit of news here, some more there, but both men had eluded him so far, seeming to have vanished on the frontier. Finally, he had discovered a Macaffee daughter living in St. Louis, but that vacant-eyed young woman had stared at nothing and made no sound when he had visited her. A shiver went up his spine. It was as if the person inside had been removed, leaving only a husk. The nuns who cared for her had told him of another sister, though. A very rich one who travelled all the time and sent more than enough money to pay for her sister's needs. They used the extra funds to help others less fortunate. How they could practically enshrine the rich sister in sainthood was beyond him. No Macaffee could be good. To his mind, the money allowed the rich woman to ignore her helpless sister. At least he had a name now, and he was following it up. In fact, he was looking forward to meeting this paragon of virtue. And once he found the sister, he would find the father. He could feel it in his bones.

Shouts and gunfire resounded throughout the narrow valley. Hud peered down sharply, grabbing his pistol. The boys were whooping, spinning their horses in tight circles, and firing guns in the air. He grinned and carefully reset the hammer. Somebody was losing a big stake down there, and he had a feeling he knew who it might be.

One of the boys tore through the trunks and bags on the top of the coach. Clothes and mail flew everywhere. He was too far away to hear what the gang member called out, but it was clear they'd gotten everything to be had.

A couple of last whoops of celebration and the gang rode off in the direction opposite him, back down the valley floor. Hud let out a breath and stood up. He was glad he would be able to speak well of the Winslows before the judge. It would be a shame to hang them, but at least they'd go to their Maker with some goodness intact for Judgment Day.

He turned around and climbed back toward his horse, Brown, named in defiance of the tradition that called all horses from light to black "bays."

No home, no family, just a misnamed horse, a risky job, and a mission of revenge, Hud thought. Maybe he was becoming a damn fool in his old age.

Mary Alice let loose a string of curses as she watched the robbers ride away, all her lovely, hard-earned money going with them. Fury and frustration ran like twin devils through every inch of her. She had had to clamp her jaw shut to keep from shouting vindictives at the holdup gang, knowing that to provoke them was to get herself shot or worse. She ought to feel grateful no one had been molested beyond some verbal taunts, but she couldn't.

"They're giving a bad name to the West!" she proclaimed out loud. What had ever happened to honor among thieves?

"That's real true, miss," the driver said, climbing down off the seat. "Thieves are everywhere."

Mary Alice started, thinking he was talking about her.

But the man added, "The Overland Company don't appreciate their stages getting robbed, neither. As soon as I get Mickey patched up, I'll get you folks to Blossom City and report it."

The driver helped his lookout down off the bench, taking care with the young man's wound. He was whimpering with his pain. The other woman immediately went over and offered to bandage him. Mickey nodded once, his face pale and sweaty.

"The Overland's lack of appreciation is doing me no good," Mary Alice muttered under her breath, whirling around. She couldn't watch the proceedings; her stomach was already roiling at the glimpse of raw muscle and exposed bone. The land never stopped leaving its mark of tragedy on people.

She spotted a man riding into view.

"We've got nothing left!" she called out in complete disgust, fearing they were about to be robbed again.

The man said nothing as he rode up on a huge bay. The monster cut a swath through the grasses that were still plentiful along the trail, halfway between the plains and the mountains. Had to be a stallion, Mary Alice thought, admiring the animal. She glanced up at the man, noting his dust-stained clothes, and found her gaze caught in his.

He stared at her for one long, breathless moment, not saying a word. Although she was furious that they'd just been robbed, Mary Alice couldn't help staring back. She forced herself to look elsewhere. Anywhere. Then she looked at the rest of him.

It was a mistake.

His hair was dark, nearly black, and in need of a barber's shears. It hung shaggy under his crumpled hat. He had the beginnings of a beard and his face was all angles, hard-edged, lean, and not handsome, but drawing the eye. Like a predator's face, she thought. His body looked hard-edged and drew the eye, too, his well-worn leather chaps and long, beige duster hiding little from her scrutiny. He sat tall in the saddle and clearly would easily top his stallion's shoulder if he were standing.

A bedroll was lashed to the back of the saddle, and Mary Alice had a feeling the man didn't need much more in the way of amenities. Nor want them. Something started deep in her abdomen, like thick, hot syrup, making her want to soften for him, give him the gentleness he seemed to lack.

The notion scared her to death. She turned away, shocked by her reaction to the stranger. She must be losing her mind, she thought anxiously.

He stopped the horse and leaned forward on his knee, his gaze going to the wounded man. His facial muscles never changed. Clearly she hadn't had the same effect on him. Mary Alice didn't know whether to be angry or grateful.

"He okay?" the stranger asked the driver, dipping his head toward the lookout.

"Looks like the shoulder's shattered," the driver said.

The stranger nodded and straightened. "I'm the marshal here."

"Thank heavens," Mary Alice said in relief, immediately thinking he'd go after the bandits. Then she realized a marshal might not be good for her own continued health. But she wanted her money back—now—and this man was the only way to get it. She immediately fell into the role of the Countess. "You'll be going after those . . . those evil men. They threatened us with bodily harm and took all the money I had in the world—"

"Too bad," the marshal said, interrupting her.

Mary Alice gasped. "Too bad!"

"I'm not going after them until I have a posse, and I won't get a posse until I go into town."

"But what about my money?" she exclaimed. "They'll be miles from here by nightfall!"

"You better hope they don't spend it all in one place." He pointed to the lookout. "Get him inside the coach and let's get moving."

"Right." The driver and the male passenger helped the injured man to his feet and into the coach.

"That's it?" Mary Alice asked, wide-eyed in astonishment. "What the hel . . . what kind of marshal are you?"

"A live one."

"A lousy one!"

His face turned to stone. Mary Alice swallowed, never having seen such a phenomenon. Her remark had obviously made him angry. Shoot-'em-dead-without-a-backward-look angry. But she needed that money desperately. She'd worked hard for it, very hard to gain Redback's confidence, and in one stroke of bad luck it was gone. Well, she was damned if she'd see that money go without a fight.

"I demand you retrieve our valuables," she said with as much dignity as she could muster.

"Get in the coach, lady," he said, seeming to ignore her.

She raised her chin, giving him her best regal look. "I am the Countess Elizabeth of England and a guest of the Governor of the Colorado Territory. I demand you retrieve my money, all our belongings that were stolen by that gang of ruffians, or I will report you to the Governor myself!"

"Get in the damn coach, lady," he repeated wearily and turned his horse toward the front of the stage.

Mary Alice stared after him, flabbergasted. He hadn't even responded to her "title." The threat of the Governor hadn't even given him pause. She had a feeling this man would be fooled by very little.

She got into the coach.

Hud rode alongside the stage. The driver kept the team at a gentle trot so the wounded man wouldn't be too jarred.

Hud thought about the woman inside the coach. Up close, she wasn't pretty in the china-doll blonde example of ideal womanhood. Instead, her features were striking, like the fine marble of a greek statue's, her skin like smooth cream. Her mouth was made for kissing. He'd had the urge the moment he'd looked at her. The rest of her was just as striking, tall and slender. A jealous person would be tempted to call her skinny, but she looked just fine to him.

He thought of the way she'd expected him to go after the Winslows all by himself, and his pride admitted it liked the notion. What he didn't like was her mention of the Governor. He didn't need any trouble with his job. Maybe he ought to soften for once and try to appease the lady. He could see her profile in the stage window and angled his horse as close as he could.

"I'll do my best to get your money back," he said above the noise of the wheels, by way of apology.

She gazed at him for a long moment. "Thank you, sir, although I confess I don't expect you to have much success starting out so late as you will."

"Trail's not so cold yet."

She had seemed to forgive him for his earlier

harshness. He felt better. It had been a long time since he'd been in the company of a genteel woman. Years, he thought, remembering his mother before the war. He'd forgotten himself and his manners. But any maternal comparison ended as he found his gaze drawn to the curve of her breast. Her travelling jacket was heavy, but couldn't hide the jut of her body. He cleared his throat. "Where are you from?"

"England," she replied. "I'm here taking the Grand Tour with friends. Unfortunately, we've become separated. I hope to meet up with them soon."

"This is dangerous country to be touring in," he warned, although he knew the European nobility were visiting the West in droves for the hunting and the adventure. But seeing a woman was out of the ordinary. Wanting to emphasize that today's incident was only one of the dangers in these parts, he added, "Seems like every rat is exploding out of his hole since the big blizzard last month."

"I'm sure I will be safe with you guarding the territory," she said, smiling at him.

It was a wonderful smile, filled with confidence in his abilities. He resisted the urge to pull her right through the window opening and kiss her like she'd never been kissed before. Unfortunately, her praise was misplaced. He didn't have the heart to tell her he was fighting a losing battle.

But he allowed himself to bask in her radiance for one long moment, anyway.

* * *

Blossom City neither smelled like a blossom, nor was a city. In fact, it didn't look much different from Redback, nestled in another look-alike valley, the Rocky Mountain foothills rising sharply on either side.

Mary Alice stepped down from the stagecoach, which had stopped in front of the hotel, and looked around the town. She ignored the man climbing down off his brute of a horse and noted, instead, the three false-fronted buildings Blossom City sported—the hotel, the saloon, and the bank. All of them belied a town's first attempts at respectability. The rest were of rough-hewn wood hauled into this place in the Rocky Mountains. The couple came out of the coach behind her, sighing in relief at the signs of civilization.

The marshal strode down the dirt-packed street and into the shebang. After a few minutes, a group of people, clearly the town's most reputable citizens from their Sunday-best clothes, came rushing out of the store the marshal had just entered, their excitement almost tangible in the air. Word of the Countess must have reached them already. Mary Alice straightened her hat and wished she'd had a few minutes to clean up before meeting her new "hosts." First impressions were crucial in her business.

She smiled as the group bore down on her . . . and passed her by, crowding around the couple. Mary Alice gaped at them.

"Welcome to Blossom City, Mr. Farley!" a large, red-faced man said, grasping her fellow traveller's hand and pumping it vigorously, his muttonchop whiskers quivering with eagerness. "I'm Mayor Bartram and our community is pleased to have a blacksmith of your caliber settle here. We've got a barn all fitted out for you and there's a nice big house, a number 10 direct from Lyman Brothers Ready-Made Houses in Chicago, behind the barn for you and your pretty wife."

"We were attacked by robbers!" the man blurted.

Every single soul in the group groaned in unison.

"You won't leave on that account, will you?" the mayor asked anxiously. "We'll make it up to you, you can bet your boots on that. We need a blacksmith here in Blossom City. Hiram Goshen darn near crippled three horses trying to fill in after our last one left to mine silver in Idaho Territory. In fact, we've all been talking about offering you two building lots on top of the house and the barn . . ."

The man looked at his wife, then back. "Well, I suppose we could stay."

People began slapping the man on the back. Mary Alice ground her teeth together. Getting bypassed for the new town blacksmith topped everything. She watched them take the wounded lookout from the coach's interior. The poor man had been left to rot while everyone fawned over a damned blacksmith. Even the "I'll get your money back, don't you worry," marshal was now lounging against the wall, clearly in no hurry to round up a posse. He wasn't a handsome man, but he was compelling in some deeper way. She could feel an intangible attraction luring her toward him.

Mary Alice came to a decision. She'd get the marshal back and she'd get this town back, too.

Hud Jackson had been watching the scene with amused disgust. The town elders had been waiting in the shebang for the stage and had rushed out before he could barely get in a word. Maybe he ought to go into the blacksmithing business. Blossom City was practically giving itself away to keep the man.

The Countess didn't look too happy, either. Hud shifted his gaze to admire the straight line of her back and regal column of her throat. She looked it. Even in the midst of a robbery, she'd looked it. Certainly she was much too fine for small, grubby towns and grubbier marshals.

Oddly, the notion hurt. He'd been on the trail for weeks now, nowhere near a bath and laundry. Then he cursed. Why should it bother him that he wasn't at his best? What should he care what a Countess thought? It didn't matter to him. Nothing mattered, except doing his job and finding his brother's killers. But he also had to admit he'd admired the way she hadn't backed down out on the trail. She hadn't shown any fear of him. Most people did. And he'd cultivated it. Any marshal who didn't usually found himself sporting a bullet in the chest. And then she'd been . . . nice, easy to talk to.

She bothered him in a way other women didn't. He told himself to ignore it. A man took relief in a woman's body. That was their usefulness. There wasn't time or need for anything else. And a Countess definitely wasn't for him.

Taking out his gun, he casually fired it into the air. The blacksmith's wife shrieked, but beyond that the loud bang had the effect of jerking everyone else into quiet.

"Folks, I'm Marshal Hud Jackson," he said, now that he had their attention. "As the blacksmith told you, the stage was robbed. It was the Winslows. I'm needing to get a posse together to go after them."

"You didn't need to shoot off your gun and scare everyone half to death," the mayor began.

Hud pointed his revolver directly at the mayor's good-livin' belly. "I'm sorry to break up the greeting, but I'd like a little help, Mr. Mayor. You wouldn't want Blossom City to get a bad reputation among the marshals about its cooperating abilities, now would you? If it did, we just might not show up when trouble started here."

Out of the corner of his eye, he saw the Countess grin broadly. He appreciated an appreciative woman.

The mayor swallowed visibly. "Naturally, Marshal. I wasn't trying to neglect our duty. Jim, Bert. Hie yourselves over to the saloon and get some of the boys for the marshal."

"Sober ones," Hud said.

"Sober ones," the mayor repeated.

Hud let the hammer down easy against the chamber. He'd been doing it for so long, it was almost second nature. He tipped his hat to the Countess.

"By the way, Mr. Mayor. You've got a Countess in town, too."

"A what?"

The Countess introduced herself with a very charming smile. Hud even found himself being charmed by it. She added, "I and my travelling party were guests of the Governor's for a hunt, but I seem to have lost them—"

"Do you know that Grand Duke . . . what was his name?" the mayor asked, interrupting her.

"Alexi," several people announced, putting the emphasis on the "i." In none-too-subtle fashion, they shifted around to the Countess.

"That's right." The mayor nodded. "Alex-i. Why he was out here for a big hunt with Bill Cody and General Sheridan over by Kit Carson last year."

"I have met His Royal Highness," the Countess said. "A most handsome and charming man."

"Yep, yep, that's him," the mayor said expansively.

Hud strolled away from the crowd, knowing he wouldn't find the people selling illegal guns by standing here being entertained. He admitted with a chuckle that he didn't mind seeing the blacksmith and his wife temporarily abandoned, although he was discovering that Countess-watching could be a very pleasurable pursuit. Anyway, he felt an obligation to ensure she got some of Blossom City's hospitality, too. He kind of owed it to her, after she'd expected him to catch the Winslow gang single-handed. Just plain ignorance of the frontier, he thought. One had to allow for that with pampered women. There was a lot of pampering he'd like to do with her . . . but she was a lady. Too bad.

Still, he'd discharged his duties, and it was clear the Countess would be well taken care of now.

That was all that mattered.

Chapter Two

"My stay with you has been absolutely delightful," the Countess said, carefully tying her reticule strings against the new set of bulging double eagles. She added for the banker's benefit, "I'm sure you'll find my bank most swift in making this transaction."

The banker was holding her letter of credit and draft up to admire. "I have to admit I've never seen Bank of England issue before. I'd like to style the Blossom City National's papers after this. Do you think they would mind?"

"I think they would be honored." She held out her hand for her letter of credit. After one last admiring glance, the banker reluctantly put it in her palm. She lowered her gaze shyly. "I need to . . . freshen up. May I use the . . ."

She trailed her voice away and wrinkled her nose at her forced indiscretion.

The banker straightened proudly. "Of course. To the right." Then he blurted, "It's the only indoor convenience this side of Denver!"

The Countess's eyes widened. "How remarkable! Thank you, sir. I'm honored."

The moment Mary Alice closed the door to the convenience room, she yanked up the jacket of her travelling suit and undid her money belt. This time she wouldn't be losing it to anybody, she thought in determination. She managed only five-hundred this time, a further loss on her original take. A girl couldn't even make a decent living anymore. At least she hadn't had to sing—just give recitations. If she had had to "count the ways" one more time, she would have brought the contents of her stomach back up for inspection.

Two coins slipped through her fingers and dropped to the floor, one rolling behind the Chinese screen hiding the necessary. Cursing, she fumbled around for them. She had to be quick. It wouldn't do to give the banker too much time to think. If he began to think, he might begin to have doubts, and doubts were deadly in her business.

Besides, she wanted to get out of town—*way* out of town—before that disturbing marshal returned. He had angered her over his refusal to rescue her money. In fact, the more she thought about it, the more angered she'd become. And anger wasn't the only emotion he stirred in her. He had lurked in the back of her mind like a wolf skirting the edge of the woods observing its prey. Her body seemed to crave something. A slow, heavy liquid pulled along her veins every time she thought of the man. For some strange reason, her brain had the notion that only he could stop these feelings.

Mary Alice forced away the thought. She'd made enough in the last four towns to ensure Harriet's care for a long time to come. It had been a great pleasure to take Blossom City right under the marshal's nose. And he wouldn't even know it . . . if she hurried. The stage to Boulder was due at any time now.

As she tucked the last of the double eagles in her belt, she heard the outer door to the banker's office burst open with a loud bang.

"Where is she? You didn't give her any money, did you?"

"Uh-oh," Mary Alice muttered, recognizing the voice of Mayor Wilkens of Redback. In desperation, she glanced around the small room, instantly spotting its narrow window. She stepped over on tiptoe and eased the sash open as the shouting on the other side of the door grew louder. She poked her head out of the window, finding the alleyway between the bank and saloon empty. She tried to put her leg over the sill, but her skirt and hooped petticoat-bustle hampered her.

Someone pounded on the door. "Come out of there! We know all about your swindle in Weldona, Miss Fancy Countess!"

Weldona had been four towns back! Mary Alice didn't hesitate. She untied her hoops, petticoats, and bustle and dropped them right on the bright little flowered carpet. Wrapping her skirt over her arm, she climbed out the window.

She took a moment to ease the window closed,

wanting to gain a few more seconds while they puzzled over how she got out of the room. She scurried down the alley and behind the bank, keeping her body low. She went by the third fancy building on tip-toes, then several more of the rough timber ones. Children watched her curiously. She smiled at them as she sprinted past. Finally, she came behind the blacksmith's spanking new house at the edge of town. Some clothes flapping on a drying line gave her an idea. Without missing a step, she yanked them off and headed straight for the outhouse.

Ten minutes later, while one end of Blossom City was in a complete uproar, a boy, his hat pulled low over his eyes, strolled into the blacksmith's barn.

"Got a horse for sale?" he asked in a gruff voice, halfway between child and man.

Ignoring the boy, the blacksmith plunged the glowing horseshoe into the barrel of water. It hissed loudly, kicking up a large head of steam. He pulled the dripping-wet, black horseshoe out of the water. Satisfied with his work, he wiped the sweat from his forehead with the back of his arm and looked up at the young male.

"There were a couple here when I came for rent," the smith said. "But nobody's been renting, and they're just eating their heads off. I suppose I could sell you one . . ."

"Twenty dollars," the boy said.

"Done." The creature would cost him more than that in feed before too long.

The boy slapped a coin on the anvil. "Which one?"

"Over there." He nodded toward the back stall. A roan munched apathetically on the hay in the manger.

The boy reached up for one of the bridles hanging on a peg.

"That's six bits extra," the blacksmith said, grinning broadly.

The boy dropped his hand away and walked into the stall. He clucked to the horse, pushing against its shoulder. The animal backed out of the stall and docilely followed the boy over to a wooden box. The boy stepped up onto the box, then threw a leg over the horse's back.

"Thanks, mister," he said, riding the horse out Indian-style. The pair turned north.

The blacksmith raised his eyebrows. The boy had been wearing ladies' shoes. This Blossom City was stranger than he'd thought, much stranger. He was beginning to be grateful for his Abigail. A wife might just keep him out of mischief he didn't want to get into—even a clinging, whining one.

Still, the boy did have fine taste in the rest of his clothes, although they were a little big. The coat had bagged on the thin body. He'd certainly liked the lad's wide-brim hat. He ought to, the blacksmith thought, grinning.

It was just like the one he'd bought in Sterling.

Four days after he rode out of Blossom City, Hud rode back in, more tired and empty-handed than when he'd left.

He handed his posse their pay vouchers to

collect at the bank, then headed Brown straight for the saloon. When the horse stopped in front of the hitching post, Hud wearily swung his leg over the bay's big back and dropped to the dusty-grey road. The sun blazed hot overhead, giving the month of April a summer-like feel.

"Just let me get a bottle and then we'll take care of you, boy," he promised, patting Brown on the neck. The horse whickered and lowered his head to the watering trough, drinking deeply. Hud half-wished he could strip down and plunge in himself. As soon as he was done seeing to Brown's comfort, he'd find the nearest bath house and see to his own. Then maybe he'd look up that Countess. She'd haunted his thoughts on the trail.

More than haunted, he admitted. Somehow, she had lodged herself into his brain and he couldn't shake her out. She was unusual, a gem only a discerning man could see. Despite the fluff and vapors most women had, he couldn't imagine her helpless and clinging. She was too self-assured for that. He wondered what it would be like to undo those clothes inch by inch and find the womanly flesh underneath.

Brown turned his head to look at him, water dripping from the horse's mouth onto his boots. Hud realized he was still standing in the street. "All right, all right. I'm going."

Unfortunately, he didn't even make it into the saloon.

"Marshal! Marshal!"

Hud turned to find the entire town bearing down on him. At least it looked that way.

"We've been swindled!" the mayor exclaimed as everyone crowded around. His muttonchops were bristling with indignation. "By that fancy Countess woman you brought into town."

"I didn't bring anyone into town. She came on the stage," he reminded them.

The mayor waved a hand. "However she got here don't matter. She took five hundred dollars from us! And Redback! And Weldona! Weldona had a party come in, a fancy English fellah with them. They thought it was her lost people. He told them there was no Countess Elizabeth Barrett Browning! The real Mrs. Browning was some famous poet lady, but she never been no Countess. She took two hundred and fifty dollars from Weldona, all they had—"

"Weldona has always been poorly for a town. Not like us," someone commented proudly.

"—And one thousand from Redback!" the mayor continued, ignoring the interruption.

"Redback always was too highfalutin for its britches," said someone else. "Taught them a lesson."

People murmured appreciatively.

"You fools!" the mayor exclaimed. "Who cares what Weldona and Redback gave her? She took five hundred of *our* money, that's what counts. Marshal, she just disappeared right out of the bank two days ago!"

Hud scratched his bearded chin. "Disappeared? How do you mean she disappeared?"

"Just what I said. One moment she was in the . . ." The mayor reddened. "Well, she was in a room by herself."

Hud nodded, getting the man's drift.

"And then she was gone, right out the window. She never boarded the stage, we searched everywhere in town and outside it, and didn't find a trace of her. All she left behind were her petticoats!"

"Five-hundred dollars for a bunch of petticoats doesn't seem like a fair trade to me," Hud conceded in a calm voice. Inside, his blood rode hot at the thought that he'd actually felt guilty about not going after the Winslows for her. Worse, he'd introduced her to the town, giving her a kind of stamp of approval. And then she'd taken them for their savings.

Not that he cared for the windbags of this town or any other. If they were going to be fools for a fancy name, then they got a lesson they deserved. But it burned his backside to know he'd fallen for it, too. And worse, he'd been attracted to her . . . more than attracted. He should have known better; he might have, if he hadn't been duped by a striking face and body.

"It ain't a fair trade!" the mayor shouted, waving his arms. "Get after her, Marshal—"

Hud turned around and walked into the saloon.

"Marshal! Marshal!" The mayor puffed up behind him. "Where you going?"

"To get a drink," he replied, heading directly for the long oak bar. A handful of men occupied the tables, all of them eating breakfast. Hud's stomach growled.

"But what about that thieving Countess?"

"What about her?"

"You have to go get her and get our money back!"

Hud paused in the middle of the dimly-lit room. "Which way do I go? You folks lost her."

"But . . . but . . ."

"Tell you what," Hud said. "As I make the circuit, I'll keep an eye out for your Countess, Mr. Mayor."

"But she'll have spent all our money!"

"Can't help that." Hud turned back to the bar.

"What kind of lousy marshal are you?" the mayor demanded. "Why, I ought to report you to the Governor—"

Hud slowly rounded on the man. He stared at the mayor until sweat broke out on the official's forehead.

"I didn't get my money taken by a pretty face and a fancy manner," Hud said in the softest of voices. "I'll look for the lady, mayor, because she broke the law. But I'm having a drink first, then taking care of my horse, and then I'm having a long, hot bath. After that, I'm going to sleep for about three days." He touched the revolver strapped to his leg. "Anyone thinking about rushing me better think again. You got me?"

The mayor swallowed and nodded.

"Fine."

Hud bought his bottle of whiskey, looking at the pale amber liquid with a jaundiced eye. It looked watered-down some to him, but he let it go. Sometimes a straight batch gave a kick that blew out a man's stomach and nearly everything else, too.

Twenty minutes later, fueled by several swigs of whiskey and pleased with the smooth fire it produced, he was rubbing Brown down in the back stall of the livery stable. The blacksmith had left off his bellows and was sweeping out the stable.

"Damn fools in this town," he commented to Hud. "I'm thinking of moving on before they give away everything to the next confidence man who comes to town. You going after that woman?"

"Eventually," Hud said in a clipped voice, stroking the curry brushes along Brown's dusty flank. The comforting smell of horse, warm and musky, filled his nostrils.

"Well, I'd like for someone to find that boy who stole my hat and clothes," the blacksmith said. "Damn fool kid pays twenty dollars for a horse and steals clothes. It's sinful what these kids get up to nowadays. A good hiding—"

Hud interrupted the man's monologue. "You say the boy stole your clothes?"

"Right off the line! My wife had 'em drying. He even went inside the house to get my hat when she was busy making a pie!"

"When?"

The smith frowned. "The other day. Same day that Countess ran off with the town's money. At least the boy had enough sense to know stealing a horse is a hanging offense . . ."

"Did you happen to see which way the boy left town?"

The blacksmith glanced up hopefully. "West.

You gonna go after him and get back my clothes and hat?"

Hud smiled to himself and went back to currying Brown.

"Eventually."

Mary Alice carefully poured the tablespoon of turpentine into the small bottle, then jammed the cork in against the overpowering smell. She straightened and stretched her aching back, shaking the bottle of pale amber liquid vigorously. The turpentine mixed into invisibility.

Bottles of all sizes and descriptions lined every inch of surface in the tiniest room in Boulder's only hotel, each one filled with the amber liquid. Only a quarter of them were corked. She set the bottle beside its fellow and went on to the next one, following the same procedure.

One had to follow the recipe exactly, she knew. That had always been Otis's failing. He added too much turpentine. It needed just a touch to cover the odor of watered whiskey and to burn going down. If it didn't burn, no one thought the elixir worked. Funny thing was, she'd seen it actually work on some sick people. Otis often said that what they were really selling was hope mixed with a little magic.

Her eyes watered and she swiped at them. The wide-open window wasn't doing much good. The room smelled like turpentine makers were holed up inside on a three-day drunk.

She wished she didn't have to resort to this, but

the Countess would have to disappear for a while until the furor died down. That meant Earnest John Nelson had to appear. Earnest John had been a creation of Otis's and her first alter-identity. She and Otis had worked the towns and forts from New Mexico to North Dakota, her role always that of the "cured" patient—sometimes right before everyone's eyes. Even the Indians had had a certain respect for Otis and his "magic." It had been a hard life, downright dangerous at times, but satisfyingly independent. It still was.

The laconic marshal came unbidden into her mind. She'd never met a man more emotionally and physically unnerving, Mary Alice admitted. She couldn't help feeling she'd escaped more than a tar and feathering, when she'd escaped from Blossom City. He probably knew all about her by now. If he caught up with her . . . she refused to think about that. She was safe enough, anyway. He was looking for a fancy woman, not an earnest young man.

Mary Alice concentrated on her work. Boulder held no dangerous marshal, thank goodness. Unfortunately, she had had to leave her carpetbag, with all her usual equipment, behind. That had meant an outlay of cash here. Also, Earnest John didn't bring in nearly the money that the Countess did. Still, the good part about Earnest John was that he could always be drawn upon in a pinch. Tomorrow was Saturday, and that meant market day.

Mary Alice smiled, thinking of all the surrounding settlers and miners who would be coming into

Boulder. She just hoped the good townspeople appreciated the "miracle" she was about to give them.

The next morning, a young male in the first "bloom" of manhood climbed up on the back of a wagon tied in front of the shebang. He was dressed in clothes too big for him. A bandana was bound around his head, under his hat. He set his basket of bottles down on the backboard and straightened. His dirt-smeared face held an expression of earnestness that hadn't been seen since the Mormons had passed through the territory.

He gazed around at the people who were slowing to stare at him as they went about their market-day business. When he felt he'd attracted enough interested parties, he began to sing.

"I dream of Jeannie with the light brown hair . . ."

The young man sang in a clear, very loud soprano. A near-miracle in itself, he thought with amusement, considering that castrated singers had gone out of fashion hundreds of years ago.

People gathered around the back of the wagon, knowing their attention was desired. More came out of the shebang and the saloon. Riders reined in at the back of the growing crowd of the men, women, and children of Boulder.

Finally, the young man finished his song and his audience burst into applause. He smiled at them and dipped his head slightly in a bow. Then he got down to business.

"Folks!" he called out, while taking a bottle out of the basket. His speaking voice was more strained and gruff than his singing one. "Have you had trouble sleeping? Have you felt poorly, been given to an irritable digestion, experienced the grief of liver flukes and suffered peculiar pains in the elbows and knees?" Heads nodded in acknowledgment. He pointed at several women. "Ladies! Have you suffered from the agonies of femininity? Have you experienced the anxiety of the tightening of the breath? A weariness of the brain? A marked increase in aching limbs and swollen feet?"

More nods came from the female contingent.

"My name is John Nelson." The young man tapped the bottle. "And I have here Dr. Otis Wainwright's patented *Elixir of Bitters* and its companion product, that wonderful tonic, *The Woman's Regulator!* These two medicines alone will cure all the ailments I have spoken of." He leaned forward. "Ladies, you'll feel and look so well, it will draw your husband back to the bosom of his family."

"What if I don't want him back?" someone called out.

"Then a few teaspoons of this directly in his morning coffee and it'll drive him away!"

Everybody laughed.

John Nelson paced the width of the small wagon while continuing to extol the medicine and its maker's virtues. "Dr. Wainwright is a renowned physician who's treated the King of Germany with his bitters and restored the man's congenial disposition. Why, there hasn't been a war in near on thirty years! He's treated all the elite of Paris, London, and New York. Even Mr. Barnum himself swears by the doctor's elixir—that's why his circus is such a success. It's been said by wags from Rome to Washington that if Marie Antoinette had had the doctor's tonic available there wouldn't have been a French Revolution. The good doctor, being the exemplary Christian and wonderful samaritan that he is, in an effort to bring unfortunates everywhere the benefit of his wisdom and talented gifts, has begun to send his patented medicines to the grand Western Territories of these United States. His philanthropy will be remembered for a thousand years!"

Mary Alice noticed someone moving through the back of the spellbound crowd. She watched the tall man for a swift, endless moment, her stomach dropping to the pit of the earth as she recognized the marshal she thought she'd left behind in Blossom City. Her patter faltered as fear and anticipation ran like ice water through her veins. She might be ahead on Harriet's care costs, but not near enough to keep her sister during a long prison term.

She pulled herself together and continued, desperately trying to think of an escape. She was aware of the marshal's gaze following her every move. Did he recognize her already? Surely not.

She pointed to a man with bulging eyes. "It'll help relieve your eyestrain, sir." She pointed to an exhausted-looking woman, who held a squalling babe and had three more tykes clinging to her skirts. "It'll give you back your vitality, madam." She pointed directly at the marshal, not being able to resist. "And it'll grace your face with a smile, my good man. You look as if you could use one."

Everyone chuckled, while the marshal didn't move.

"But how do we know it works?" a man in the back called out.

Every crowd had a cynic, Mary Alice thought. Thank goodness. "I'm glad you asked me that, friend. I am an earnest man, and I feel it is my obligation to give you proof of my claims. When I was a youngster, I contracted scarlet fever. Yes, I lay for two months in the nightmarish hell of that dreaded disease. My fever went so high that my skin smoked and my hair fell out. Every single strand of it! I was at death's door for so long my mother held my wake in anticipation of my demise."

The crowd stared up at her in rapt attention—except the marshal. He just stared.

She continued, broadening her smile. "But hallelujah, folks, the fever passed, and I lived through prayer and the Good Lord's Grace. But I was marked with the ill effects of that horrible experience. I had no hair left. Not a one to call my own. Can you imagine the further agonies I suffered as a child? All the tormentations of other youths tried my soul . . ."

The crowd murmured in sympathy.

Mary Alice waved her hand. "As I entered my formative years, the torments grew worse. I tried bear grease, false hair, even sleeping with garlic—

a cure made famous in China. But no hair grew." She paused, allowing a catch in her voice. "There was a girl. Jeannie. She was the most beautiful and kindest girl in all of Virginia. I sang of her earlier in my lament. Her kindness was all-encompassing, but even she could not find it in her heart to love me because of my baldness, and so she married another—"

"That elixir sure didn't help you, boy!"

"I'm just getting to that part," Mary Alice said.

"Don't rush him!" someone else called out.

The crowd was poised in anticipation. Mary Alice wanted desperately to jump off the wagon and run, but leaving such a willing crowd like this was a sin. Even Edwin Booth couldn't have held them as she did now, she thought. She reminded herself that selling patent medicine wasn't against the law. She was doing nothing wrong here, and he was looking for a woman, not a young man. He hadn't made a move toward her yet. There was still a chance she could pull it off and get away without him realizing who she was. The challenge sang through her veins.

"Yes, my Jeannie married another," she said, gazing boldly at the man. "My heart was broken, but I understood. How could I not, when I couldn't even face myself in the looking glass. I decided to kill myself."

The crowd gasped on cue.

Mary Alice nodded dramatically. She removed her hat and set it aside. "Yes, folks, I was willing to give up my life, that's how desperate my plight was. And then, at my lowest ebb, I met Dr.

Wainwright. He gave me a course of his *Elixir of Bitters.* In just two weeks my disposition improved. I accepted my lot in life, glad to live again, sure that the Good Lord had some grand purpose for a bald man. But the good doctor was not through with his miracles. Why, just shortly after my rejuvenation, I was running my hand across my head . . . and I felt it. A strand of hair. Then two, then three . . ."

The crowd gasped again.

It was the moment of truth in more ways than one, she admitted. She yanked off the scarf, and her hair came tumbling down past her shoulders, gleaming in the spring sunlight. "Thanks to Dr. Wainwright and his *Elixir of Bitters* I have hair that is the envy of men and women everywhere. Why, even Bill Cody declared my hair more luxuriant than General Custer's!"

The crowd cheered boisterously—all except the marshal.

Mary Alice bowed anyway. At least he wasn't shouting "Liar! Cheat!"

"My life was changed by Dr. Wainwright, changed so much that I felt compelled to join his company as living proof of his success and bring his good works to those who are suffering now as I once did. I know this is the Lord's grand purpose for me, to help other poor unfortunates back to the vitality of life."

"How much?" a man in back shouted.

"Just one dollar each for *Elixir of Bitters* and *The Woman's Regulator,"* Mary Alice replied. "A bargain when you consider all they can do."

People crowded around the back of the wagon.

"Follow the directions printed on the label," Mary Alice repeated over and over, as she exchanged her bottles for silver and gold. Within five minutes her batch of elixirs was gone, although the crowd milled around in front of her, clamoring for more. They effectively blocked the marshal from coming close. He still hadn't moved.

"I have more in my room," Mary Alice said, knowing she had to take advantage of the moment. "I'll go get it."

She leaped over the side of the wagon and raced between the two buildings. Boulder was more heavily populated than Blossom City and she easily made her way onto the next street toward the tent city of miners set up on the edge of town. If she made it there, it was possible to escape among that sea of poor humanity.

As she ducked past the corner of a building, something grabbed her.

She shrieked as she was yanked back against a hard body.

"My compliments, Countess," said a dreaded voice behind her. "Allow me to escort you."

It was the marshal.

Chapter Three

Hud was unprepared for the hellcat who erupted in his arms.

She fought and kicked and clawed, her hands and feet flinging everywhere as he struggled to keep his hold on her. Her fist landed full on his cheekbone; pain exploded in his face.

"Damn you, woman!" he swore, grappling her to the ground.

When she was effectively pinned under him, he raised his head and stared down at her. Her hair was all dishevelled and her face was stained and dirt-smeared. Her legs were tangled with his with no skirts to hamper or hide them. He was all too aware of every long inch of those forbidden limbs. His hips pressed her down, pelvis to pelvis, in the most shocking way. The feel of her beneath him was heady and distracting, stirring something deep inside him. He wanted to erase the notion from his mind, but even in the midst of an arrest it stayed with him.

Hud cursed again. He'd never used a weapon on a woman before, but as wily as she was, he considered unholstering his gun. He'd need all the help he could get.

"Get . . . off . . . me!" she gasped out, his weight forcing the air from her lungs.

"Don't think so," he said, although he did ease up a little. Not enough for her to start fighting him again, he calculated, but enough to let her breathe. He still couldn't believe her performance. Dressed in baggy, shapeless brown pants and a grey coat, the rounded collar of a pair of long johns peeping out from the outer garment, she looked every inch the young man. Even when she whipped the scarf off her head, he still hadn't been sure if he were imagining things. But when she leapt over the wagonside, he'd followed—and found her running. That had been enough for him, and so he'd gone to cut her off. Now he smiled grimly. "It's nice to see you again, Countess."

"I don't know what you're talking about, Marshal," she said in a deceptively deep voice. "I'm John Nelson, just passing through. Now let me up!"

"How do you know I'm a marshal?" he asked, ignoring her request. "My badge is *under* my coat."

She swallowed visibly. "Let me up."

He shook his head, a slow grin spreading across his face. "I like it fine just the way we are. But I'm willing to be reasonable and let you up *after* you explain yourself."

She lifted her chin. "It's not against the law to

sell medicine—not even posing as a boy."

"It's against the law to spread false credit and take a town's money."

"Who says I did that?"

"Weldona, Redback, and Blossom City." He was beginning to like lying with her. He'd never questioned a prisoner quite like this before.

"And how would they know I have false credit?" she asked. "It would take months to send my draft to England and receive a reply."

That logic stymied Hud until he remembered his conversation with Blossom City's mayor. "A party came into Weldona with an Englishman who told them there was no Countess Browning, that the real Browning lady is a poet and the town had been swindled—"

"And they took his word for it?" she exclaimed indignantly. "A complete stranger? Without proof? And you, a marshal sworn to uphold the law, just takes it right into his own hands on the word of a stranger who's long gone from the Territory? I'm heartily ashamed the U. S. Government has come to such a pass—"

"Shut up!" Hud growled in frustration. The thought of nearly being taken in yet again aggravated him beyond measure. She certainly knew how to kill the physical attraction, too. "You hardly look like a Countess now, Countess. Or sound like one. No one would have a hard time believing a stranger if they saw you in that getup. And especially if they'd seen your performance selling that swill. We're going over to Boulder's nice new jail, and we're going to hold you there until the circuit judge comes riding in . . ."

She began to struggle again, finding a strength he couldn't believe she possessed. She bucked under him, slamming her hips and legs against his own, her arms thrashing from side to side in a desperate attempt to get out from under him. Sweat popped out on his forehead as he grabbed for flailing hands and attempted to press her into the ground with his body. He finally got her arms pinned over her head. His face was practically buried in the base of her neck, his lips almost touching her flesh. He was seized with the overwhelming urge to kiss her.

"Hey! What the hell . . . Sweet Godamercy, Joe!"

Hud glanced back toward the sound of the voice to find two men behind him, gaping. Others were coming down the alleyway in between the building. Jaws dropping open, they crowded around the two men.

"I heard about this," the man named Joe said darkly. He drew out his gun and aimed it at the couple sprawled together on the ground. "This here's a respectable town, mister. We don't tolerate no fancy goings-on like in Chicago or Frisco."

Others murmured in sudden realization. They pulled out their guns, too. Heat rose up Hud's neck and boiled onto his face at their implication.

"This is the Countess Elizabeth Barrett Browning!" he said in outrage. The moment the words left his lips he knew he'd made a mistake. Everyone's gun hand stretched out a little farther toward him.

"And I'm the King of England," one of the men said. "You ain't a-foolin' us. If that's a lady, then why's *she* wearing them boots and pants? I ain't never heard of no respectable *woman* doing that. Now git up real slow, mister."

Hud frowned, wondering why they couldn't see she was a woman. Then he realized they literally couldn't. From their angle, only the bottom half of her was visible.

"He did this to me!" John Nelson—aka Countess Elizabeth Barrett Browning—suddenly exclaimed. "I'm completely innocent of any perverse lustfulness . . ."

Hud flung himself off the woman, deciding right then and there that he'd kill her the moment he had a chance. He hauled her to her feet. "See? It's a woman!"

"Why, it's that medicine man John Nelson . . ." one began, peering intently at the Countess.

"By gum, he's right! It *is* a woman!"

"If she's a woman, what happened to that medicine man?" another asked.

"I think that's him," someone said dubiously.

"No, that's her."

"How could that be her if that's him?"

"But that ain't him. Him is her. I think."

Everyone frowned, clearly baffled with the "magical" switch. The Countess's smile was positively angelic. Hud gnashed his teeth.

"I don't know exactly what kind of sinnin' is goin' on here," the man called Joe said, swinging their attention back to the immediate problem. "But no matter how you skin this cat, it still ain't decent sinnin' to me."

"We were not doing anything!" Hud snapped, glaring at all of them.

"You looked real busy the way we saw it," one said.

The others murmured agreement.

Determined to get them to understand, Hud whipped open his jacket. Eight gun hammers clicked back. Very slowly, Hud pointed to the badge on his chest. "Look, I'm Hud Jackson, U.S. Marshal for the Colorado Territory—"

People gasped and eyes turned even more angry. Joe, the unspoken leader, said, "I'm ashamed of you, Marshal. Right out here in the open like that, and you supposin' to uphold the law. The Governor's gonna hear about this."

"I was trying to arrest this person for swindling several towns!" Hud nearly yelled.

"I didn't see no gun drawn on him, Marshal."

"Me neither."

"None of us did."

"Looked like he was trying to draw something else."

Heads wagged in agreement.

"A picture's worth a thousand words," Joe quoted, his eyes narrowing. "Marshal, we ought to shoot you right where you are, because you're a marshal . . . well, I suppose we shouldn't. But you get yourself and this . . . this floozy of yours you're suppose to be arrestin' out of town right now."

"But—"

"Now!"

Hud ground his back teeth together, not daring

to look at anybody. If he did, he was liable to start swinging. He could see the laughter the Countess was suppressing and resisted the urge to wring her neck.

"Get his horse," Joe said. Several men ran back up the alley. They returned in a few moments, leading Brown over to Hud. Nobody got too close.

Determined to get out of town faster than even this group of vigilantes wanted, Hud put his foot in the stirrup and hoisted himself into the saddle in one quick movement. He reached down and grabbed the woman and hauled her up in front of him.

"See? Right cozy."

"Sweet Jesus!" Hud muttered furiously, and kicked Brown into a lope.

They were out of the town limits within two minutes.

Mary Alice knew she had gone too far this time. Trying to get herself free by blaming the marshal for a nefarious deed wasn't the wisest thing to do.

Still, the thought of the marshal being run out of town for lustful misbehavior tickled her. The expression on his face had been priceless. She wondered if she could imitate it for the future—that perfect blend of horror and astonishment. It might come in handy for the show. If she ever had a show again.

Mary Alice stifled a groan of disgust. She held herself stiffly away from the marshal's body, not wanting to touch him any more than she had to.

He was furious with her, for one thing, and she was half-afraid that if she relaxed against him accidentally, he would explode with rage and kill her. He looked meaner than a stepped-on rattlesnake.

Unfortunately, no matter how stiffly she held herself she seemed to be touching him everywhere. Her shoulder was tucked under his chin, her back was snuggled against the breadth of his chest, and her head was just inches from resting on his shoulder. Her hands were holding onto the saddle horn, forcing her right arm to run along the length of his thigh. Her left hip and thigh were resting on the junction of his legs. The odor of man and horse combined bewitchingly to torment her senses. She could hear his breath.

She closed her eyes, her body restless and wanting. The notion was dangerous. It was what led women to subjugate their will to men. That was something she'd never do. Ever.

Mary Alice set her jaw. The saddle horn was pressing uncomfortably against half her bottom, nearly stabbing her, actually. She decided now was not the time to complain. She also wondered where he was heading and what he would do with her. She decided she'd better not ask about that, either. Instead, she worried about how to escape. Being alone in the mountains wasn't safe, but she much preferred it to a jail. What would happen to Harriet if she went to jail?

Too bad she had left all her medicines behind, she thought. She could have fed him some and put him out of commission for a day or so, giving her an opportunity to put distance between them. Other alternatives floated through her mind, although she discarded several. She only wanted to get away, not kill the man. She would just have to be ready when an opportunity presented itself.

Tucking her arms closer to her sides, she smiled to herself. The only good part of all this was that she still had her money belt intact and snug around her waist. It was a miracle the townspeople hadn't thought to take their money back, although they might come after it. If the marshal should find it . . . she had to get away.

The air was brisk, biting into her cheeks and hinting at a cold sweeping down from the higher elevations as they wound their way along the trail. She recognized that they were heading south toward Denver. Denver had a fully-equipped jail and a judge on hand. Mary Alice swallowed. Between Boulder and Denver were outlaws, avalanches, and even the occasional indian war party. Any of them appealed more than jail. If she were lucky, they'd get all three.

Hud pulled up on the reins, slowing the horse to a stop.

Mary Alice looked around at the isolated gulch. Rocks and bushes and the occasional scrub pine were its only decorations. Boulder was just a few miles back—they hadn't come far enough for a legitimate stop. She had a bad feeling about this.

He slid off the saddle, keeping her seated on the horse with iron hands. Then he hauled her off. She was still stumbling to right herself as he whipped out a pair of handcuffs. He had them snapped around her wrists before she could blink. She'd been branded faster than a scared calf.

"That's better," he said, tying a thin rope around the cuffs. "By the way, you're under arrest, Countess."

"What do you think you're doing?" Mary Alice demanded, pushing her hair out of her face with her cuffed hands. She hadn't been physically scared of the marshal before, but suddenly she was all too aware she was a woman alone with a man and no help in sight. She couldn't rely on the western code of chivalry, especially in regard to a lady of nobility. He knew she wasn't one and he looked ominous, dressed all in black. From his boots to his hat, he could have been a modern-day Satan. The only vague relief was his silvery flowered vest.

"Brown can't carry both of us all the way to Denver," he said, glaring at her like she was an idiot. "So you walk. I'm making sure you *get* there."

"I'm not walking all the way to Denver!" she snapped, wiggling her wrists. The cuffs were tight.

"Lady, you're lucky I don't horsewhip you all the way to Denver after what you did back there!" he snapped back, grabbing up her hands and checking them. Once satisfied, he dropped her hands like they were rocks heated white in a fire. "Damn you, half of those people still aren't sure you're a woman. You ruined my reputation and it's going to be all over the territory before the week is out that I'm a . . . ! If I have a job by the time we get to Denver, I'll be damned lucky. And if I don't, I swear I'll strip you bare naked in front of the Governor, just to prove you're a woman and I'm . . . virile."

"I don't know," she said, in a dubious tone. "What'll they say when they find out you were only trying to arrest me? Where was your virility then?"

He shook with anger. Sputtering an oath, he yanked the loose end of the rope around the saddle horn several times, remounted and tapped Brown into a slow walk. Mary Alice was jerked forward. She tried to dig her heels in, but the horse just dragged her along.

"You are no gentleman," she said, finally forced to walk beside the animal. She had to admit the pace was gentle.

He smiled. "You're no lady, Countess, so we're even."

"And I'm not what you're thinking, either," she told him. A perverse anger ran through her at what was clearly on his mind. "You don't know who I am or anything about me! I have a very sick sister who needs money, and I'm the only one who can get it for her. And get it I will!"

He didn't say a word. He didn't have to. Mary Alice knew he didn't believe her. She could feel the heat creeping into her cheeks. Why should she care what the high and mighty marshal thought of her? Then she realized that what she had said was tantamount to a confession. She wished she'd never shot her mouth off like a cowboy on the Fourth of July.

She changed the subject. "You can't walk me all the way to Denver! It's a hundred miles, all uphill!"

He grinned. "It's about forty-five, and there's some downside."

She tried to force her wrists apart. "If I ever get myself free, I'll give you a downside you won't forget."

"Threatening the arresting officer will get you another year from Judge Bailey," he said. "If not two."

Mary Alice glared at his handsome face, all the while playing with her wrists. If she could get the cuffs to work loose slightly, then she had a chance of getting free.

"Keep that up and I'll tie you over the back of Brown here," he said in a deadly-calm voice.

"Does it make you feel better to threaten a woman?" she asked, although she stilled her movements.

He pulled up the horse and rounded on her. "The last thing I need is to trek you all the way to Denver. I've got someone selling guns to the Indians, creating all the makings of an uprising in the northern end of the Territory. But thanks to your shenanigans, I can't leave you in the Boulder jail to go after the gunrunners again and there isn't another jail until Denver. By the time I get back, the trail'll be so cold even Hell couldn't fire it up again."

Mary Alice smiled happily. "Then let me go, right here. Nobody's going to know—"

She was jerked forward into silence as he kicked

the horse into a trot. Stumbling along, she grabbed his leg, trying to regain her balance. He immediately slowed the horse to a walk again.

"It was just a suggestion," she muttered, pushing her hair out of her face.

He never said a word, just kept moving the horse forward. Mary Alice cursed him.

Three hours later, he still hadn't said a word and Mary Alice was still cursing him. Instead, he moved them both along without a break. She placed all her concentration on keeping her feet one in front of the other. They had been steadily climbing most of the time.

When he finally stopped his horse near a stream, she collapsed against the animal. She gasped for breath, the air more rarefied than she was used to. Her legs ached, and she was positive her feet were swollen. Her shoulders were stretched taut from her arms being forced together in front of her. The marshal had a lot to pay for, she decided. A lot.

Hud swung off the horse, dropping the reins over the animal's head so Brown could graze free. He pulled his rifle from its saddle holster and took off the saddlebags and canteen. He turned his back on her and walked over to several sheltering rocks.

Mary Alice raised her head, watching over the saddle's seat as he dropped the bags and set his rifle aside. He opened the canteen and drank deeply. She licked her lips, tasting the salt of her perspiration and the dryness of her mouth. He knelt down and began rummaging through the bags. She slowly brought her hands up to the saddle horn. In one leap, she could lift herself onto the horse . . .

"Don't even think it," he said, without turning around.

"I wasn't thinking anything," she snapped, snatching her hands back. "Am I supposed to stand here while you rest? I won't make it even a quarter of the way if I don't rest, too. I'm not an animal, you know—"

"And you don't know how to be quiet, either," he said, getting up and coming toward her.

She eyed him as he untied the rope from the horn. "You don't think much of women, do you?"

"Nope." He handed the rope across to her. "The amenities are behind that pine. Don't wander far. Escaping an arrest is an automatic no parole and another five years from Judge Bailey. Besides, I'm not in the mood to chase you down."

Mary Alice glared at him. She looped the extra rope up in her wrists, grateful that she could still move her fingers. Except for a slight reddening, they were fairly flexible. She had to admit he could handcuff a person and still keep the circulation going.

She managed to take care of the "amenities," although doing the pants buttons with her cuffed and tied wrists was a course in frustration. She gazed out across the deserted ravine longingly, wondering if she could "wander" away without him becoming aware of it until she was gone.

The thought of being alone with him frightened and excited her at the same time. Panic welled up inside her. She couldn't go to jail. She absolutely couldn't. Harriet wouldn't survive it. Glancing around, she wondered if she could find a hidey-hole among the rocks. Maybe even a cave or a thicket. She'd gladly risk bears and brambles if there was a chance he wouldn't find her. Unfortunately, she didn't know what was out there to shelter her, or if she could be sheltered. The marshal had also, in his crafty way, picked a spot on the bend of the stream that allowed him a complete view of the ravine. He could even see the tree clearly, but not whoever was directly behind it. She wasn't willing to risk five years of her life if the odds weren't in her favor. She'd wait.

She turned back and walked over to the stream. It bubbled like champagne among the submerged rocks, the icy mountain snows almost visible in the white foam. Kneeling down, she splashed water on her face. Her skin rejuvenated instantly. She licked at her lips, taking in the refreshing wetness. It wasn't nearly enough. With her hands tied, she couldn't make a cup from them. She wanted water—clean, clear, crisp water. There was only one thing to do.

She plunged her face right into the stream, drinking water in great gulps until her breath ran out. Fortunately, about that same moment her thirst was quenched.

Water streamed off her face when she finally emerged. It ran down everywhere. Rising back on her heels, she laughed and blotted at her cheeks and chin with her forearms, letting the coatsleeves absorb as much water as could get to them. Her tied hands made it awkward.

"Couldn't wait until you got the canteen?" Hud asked, amusement in his voice. He was slightly forward of where she was, allowing him a full view of her antics.

Mary Alice lowered her arms and grinned. "I wasn't sure if I was getting it."

"Maybe you won't now. I kinda liked the show."

"You're the marshal." Feeling the water dripping down under her shirtfront, she reached up and fumbled with the chain around her neck. Finally she was able to hook a finger around the chain, and she pulled out her father's watch. Since it didn't work, it wouldn't hurt to get the watch wet, she thought, rubbing it against a dry spot on her coat front. Still, she'd hate to ruin the case. It was all she had left of her happier past.

She sensed the marshal walking toward her and looked up. He paused in front of her, staring down at her chest.

"Where did you get that?"

She glanced down, looking to see what he was looking at and half-afraid she was accidentally exposed. "What?"

His eyes narrowed ominously, and he pointed to the watch. "That."

"My father gave it to me."

"A father!" he scoffed. "How could someone like you have a father? Who was the man you were with who gave that to you?"

"I have never, *ever*, been with a man!" Mary Alice exclaimed, furious at the accusation and a little fearful of the anger on his face. "I may be a lot of things, but I'm not a whore. My father gave me this watch."

Suddenly, his eyes widened as if he'd been jolted by lightning. "Sister! Your sick sister! She's in St. Louis with some nuns, isn't she?"

She gaped at him. "How do you know that?"

"I should have known it right away," he muttered, not answering her question. "If you're the woman I've been tracking since last year, you're Mary Alice Macaffee, Cullen Macaffee's younger daughter. Where is he?" He grabbed her shoulders and shook her almost violently. "Where is your father?"

"Dead," she nearly shrieked in her fright. "He died of cholera on the Santa Fe Trail nine years ago."

He let go of her so abruptly she stumbled back. He stared at her, his jaw working.

"I'm sorry to hear that," Hud said at last, in a cold voice. "The son of a bitch left my brother for dead during the war, and I've been looking forward ever since to sending him on to God myself."

Chapter Four

She jumped up and slapped him so fast with the power of both her hands that Hud heard the crack of her flesh against his cheek before he felt the sting.

"Jesus!" he snapped, holding his hand against his smarting skin.

"My father left no one for dead," she said with great dignity, a state difficult to manage with her hair hanging in wet ropes about her face. But somehow she did it. "He was an honorable man from one of the finest families in Mississippi. He rode with Jeb Stuart—"

"And he was sent on a special mission to bring back gold from California sympathizers for the Confederacy," Hud interrupted in a near snarl. The deep, abiding anger that had fueled him for so long burst forth. "It was after the South tried to cut off the West for its gold in '62. Twelve men, all "good and true," my brother among them, were sent to bring gold back overland. Only they were attacked by Indians on the trail, and John was left for dead with a broken leg by the other two survivors. *For* dead! He wasn't dead." His voice hardened. "Some friendly Indians found him five days later. He lost his leg to gangrene, and then he lost his life, screaming like a woman in his pain."

"My father would never have done such a thing!" she shouted.

He had been determined to treat her as any other prisoner at first, but he had begun to feel like a cad as she walked alongside Brown. That was why he'd called a halt long before he should have. He even intended to put her on the horse from now on. When she had stuck her head straight into the stream and laughed at herself afterward, he'd found himself liking his prisoner and almost wishing he didn't have to take her in.

And then he'd seen the watch. He knew that watch. He had one just like it. All the laughter had dissolved in one blinding bolt of disbelief and fury. The paragon of virtue had turned out to be the liar and cheat right under his nose all the time.

"How do you know my father did this?" she asked. "Whoever told you was mistaken—"

"There's no mistake," he said coldly. "My brother wrote down the names of the two bastards who left him behind in his letter to me. He lived long enough for that. The other man was Roger Ward."

"No," Mary Alice said, her chin rising in defiance. "Not my father. The other man left your brother—"

"Your father got out." Hud's blood boiled at her

obtuseness. "And he didn't take my brother with him."

"He wasn't there!" she screamed at him, fury in her eyes.

"He was there," Hud repeated. "Everyone who went on the mission got a watch, the same one." He reached in his vest pocket and pulled out a watch, its scrollwork on the casing the exact likeness of the one around her neck. "Davis himself gave them as gifts of appreciation for volunteering for such a dangerous mission. Of course, he didn't know how he and the cause would be betrayed."

"Shut up!" she snapped, turning away from him.

"The watch doesn't work, does it?" he said. "It never has."

She turned around. Tears threatened to spill over in her eyes.

He almost didn't want to hurt her, but it would be a form of revenge for John if he could convince the daughter of her father's betrayal. A pale one, maybe, but it would do. He continued. "It doesn't work because there's a paper inside it. A portion of the map my brother and your father and Ward made of the place where the expedition hid the gold before the Indians hit them. My brother told me they tore the map in thirds, each keeping his portion in the watch. They took my brother's map after he broke his leg, but left him the watch. At least they did that much for him. Open the watch, Mary Alice Macaffee, and find the soiled legacy your father left you."

"No," she whispered, her eyes wide and staring. Her fingers clutched at the piece as if to hide it from his words. She still didn't cry.

"Open it."

"No! You won't take the last thing I have, damn you."

He reached out and yanked the necklace from her hands, then pulled it over her head. She tried to grab it, but her bound hands hampered her. She kicked at him, beat at him with her fists. Hud fended her off easily. She sat down on the rock again.

"What's the matter, Mary Alice?" he asked, sarcasm dripping from his voice. "If your father's what you claim him to be, then there won't be a map. Or are you afraid to find out the apple hasn't fallen far from the tree?"

"Bastard."

Ignoring her, Hud took out his knife and gently pried open the back of the watch. Folded small and nestled against the tiny gears and mechanisms were two pieces of paper, one larger than the other. He heard Mary Alice's sob of despair and hardened his heart against the sound of it. Carefully, he withdrew the papers and snapped the watch casing closed. He turned to hand her back the watch, but she had walked away to sit on a large boulder. Her face was hidden from him as she looked out over the ravine.

Somehow it bothered him to have her hurt like this. She might be a confidence trickster, but clearly she'd cared very much for her father. He knew what it was like to have illusions about someone and be forced to face the reality of who they truly were. His proper ex-fiancée, who had pledged undying love to him and then married the first Union officer to cross her path, had been one.

He realized his revenge was hollow. The sins were the father's, not the daughter's. He walked over to her and held out the watch.

"Here," he said in a gentle tone. "It'll work now."

She took it from him and tried to put it back over her head, but couldn't open the chain wide enough. Hud took the watch and spread the chain with his fingers, then slipped it over her head. Her hair felt like silk, sable-colored silk. He resisted the odd urge to run his fingers through the damp tresses and feel the fineness.

"Thank you," she murmured in a low voice.

He nodded.

She said, "My father wouldn't have wanted to leave your brother."

"But he did."

She gave no answer to that. Finally, she raised her head. "How do you know about my sister?"

"I've seen her."

Her grey eyes widened. Like a fawn's eyes, he thought. Innocent and vulnerable. "You have? How is she? Is she better?"

He thought of the woman in St. Louis. "I . . . I don't think so."

She slumped, the moment of hope gone in an instant.

"You do what you do to pay for her care, don't you?" he asked, the truth suddenly dawning. All of the anger went out of him.

"Yes!" She spat the word out. Twin tears tracked their way down her cheeks as she lifted her head. "She's under a doctor's constant supervision and the nuns need the money for her upkeep. She saved my life once, and it's all I can give her now."

Everything snapped into place like a bolt into a lock. Sympathy welled up inside him. She might have broken the law, but she was no criminal. The apple *had* fallen far from the tree, after all. That thought meant more to him than he cared to admit.

"I see," he said. "But you wouldn't have had to resort to cheating towns of their money, would you, if you hadn't taken on the cost of all those other people the nuns have—"

"What other people?" She frowned in puzzlement.

"The others," Hud reminded her. A vaguely uneasy feeling came over him. "At the nuns' hospital. People sick in the mind like your sister. The nuns said you send extra money for their care—"

"I do not!" she exclaimed in outrage, sitting up. "The money I send is for my sister. Do you mean all that extra I've sent for her future they've been using for *others?*"

He nodded. "That's what the Mother Superior told me."

"No!" She burst into tears. Shocked, he watched her weep copiously. She hadn't cried for her father, but she cried for this. "I was . . . getting ahead . . . in case anything . . . happened to me. How could they? How could they?"

Hud couldn't answer her. But as he remembered the kindly, naive faces of those women, he knew how they had. It wouldn't have been in their hearts to say "no" to others in need, especially when they thought they had a benefactress.

Feeling sorry for the reluctant female Robin Hood under his arrest, he walked over to his saddlebags and sat down. He unfolded the two papers and found himself looking at a crude map—or part of a crude map. Hills were marked but unnamed, and a stream ran through the smaller bit, John's part of the map. An "X" was on the other near what looked like a hill, but contained no writing. John's bit held several words—"Hard . . . stream . . . cave"—in a spidery scrawl that made no sense, his map having been separated between some instructions. There was no clue about which area of the country the map defined. All John had ever noted was "Indian Territory." That could encompass anywhere from Kansas to California where there were millions of streams and caves. Hud pushed the thought away that his brother had been trying to keep the location back for a personal reason. John just hadn't wanted the place to fall into the wrong hands.

"Does it tell where the gold is?"

Hud looked up. Mary Alice's eyes were red and swollen, but her expression was curious. He shook his head. "No. You need the other parts for that."

"Are you going to go after Roger Ward?"

Hud smiled grimly. "I've been after Roger Ward

for as long as I've been after your father. I haven't found him yet. In his case, there's no family to trace either."

She glanced away and then back again. "Are you going to look for the gold?"

Hud gazed down at the cryptic pieces of paper. It was like having a cherry pie without the sugar. A major ingredient was missing. "No. I never intended to. Rest time is over."

He stood up.

"But I've barely sat down!" Mary Alice protested. She crossed her legs defiantly. "I'm not moving until I've rested and eaten. Or are you planning to starve me?"

The fragile creature of the moment before had been replaced by the tigress he had come to know. In appeasement, he began, "You can ride Brown—"

"The horse isn't even rested yet."

"—And eat biscuit and jerky while you're doing it," he finished. He looked her up and down in those shapeless clothes. "I don't think I can afford to starve you—you're too skinny as it is."

She gaped at him, then narrowed her eyes. "You wouldn't know a womanly figure if you saw it."

He grinned. "Maybe we should try with you."

She thrust out her chin. "I can't ride and eat at the same time."

Hud raised his eyebrows. "Even though most of the tribes have moved on, war parties have been out this spring. Remnants of some of the Cheyenne dog soldiers, the Arapaho, and even the Sioux have been raiding more and more around here. They're all raising hell over the way the treaties of '67 and '68 cheated them by allowing the railroads into their lands. They've been doing a slow-burning fuse and now the settlers are really coming in. That's the powder keg setting them off. They're building up to something big, and I ought to know because I've been tracking it. Hell, I don't blame them for being mad, but I don't intend to be caught out here in the middle of nowhere . . ."

She uncrossed her legs. "I'm ready."

Hud scratched at his day-old beard. "Thought you might be."

She walked over to Brown and before he could help her, she grabbed hold of the saddle horn, put her foot in the stirrup, and hoisted herself into the saddle. Hud admitted he would have liked to give her a "leg up," especially when he'd be touching her leg to do it.

After taking out some biscuit and jerky and handing them over, he slung the saddlebags over Brown's back. The canteen he hung on the saddle horn. Mary Alice tucked the stringy, tough meat in between her legs while she nibbled on the biscuit. Hud found himself wishing he were the lucky meat. She had a fire to her, a fire he wanted to explore further.

Forget it, he told himself. She was just another prisoner going to jail. And, innocent or not, she was Cullen Macaffee's daughter. Her heritage alone ought to kill any allure she might hold for him.

He picked up the reins. Slinging his rifle on his shoulder, he began walking toward the other end of the ravine.

"Why aren't you going after the gold?" she asked.

"Because it isn't mine. Besides, the map's not complete."

"The gold isn't anybody's anymore, you know," she pointed out.

"It still belongs to those who gave it," he said.

"But they already gave it to the Confederacy, so that means they gave it up. And now there is no Confederacy. That means the gold's free."

"I don't think so."

"Are you crazy?" she demanded. "Of course it doesn't belong to anybody. Who would you give it back to if you found it? Jeff Davis? He's gone. The sympathizers? Who are they? There's no way of knowing." She paused. "I suppose if it belongs to anybody, it'll be the government's now. I mean, it was given to a legitimate government of America, but since that government lost the war, the Union government would take over their claim as the winner. I don't know about you, but I wouldn't want them to get it."

Hud had to agree. It did seem a shame to leave it lying out there for any fool to stumble across, but then again, the pieces of the map didn't tell him where the gold was.

"I think . . ." Mary Alice began, in a musing tone. "Snatches of conversation with my father are coming back to me . . . when we were travelling west, he said something about Colorado being the land of milk and honey, riches flowing free . . ." Her voice quickened with excitement. "It's here in

Colorado! I know it. In fact, he even said . . ."

Her voice trailed away.

"What?" Hud asked, picking their way along the rock bed by the stream to cover their tracks. "What did he say?"

"He told me where it was," she said with great satisfaction.

Hud whipped around so quickly that Brown bucked back, startled, and nearly threw her off. "What?"

She grinned at him. "I just realized it. Something else he said clicked in my head."

"Where?" Hud asked, getting caught up in the excitement.

"Well, I'd be happy to tell you," she said, "but there's a little problem. I'm going to jail."

"Dammit, woman!" he snapped. "What the hell game are you playing at?"

"I'm not playing at anything," she replied, staring down at him. "You want the gold. I know where it is. I'm going to jail, and I don't want to go to jail. You want to know where the gold is. Don't send me to jail and I'll be happy to take you to it. A simple solution to a simple problem."

"Telling me is just as simple."

"Telling you doesn't get me out of jail."

A red haze of anger clouded around him, and he felt as if she had tricked him again with her crying and need to defend family honor. He should have known she wasn't normal. "I ought to . . ."

"What?" she scoffed. "Shoot me? That won't get you the gold. You can torture me, and I'll be damned to Satan before I tell you anything! It would give me more satisfaction to die first. You've taken the last thing that was precious to me. My father's honor. I will never forgive you for that."

He knew she meant it.

Furious, Hud turned around and tugged on Brown's reins, determined to walk off his frustration. Behind him, Mary Alice began to hum a tune.

He set his jaw against yelling at her to shut up. He must have been crazy to think she wasn't a criminal. She was as wily as they came. She was going to jail. She'd have a trial and the judge would pass a sentence or set her free. He'd speak to the judge about her sister in St. Louis. But it wasn't for him to take the law into his own hands, and he wouldn't do it for a pile of gold. Still . . .

John had left a wife and children behind. If the gold belonged to anybody, it belonged to Missy and the kids. They were eking out a living on a small farm in eastern Kansas now, young John just old enough to take it over from his mother. Hud sent money when he could. All that gold would restore their lives to what they had been—and maybe help make up for John's loss.

"You probably don't even know," he said, remembering she was a liar of the first water.

"I know," she said confidentially, from behind him. "Besides, can you afford to take the chance?"

"Yes!" The word was forced out between his clenched teeth. Damn her, he thought. She was toying with him. How could she know? What could her father have said that gave her an exact location? And if he had, then why had she never known about the gold?

He realized the precious metal was already exerting its power over him, luring him into straying from his duties. Gold Fever. He cursed himself. He hadn't even seen gold yet and he was already succumbing to it—and to a fiery temptress. Mary Alice Macaffee hadn't matched her prim and proper name. She'd already lured him once into believing she was a Countess, and she was luring him now with the thought of unclaimed riches for the taking.

"Thinking about it, aren't you?" she taunted.

"No."

"Well, I'm just as glad," she said. "I'll serve a few years in prison, probably at most—if a judge believes I'm guilty. And the gold will sit there waiting for me after I get out. The Good Lord knows it won't spoil."

He hated the thought of her getting it all, although he could see her sister needed it. But his brother had paid the biggest price for that gold. His brother's family deserved it, too.

"Ward probably got it years ago," he said, in an attempt to stifle her grand scheme and bring himself back to reality. "He could remember where it is, as well as your father."

"But then why would they have made a map if finding it were that easy?" she asked logically.

"Then how could you know where it is?" he asked, just as logically.

She was silent for a moment. Hud smiled in satisfaction. He'd caught her in the lie.

"I may know where it is, but I don't know how to get there," she replied. "That's the part you have."

He laughed. "Then you can't get it without me, and I'm not going."

"But I'll have plenty of time and plenty of people in prison to ask about the way," she mused. "A question here, a question there, and eventually I'll know what's on the part of the map you have."

"Shut up," Hud practically growled, jerking Brown faster along the trail.

"Okay," Mary Alice said. "Anyway, it'll give me time to think. Maybe I'll remember even more my father said . . . now that I know what to remember."

He wondered what she was thinking, then scoffed at the idea. She was a treacherous woman, he reminded himself. An actress Edwin Boothe would have admired. She didn't know anything. There wasn't anything more to remember.

Hud pulled Brown along the stream bed. They were both silent for another hour. The sun lowered, turning into a red-orange ball that streaked the sky with its colors. Birds cried overhead, startled at the sudden invasion into their domain. They rounded a bend to find several deer drinking water. The animals lifted their heads, their ears flicking in unison; then fled in a scattering of white tails.

As they covered more miles in silence, he tried not to think about the gold, the map, or Mary Alice. He was taking her in, just as he was supposed to do. Then he was going after the

Winslows and the trail of the gun sales. He hadn't been lying about the Indians. The young Cheyenne warriors were tired of being penned up in Oklahoma Indian Territory or driven north. They were resurrecting the dog soldier societies—or trying to. Rumors abounded that Bull Bear would come out of retirement to lead them again, and that their great warrior Roman Nose had arisen from the dead to bring death to the whites. The war bands were raiding everywhere, it seemed, throughout western Kansas and eastern Colorado. Tribes who had been enemies for centuries were joining up to fight. And they were getting the weapons to do it.

Like a lot of Denverites, Hud had found himself sympathizing on more than one occasion with the desperate men. They'd had their lands taken and whole villages massacred at Sand Creek and Washita where the great peace chief Black Kettle was killed by that son of a bitch Custer. There had been a lot of wrong done, but more wrong wasn't the answer. People were going to get hurt if the gun traffic wasn't stopped. He couldn't just walk away from the job and go after some fool's gold—especially on her word. It was long gone

But what if it wasn't? Didn't John suffer the most from its evil? Wouldn't John want him to find the hidden cache for his wife and children, rather than Ward or Macaffee's daughter?

Hud pushed the thoughts aside even as he pushed ahead. At the rate they were going it would take them three days to get to Denver. But they were going to Denver. She was going to jail to await trial, and he was going after the gun runners.

And then he would go after the gold, he decided. Instantly, he hit a snag. He would need her to get it . . . if she weren't lying, a big "if" in itself.

"Shit," Hud muttered under his breath.

"Are we ever going to stop?" Mary Alice asked. "I'd like to eat before my stomach caves in on my backbone."

"You just ate," he said, without turning around.

"That was hours ago. It's going to get dark soon, too dark to keep moving on."

Hud pulled up and looked around. He realized they had come too far south and west. He had completely missed the triple rock column that led to the easterly trail for Denver. He cursed again.

"I would hardly put it that way," Mary Alice said. "But I suppose we ought to stop for that, too."

"I missed the trail to Denver."

"Been thinking about the gold?"

"No, I haven't been thinking about the gold," he snapped.

"Could have fooled me."

He set his jaw against an answer, then yanked Brown's reins and walked out of the creek bed toward the pine and aspen forest.

Once they were deep under the canopy of green leaves, he kept the weak light of the setting sun at his left shoulder as he cut a diagonal backtrack to the triple rock column. Mary Alice said nothing, and he was grateful to her. The last thing he needed was her needling him about the gold. It was nearly dark by the time they could see the triple rock column in the distance again.

"We'll stay here tonight," he said, stopping in the shadow of a group of boulders that formed a makeshift protective circle.

"Here?" she questioned, looking around dubiously. She frowned. "Can't we keep moving until we come to a town?"

"There isn't one for another ten miles," Hud said.

"Well, let's move on then," she said firmly. "We can make it—"

"No, we can't. It's too far, too dark, and I'm not about to be caught out in the open at night."

"If we really push it . . . yipe!"

He lifted her down off the horse, ignoring her shriek of surprise. Through the heavy coat, he could feel an extra roll of flesh at her waist. It surprised him; she didn't look heavy. In fact, she looked damned good to him. The moment her feet touched the ground, she scooted away.

"I thought you were hot to get me to jail," she said.

"Not hot enough to get myself killed," he answered, losing patience. He unstrapped his bedroll and tossed it to her. It fell at her feet. "Here, make yourself useful."

She didn't pick it up. "What am I supposed to do with it?"

"Set it up by those rocks," he said, wondering if she'd gone crazy on him. "We'll be out of the wind at least."

Mary Alice stared at him for one long moment, then slowly picked up the bedroll. As she walked over to the spot he indicated, she knew she was desperate to keep out of jail. But how desperate was she?

Not that desperate, she thought, resolving to fight him if he tried anything. She hated him for what he had done to her today. But a part of her mind wondered what it would be like to be kissed by him, to feel herself lying under him again, not in anger but in passion. Flashes of their struggle in Boulder came back to her, vividly reminding her of the strength of his legs as they tangled with hers. The weight of him pressing her down . . .

Shocked at what she was thinking, Mary Alice forced her mind away. She would never be desperate enough to risk her sanity for a moment of a man's pleasure. Especially not for Marshal Hud Jackson's.

She dumped the bedroll by the rocks and sat down. The things he'd said about her father were lies, she thought. They had to be. Her father had been good and kind. He would never leave a man to die. Never. It had to have been that other man, Roger Ward. *He* was the one; he had forced her father, surely. There was some other explanation for the map in the watch—a very innocent one.

She watched Hud brush the horse down with the saddle blanket and hobble the animal to graze. He'd given her doubts about an honorable man. She could never forgive him for that.

But then there was the gold. All those lovely shiny yellow coins just out there for the taking.

Maybe it would be bullion, Mary Alice mused. Bullion was lovely, too.

Dammit, that gold was hers, she thought. She had as much claim to it as anybody else. More. If she found it, she could provide for Harriet for as long as her sister lived. And she would never have to play the Countess or Earnest John or anybody else again. All she had to do was stay out of jail, get her hands on his half of the map . . . and figure out the rest.

What the marshal didn't know wouldn't hurt him.

"Thinking about the gold?" he asked, coming toward her, carrying the saddle and the bags.

"Unlike you, I'll be honest. Yes." She toyed with some small rocks next to her. "Just remembering what my father said."

He snorted his disbelief, then set down the saddle. He handed her the canteen and a small bag. "No coffee tonight, Countess. We can't risk a fire."

"I won't argue with that."

He smiled and said in a very dry tone, "I'm grateful."

He set the saddle on the ground, then spread out the horse blanket next to it for them both to sit on. He sat and crossed his long legs Indian-style, leaving her a bit of space on the other end.

She sat on the edge of the blanket and rubbed her hands together, wishing things could be different about the coffee. It was chilly, a brisk breeze kicking up through the pass. Even in the leeway of the boulders, she could feel it infiltrating her corduroy pants. Hard to believe it was spring, she thought. The blacksmith's coat was heavy enough —at least for now. Unfortunately, in the mountains it would get colder before it got warmer.

She found herself watching Hud, watching the way his hands moved over everything with an innate self-assurance. Those same hands must know how to please a woman. What would it be like to see that hard line of his mouth soften? She swallowed, her mouth devoid of moisture.

He handed her more biscuit and jerky. She broke off a piece of the biscuit, ignoring the dry, hard staleness of the bread, and chewed, determined to regain her composure. She had never reacted like this to a man before. It was both heady and very frightening.

"Not bad," she commented.

"You *are* hungry." He raised his eyebrows. "I've never seen a woman with such an appetite. I hope I've got enough to last."

She smiled. "You could always let me go—"

"Don't start," he muttered, breaking off a piece of the biscuit and jerky. He popped them both into his mouth, chewing vigorously.

Knowing he'd be too occupied to talk, she began. "I really think you ought to seriously consider my proposition over the gold—"

The gun coming out of his holster interrupted her. He held it up, examined it, then set it on the ground next to him. He gave her a meaningful look. His mouth might still be chewing but he'd certainly gotten his point across.

The rest of the meal was finished in silence.

Mary Alice watched him flick the last of the

biscuit crumbs from his shirtfront. He stretched out on the ground, rested his head on the seat of the saddle, and set his hat over his face.

"Let me know if you see anything," he said from under the hat.

"Like what?" she muttered, staring out into the growing pitch of the night. She could barely see the horse.

"Use your brain. I know you've got one. And remember what I said about the judge and escaping."

"Five more years, no parole."

"Good girl. Wake me in a couple of hours. You can have the bedroll."

Clearly he wasn't going to expect any "favors" from her. Mary Alice was grateful . . . and yet the thought that he didn't find her attractive enough gnawed at her.

Don't be ridiculous, she told herself. It wasn't what she wanted; it never would be. As far as she was concerned, the marshal could take a nice long nap. She'd be happy to stand guard all night.

She peered into the darkness and listened intently for the slightest unnatural noise. The wind whispered through the trees. An owl hooted. The horse chomped on the sweet grasses. The owl hooted again. Something scurried through the bushes. The owl hooted a third time.

Mary Alice tapped the marshal. "There's an owl out there."

"No kidding," came his voice from under the hat.

"Maybe it's not an owl," she whispered. Maybe it's an Indian—"

"It's an owl."

"Are you sure?"

"It's an owl."

She took a deep breath.

"It's an owl, dammit!"

"Okay," she muttered. "It's an owl."

She stopped and listened to the owl hooting its head off. It sure didn't sound like any owl she'd ever heard before, and she'd tell him that right before the Indians scalped them both. She and Otis had been on the trails camping out many times, but her senses had never been this tense. Every breeze, every rustle seemed to shout through her system. What was wrong with her?

Mary Alice put the thought aside, having a bad feeling the answer was lying next to her. The marshal seemed to be sound asleep. Certainly he hadn't moved from his position on the blanket. The minutes were agonizingly long as she watched and listened.

But nothing materialized out of the darkness, and she woke the marshal as close as she could tell to the two-hour mark. He came awake instantly. "Everything okay?"

"Except for a maniacal owl, yes." She shivered. The temperature had dropped with a quickness that already had her hands and toes frozen.

"Why didn't you take the blanket out of the bedroll?" Hud asked, untying it.

"A slight problem." She held up her still-tied-and-cuffed hands.

"Oh." He cut the knot of the rope and unlocked the handcuffs.

Mary Alice pushed the hateful loops off her wrists. She flexed her fingers, feeling the slight tingling. "Aren't you afraid I'll escape?"

"Why should I be? I'm awake now."

"Of course." She scrambled into the roll, burrowing down into the blankets for warmth. She ignored her continued shivering, knowing it would stop once she warmed up. Her hands were free at last, but she was too tired to think of anything. She'd just sleep for a little while, she decided, closing her eyes. And then she'd come up with something. Something that didn't entail an angry judge, five extra years, and no parole . . .

Hud watched his intriguing prisoner shiver herself to sleep. The temperature had dropped alarmingly during the last few hours. Common sense told him what he had to do if he were to keep her and himself alive through the night. But he hesitated, knowing the torture it could cause. Finally, logic won out. With a curse, Hud pulled up the blanket and slipped in beside her, tucking her body against the length of his.

Even through the heavy clothes, he was all too aware of the soft woman's flesh underneath. Her hair seemed to flow around his face, the fine strands exactly like those threads of silk he'd compared them to earlier. The scent of female filled his nostrils. It had been a long time since he'd held a woman and never such a vital, intriguing woman as Mary Alice Macaffee.

The torture had already begun.

Mary Alice didn't know how long she'd been asleep, but slowly she became aware of a heat and a weight against her back. She snuggled into it to drive out the chill. An arm came around her. A strong, comforting, protective arm.

She practically shot out of the bedroll.

"What the hell do you think you're doing?" she demanded, sitting up.

"Keeping warm," Hud said, still lying next to the spot where she'd been. "And will you lower your voice? Sound travels far at night."

"I thought you were guarding us," she whispered, conceding to his request.

"I am. But you were shivering in your sleep, and I'm freezing, too. I figured our combined body heat would—"

"I'm not interested in . . . in . . ."

"Neither am I," he said. "But I don't want to die frozen like an icicle because I'm too stupid to bundle with you. The blanket's between us, plus clothes. You wouldn't be any safer with the Temperance Union. Now get back here before we both freeze in mid-argument."

The darkness hid his expression, but she didn't have to see his face to comprehend his disgust. Every nerve in Mary Alice's body screamed a protest at the thought of bundling with him. It was too dangerous for her well-being. And yet she knew he was right. They had no warmth but each other's bodies, and they would have to use them together to survive.

"Why couldn't I have gotten arrested in the middle of summer?" she muttered, very slowly crawling back next to him. It had been the worst day—and now night—she'd ever had in her life . . . and she'd had plenty of bad ones.

She didn't look at his eyes before she turned her back to him. He pulled her close against him again. Mary Alice swallowed, feeling every inch of him curved along her body. Odd butterflies flitted along her abdomen and thighs, while a hollow pit opened in her stomach. He made no other move toward her, just his arm around her waist to hold her in place.

She didn't sleep a wink for the rest of the night.

Chapter Five

"I need a dress."

Hud turned around and stared at Mary Alice as she sat on the horse. The request was a simple one and she looked as placid as Brown, but he didn't trust her for one moment.

"I'll need a dress if you want everyone to think I'm the wicked Countess," she continued. The leather creaked as she shifted in the saddle. "I certainly don't look like one at the moment."

She had a point, he conceded to himself.

"Besides, I'd like to look presentable before the judge," she added. "It would help my cause. You can't deny me my rights without appearing to be an ogre. I'm a woman alone in the West, after all, to be given full courtesies. People won't like it if you don't."

She had a point there, too.

But she also had something up her sleeve that entailed getting a dress. She was too damn clever, Hud thought, trying to see what havoc a dress could cause.

"I pick the dress," he said.

"And you pay for it."

"Now just hold on a minute," he began indignantly.

"If you pick it then you pay for it." She lifted her chin. "I have no money, and the Territory cannot deny me appropriate clothing for my trial."

Hud grumbled under his breath and yanked Brown's reins after him as he trudged along the wagon-rutted dirt road. They were on the outskirts of Denver, and he was tired from lack of sleep and walking while she rode. Last night, he had watched her shake with cold and had known he'd have to bundle with her. But to lie there with her back against his chest, her curved rear spooned along his thighs, had nearly undone him. Even the cold and the thick layers of coats and blankets between them couldn't rid him of the vision of her naked and cuddled to him after lovemaking. He hadn't had to wake her to play guard for the rest of the night. Why bother, when *he* wasn't getting a wink of sleep.

All he wanted now was to get her to the jail, go to his room at Mrs. Jerome's Boarding House, fall into his bed, and stay there for a week. He'd buy her that damn dress, and if one thing happened, one little thing, he'd strip it off her himself.

That settled in his mind, they came down out of the hills and into the thriving city of clapboard houses, straight streets, and elegant hotels. This was the new Denver, the old one having been built along the banks of the Cherry Creek and nearly wiped out in the flood of '64. Streetcars competed with wagons, carriages, and riders in a traffic jam of horses and noise. One streetcar whizzed by them on the downgrade, the horse who had pulled it up the grade now freeloading a ride on the trolley's back platform.

"Ah, Denver, Queen City of the West," Mary Alice said, great satisfaction in her voice. "Civilization and sophistication within a day's ride of the wilderness."

Hud squinted up at her in speculation. "Been here much?"

"My first visit in several years." She sighed loudly. "How I wish I could enter this fair city under less humiliating circumstances."

"And have you tricked Evans, Hill, and Cheeseman out of their money?" Hud shook his head. If she ever got loose in Denver, those three biggest citizens had better run for cover. They'd be lucky to have their shirts on before she was through.

On the other hand, having her leave him only in his shirt in another form of seduction teased at his mind. Hud shook his head to clear it.

"Cheeseman might not be so bad, you know." Mary Alice leaned forward, her hair coming around her face like a veil. "Everyone here is still smarting over his water monopoly."

"I thought you hadn't been here in years," he said, knowing she was talking about one of Denverites' major bones of contention.

"I haven't. However, knowledge can bring one a wealth of riches."

"Especially someone else's," Hud muttered. A building sign caught his eye. "Here's a dress shop."

He pulled Brown over to the nearest hitching post and wrapped the reins around the scraped log. Brown lowered his head to the trough. Hud watched as Mary Alice slid a long leg around the horse's rump and stepped down out of the stirrup. People stared at her as she walked nonchalantly into the dress shop. Hud followed behind, stifling a grin. She had nothing to worry about. Even dressed in men's clothes, her hair unbound and hanging down her back in all its chestnut glory, Mary Alice Macaffee had still managed to make a grand entrance into the great city of Denver.

Inside the shop, the owner, a small, plump woman in a high-collared black dress, stared at Mary Alice.

"We want a dress," Hud said.

"For me." Mary Alice smiled sweetly.

Hud gritted his back teeth. She was never going to let him forget Boulder. "I'm Marshal Hud Jackson, and we want the dress for the *prisoner.*"

The shop owner looked at Mary Alice as if she'd suddenly grown two heads.

"Ah . . . we have few ready-mades." She waved toward several dresses displayed on wall pegs.

Mary Alice frowned as she examined a black muslin mourning dress. "I believe that would be inappropriate."

And probably premature, Hud thought. One wore black *after* the hanging.

She turned her nose up at a purple wool dress

trimmed in lace fringe with a very wide skirt.

"What's wrong with it?" Hud asked.

Her eyebrows rose in astonishment at his question. "Hud, it's at least ten years old." She turned to the owner. "Have you anything in the latest fashion?"

The woman walked to the other side of the shop. "There are several over here, but they're my displays—"

"They'll cost too much," Hud said, following behind Mary Alice.

"Nonsense," Mary Alice replied.

He pointed back to the purple wool. "We're buying that dress, Countess, and no more of *your* nonsense."

"Hud, do you want me to sully your reputation by going to jail looking like something out of Atlanta during Sherman's march to the sea?" Mary Alice asked, her hands on her hips. She whirled around and pointed to the newer dresses. "I'll try on the white muslin with the blue and green spot pattern. That's not too outdated. And the grey silk with the double skirt and rosettes. The marshal will pay extra since they're displays."

"I will not!" Hud exclaimed, glaring at her. His prisoner ignored him.

"Have you any . . ." She leaned forward, whispering loud enough for him to hear. ". . . Underthings, madam? I am afraid I am sorely lacking in necessities."

The woman blinked. "Ahh . . . I believe we can accommodate you. You can try on the clothes in the back."

She led Mary Alice through a curtained doorway. They both turned when Hud followed them into the long hallway.

"What *are* you doing?" Mary Alice asked.

"Just watching over you, Countess."

"You are not coming with me."

"Is there a window back there?" he asked the shop owner.

Startled by his question, her jaw dropped open. "Yes, but—"

"Then I'm coming in, too."

He walked past the women and into the back room. It was long and narrow with two windows and a dressing screen in one corner. The sewing machine took up most of the area. A young girl sat in front of the Singer, working the treadles and feeding material under the needle. The girl stopped her work and looked wide-eyed at the male invader. Hud smiled at her and leaned against the wall where he had an unobstructed view.

His prisoner glared at him.

Hud smiled innocently. "Let's get moving, Countess." He turned his gaze to the shop owner. "And bring her the purple wool."

The dressmaker scurried to do as he asked. Mary Alice narrowed her eyes at him. "You son-of-a—"

"Swearing is a fifty dollar fine and two days in jail."

". . . Bitch. It's worth it."

"Suit yourself." Hud couldn't help grinning at her.

Mary Alice swept behind the changing screen

and sat down on the narrow stool. She would kill him, she thought. As the Good Lord was her witness, at some time and some place, she would kill the man. And damn what the judge would say!

She took a deep breath and exhaled. Giving in to one's fury was all well and good, but it didn't get her out of this mess. She wasn't going to prison. Surely, he didn't really mean to put a woman in jail for a prison trial. Her stomach churned at how close the masquerade had already come. Prisons were filthy, horrible places where people did filthy, horrible things. Like in the war.

Visions from the past rose up inside her brain, swiftly and with great devastation. Mary Alice gasped out a sob of despair and swiped at the sudden tears. Ever since she'd met Hud Jackson memories had been stirring up again. Memories she'd thought were long gone from her mind.

"Oh," said the shop owner as she came behind the screen and saw her customer's distress. Her arms were filled with dresses, clearly showing she was ready for even the remote possibility of a sale.

Mary Alice immediately turned her hand and pressed her fingers against her cheeks, wiping away the trickle of wetness. It sickened her to think that the woman had caught her like this.

"I'm sorry," she said, a plan forming in her mind, more satisfying than her previous thoughts. "Please, I did not mean to be so . . . critical about your merchandise earlier. But that marshal . . . he just will not listen to reason." She kept her voice low, barely a whisper, as she continued. "I've tried to tell him he's made a terrible mistake, that I'm not the person he seeks. I'm a Countess of the Realm, Queen Victoria's lady-in-waiting, and I'm lost from my travelling party. Can he not tell even from my speech that I am a gentlewoman?"

"I certainly can," the woman admitted, wide-eyed.

Mary Alice smiled and nodded her head in acknowledgement. "Of course you can. You are an extremely reasonable woman. One knows."

"Thank you." The woman smiled back tremulously.

Mary Alice reached out and took the woman's hands, looking her straight in the eyes. "Can you help me? He . . . the marshal frightens me." She paused dramatically. "He spoke of the old days with a man named Harrison and how 'they' would make Denver know its place again."

The woman gasped at the name of the ringleader of the Bummers, a gang of hellions who caused much anarchy in the city during the early years of the war. A little knowledge, Mary Alice thought.

"I somehow knew that name was dangerous to this fair city," she said. She tightened her grasp on the woman's hands. "Can you help me?"

Wariness came into the woman's eyes and she glanced behind her as if Hud were there. "Oh . . . ah, I don't know."

"Could you just go to Mr. William Byers of the *Rocky Mountain News?*" Mary Alice made her voice more urgent. "Please. I have heard of him and heard he is a man with much honor who's righted many injustices through his newspaper.

He has the power to help me now."

The woman nodded.

Both of them jumped as Hud called out, "I don't have all day, Countess!"

"You see?" Mary Alice whispered. "Just go to Mr. Byers and tell him to come to the . . ." She frowned. "Where will he take me?"

"To the sheriff's office at the Court House, I suppose," the woman said. "That's usually where prisoners are held."

"Then tell him to come there. I'm a woman alone and desperately need his help."

Hud called out again. "You're not trying on that one from Paris, are you? I said no. And I meant it, dammit!"

"Go." Mary Alice let go of the woman's hands. "Act like nothing is wrong and after we leave, go to Mr. Byers. Promise me."

"I promise."

Mary Alice tapped her on one ample shoulder and then the other. "I hereby make you a Lady of the Realm for your good deed and swear all fealty for your bravery."

The woman's eyes were wide with wonder. "You mean I'm a—"

"Yes, you are," Mary Alice said, pushing her toward the entrance. "Now, remember. Act natural and go to Mr. Byers right after we leave."

The woman nodded. "You can rely on me."

"I hope so," Mary Alice muttered as the woman scurried out.

Hud appeared at the side of the screen after the woman had gone. He looked like he'd just bitten a rattlesnake. "What the hell were you doing with that woman?"

"Trying on a dress," Mary Alice said innocently. That she was in her same pants and shirt didn't disconcert her.

"Then why are you still holding the thing?" He glared. "And it's not the purple one. Dammit, Countess—!"

"All right, the purple one." She would look like an elephant in the crinolines required, but she was desperate to divert him.

"Now, what scheme were you trying to pull with the woman?"

"Nothing."

He stepped behind the screen. If the area had been tiny before, now it was like a coffin. "What were you doing? Answer me. Were you trying to get that woman to help you escape?"

"Yes," Mary Alice hissed. Then, in a calculated move, she added, "But she refused. Happy now?"

He released a breath of air. "No. But you're probably telling the truth."

As far as it went, she thought, without moving a facial muscle.

He snorted. "Take the grey if it fits."

Mary Alice stared at his back as he turned and walked away. That had been quite a concession. And better still, the grey had the advantage of subdued dignity. Mr. Byers would be most impressed.

Mary Alice began stripping off the men's clothes she'd been wearing, all the while thinking up what she would say to the newspaper editor. It had to be good. It had to be better than good.

It had to be perfect.

"Got a prisoner for you, Mike."

The deputy sheriff turned away from his game of solitaire and grinned. "Hud Jackson. We been wonderin' about you."

Hud smiled thinly. "I have a prisoner to be held for the federal judge."

"That pretty lady?" Mike asked, smiling appreciatively. "What'd she do?"

"Confidence trickster." Hud had the overwhelming urge to smash that smile off the man's face. He'd never liked Mike O'Hara, but the way the man looked at Mary Alice was enough to get his blood boiling.

"Well, well," Mike said, raising his eyebrows. "Business has been a little slow today. She'll liven things right up, I reckon."

"She's to be held in solitary and treated with all due respect," Hud said, leaning forward. "Or you'll be lucky if I only beat you to death."

"No need to get huffy just because I'm admiring the lady, Hud." Mike rose to his feet.

Hud took Mary Alice's arm to walk into the back of the jail. She didn't budge.

He turned around to find her staring at the large iron-studded door that separated the office from the cells. Her face was completely white and her eyes were hollow and staring.

"Countess," Hud said softly, frowning. "Wake up."

She just stared at the door.

"Countess."

"No," she said finally. Her voice rose. "No! No! No!"

Hud stared at her in astonishment. He'd expected yelling and screaming, but not this kind of genuine fear. He immediately reminded himself that he had seen her transform into anyone she wanted to be, that she had even tricked him into believing her before. He hardened his heart against the sight of her.

"Come on," he growled, pulling her into the back. She felt like a rag doll in his hands.

The three holding cells were empty, although the dirty mattresses and unemptied slop bucket attested to recent former occupants.

"Clean up the place, damn you," Hud said to the man. He whisked Mary Alice out of the back room.

She was shaking, her body trembling violently.

"I'm sorry," he said, not knowing what else to do. He cursed O'Hara for his laziness.

"Don't put me in there," she whispered. "Please."

Something inside him broke at her words. If she'd screamed or cried, she never would have even dented his mental armor. But that fear in her low voice swept right through as if he'd been thin, worn cotton. Hud swallowed, took a deep breath . . . and hardened his heart.

"I have to," he said. "You broke the law, Mary Alice. Now I have to do my job. It's the only honor left to me."

She seemed to shudder inside herself at his words. A stiffening drew through her, like a rod slowly asserting itself. "If you can do this, then you have no honor."

Hud clamped his jaw around his anger. "Where was yours?"

"Left back in Alabama with those murdering Yankees." She turned her head and looked at him with forthright brown eyes. "I make no excuse for that, Marshal."

He nodded. "I'll speak to the judge. See what I can do for you . . . and your sister."

Her expression turned colder. Hud had a feeling he'd said exactly the wrong thing.

"Cleaned up," Mike said, emerging from the back. He looked at the two people who paid no attention to him.

Hud stared at Mary Alice, hesitating, not feeling right somehow over what he was about to do. Mary Alice's gaze never wavered from his. It never pleaded, either.

"I'm sworn to uphold the law," he muttered, pulling her back into the cell area. He steered her into the semi-clean one and banged the door shut behind her, mentally flinching at the sound. Turning the key in the lock with a final click, he said, "I'm sorry, Countess. I'll see you've got your comforts."

She never turned around. Never said a word.

Hud stared at her for one seemingly endless moment.

Then he walked out of the room.

* * *

Mary Alice sat on the very edge of the dirty mattress and closed her eyes against her fate.

This was only temporary, she told herself as the panic welled up inside her again. She could easily talk her way out of this. In the meantime she would endure what she had to.

She had hate to strengthen her. Hud Jackson would pay for what he'd done. He claimed he was a man of honor, but no man with the least shred of honor would have left her in this hell-hole. And he'd enjoyed her humiliation. That had been so obvious.

He'd taken away her freedom and taken away her father. Soon, her sister would know great suffering because of him. Her hate burned at the thought. She would avenge herself against the marshal.

And then she would avenge her father's honor against the third man, Roger Ward. He had been the one to leave Hud's brother. She knew it. Not her father. Never her father.

Mary Alice curled her fingers around the iron bed-frame and vowed she would take vengeance against them all.

And once she did, the gold would be hers.

Chapter Six

The harlot's face was painted white and tinged with red, like a clown's. Her hair, questionably clean, hung in lank handfuls around her face. Her expression was hard and cold as she stripped off her dress slowly for the customer lying on the bed.

Richard Walker stared at the woman, half in revulsion, half in fascination. She was everything he hated, dirty and knowing. To her, he was the next gold dollar. To him, she was another break with the past, a past he never allowed himself to think about. A past long forbidden to him by his own actions.

And yet lately it had risen up again like ghosts on Hallow's Eve. Like his real name, he had buried his former life so far inside himself that he'd never thought a whisper of it would cross his mind again.

Maybe it was the trade with the Indians, he wondered. They had thought it a joke to be sold guns by whites for raids on whites. Fools, Richard thought, knowing the railroads were beginning to proliferate now that the Denver Pacific and Kansas Pacific connections were complete. Soon, building of the side branches would begin, and in fact was already beginning close to Denver. With help from a friend in the railroad office, he'd calculated where they would go next and had begun creating the Indian raids to drive out the settlers along those paths—or at least make them sell out to the well-meaning man who felt sorry for them. And the Indians posed no problems. The army would move and wipe them out in retaliation for the settler raids. And all the while he sat in nice, distant Denver and waited for events to take their natural course. After they did, he'd hold all the major right-of-ways in two territories—if his creditors didn't close in on him first.

The prostitute drew his attention as she began to unbutton his pants, exposing him. He watched her, unmoving. She was dressed only in garters and stockings, which were laddered throughout on both legs. She hesitated for a long moment, then buried her face in his crotch.

Her effort produced absolutely no effect. In disgust, Richard pulled himself away.

"You have to pay me anyway," she said, wiping her mouth.

He glared at her, then got up from the bed. He slammed a coin down on the table. "Whore."

She picked up the coin and then began to pull on her clothes, unconcerned with his epithet. When she was dressed, she opened the door to the saloon's upper rooms and said, "Honey, the Good

Book says to follow the Golden Rule, so make sure you can at least 'do' unto others before you start callin' names again."

Richard cursed as she scurried out and slammed the door behind her.

"Bitch," he muttered.

He rolled over on the bed, burying his face in the pillow. It didn't matter, he thought. No man in his right mind would take to a woman like that one. Someday, when he'd made his money, he could come out into the open again rather than stay holed up in Denver's worst saloons. He would be the person he once had been. And he would have money. He'd aleady lost more than he cared to remember. He didn't dare remember.

It didn't matter, he mused. Money was money, no matter where it came from. And money was what counted in this world.

This time it wouldn't slip through his fingers.

Hud slid down into the tub of water, luxuriating in the feel of the soapsuds and warmth against his skin. It was his third bath since he'd seen the Countess off to jail last night . . .

It didn't seem fair somehow for him to have this pleasure and deny it to her. Certainly, he gave her no opportunity for one. Hell, he thought. She probably would have escaped if he had. Then he smiled. He would have had to guard her very closely.

"Damn," he muttered cheerfully. Next time he had to be quicker.

The memory of how he'd left her surfaced in his brain. Guilt washed through him as he remembered her stricken face. She had been scared to death for a moment—she hadn't been playing false on that.

But that didn't change what she'd done. And it didn't change what he'd had to do. He'd talk to the judge first thing this morning and see what arrangements could be made to lessen her sentence. Then he'd go visit her. He hadn't left her in the best of circumstances, after all. She was safe enough with Mike; the man knew Hud would kill him if he touched her. Still, he'd have to see about better arrangements. And a bath.

The curtain partitioning him from the others in the bath house was pushed open by the proprietor. "You want a newspaper, mister? We add two cents to your charge for delivery."

Hud grinned. He'd always liked this bath house best when he was in town. They didn't run the patrons off with a quick swipe.

"Sure," Hud replied.

He sat up in the metal tub and unfolded the newspaper, carefully keeping the edge of it out of the water. The headline blared its news around a drawing amazingly like Mary Alice Macaffee. In jail. With the saddest look on her face as she gripped the cell bars. He read on . . .

DENVER'S DISGRACE

"The law dirtied its own hands this time when a lovely woman, a brave flower of

English Society, was arrested in circumstances so heinous that I have never seen their like in my fifteen years of publishing this paper.

Countess Browning, lost from her travelling party and accused of thievery under highly questionable grounds as far as this reporter can determine, has been dragged across this territory without care for her needs, given one thin dress to ward off Colorado's chill spring, and thrown into a jail cell inhabited by murderers and other hardened criminals. What has our justice system come to when a woman, unworldly and innocent before the law, is treated in so reprehensible a manner? What does this say about our fair city's practices that we allow those who enforce our laws to have no concern for the unjustly accused? The law should take itself into its own hands and acquit this woman and punish her jailers for the scandalous treatments she has been forced to endure . . ."

"I'll kill her," Hud shouted, crumpling the paper into a ball and scrambling to his feet. Water sluiced down his body unheeded as a red haze stormed through every inch of his being at Mary Alice's latest stunt. His clothes were lying on a chair next to the tub. He pulled on his pants, cursing at the way they stuck to his wet skin; staggering around, he lost his balance.

The proprietor yanked open the curtain. "Anything wrong, mister?"

"Everything." Hud reached in his pants pocket and flipped the man a coin. "Get out."

The man disappeared. Hud managed to struggle into the rest of his clothes and was down the hall and out the door in a blur. It took him two minutes exactly to run to the jail.

He burst through the door.

"Hud," Mike began, straightening up from his chair.

Hud ignored him and grabbed up the key to the cell area, unlocking the thick wood door. He was inside the moment the door gave on its latch.

"What the hell have you—?"

His voice trailed away as he stared at Mary Alice's cell. Yesterday, it had been filthy. Now, a new mattress and gingham quilt, stuffed to the straining point, graced the bed frame. A rocker sat in one corner and a small screen hiding the necessary bucket was in a place of prominence opposite. Several dresses and shawls hung on a pegboard that hadn't been there the day before. Pies and cakes were on the bed and a plate of cookies was on a small table along with a decorative pitcher of crocuses and snowdrops. The jail still had no other occupants, it being a Tuesday.

"Good morning, Marshal," Mary Alice said, smiling graciously. "Would you care for some cookies? Or a slice of pie? We have some lovely cakes—"

"WHAT THE HELL IS THIS?" he roared.

"Donations from the fair citizens of Denver.

Mrs. Byers arranged it with some of her fellow Ladies' Club members. I can see we are dyspeptic today," she added with wide-eyed innocence. "Maybe you would care for some hot chocolate, courtesy of the Windsor Hotel? Or some *boeuf bourguignon?* It's on the stove in the other room. Michael!" She called out. "Bring the marshal a plate of the *boeuf.*"

"I don't want any damn 'boof!'" Hud exclaimed, deliberately butchering the word. "What the hell is going on here?"

Mary Alice shrugged. "Kindly people have tried to relieve my plight. I don't know what you're fussing about—"

"I'm *fussing* about that newspaper article." He wrapped his fingers around the iron bars separating them, gripping the metal with all his might, as if he would lift them away in sheer anger. She must have thought so, too, because she took a step back. "I want a straight answer, woman."

"Mr. Byers heard about me and came to interview me." She stared at him. "I can't help what he wrote."

She stood there in the cell, beautiful and smart and defiant. Despite her confinement, she had outwitted him yet again.

"The hell you couldn't. How did he find out about . . . the woman in the dress shop," Hud said, answering himself as he noticed she was wearing the Paris creation they'd argued over. The white muslin fit her like a glove, outlining her figure to perfection. He forced the thought away. "You're wearing that damn dress I refused to buy for you. It was her, wasn't it? She was the only contact you had. Besides Mike."

Fury shot through him at the thought of a deputy sheriff actually arranging an interview. His next victim walked into the room right on cue.

"I got that stew like you asked, Countess," Mike said. Hud spun around at the sound of his voice. The deputy was walking carefully as he held a bowl with both hands. The rich aroma of beef and wine wafted through the room. "I kept it off to the side so it would just simmer but wouldn't burn."

"Have you lost your mind, O'Hara?" Hud asked, incredulous. Yesterday, the man had been leering. Today, he acted like a pet puppy.

"No, but you lost yours," Mike snapped.

"Me!" Hud gasped. "You arrange for Byers to interview a prisoner—"

"I didn't arrange anything," Mike said, aggrieved. "He already heard of her when he got here last night. Boy, did I get an earful—"

"But you let her be interviewed," Hud interrupted. "How the hell could you do that?"

"I couldn't stop it. Besides, I'm not the idiot who brought her in." Mike glared at him. "Arresting a fine woman like this and putting her in jail! It's embarrassing is what it is. And you ought to be ashamed, Hud. People come in all day with food for her, after they heard, and they're cursing at me now. Like I done it!" He shoved the bowl into Hud's hands. "Here. Don't know why the Countess is wasting it on you."

Hud stared down at the bowl. Everything inside

him culminated in one overwhelming rush of madness. He threw the bowl of *bourguignon* against the wall. It shattered into pieces, the brown-red juices hanging for an instant, then sliding slowly down the rough-hewn wood.

Mike shook a finger in his face. "You'll clean that up, Hud Jackson! Right now!"

"The hell I will," Hud muttered.

"Gentlemen, please." Mary Alice's voice was soft yet firm. "Mr. Jackson is testy today, Michael. It's best we leave him alone."

"Well, who's gonna clean this up?" Mike asked. He pointed his thumb behind him. "I don't want those people out there cursing at me again."

"What people?" Hud asked, feeling like events had spun far out of his control and into a quicksand already closing over his head.

"The people out in the office waiting to visit with the Countess." Mike smiled. "They brought more food."

"Oh, dear," Mary Alice said, looking around to find a place for her new culinary treats.

"That's it!" Hud snapped, waving his arms wildly. He practically put his face between the jail cell bars and said, "I don't know how the hell you managed to do what you did, but it's stopped now. Do you understand me? It's stopped now."

He turned and strode out of the room . . . and into an even worse encounter. A gaggle of people stood in the office area and the moment they caught sight of him, they swept toward him like a tidal wave, voices raised in outrage.

"How could you? You animal!"

"There's no decency left in this city, thanks to people like you."

"I'm asking the Governor to remove you from your job! How do you like that?"

"Suits me fine," Hud shouted, pushing his way between them.

"Take that, you monster!" a woman cried out, whapping him on the backside with her parasol.

His butt tingling, Hud stormed out of the office, afraid of what he'd do. He hated to leave the Countess to "hold court." No doubt she would. The heels of his boots thumped along the wooden planks of the sidewalk. The town had gone insane. That was it. Stark, staring, raving insane. Or somehow she had hypnotized them all, a distinct possibility if one were talking about Mary Alice Macaffee.

However it had happened, one thing was clear. She had the support of Denver's leading citizens. She would get off, Hud acknowledged. No judge in his right mind would even consider putting her in prison without fear of being lynched himself. It would be a miracle if she even went to trial now.

And she'd be right after that gold. There was no question about that. She'd fill in the missing pieces to the map. She'd be a dog with a bone until she did. One thing was sure in all this—he wouldn't have a job when she was let go. The Governor couldn't afford to have him any longer. He didn't even have to hear the words to know the truth of it. Hud cursed under his breath . . . and kept cursing.

Eventually, his anger was dissipated by common sense. What did the gold matter? It was ill-gotten in the first place and no good had ever come from it. Instead, it had brought tragedy and death. He didn't want it. Not really. Maybe for a wistful moment or two, but that was all. Miss "Countess" Macaffee was welcome to it. He'd earn his fortune the way nature intended—through hard work. It'd be a cleaner wealth, and one he could live with for a lifetime.

Pondering the question of how to handle her trial, or possible lack of it, with his conscience, Hud headed for the post office to get his mail. He never made it. Coming down the street toward the marshal's office was a woman with children trailing behind her. Hud blinked and rubbed his eyes, then stared at the mirage which looked exactly like an older version of John's wife, Missy.

The woman paused. "Hud? Hud, is that you?"

He stepped forward. "Missy?"

His sister-in-law flung herself into his arms, bursting into tears. "Thank God we found you."

"What are you doing in Denver?" he asked, astonished, trying to hold her upright. She was in complete collapse.

"I sent . . . you letters," Missy managed between sobs.

"I guess you beat them here." Hud looked heavenward for help.

"Uncle Hud?" The tall boy behind Missy spoke, drawing his attention.

Hud peered at him. Fair-haired and about sixteen, the boy looked anxious and as if he were trying to keep from crying. "You can't be young John."

The boy nodded, then pointed to a girl just beginning adolescence and a ten-year-old boy. "That's Jeannie and Jeff."

"But what are you all doing here?" Hud asked.

"We . . . we lost the farm," Missy gasped, swiping at her tears. She looked worn out. So did the kids. "The rains didn't come and we owed so much already, we couldn't pay without crops to sell. We couldn't get seed for this year's planting. We couldn't live. We had nowhere else to go, Hud. Nothing's left back home for us."

Hud patted her back. He'd known she'd been more desperate for funds this past year when the crops had failed, but clearly she'd been keeping from him just how serious things were. "It's okay, Missy."

"I can work," John said, straightening. "I just need a stake to go to the camps."

Hud cleared his throat, not knowing what to say to this latest complication in his life. "Let's get you settled first, boy."

He headed his family toward the boarding house he roomed in, his only permanent home. He had no idea how he was going to support them all; the money he'd been sending had been to supplement their income. It wasn't enough for all of them, he knew that. He smiled at them encouragingly.

Inside, he was sick at heart.

* * *

Mary Alice pushed a pie and cake to one side, then sat down on the quilt comfortably padding her cell bed. Her stomach protested the slightest movement, its fullness straining against her insides.

She sighed heavily, lethargic and yet content. She shouldn't have eaten so much, but all of it had been too inviting. Looking around her crammed "home," she decided that next time she was arrested she'd have to organize her gifts better. Baskets lined one side, each filled to the brim. All kinds of cakes and pies had been delivered, so many that Mike had had trouble storing them, even in the outer office. And then there were the clothes and other creature comforts. Mr. Byers had done a second article on the newfound kindliness of Denver's citizenry for a special evening edition, and the outpouring had doubled.

Mary Alice smiled ruefully. It wasn't money, but it would more than do this time. No judge would convict her now, not even Hud's evil Judge Bailey. After all, he had to live with these people afterwards, while she would be long gone. And long gone she would be. Still, she'd have to give up the Countess after this. The persona was too well known now and would never be effective again. The loss of that income was saddening.

But the look on Hud Jackson's face when he'd seen her jail cell had been worth it, Mary Alice admitted with a chuckle of satisfaction. He'd been priceless in his fury. Thank goodness solid iron bars had separated them. At one point she had been terrified he'd actually wrench them from their moorings to get at her.

What had he expected? That she would sit here meek as a lamb waiting for the trial? More fool him if he had, she thought in disgust. Maybe before she abandoned the Countess forever, she could take advantage of the citizenry's current good will . . .

Her conscience rose up in protest at the thought and Mary Alice had to agree with it. People had been good to her already, and their generosity practically ensured the outcome of any trial. Still, it seemed almost shameful to leave something so ripe for the picking.

She'd gotten Mr. Byers to put a personals ad in the newspaper, too. If that brought results . . .

Voices in the outer office caught her attention. Her nerve endings prickled with an odd shiver as she recognized Hud's. The earlier confrontation had held an undercurrent of something that created the mixed emotions of eagerness and dread. She wanted to provoke him at every turn, and yet the clash scared her because of what it evoked. Every nerve inside her was on edge. Her body seemed to sing with its aliveness. Certain parts of her, hidden parts, swam with a warm, molten liquid. The very air almost glittered around them.

He came into the cell area and the air immediately began to change. "I see you've had more visitors."

"Yes, I have." She stared straight at him, not

daring to look away and show any vulnerability.

"Right." He spun on his heel and left the room. The light went out instantly.

Mary Alice frowned. Was that it? If so, it was the oddest visit she'd ever had. She shrugged, dismissing it. He could be as cryptic as he liked.

She settled back among the cushions on her bed, feeling nice and safe and warm. There was a time she'd never have thought a jail could produce that kind of sensation. But as the Good Book said, the Lord helps those who help themselves.

And nobody helped herself better than Mary Alice Macaffee.

The scrape of metal against metal woke Mary Alice several hours later. She opened her eyes and straightened up from her cramped position on the upper end of the bunk.

Hud stood in her cell.

"You win," he said in a low voice filled with loathing. "Come on."

"Come on where?" she asked.

"Out."

"Out where?"

"Just out, goddammit!" He snatched up her shoes. "If you want out of here, this is it, Countess."

Very carefully, she said, "Are you breaking me out of jail?"

"Yes, I'm breaking you out of jail."

Mary Alice was positive she hadn't heard him right. But his expression was so filled with anger that she was surprised it didn't crack his features right off his face. This was quite a turn of events, one she'd never have expected.

"But I don't want to go."

His curse would have raised the rafters if they hadn't been made of solid adobe brick. "Oh, you're going all right. Now!"

"Look," she said. "You brought me here to stand trial. Why wouldn't I want a trial now? I'm damned if I'm going to be a fugitive for every bounty hunter around when I'll get off in just a few days, completely vindicated."

"That's exactly why I'm breaking you out now," he replied. "I'm damned if you're going to get off scot-free and go after that gold all by yourself."

She grinned. "Been eating at you, hasn't it?"

He glared at her. "Get your stuff and let's go. The laudanum I put in Mike's coffee on my earlier visit isn't going to last forever."

"But I'm not—"

"Don't," he interrupted. "Don't argue with me. God knows what I'll do if you do."

Mary Alice realized she was toying with a powder keg, the fuse already halfway gone. She swallowed. Defiance only went so far, before one became foolish. Better to defy another day.

She stood and began to gather up as much food as she could and all the lovely dresses she'd been given.

"No," Hud said. "Leave them."

"Leave them!" She rounded on him. "Are you crazy? I'm not leaving this food. And certainly none of these dresses! They were given to me—"

"Leave them," he said. "Leave everything except what you're wearing. You're going to be the 'Disappearing Countess'."

She stared at him, agape. "I'm *what?*"

"You're going to vanish right out of this cell." He smiled slightly. "Everything still here, untouched. Mike on guard in the other room, the keys still hanging on their hook. Just you gone in a mystery no one will ever be able to decipher. A gentle noblewoman, 'wrongly' accused of chicanery, disappears from her cell in a flash of the Almighty's justice. The Countess will be the stuff of legends like the seven cities of gold or the white buffalo."

"I think you're in the wrong profession," she murmured in awe.

"Hardly."

Mary Alice considered his idea. She couldn't use the Countess again; she already knew that. But what better way to go out than with a finale that would be talked about for years? Maybe even written about in one of those dime novels. There was no guarantee that even with the townspeople's support, the judge would dismiss the case. And vanishing like this meant that no bounty hunter would come after her at some point in the future. It was brilliant.

"I hate to leave the food," she said regretfully.

"I never saw anyone eat like you," Hud said, shaking his head. "Come on."

She smoothed out the wrinkles on the skirt of the green sprig muslin dress she was wearing, the shopkeeper's latest "Paris creation." "The Countess has to go with one dress, after all."

"As long as I didn't pay for it," Hud said. He waved a hand. "After you, Countess."

The Countess Elizabeth Barrett Browning strolled out of the cell and into oblivion.

Chapter Seven

Hud poked at the fire, stared at it mesmerized. It was easier than thinking about what he'd done.

Unfortunately, he couldn't keep thinking about it. He was appalled at his actions. Somehow, they had gotten out of the jail unseen. Mike had been snoring with the effects of his laudanum, his head flat on the desk top. Outside, the street had been deserted. Hud had put Brown and the other horse, a buckskin he'd brought for Mary Alice, on the side of the jail, out of sight of the street. They were camped several miles out of town in a small gully.

"Damn," he muttered, closing his eyes. A little voice inside him asked how he could call what he'd done "justice." He'd been sworn to uphold justice. That was what he believed in, lived his life by. But the Countess had bamboozled everybody into believing her. He had had to do something to stop the nonsense, to bring some kind of justice to bear. At least she could never play the Countess again. It was all the other people she could play that worried him now.

Mary Alice emerged from the bushes, catching his attention. Her fancy gown was slung over one arm and she was dressed in the pants and shirt he'd lent her. Her dark hair tumbled down her back, a sensual contrast to the roughness of the shirt. She had the shirttail tucked into the black pants. The latter were a little baggy on her frame so she had them cinched with a belt, but the result was startling. Her curves were visible, the forbidden lower limbs outlined to the junction of her.

Sweat trickled down Hud's temples. He turned away. He'd seen her like this before, so why did she cause such a vivid reaction now? Well, she had in the past, but not this vivid. Gritting his teeth, he admitted she caused all kinds of reactions in him. The better question was, why should this be any different?

And the most important question of all was, what was he supposed to do with her now that he had her?

Mary Alice folded up the dress carefully, almost lovingly, running her hands along the material. She sighed. "Good-bye, Countess. You were wonderful."

Hud made a rude noise. That the Countess was vanishing only added to his anger at himself.

She ignored him as she packed away the dress. After she was done, she pulled the saddle blanket around her shoulders against the chill air and hunkered down by the fire. She put out her hands to warm them. "It occurred to me that my vanishing is marred by your vanishing. I'm sure someone will catch on that the marshal who arrested me is no longer around, either."

He glared at her, then looked away again for a brief moment. He looked back. "I resigned."

"What!" She stared, round-eyed.

He shrugged. "I resigned."

"I don't believe it," she said. "You're teasing me."

"I wish to hell I were," he snapped. "I was sworn to bring justice to this territory. And leaving you in jail was an injustice, what with what you were doing to those people. I couldn't break you out without breaking my vow. And I couldn't leave you in to shred the law the way you were doing. So I resigned. It was the only way to keep you from being the Countess and wreaking more havoc, and it was the only way I could take the law into my own hands."

She stiffened. "What do you intend to do? Hang me yourself?"

"Hell, no." It was incredible, the things she was willing to believe of him. "I'm just making sure you don't break any more laws with the good citizens of Denver. Now you can't be the Countess without getting yourself arrested in two seconds flat. No one will believe you. You know they won't. Besides, I figured the Governor wasn't about to keep me on after your antics so I just beat him to it. I still had a job to do, too. Now it doesn't look like it'll get done." The thought of the gunrunners and the further tip he'd received in Denver bothered his conscience as much as she did. He'd never let go of a trail before until he either found the end of it or the body. He got up and began pacing. "I would have had to quit anyway. My brother's wife lost their farm so I have to help her. She deserves that gold more than you, lady."

Missy and the kids were already settled at Mrs. Jerome's. Their coming had been the final straw to force his hand. He'd had no choice but to succumb.

Mary Alice smiled. "Well, well, so that's it. You do want the gold—"

"For my family," he broke in, determined to correct her.

"For your family. Sorry, I forgot." He wanted to wipe that knowing smile off her face. "So when do we leave to get it?"

Thoughts of the nebulous gunrunners pounded through his brain. He couldn't do it, he thought. He couldn't just chuck his personal pride and every moral value he believed in—that had never wavered through an entire war of injustices. To leave them out there inciting what was left of the tribes in their bitter state . . . an uprising was easy to predict. Very easy.

Telling Mary Alice, on the other hand, was a whole different story. He had a feeling she wasn't going to like it. In fact, he dreaded the explosion. Who wanted to be around that?

"We'll get the gold," he said, looking away. Taking a deep breath, he looked back. "But first, we're going to get my gunrunners, the job you so happily interrupted back in Blossom City."

She leaped to her feet. "I am not getting myself shot for any gunrunners! You're stark raving crazy if you think that!"

"You'll go," he said. "If I have to tie you to Brown myself, you'll go."

"No, I won't!"

"You'll go."

They stared at each other across the small, flickering fire. Awareness slowly crept through the anger. His blood slowed, then pounded and quickened. Women were supposed to be meek and retiring, subject to the vapors and other elusive ailments. Not this one. He couldn't imagine her being anything but defiant and magnificent. She met him head-on as an equal. She was superior in some ways. And those ways challenged him, forced him to stretch himself to match her.

"You'll go," he repeated. "Or you'll find yourself back in jail so fast your head'll spin. I don't think the good citizens of Denver are going to appreciate your sudden reappearance. It would spoil the fantasy."

She cursed him. He stood and took it because he knew he was right. That the job was going to be doubly dangerous with a woman along seemed somehow even more exhilarating. He promised himself that he'd make sure she didn't get hurt. Really, all he needed to do was find out exactly where the gunrunners were and inform the local marshal. His conscience would be satisfied with that.

And then he had the oddest thought. He told himself he *wasn't* keeping her with him because he just couldn't let her go. That was loco, as the locals would say. Of course he could let her go. Hell, he ought to be desperate to send her on her way. She was nothing but trouble.

"Sit down, Countess," he said, forcing his disturbing notions away. "You might as well get some sleep while you can. It's going to be a long ride in the morning."

She cursed him again, very thoroughly. He grinned. For once, he had the upper hand with her.

And it would stay that way.

They didn't bundle during the night.

Mary Alice shook out her blanket and told herself she was eternally grateful for small favors. But for some strange reason, her body insisted on disagreeing.

She forced away the thought. No one infuriated her more than Hud. But she knew he was right about her "reappearance." All the mystique would be stripped away. He had outwitted her, actually outwitted her.

The realization pricked at her pride and her determination to outwit him. The last thing she wanted to do was go on some damn hunt for gunrunners. Was he crazy? He must be, and he'd get them killed. Well, she wasn't out of jail for *that*. She'd considered sneaking away during the night, but she'd known he'd come after her and wouldn't rest until he'd found her. She had a feeling she'd be his life's work if she escaped. Besides, he'd been awake all night as far as she could tell, staring into the fire. And as she'd washed her face and brushed her teeth with her finger at the stream burbling nearby, she could feel his gaze on her back the entire time. Not only did that leave no room for escape, but her body was now tight with nerves from his constant watching.

Across the burning branches, Hud rose and stretched his arms out behind him and over his head. His upper arms knotted with strong muscles, visible through his shirt. She felt the urge to run her fingers along them, to feel the steel under his smooth skin. Ridiculous, she thought. His chest expanded as he drew in a deep breath, while his belly grew taut. A bulge at the junction of his legs was suddenly noticeable—and Mary Alice noticed.

She turned her face away and busied herself with finishing rolling up her blanket. The heat in her cheeks burned her skin. And yet her mind's eye refused to let go of the image. Over and over, she saw the stretch, the tightening of his torso, the soft pouch at his thighs.

"I'm going to wash up," he said.

She nodded. "Fine."

Her voice croaked out the word. She cleared her throat loudly.

"Why don't you get some coffee started?" he suggested. His voice was perfectly normal. "You sound as if you could use it."

"Son of a . . ." she muttered under her breath, but she only nodded her head.

She didn't look up until he had walked away, down to the stream. It was a mistake.

He took off his shirt—almost leisurely, to her mind. His union suit fit like a second skin, emphasizing the lean lines of his body. He reminded her of a triangle, his shoulders unbowed and wider than his narrow hips. She had no idea why a man's body should be so fascinating, but it was.

He pushed the sleeves of his union suit up past his elbows. His arms were dusted with dark hair, not unappealing. Not unappealing at all, Mary Alice thought, rocking back on her heels. He splashed water on his face, sluicing it against his skin in movements so rhythmic they were almost erotic.

"Dear God," Mary Alice whispered.

She wrenched her gaze away. Her blood was like thick, hot syrup pumping slowly through her veins and there was a tingling along her inner thighs. What was wrong with her? Was this . . . sex? It felt . . . pleasurable. But that was only supposed to happen in men. She knew that. Women weren't supposed to like it. In fact, they were supposed to be barely tolerant of it, and only in marriage.

Cold fear raked her spine. She was already nearly living "in sin" with him. Their ride into Denver and now this trip that promised days together certainly qualified as living together. Maybe not in a house, but being with him day and night was probably within those bounds. How was she to stay with this man if these feelings continued?

Hud walked back over to her. Mary Alice found

she couldn't move, couldn't do anything but watch him like a rabbit frozen in front of a wolf. Somehow, her entire body seemed to be watching him.

"Are you going to sit like that all day with the blanket rolled up in your arms?"

Lord, but he was big, she thought, staring up at his face. She didn't dare look anywhere else.

"I thought you were going to make coffee," he said.

"I thought you wanted to get those criminals you were harping on last night," she countered, finally finding her voice.

"After coffee. You look as if you need it."

"Thanks." She struggled to get to her feet, but her armload of blanket hampered her. Hud reached out and took her arm, pulling her upright. His fingers were strong around the softness of her flesh. His touch sent her blood throbbing through her veins. She stared up at him, wide-eyed and open-mouthed. She couldn't stop herself.

His lips came down on hers. She didn't even know how it happened, but one second she was staring at him and the next he was kissing her. His hands were on her back, pulling her to him until she was pressed to his chest. Her arms were trapped between them by the blanket she held, and she could feel the hard wall of his chest against her arms. She had only to turn the fingers of her left hand, and she would be touching him in the most shocking manner. His mouth was firm, almost demanding in its fervor. The sensation was scandalous and heady at the same time. She leaned against him, caught up in the feel of his mouth on hers.

Abruptly, he pulled away from her, almost like the snap of a cord suddenly being broken. Mary Alice shuddered and opened her eyes at the same time. Hud's jaw was set tight, waves of anger emanating from him almost visibly.

"Make the coffee," he said, then turned away and went over to the horses. They'd been hobbled for the night, but had drifted to the sweet grasses along the edge of the stream.

"You make the damn coffee," she muttered to herself, flipping the blanket around and around her arms in sharp, jerky movements. Her face burned with humiliation this time. She couldn't believe her own brazenness. She could imagine what he was thinking, and she vowed he'd find a rattler in his bedroll before he ever found her there.

She realized her attempts to make a tight roll of her blanket were a complete failure, and she flung it to the ground. She grabbed up the coffee pot and got water from the stream. She fixed the coffee in silence. He saddled the horses in silence. They drank the coffee in more silence, she by the fire, he by the stream. They buried the traces of their camp and rode out, all without a word.

Mary Alice stared at Hud's straight back as he rode in front of her. A wealth of emotions ranging from anger to more anger ran through her at the way he treated her. She felt the money belt hanging heavy at her waist. The first town they came to she would buy a gun.

Hud Jackson might find a rattler in his bed, but

if he crawled into hers he'd find something far more dangerous.

"Do you have a plan?"

"What?" Hud turned around in his saddle, the leather creaking under his weight.

They were the first words she'd spoken in the hours since breaking camp—not that he'd been saying anything, either. The only sounds had been the clump of the horses' hooves, the breeze rustling through the trees and grasses, and the occasional creak as one or the other of them had shifted in the saddle. The velvet scent of pine was almost overwhelming in the air.

"Do you have a plan?" Mary Alice repeated, guiding her horse around a low-hanging branch. "For finding the gunrunners. Do you have one?"

She sat well on her horse, her back erect and her arms easy at her sides, the reins loose in her fingers. He admitted he was surprised she was still with him. He'd been braced for her to bolt once they cleared Denver.

"Just to ask around," Hud said finally, turning back in his saddle. He couldn't look at her without thinking about that kiss. She had a mouth like honey, smooth and incredibly sweet. He wanted to make a habit of tasting her and that scared the hell out of him. But it was as if a door was opened now, one he couldn't close again.

They were slowly and steadily climbing down out of the mountains to swing easterly around the city, then north to take up the trail again. He let

Brown pick his way along the down-slope, rather than guide him. The horse knew better than he where its hooves ought to go on the sharply-angled slope.

"You're just going to ask around?" She snorted in disgust. "Hello, I'm looking for some gun-runners to arrest them. Have you seen them?" I'm sure everyone will fall all over themselves to tell you."

He smiled. "If they're smart, they will."

"People aren't smart, Hud. If they were, I'd never be able to make a living. Besides, they don't like the law unless they're the ones in trouble."

She had a point.

"You need a plan," she continued. "One that won't get the two of us shot to pieces."

He glanced back. Her face was set in concentration. That was another thing that scared the hell out of him: her thinking. He couldn't imagine anything more dangerous than Mary Alice Macaffee thinking, not even a thousand buffalo stampeding and not a ditch in sight to throw himself into. Still . . .

"What do you suggest?"

"I don't know," she said, musing. "Something that will put people at their ease, open them up to talking. And boasting. That's usually when you find out something they don't want you to know. We'll have to be disguised—"

"Disguised!" Hud turned and gaped at her. "I'm not wearing any disguise!"

"Well, you can't go in as the former marshal," she told him. "Better turn around."

"What?" He turned around and was immediately slapped in the face by a pine branch. His cheek stung where the needles had whipped against it. He spat out a stray wisp left behind, the oils numbing his tongue.

"I tried to warn you," Mary Alice said innocently.

"Thanks," he muttered.

"I don't think we'll find these men in church, do you?" Clearly, she was back to the subject at hand. "Or at the local Women's Society social."

"There aren't any where we're going," Hud said, watching ahead of him instead of behind. "It's mostly mining towns up north. My latest message said they were selling to the Utes on the west side of the mountains and what's left of the Cheyenne and Arapaho on the east side and in the Wyoming Territory."

"That's a lot of Indians when you add them up."

He nodded, not looking back again. "That's what worries me. And there are a lot of settlers up that way, too. Someone seems to be encouraging them to mass and attack, and supplying them with the wherewithal to do it."

"I think I'd like to go back to jail now."

Hud grinned to himself. "That's not the way to the gold, Countess."

"But it's the way not to get my backside shot off."

"I'll guard it carefully. Trust me."

She didn't answer at first. He was about to tell her the kiss wouldn't be repeated, when she said,

"If you try to get under my skirts, Marshal, I'll blow your head off."

"I make love to a woman, Countess," he snapped. "I don't get 'under her skirts' as you so crudely put it. I don't have to. They come to me."

"Well, I'm not coming. Stay on your side of the blanket and everything will be fine."

"You've got an inflated opinion of your charms if you think I'd be anywhere else." He'd be damned if he told her how she could affect him.

"Why, you . . ." she sputtered, then immediately shut up.

Hud smiled to himself again. For once he'd actually won an argument with her.

Things were definitely looking up.

The town they rode into late that evening was small and homey, with one saloon and a church.

"I don't suppose there's a hotel," Mary Alice said ruefully.

Hud shook his head. "Don't see one, so I don't think so. Anyway, I can't afford it. I'll get us rooms over the saloon. It looks decent enough."

In many towns the saloon was a fairly respectable establishment for travellers, often the only one. Hud acknowledged that this one, with its clean appearance and quiet atmosphere, looked like it fit the bill.

"*Two* rooms," Mary Alice emphasized.

"If they have them," Hud said, teasing her a little.

"They have them."

It turned out she was right. As Hud paid the money, he wasn't sure whether to be glad or disappointed. Mary Alice waited outside, wearing his hat low on her brow to hide her hair. She looked like a small man at first glance, Hud thought, emerging from the saloon. Somehow she had hardened her jaw, eliminating the softer feminine edge it usually had.

"Get two?"

"Got them." He sighed.

"Let's go bed the horses at the livery stable," she said, smiling smugly. "And then I need to buy some things."

Immediately, he was suspicious. "What things?"

"A dress . . . and things."

"You have a dress," he reminded her, untying his horse from the post.

"The Countess's dress. I can't very well wear that, so I need another, more ordinary, one." She swung her horse away from the post and headed for the stable.

She made sense and that made him nervous. Last time she got a dress, she turned an entire city upside down.

"All right," he finally agreed.

Once the horses were taken care of, they visited the general store. "It isn't a shebang," Mary Alice commented, "because it doesn't have the whole shebang in it." The dress she picked was modest cotton, with a high neck and sleeves. Hud had no idea what plan she had, but this looked innocuous. When they were back at the saloon, she arranged for a bath to be brought to her room.

"I'm not coming out for hours," she said with great satisfaction.

"You're entitled." He remembered his own guilt over his baths when she was in jail and had to admit that far outweighed the extra money carting all that hot water upstairs would cost him. He also had to admit that his senses stirred at the thought of her naked, trailing a stream of water over her creamy skin. Would her breasts be full and the nipples deliciously tipped up? Would they fit his hands as if they were made for them? In his mind's eye, he could see her leaning back in the tub, eyes closed, drizzling water between her breasts. His mouth went dry with sudden thirst . . .

"I'm going for a walk." Hud jammed his hat on his head and strode out the door of the saloon.

It was hours later when he returned, his body finally under control. He'd also taken advantage of being out to "jaw" with folks. No one had anything of interest regarding guns to the Indians, just the usual persistent rumor that something was happening.

He'd also reached a conclusion about his Countess. He would be the one in control from now on—control of the situation, and of her. He would get her out of his system, too. Whatever she was, she wasn't a "good" woman, and he'd be damned if he would deny himself any longer. Mary Alice would find things changed drastically. Beginning tonight.

Pleased with himself, he walked into the saloon, intending to go right up to her room and drag her from her tub if need be, to begin her "rehabilitation."

He didn't have that far to go.

Mary Alice was seated at a table, surrounded by men. Playing poker.

She was at it again.

Chapter Eight

"This is my brother, Hud . . . Huddleston. People call him 'Stone' for short. These kind gentlemen were teaching me to play cards while you were out walking. They've heard of our tragedy and wanted to help me take my mind off our troubles."

Mary Alice looked pointedly at Hud as she spoke. He gaped at her. The men, who seemed to be two local ranch hands and three businessmen by their dress, quickly assured her "brother" that this was all innocent.

The plan she'd outlined on the trail had been moving along nicely. In fact, much sooner than she'd expected. When she had come down from her bath, opportunity had presented itself in the form of curiosity as she chatted with one or two of the men while ordering coffee. A woman in a saloon wasn't *de rigueur* and these men were wondering exactly who she was. While they were trying to find out, it made sense for her to try to find out information for Hud. "Guiding" them into suggesting a game of poker had been simple. Until now.

Hud's face turned a dull red. Mary Alice practically curled her lip to get her message across to him, but his expression didn't indicate that he realized she was helping him. He was convinced that the sooner they wrapped up his mission, the sooner they could get on to the gold. She knew she should have consulted him first, but he hadn't been there to consult, of course.

I hope the idiot doesn't blow it, she thought, eyeing his jaw. Clenched any tighter and the thing would explode.

"What do you think you're doing?" he demanded, glaring at her.

The men seated at the table stiffened. Mary Alice swallowed back a curse and rushed into the breach. "Stone, please. These good men mean no harm. You, too, could use some entertainment. Come, sit with us. We cannot bring back our belongings so cruelly stolen by those thieves. Or my husband . . ."

The men made noises of sympathy and assurances that they truly didn't mean to sully his sister's reputation.

Hud stood for the longest time. Mary Alice held her breath. A shudder, barely visible to the naked eye, seemed to run through him, then he pulled out a chair from another table and sat down opposite her.

"I suppose you're right . . . Sis," he muttered grudgingly.

She relaxed mentally. He'd accepted his role in her scheme. She found herself wishing he *was* her brother. Instead, she remembered how his mouth had captured hers in a most unbrotherly manner. It had held gentle fire and primitive demands—and evoked the same from her. She could feel his lips moving on hers, tasting and insistent. And she'd responded.

She forced the thought away. "I was learning Blackjack, as I believe it's called. It's very easy. Have you played it before, Stone?"

"Once in a while," Hud replied.

He still looked like he'd swallowed an entire bottle of castor oil, she thought.

"Well, I'm getting good at it," she announced in a very innocent tone. The men grinned indulgently.

"It's even more fun when you bet money," one of them suggested.

"Really?" She widened her eyes.

They nodded.

"We have no money," Hud began forcefully.

"Well," she interrupted, drawing a coin from the folds of her skirt. "I did manage to hide several of these."

She held up one of the double eagle gold pieces she'd taken from her money belt to pay for a special purchase she'd made earlier, the gunsmith being conveniently located two doors down from the saloon. She hadn't returned the extra money to her belt yet, and now, unfortunately, they had to have some stake for the game.

Hud's eyes bulged with shock and she knew she

would have some fancy explaining to do later.

The cards were dealt around the table so fast, her "brother" had no time to protest. There had been enough hands played in fun before Hud joined them for Mary Alice to have a pretty good idea of what order the deck was in. She calculated the gentleman to her left held the winning hand at the moment. The betting was for one dollar. She deliberately busted, allowing her double eagle to be changed.

"This is fun," she announced happily. "Oh, could I deal? Please?"

The men looked at each other, then chuckled as the dealer handed over the cards. Hud looked just plain livid. Mary Alice dealt them out.

Hud had the winning hand this time.

"How wonderful!" she exclaimed. "Gentlemen, this is just the tonic I needed. That robbery was so shocking. How long have those despicable men been waylaying travellers in these parts?"

"First I heard of 'em," one cowboy said. "And I've been here for years."

The others agreed with him.

"Well, I hope you can bring them to justice. Don't you, Stone?"

"Stone" was in the process of lifting his down card. He froze. Mary Alice smiled, knowing he had a king and a ten.

"Stone?" she prompted.

"What?" He blinked, then lowered his chin and gazed straight at her. "I would certainly like to see some justice around here. In fact, it may be coming sooner than you think . . . Sis."

"I hope you're right," she murmured, concentrating on her three and five.

"We had some troubles last fall," one of the businessmen volunteered. "Ranchers and farmers were being raided and burnt out. Those hit the worst gave up cheap. I forget who they sold to, but I wish I'd bought them out. The railroad came through here a couple months later, wanting most of that land for branch lines. I could have made a bundle from them."

Mary Alice wished the Countess had come through here right after the railroad. She would have been swimming in double eagles if she had. And she might not have been in this mess, either.

Hud won the hand again.

Mary Alice frowned, having a feeling that he was extremely angry with her. Some anger she could understand, simply because she didn't understand him. But the set of his chin, the clenching of his hands, and the blaze in his eyes spoke of suppressed fury. She had no idea why he should be so angry. Certainly, he didn't expect her to lose her money in the game? That was ridiculous. And it would have been ridiculous if she'd been winning, supposedly never having played before. The men wouldn't think anything about him, except that he was a shrewd player.

Several more hands were played. Hud lost two and won another three.

"My sister looks tired," he suddenly announced, rising from his chair. "If you gentlemen will excuse us . . ."

"Stone . . ." she began.

"No. I insist," he said, staring at her meaningfully as he came around the table. "You are exhausted, now admit it. And tomorrow we must begin our journey again to . . . Oregon."

"I thought it was Idaho," one of the men said.

"You've given up the notion of mining!" Mary Alice exclaimed in a delighted voice, covering the mistake. "Oh, Stone, Mama and Papa would have been so proud."

"Yes . . . well . . . the camps are no place for you." He grabbed her arm and practically yanked her out of the chair.

"Good evening, gentlemen," she said, inclining her head.

Hud tossed the money he'd won back onto the table. "For the local church fund. Will you see that it's distributed?"

"Of course!" The men cheered instantly.

Mary Alice stumbled along behind him, shocked at what he'd done. In a bare whisper, she demanded, "Are you crazy?"

"No, damn you," he muttered back.

They were up the stairs so quickly, she was huffing with exertion. Hud opened his door and practically shoved her inside before she could resist. He slammed the door shut.

"What the hell were you doing, woman? Trying to have me shot for cheating at cards?" His voice was a whipcrack of anger. "And where the hell did you get that money?"

"Shh," she hissed. "People will hear you, and then we'll be shot for sure. I was only trying to get information for you about the gunrunners."

"Get information!" His voice was lower, but he took an ominous step toward her. For one horrible moment, Mary Alice thought he would hit her. "There's no information in this town!"

"You said north. We're north of Denver now."

"We're not even twenty miles from Denver! None of that was happening around here—"

"What about those farmers and all?" she asked triumphantly. "Maybe that was part of it."

"But the last place the gunrunners were wasn't," he snapped. "That game was a dangerous waste of time. Damn you, playing with me like that! And you didn't answer my other question."

"What question?"

He bent his face to hers. "Where did you steal that money?"

She reared back in outrage. "I didn't steal it! I . . . earned it."

He stiffened. "How?"

"Well . . ." she began, scrambling for a plausible lie.

His features darkened. "That fast you had a man up here? I doubt you were worth that double eagle—"

She swung at him, but he grabbed her wrist before her hand made contact with his face.

"Bastard!" she spat out. "I earned that money as the Countess. I don't need to take a man to my bed for coin when I can make an ass out of him to get it."

He yanked her against him. "Maybe a man is exactly what you need. The last thing I am is your damn brother!"

She could feel every inch of his body hard against hers. Panic shot through her, knowing they were alone in his room, her recent "purchase" in the next. But she glared up at him defiantly, her spirit and instinct demanding she not show her fear.

Suddenly, he pushed her away. "I wouldn't dream of sullying myself with you."

The words stung. Mary Alice drew in a ragged breath to control herself, not wanting that to show either. "Are we done here? May I go to my room?"

"Gladly. And you damn well better be in it come morning." He strode the two steps to the door and opened it. "We ride out at dawn."

She swept over the threshold without a word. Normal noises came from downstairs in the public area. Clearly, none had heard the argument between "brother and sister."

The moment she was in her room, the door locked behind her, she sat down on the bed. Her hands shook as emotions boiled inside her. The man was infuriating. He never told her anything, just dragged her along like baggage. Never had she wanted so much to pack her things and run. Maybe she ought to . . .

But that meant leaving him with two-thirds of the map. She wasn't ready to give up on that yet. Besides, deep in her bones she knew he'd come after her if she ran. He wouldn't stop hunting her . . . not until he was ready to let her go.

Instead, she checked the revolver she'd purchased earlier. It was loaded.

That was the last time she'd help Mr. Hudson Jackson, she vowed. Next time, she'd help herself.

Several towns later, Hud smiled in determination as they rode into sight of Longville.

"This was the last place I've had word of them."

"This is too close to Boulder," Mary Alice said, stopping her buckskin alongside Brown.

Hud grinned. "Afraid you'll be recognized?"

"You ought to be afraid you'll be," she retorted.

He grimaced. She had a point. After all, they'd been run out of Boulder for . . .

"Shave off your mustache," Mary Alice said.

"What? Why?" He touched the hair that had graced his upper lip for many years.

"Because you won't look quite the same." She appraised him. "We'll part your hair down the middle, too. If anyone from Boulder's in town, they'll have trouble recognizing you."

"What about you?" he asked, staring at her men's clothing. "You look like that snake-oil salesman—or woman. I bet they still can't make up their minds."

"Rejuvenator of life, we prefer to be called," she corrected.

"You'd rejuvenate them right into the poorhouse." But he couldn't help grinning at her, enjoying the upper hand. Well, mostly.

She ignored his comment. "I'm going to become your sister again."

"We need to talk about that," he began. "I don't want any damn sister—"

"And I'll put myself back in jail before I play your wife," she broke in. "Besides, it won't work as your wife. People will wonder why you're allowing me certain freedoms. As a widowed sister, no one will be too shocked if I take a slight liberty or two."

"No," he said, stiffening. "We're not doing poker games or anything else. We'll get rooms and I'll ask around for information about a man with a scar burned across his right hand and his companion who's skinny and mean. That's worked for me for years."

"Not as much as you think." She leaned back in the saddle.

"That's how we're doing it," he said firmly, turning his horse into town. "No more damn nonsense. Just straightforward behavior. Do you understand me?"

"Okay." Her voice held an air of amusement.

The hair on the back of his neck rose in warning. Mary Alice amused was a dangerous thing. Seeking to turn the conversation, he said, "By the way, you're paying for the rooms this time—"

"I am not!"

Hud grinned. "You've got more money than me. Besides, it ought to be put to some good use."

"You're crazy if you think I'll use my money. That's for my sister—"

"You can spare a little to fund justice, Countess."

She was still grumbling when they rode into Longville. The mountains loomed over the small mining town. Buildings, built years ago with precious woods and fancy storefronts, were abandoned when the local mine went bust. Those who had stayed were mostly ranchers eking out a harsh living on slopes grassy just a few short months of the year. The only place with rooms was a boardinghouse with a drinking parlor. An hour later, Hud left the place, whistling contentedly to himself. Mary Alice had paid, grumbling all the way. It had been a sweet victory.

He touched his bare upper lip, feeling halfway to naked without his mustache. His hair had been parted in the center and slicked down. After viewing himself in the mirror, he had had to admit she was right. He did look different. Taking her advice hadn't been easy, but he wasn't about to be so stiff-necked with her as to ignore reason. She made something else entirely too stiff, and that was enough to cope with.

His business didn't take him long. In fact, it was dismally short. He stomped back into the saloon and up the stairs without a word to anyone. He banged on her door. "It's me."

"What do you want?" Her voice was muffled through the wood, but the suspicion was easy to discern.

"Just open the damn door!" he snapped, aggravated with her unnecessary caution.

It took a while but the door finally opened. Hud stepped inside and glared around at the sparse, threadbare furnishings. He refused to look at Mary Alice, but his brain burned with the images of the people of Longville eyeing him with suspicion as he'd questioned them about unusual happenings and the two men. Facial expressions had literally slammed like doors and suddenly no one knew anything. He worked his jaw, trying to press them open to say what he had to say. Finally, he clipped out, "Get the cards . . . Sis."

"I told you so," she said, grinning.

"I didn't ask you for your damn opinion."

"But you'll get it anyway."

Mary Alice put the finishing touches on her neatly pinned hair, humming contentedly to herself the entire time. Hud gritted his teeth together against the building explosion of anger inside him.

He hated happy people. He really did.

Mary Alice counted the winnings as she swept back into her room.

"Not bad," she said, smiling to herself for snatching it off the table before Hud could "donate" it back to the losers.

Hud followed behind her, closing the door.

She turned around, suddenly aware of her vulnerability. "You can leave now."

"In a minute."

She put her hands behind her back. "I'm not giving back the money."

He stared at the grimy window. It was nearly impossible to look out of it. "I want to thank you."

"You do?"

"Yeah, I do. Thanks to the game, we found out

Burn-hand and Skinny moved on northwest. Now give me the money."

"Oh, no," she said, shaking her head vehemently. "You're not giving it away to anybody. This is mine."

"No, it's not—"

"Yes, it is!" she interrupted angrily. "And don't try to tell me I cheated those men downstairs. You saw their faces and their greed when they thought we had a little money they could win away from us. Do you think they cared a hoot about whether it was the last of our lifesavings? No! All they cared about was making a fast dollar without working for it. Don't tell me they're better than I am, because they're not! Those people are hypocrites. They cheat six days a week, and sit in church like pious sheep on the seventh. Give me a crook every time. At least he's true to himself."

"Are you done?" he asked.

"Barely."

"That money's ill-gotten, and it'll just bring bad luck," he said. "It's best to give it to the local poor."

"But that's everybody in town!" she protested.

"Hell, they need it worse than you or I. Come on, Countess," he coaxed. "We're riding into danger, so we don't need to jinx ourselves more than we have to."

"I'd make a fortune from you," she said, shaking her head at his funny superstitions.

"Probably," he agreed. He held out his hands. "No bad luck. We've got enough as it is."

Her fingers tightened around the coins, then she

slapped them into his palms. "I hate this."

He grinned. "Well, the poor here will love you just like those nuns in St. Louis do."

"Don't remind me," she said sourly, turning away. At least she still had her money belt.

This hadn't been easy for her, he knew. He set the coins down next to the pitcher and bowl on the only table in the room and walked up behind her. He put his hands on her shoulders in an awkward attempt at comfort. "It isn't good to carry bad luck with you, Mary Alice."

"But hate and revenge are fine."

She tried to step away from him but he tightened his fingers. "I don't have hate and revenge. All I have left is my honor. When a man lets go of his honor, he's got nothing at all."

With the way her hair was swept up in a neat bun, he could see the slender line of her neck above her dress collar. Her skin was creamy white, a sensual contrast to her dark tresses. A pulse in her vein throbbed steadily . . . temptingly.

"Do you know what it was like," she began, "watching your home burned, your mother killed? Having nothing to eat for days on end and no one who cares about a child? Or being left out in the middle of nowhere, knowing your father is already dead? Or having to care for a sister who cannot even say her name, because Union soldiers have . . . raped and beaten her senseless? What can honor give you of that, Hud?"

"The will to fight it all." It was the only thing he could offer her.

She laughed bitterly. "I tried honor once. After

Otis died. I worked as a hurdy-gurdy girl. A lot of girls do it because you just have to dance with the customers. Nothing else. They were miners mostly, well-meaning, and just wanting feminine company. I made twenty dollars a night, seven nights a week. But I couldn't take the way the owner treated us worse than slaves and cheated us out of our money half the time. I knew I'd never have the stamina to last a hundred and more dances a night. My way has its own honor, and it ensures my sister gets the care she needs for years to come . . . at least, it did."

He sensed her pain and pulled her back against him, instinctively wanting to give her comfort. He had a feeling that somehow, for all his own trials, he'd had more comfort than she. Many things made up Mary Alice Macaffee, things he understood. And in a lot of ways he couldn't fault her, despite the continual aggravation she caused him.

They stood together quietly for long minutes.

Then Hud ran his hands down her arms, feeling the soft strength in them. Then he turned her to him and stared down at her face, drinking in the wide, vulnerable eyes, the slight flush to her cheeks, the way her nose tipped up, the defiant set of her chin. The perfect full shape of her lips.

He brought his mouth down on hers.

Chapter Nine

Mary Alice wanted to pull away, a small voice inside warning her she'd exposed too much of herself to him. If he had been cruel or selfishly demanding, she might have succeeded. But her defenses were sluggish against the velvet onslaught of his questing lips.

Her fingers gripped his arms, feeling the strength in the corded muscles. He enfolded her in his embrace, his hands spread wide against her back. He could easily overwhelm her and yet she felt safe with him, soft and protected. How he could evoke that emotion, she didn't know. He just did.

His lips pressed hers more open and his tongue slid inside to taste her. She entwined hers with his, and all her senses spun into a dark satin, lifting her away and into the enticing nothingness. Deep inside, she admitted she'd craved this since the first time she saw him.

Gentle and light, questioning and answering,

giving and taking, the kiss went on and on, drowning her in the sensations it created. Her body never seemed more alive . . . and more wanton . . . and more right. She knew what happened between men and women wasn't always the brutal rape of her mother and sister. She'd been in enough camps when travelling with Otis to have seen the knowing smiles and pats and giggles. Otis had talked with her, too. But he'd never said a kiss would feel like dreaming through a cloud. It was . . . heaven.

Hud lifted his head. Mary Alice opened her eyes, feeling lightheaded and not quite awake.

"How do you do that?" he whispered.

She stared up at him, mesmerized. "Do what?"

"Hell, I don't know. This."

His mouth claimed hers again, this time rougher with a need that dragged her down into its swirling depths. Her breasts were crushed against his chest. Her skirts did nothing to keep her legs from touching his. Her blood ran slow and thick in her veins, and a pulsing ache began deep in her belly. His hands swept down her back, the flat of the palms hard against her skin before his fingertips settled at the dip of her spine. Something inside her shockingly wished they would go lower.

The thought brought her senses to the surface and she pulled back from the kiss. Unfortunately, her action brought her pelvis even more closely to his. She could feel a hard bar between them. Mary Alice gasped in panic, even as Hud buried his lips in her throat.

"I knew you wanted me," he murmured, his hands curving around her derrière.

"Hud!" she exclaimed, pushing back from his shoulders to extricate herself. It brought her lower regions more solidly than ever to his.

"Yes, say my name, Countess." He pressed his face to her breasts, kissing her through her clothes. His hands squeezed and kneaded her buttocks.

He held her so tightly, her breath was coming in short gasps; she was bent so backwards, she thought her spine would crack at any second. She could barely move.

"Hud, please," she managed.

"I'll be gentle," he promised.

"We . . . can't . . ."

"I'll be careful," he vowed, just before his mouth came back to ravage hers.

His lips pried hers open somehow and his tongue plunged inside. Mary Alice made squeaks in the back of her throat, trying to protest. She clawed at his back, digging her fingers into the hard muscles of his shoulders.

"God, but you're ready," he said, breaking the kiss.

He lifted her off the floor and spun her around. She actually found herself grabbing onto him to keep her balance as he brought them both down on the bed. She sank into the old mattress, literally, Hud on top of her, his weight pressing her even further into the smothering confines.

He exploded into a flurry of action that she could never quite avert. His mouth roved her face, spreading quick kisses across her cheeks, neck, and shoulders, then coming again and again back to her lips. She tried to speak when she could, but his weight was suffocating, like a buffalo sitting right on her lungs. And his hands were everywhere. She grabbed his wrist and pushed his hand down from her breast. He seemed to take it as a signal to begin exploring her thighs, twisting her skirts up high in the process. After long moments, she managed to push his hand away. To her horror, it wound up *between* them in the most intimate of places.

"Hud!" She clamped her legs around his hand to stop him.

"I can't wait, either," he muttered, kissing her. "God, but you're a tigress."

But he did stop fondling her. Mary Alice sighed in relief, relaxing slightly when his hand left her. His fingers fumbled around, and then he grasped her drawers and yanked. The thin batiste tore away from her body like paper.

Mary Alice gasped. "Hudtt . . . !"

"Yes," he practically growled, bringing his lower body against hers.

He was naked there, as naked as she!

"Noooo!" she cried out, as something pressed and widened between her legs.

It plunged inside. Pain ripped through her, tearing her in half. She cried and thrashed and butted in an attempt to stop the pain, but it only made it worse. She held herself abruptly still. The bedsprings squeaked loudly as Hud's body moved quickly, almost frantically. Then he stiffened and groaned. The bar of pain was swept from her body as he finally collapsed against her.

"Oh, God, but that was good," he said.

"Good!" she shrieked, pushing him off her. Now that it was all over she had the strength of ten men. She balled up her fist and hit him squarely in the chest. "Good! How could you? How could you!"

Holding his chest, he looked at her as if she'd gone crazy. "Jesus, Countess, I didn't do anything that you didn't want!"

She swiped at the moisture on her cheeks. Inside, she felt pain and stickiness and shame. "I was fighting you, damn it! Couldn't you tell?"

"But you were kissing me back!" he began indignantly, hitching up his pants. Mary Alice gasped in shock at what was nestled at the juncture of his thighs and scrambled off the bed. She glanced away, her cheeks burning. He continued. "You were all soft and sweet in my arms—"

"I couldn't breathe!" she snapped. "And you wouldn't listen whenever I did try to tell you! Get out!"

"Countess, look—"

"Get out!" Her voice rose to a shriek. "GET OUT!"

He climbed off the bed and walked over to the door. He turned back . . .

"Get out!"

He left the room.

Mary Alice stared at the door, fury and frustration running twin races inside her. Humiliation raged through her body. She became aware of a wetness on her petticoat and realized it was from their . . . sex. Feeling suddenly, desperately unclean, she went to the pitcher on the nightstand. The vessel was empty. It was the final embarrassment not to be able to wash Hud away from her. She staggered over to the only chair in the room and sat down, wincing as the hard wood came into contact with her sore bottom. It was a further reminder of the disgrace she'd just suffered.

Now it was finally true, she thought, fresh tears streaking down her face. After years of keeping herself pure, she'd become a whore in ten minutes time. She'd led herself down that path the moment she'd kissed him back. All the pride she'd been able hold onto in her life had been shredded. How could she have done that? How could he?

A preacher would say she'd gotten her just deserts for her wicked life. She'd always thought herself clever, but never wicked. Maybe the preacher was right.

She remembered the gun she'd purchased and realized that never once in the midst of everything had she given it a thought. It was still sitting pristinely clean in her bedroll—the very means of protection lost in panic.

"Damn him," she muttered.

Now what would she do?

Hud walked along the rutted main street of the town. The late afternoon sun blazed red just above the horizon. Few people were out and those who were seemed to be hurrying home. Hud paid them no attention. He'd been walking for some time, not wanting to go back to the boardinghouse.

He didn't understand her. How could she accuse him of taking her? She'd been a willing partner . . . hadn't she? He'd never believed her story of being a virgin. How could a woman so knowledgeable in so many ways not have taken a man as a protector out here? How could she survive without one? It was unthinkable . . . wasn't it?

In his mind, he went over the events. She'd kissed him back, kissed him pretty thoroughly. In fact, he'd found himself forgetting everything except the honeyed taste of her mouth. It had been unique, dragging a man in and enveloping him in her softness. He remembered her breath heaving in and out of her lungs . . . her hands tightly gripping his shoulders . . . she even cried out his name several times in the heat of her passion. He remembered that part vividly. She'd sounded so desperate for him . . .

Hud swallowed back a trickle of uneasiness. Maybe she *had* been fighting him. Don't be a dunce, he thought. She'd wanted him badly. She'd even taken his hand and placed it right on her legs. Or, a little voice inside him wondered, had she just been trying to get it away from her breast?

The uneasiness came back in a rush. Maybe she hadn't said much because she really couldn't. She did seem to gasp a lot. Maybe he was holding her tighter than he'd realized. He had to admit he didn't know a lot about women. He had been overwhelmed by the feel of her, and he'd been a long time without feminine companionship. If he were to be completely honest with himself he also had to admit that his attention to subtleties hadn't exactly been in the forefront. And that one time she did say, "We can't," he'd thought she'd been talking about keeping her from becoming pregnant. He'd pulled out before . . .

He almost hadn't, Hud remembered. He'd wanted to be inside her so badly.

And then he remembered the tinge of red on his own body when he'd pulled up his drawers afterwards. He'd had a fleeting thought that her time was either starting or ending. Or it could be she was a virgin.

A slow burning rose up his neck to his face as he realized he'd gotten everything completely wrong. If he had, that was a real good explanation for why she'd been so distressed afterward. What if people in the boardinghouse had heard them? The burning on his face turned white hot in humiliation. Mary Alice would probably shoot him. Good thing she didn't have a gun.

Knowing he couldn't wander the streets forever, he turned his steps back to the boardinghouse. He had to face her sometime, so it was better to get it over with, he decided.

He managed to get in through the back stairs without a soul seeing him. No sound came from Mary Alice's room as he neared her door. He hesitated for a long moment, then passed by, cursing himself for his lack of courage. She was just a woman, so why couldn't he face her? Inside his room, he found his water pitcher empty and he took it back downstairs to fill it. Several people in the parlor stared at him, but he felt no knowing in their gazes, just curiosity toward a stranger.

When he returned with the filled pitcher he did stop at her door. And he knocked. "Countess?"

"What?"

Her tone was flat, lifeless. That bothered him more than anything, it was so unlike her. He took a deep breath and immediately had no idea what to say. Finally, he began lamely, "I brought you some water."

A silence ensued. He wondered if he should just walk away, but the door opened. He noticed Mary Alice was still dressed in the same dress, rumpled now from their lovemaking. He corrected himself that the event was in dispute. Her hair was pulled out around her face, with what was left of the bun flopping on her neck. She looked as awful as he felt. Somehow he knew she'd been telling the truth about her virginity and her attempts to stop him. He hated himself.

"I thought you might like some water." He held out the pitcher, his gaze focused on the peeling violets on the side of it. She took it from him, carefully not touching him in the process. An idea came to him. "We can move on now."

She said nothing.

"If you like. I've gotten all the information I can from this town so we can leave immediately. If you're coming with me."

"Do I have a choice?" she asked bitterly.

He winced. "Not really." He held out his ace card. "And not if you want the gold."

She said nothing again, just took the pitcher from him. She shut the door in his face.

"Mary Alice?"

"I'll be ready to leave in fifteen minutes."

He nodded at the poorly-painted wood. "I'll be at the livery getting the horses ready."

He fled the boardinghouse as fast as he could.

Nearly a half-hour later, Hud didn't think she was coming.

"Damn," he muttered, knowing she must have skipped out on him. With a vengeance, he tightened the cinch on Brown's saddle for the twentieth time.

Mary Alice walked into the stable. She carried her bedroll and was dressed in her pants and jacket. She strapped the roll to the back of her horse's saddle, then, with an economy of movement, swung up into it. "I left the money."

He had forgotten all about the winnings. "Fine."

Hud put his foot in his stirrup and settled in the saddle with a creak and a jingle of leather and metal. Once seated, he spoke without looking at her. "I'm sorry. It won't happen again."

"No," she said. "It won't."

She led her horse out of the stable.

Hud followed behind her.

Mary Alice sat huddled under her blanket and stared at the campfire which Hud had decided to risk. She tried to ignore the chill in the night air and the man sitting across from her.

She was selling herself out for the gold. That was the only reason she was here. The thought made her half-sick and ashamed, but she had her sister to think about. That gold would pay for a lifetime of care for Harriet and all the other people she'd been unknowingly supporting. If they could figure out the map.

Don't even think about it, Mary Alice told herself. Getting the gold was the only thing keeping her going right now.

The wind whistled through the upper branches of the spruce pines, calling to itself in a moaning voice. The eerie sounds were almost welcoming. They fit her mood. Across from her Hud stirred the bacon in the pan over the fire, then slid it onto plates.

"Coffee's ready," he said.

She didn't feel like coffee or eating. She also wondered why she hadn't shot him. Granted, she'd never killed a man before, but this was more than reason enough. If she shot him, she could just take the pieces of the map and go after the gold herself.

But his bringing of the water was an unexpected gesture of kindness. That had thrown her, especially after what had happened between them. And so had his offer to leave. In truth, she couldn't stand being there in that room another minute. He did say he was sorry, too. Men usually didn't apologize for what they took. Even this fire tonight had been a kind of consideration for her well-being, too. Maybe that was why she didn't shoot him.

She was getting soft. He'd ruined her, and she ought to remember that.

He cleared his throat. "If there's a baby, I'll take care of it. And I'll take care of you before it comes."

Mary Alice moaned in horror, pulled the blanket over her head, and collapsed over onto the ground. A baby! She hadn't even thought of that. The nightmare was turning even more frightening. A baby! God help her.

"There shouldn't be, though," he added, his voice easily penetrating through the blanket. "I was . . . careful. But just in case, I wanted you to know."

"You're disgusting," she muttered.

"I guess I deserve that." He paused. "Eat some food. You'll feel better."

"I feel sick."

The silence was deafening, until Hud finally said, "Don't women with child become ill—"

"No!" Mary Alice shook her head violently, then reached out and grabbed up the hot bacon, stuffing it in her mouth. She shook her stinging fingers and blew air in and out of her burned mouth to cool it, even as she chewed vigorously. "See? Not sick."

She'd be damned before she would even consider the possibility that there was a baby.

"Well, I just wanted you to know," he said, searching her gaze with his own. "I believe in taking my punishment."

"Thank you very much," she said tartly, glaring at him. She had no idea why his words annoyed her so. But they did.

"I didn't mean to offend you."

She flipped the blanket back over her head. "You're breathing. That offends me."

"Look, I didn't understand you. And I said

I'm sorry. And I said I'll take care of you and the baby. What more do you want? My hide on a platter?"

"That's a start," she muttered, closing her eyes. The wool was rough against her face and hands. "Leave me alone."

"All right!" Silence began. "Don't you want to eat?"

"No, I don't want to eat. I want to be left alone. Especially by someone who has babies littered all over the face of the earth!"

"I don't have babies littered all over the face of the earth!" he exclaimed indignantly. "I don't have babies anywhere, damn it!"

"Well, you sure sound like it with your plans and all." She cursed under her breath. What did it matter to her if he had a set of manners all worked out for women with child?

"Well, I don't have babies everywhere that I know of. And come out of that damn blanket!"

"No." She curled the edges of the wool between her hands. "I told you to leave me alone."

"Fine. I'll leave you alone."

The blanket kept her from having him in her sight. But other things penetrated the fabric. She could hear the clink of his fork against the tin plate. He sipped at his coffee, with a slight intake of breath. And she could smell the roasted beans, rich and hot. The aroma of bacon, salty and crisp, penetrated her coverings, followed by the scent of beans sweet with molasses and yeasty pan biscuits. Her stomach growled.

"I heard that."

She turned around and faced away from the fire. "I'm not hungry."

"When you are, there's a plate warming at the edge of the fire."

She hated the thought of taking food from him. Or anything. She just wanted to get her time with him over with and move on.

After a few minutes, she heard him scrape off his plate, the fire hissing with its added contents, then the thump of the flames being put out. With a creak of leather, he settled down in his bedroll against his saddle. She didn't have to see him to know that he was tilting his hat over his eyes.

Her body tensed. Her muscles tightened to knots as she remembered the events of the afternoon.

"I won't touch you again, Countess," he said, from under the hat. "You have my promise."

"Don't make me laugh," she snapped, without turning around.

"I won't. Don't try killing me in the night. I don't sleep that sound and, with you, I watch my back."

"That's not where you should be worrying about," she muttered in a tiny voice.

"Let me know if you hear anything."

It was a quiet night.

"Roger Ward. Three is the way, and hope is found only together. If you wish to find the way, leave message with post office on where to contact. Jackson and Macaffee."

Richard Walker read the missive in the personals column three times, his mind not quite comprehending what his eyes were seeing. Jackson and Macaffee. He crumpled up the paper and threw it down on the table. The barkeeper merely raised his eyebrows but kept polishing shot glasses.

It couldn't be, Walker thought, his consciousness draining out in a grey mass for one long moment. The world returned with a rush and a roaring in his ears. He was back in the quiet morning of the saloon on Denver's west side.

Those two were dead, long dead. Macaffee had gone back South to get his daughters, while he'd waited here in Denver with his portion of the map. But Macaffee's wagon train had come upon cholera on the trail and been wiped out. He'd heard about it long after. Unfortunately, that had left him, Walker, with only a part of the map. He'd never find his way through those cliffs and ruins without the whole.

He knew Jackson was dead. He knew it all too well.

Because I killed him, he thought. He wiped his hands over his face and was shocked to find them trembling.

Someone was playing a joke. Someone who knew something about his past, about him now. Otherwise why in the wide world would they have put a personal in the *Rocky Mountain News?*

He wouldn't answer it, Walker decided. He wouldn't answer it.

He picked up the paper, intending to throw it in the trash barrel. Something stopped him. He tore out the personal and tucked it in his pocket. Somebody was looking for him. It wouldn't do to lose sight of that, especially with what he'd planned for the next few months.

Maybe it would be better if he found that somebody first.

Chapter Ten

"Watch. It's slippery."

Hud issued the warning to Mary Alice as Brown skittered down the slope, practically sitting on his haunches. Hud let the animal go, knowing he'd never be able to guide the stallion as well as the creature could find his own footing. They were heading into the Medicine Bow Mountains and the land was getting more treacherous, with near-vertical slopes like this one.

Well to the left of him, Mary Alice also let the buckskin have its way. She kept low in the saddle so the lower branches of the pines wouldn't grab at her and pull her off her horse. Her dark hair was plaited in a thick braid that clung to her back. She looked young and determined and vulnerable.

He was half-surprised she was still with him. All surprised, he admitted. It had been days since the incident in Longville. Days in which she rode with him, but she wasn't *with* him. She'd speak sometimes and then she'd withdraw mentally. He knew he'd added insult to injury that first night, but he wasn't sure how. He hadn't treated her well. It had been her first time. First times deserved to be so much more than a quick burst of need that rode roughshod over feeling. It was amazing that she'd managed to keep a personal moral value in these times. With all the spirit and stubbornness she'd shown, he shouldn't have been surprised. And he didn't know how to make it up to her.

What, he asked himself for the hundredth time, did it matter what she thought of him? With her life, it was just a question of time before it happened anyway. Inside, something rebelled at the notion. It may have only been a question of time, but it didn't have to be *him* who dishonored her . . .

A tree branch reared from nowhere and smacked him square in the chest. Hud suddenly found himself flying backward out of the saddle. He landed with a bonecracking thud, then rolled helplessly down the slope, his lighter weight catching up far too quickly to his horse's dangerous bulk directly in front of him. Too direct—he was nearly under the beast. Rocks raked his back and legs sharply as he tried to brake his control and veer his body away from Brown's.

A tree trunk loomed up on his right, speeding by horribly fast. Hud grabbed it, his arms nearly yanked from their sockets as his body was abruptly brought up short.

He clung to the tree, slowly becoming aware of dirt and blood in his mouth and a general screaming pain everywhere. A voice seemed to filter through the grey mist in his brain.

"Hud! Hud! Are you okay?"

He focused on Mary Alice as she scrambled back toward him on foot. He looked up as she finally made the last few feet to the tree. He decided that nothing looked more beautiful than her swimming face peering into his.

"Where're the horses?" he whispered.

"You're okay." He wasn't sure he agreed. She smiled slightly. "By the way, you can let go of the tree now. You only had about twenty feet to go before you hit bottom anyway."

He relaxed his grip on the pine cautiously, then asked again, "Where're the horses?"

"At the bottom of the slope. You better clean up. You've got a lot of scrapes."

"I bet." He touched his face gingerly, feeling the seeping fluid.

"Didn't you say to be careful?" Mary Alice asked, rising to her feet, bracing them to keep her balance against the steep angle.

"I thought I did," he admitted. He climbed to his feet and eased his way down the last few yards to the bottom. "How's Brown?"

His question was answered by the creature himself, who was grazing nonchalantly on the sweet grasses, completely unconcerned about his rider.

"Thanks a lot, friend," he muttered.

Mary Alice chuckled and pointed further ahead. "I caught a glimpse of a stream that way. I don't think it'd hurt us to take a break."

"Me, neither." He felt his arms and legs,

wincing when he hit a tenderness in his wrist. "I think I might have a sprain. I don't think it's broken."

"Then get soaking in that stream," she said. "The water's probably close to freezing. That'll help keep the sprains from swelling worse."

"No!" Hud exclaimed. "That's not going to do anything—"

"Yes, it will," she said firmly, looking him straight in the eye for the first time in days. "It will clean the scrapes out, too."

"You're not a doctor—"

"No. But you can't be a snake-oil salesman without knowing some real cures. Now, stop fussing like a baby . . . I mean, act like a man. You know this is just common sense. The horses have more of it than you do."

"Then let them go take a bath," he muttered, dreading the thought of cold water.

She just chuckled. "You should have taken your own advice about being careful."

He grumbled as he limped off toward the stream. His body was already stiff and sore. Slowly he peeled off his clothes. They were filthy from his fall, his pants especially taking the brunt. They were shredded through in several places. Fortunately, his hands were fine, thanks to his cowhide gloves.

"At least they're not scraped skinless like the rest of me," Hud said aloud, trying to flex them and finding his finger muscles stiff.

He stared down at the stream, watching the water rush pass in a chilling whitefoam of bubbles. The water was crystal clear, cold clear, and about thigh deep. There was no gradual downward shape of the bottom. Instead, it was cut abruptly in the earth like a deep groove. He'd have to drop straight in.

Hud bared his teeth, took three quick, bracing breaths and dropped into the water. His legs instantly went numb in the liquid ice straight from the North Pole.

"Sweet Jesus!" he prayed, dancing around, trying to get his body used to the water. He dipped himself in and out chest high and splashed his face. Parts of him froze up. That ought to make Mary Alice happy, he thought, grimacing at the pain.

He could take it no more and hauled himself up on the bank, panting for breath. Never again, he told himself. No matter how healing. His body began to shake uncontrollably as the brisk air made contact with his icy wet skin. His teeth chattered in a jawbreaking rhythm. Hud realized he had no towel to dry off with or get warm.

"Here's a blanket," Mary Alice called out, coming toward him through the trees and bushes. "And clothes."

He leaped behind a tree, not wanting to offend her after what had happened. "I'm out of the water!"

"Oh!" She halted about fifteen feet away as he peeked around the tree. She was silent for a moment. "I'll leave them here and you can come and get them."

"Fine." He leaned against the tree trunk, the

rough bark barely made a dent in his now iron-cold skin. He felt ill and ready to collapse. When she had gone back to the horses, he crept out from behind the tree and snatched up the blanket. He wrapped it around himself, hopping up and down, trying to get the circulation moving again in his veins. It smelled strongly of horse and he realized it had been stripped from one of the animals and was warm with its body heat.

"Here." Mary Alice was suddenly at his side, throwing another warmed blanket over him. At least he thought it was warm. It smelled like it.

"Were you trying to kill me?" he asked, looking down at her.

"Don't tempt me. Unfortunately, I have no idea where we are."

"Near Medicine Bow Mountains. There are a couple of camps up this way."

"Well, boy, that makes a difference." She shoved some clothes at him, interrupting his further explanation. "The sooner you get dressed, the sooner you'll get warm."

"How're my scrapes?" he asked, trying to wrap his fingers around the change of pants, shirt, and union suit from his saddle bag. They shook too hard to get a good grip.

"Your scrapes look clean. I'll set these here." She put the clothes on the ground at his feet. "I'll go make a fire."

"Best not to risk it," he began.

"If you want to help me kill you, then I won't," she said, glaring at him.

He eyed her for a moment. "Does this mean I'm forgiven?"

"No." Her mouth thinned, then she reluctantly added, "But I don't hate you too much."

"Make the fire." It was a better concession than he could hope for, but not even close to the one he wanted.

"Get dressed," she ordered, then whirled on her heel and went to gather wood.

A short time later, Mary Alice blew carefully on the small, smoldering sticks until they grew into a decent flame. She drew back on her haunches and, with her hands, fanned the fire even stronger.

She deliberately didn't look over toward the bushes where Hud was dressing. She couldn't, but her heightened awareness could almost "see" his movements. She had been conscious every moment he'd been down by that stream. It had been ironic, somehow, to have him naked just a few feet away. And frightening. But she knew he had to bathe away the dirt or it could fester. God knows where they'd be when that happened.

His plunge had reminded her, too, a little of Otis's fateful fall. She'd been terrified to turn and see him nearly under his horse's flanks. If it hadn't been for that tree he would have slid right under Brown. The relief had been overwhelming when she saw him moving. And he'd been damn lucky not to have broken anything.

It hadn't been like reliving what happened to Otis. Her heart had frozen like never before when Hud looked as though he could be killed at any second. She would have thought she'd be happy to have him fall off a cliff. Damn it, she would have thought she'd be *pushing* him off a cliff. She'd never forgive him for what happened in Longville, but she could tolerate him for as long as was necessary. And she couldn't hate him.

"I thought you said I'd warm up."

Hud sat down next to the little fire and began feeding it with the bigger sticks she'd collected. The side of his face was scraped raw in patches, but his skin tone was good. Rosy, almost. For all his complaining, he wasn't blue.

"You'll warm up," she reassured him.

He grimaced. "The big question is when."

She was silent for the moment. "How are the scrapes and sprains?"

"Hurting."

"You nearly went under Brown, you know."

He nodded. "I prefer to be on top."

Although the remark was about the horse, it conjured up another image. Heat flooded her cheeks and she looked away, aware of his body, his maleness, so invasive and foreign to herself. How, she wondered, did men and women live together for all their lives feeling so uncomfortable like this? She couldn't. Travelling with him was more than enough.

"How far is it to the camp you're talking about?" she asked, trying to cover her embarrassment.

"About a day. I was trying to go cross-country to get us there when we ran headlong into that gully slope," he commented, pointing up the way they came. "I don't like being out here longer than we need."

"It's lonely," she agreed.

"I . . . ah . . . I haven't said much about this . . ." Hud began, his tone very cautious.

Mary Alice braced herself. They'd talked enough. In fact, they'd talked it to death. "I don't—"

"It's about the camps. They're pretty rough places," he went on, overriding her. His blue gaze searched hers. "They're no place for a woman."

"You're always telling me I don't look much like a proper woman," she said, smiling wryly, a little relieved that he wasn't talking about them. She patted her plait. "Don't worry. I'll pass when the times comes."

"You may pass," he conceded. "But if you're found out . . . Mary Alice, these men . . . they're not mean or cruel. They're starved for companionship of the lowest . . . they take. It doesn't occur to them not to. I don't know if I can protect you—"

"You can't," she said flatly, looking away from him. Her jaw worked. "You couldn't even protect me from yourself."

"I know it. And if I can't protect you from me, how can I protect you from others?"

She glanced back sharply, his admission was so surprising. His eyes were hard, his nostrils flaring, his set jaw the only indication of his suppressed anger.

"I can protect myself," she repeated. "I've been doing it for years. Besides, I have a gun—"

"What!" He gaped at her.

She smiled sweetly. "I have a gun. I bought it back in that first town. I forget the name of it."

Hud leaped to his feet. "Goddamn son of a bitch! I give you an inch of freedom and you take the train to San Francisco!"

"Relax," she told him, disgusted. "I haven't shot you yet, have I?"

"No. But you're a prisoner. You can't—"

"We better move on if we're going to make this camp of yours anytime soon." Mary Alice got to her feet. She took up her horse's blanket and began walking over to the grazing animals.

"Now wait a minute," Hud began, following behind her. He grabbed her arm and spun her around.

"Don't touch me," she snapped, glaring at him. Her flesh seemed to burn right at the spot his hand had been. "I won't shoot you in the back, that I promise. But by God, I'll kill you if you touch me again. I'm going to the camps, to wherever you have to go until you get this stupid need to finish your last job over with. I'll stay out of trouble, that I promise, too. I'll stick with you until we get the gold. And then you and I will deal with what's between us. But, until we do, I'll carry my gun and I'll use if it I have to."

She spun back on her heel and walked toward the horses again.

"So much for being in control."

His words didn't make any sense, but she didn't bother to turn and ask what he meant.

He kicked out the fire while she flung the blankets over both horses. She hefted her saddle and tossed it on the buckskin's back. The animal never stopped its grazing on the sweet mountain grasses as she cinched up the belt around its belly. She did the same for Brown, not wanting to waste another minute in this valley. She swung up into her saddle and waited.

Hud checked Brown's cinch. Mary Alice took no offense. Besides, he probably knew she'd be more deliberate in killing him than simply loosening a buckle. He swung up in the saddle.

"Let's ride," he said.

They headed through the valley for the nearest mining camp.

The haphazard rows of tents wedged between two spires of mountains weighted heavily on Hud's heart.

This was no place for a woman. Any woman.

"Relax," Mary Alice said as if she could see into his mind. Her face was grimed over deliberately with dirt, blurring her feminine features. A piece of wool was wrapped around her head, topped by her wide-brimmed hat, completely obscuring any trace of her long hair. Her slender hands were inside bulky rawhide riding gloves. "There are more women than you know who travel this way to be safe. Many even served in the war as men. Heck, the 'bloomies' are quite open about dressing like a man!"

He had to admit she looked the part. Only he knew the incredible woman behind the facade. Despite his vow not to touch her, doing so was continually in the back of his mind. He hadn't treated her well, though, and she wasn't forgiving him any too soon.

"You look like a greenhorn," he muttered. Somehow he'd completely lost all control of her when he'd fallen off his horse. He wasn't sure how one produced the other, but it had.

"At least I don't look like a woman," she reminded him. Her voice had taken on a deep, gruff quality, like that day in Boulder when she'd been selling her cure-all. "By the way, my name is Jimmy."

"I still don't like it." But he led Brown into the makeshift town.

The pungent odors of unwashed bodies and waste were gratefully choked off by wood smoke that hung like a thick grey pall right above the camp. The air was above freezing and passageways were a sea of mud, planks laid everywhere to provide a crisscross of walkways a tightrope walker would be hard pressed to manage. Men dressed in bearskins or thin wool trudged along, oblivious of the pair travelling above them. An overall dinge was everywhere, added to by the cloudy day. On a sunny day, it probably looked worse.

"How do they live like this?" Mary Alice muttered in a low voice.

"Desperation," Hud said, surprised she didn't know the answer herself. He'd never met anyone who understood people as well as Mary Alice did.

A faro tent was set up on the far side of the canvas city. Hud headed straight for it. No noise came from the inside, not unusual for the afternoon hour. He dismounted and tied Brown up on the lodgepine tri-post outside the tent, the bark still on the wood. Horse-stealing was a hanging offense and it usually kept most folks from stepping over that line. But in a place like this, beyond untamed, Hud wondered if any rule even applied. As a marshal, he never came into these places without several deputies. A few other horses were tied next to Brown. Mary Alice dismounted and added the buckskin to the row.

"Ready to go in, big brother?" she asked cheerfully.

"Damn, but I hate that," he muttered.

He pushed aside the tent flap, then caught himself just as he was about to step aside and let her in first. Little brothers got short shrift, he reminded himself, going ahead of her. Inside, the dim sunlight barely filtered through the thick canvas. The interior was dark, everything in shadow. People and tables and chairs slowly sorted themselves out as Hud's eyes adjusted. A bar made of two barrels with a plank across them dominated the left side of the tent. A chusa wheel, cousin to the roulette from down Tucson way, was on the right.

"Drinks are ten cents. Chusa's two bits a white chip, and faro is the pleasure of the house," said a man in a black suit, sitting in a chair, flicking cards one by one into little piles. He never looked up from his solitary game. A faro box sat idle on the table. A group of men around the back table glanced once in their direction, then went back to their game.

"'Taint no work here, boys. Minin's full up,"

added the bartender.

"Just passing through," Hud said. "Me and my brother."

The word came more easily than he ever would have expected. At the bar, however, he ran headlong into his first problem as the bartender poured two glasses of whiskey. It looked like Taos Lightning, stuff so powerful as to blow out a man's brain with the first sip.

"Ahhh . . ." Hud began, wondering desperately how to get Mary Alice out of drinking the brew without causing any suspicion.

But before he could say more, Mary Alice lifted the glass to her lips and downed the drink in one smooth gulp. Her eyes didn't even water. She rapped the plank in his direction. "That'll warm ya, big brother."

Hud gave up and downed the drink, the raw whiskey burning a hole all the way to his toes. He coughed slightly, trying to clear his throat of the kerosene they were passing off as legitimate liquor.

"Couldn't never hold his likker," Mary Alice confided to the bartender, who chuckled. The man held up the bottle again, raising his eyebrows in question. Mary Alice shook her head. "Hell, even I know when to quit, friend. That's powerful heat you've got there."

"And I can't hold my likker," Hud said plaintively, staring down at his empty glass and wondering who would want to.

The bartender chuckled again, taking back their glasses and wiping off the rims before setting them back next to their neighbors at the edge of the bar.

"Well, my friend, if you're not interested in the whiskey here, and I don't blame you, then maybe bucking the tiger would suit you," the man in black suggested.

"Maybe," Mary Alice said.

Hud glared at her. "Now, Jimmy . . ."

"Let the boy play," the man said, smiling archly.

Hud narrowed his gaze at the encouragement. Mary Alice was absolutely right—people were happy to part a fellow human being from all he had. Unfortunately, these people had no idea what they were letting themselves in for. Knowing his companion, she'd own the place inside of fifteen minutes.

Fifteen minutes later, Mary Alice didn't own the place but she had a small pile of chips in front of her, having shrewdly bet on the way the faro cards would be laid out. Hud was careful to keep from watching behind either her or the gambler, knowing that would easily lead to an accusation of cheating. He had no interest in getting a bellyfull of lead for something he wasn't doing. Instead, he watched from the bar, leaning back on the planks. He even had another drink of lightning, just to pass the time politely. Half the hellfire was still in the glass, and he calculated that he could nurse it along for another hour.

He wondered what everyone thought of the "younger brother" who took the lead—and what they thought of the elder who deferred to him.

"Get us a bottle, Fred," one of the men from the

back table called out. They continued to be interested in their own luck, rather than the action at Mary Alice's table.

"Come get it yourself," the bartender snapped.

They burst into knowing guffaws. Hud decided it was some inside joke. The one who called out finally got up out of his chair and came over to the two-plank bar. He plunked down his coin. The bartender scooped it up and handed over a bottle of the Taos Lightning.

"Any of you think of breaking up the place, and I take my rifle to your heads. You understand?" the bartender asked, glaring at the man.

He laughed. "Ya can't shoot all of us at once."

Hud stared at him, too. Stared in complete shock. The man's right hand was scored with a distinctive burn across the back.

He'd found one of his men.

Chapter Eleven

Hud wanted to rub his eyes to make sure he wasn't seeing things, but he resisted the effort. More than once in his job, he'd learned the person and the crime didn't always look as if they should go together.

Certainly, Burn-hand was cheerful enough, a typical miner or cowboy with an easy-going nature. Nothing could be discerned about him just by appearance. Still, Hud knew he should have been prepared. He'd been expecting to run directly across the man's trail at some point soon.

He glanced over at the back table, surveying the men sitting there. They seemed to be having a good time together, no one looking especially skinny or mean. Maybe it was just Burn-hand here at the camp. Maybe taking one rather than both was an advantage he shouldn't pass up.

Hud opened his mouth to declare the man under arrest, then realized he'd given up that responsibility when he'd quit as marshal. He also had no hard evidence except the scar burn.

Burn-hand went back to his game.

Even if he had the guns in his hands, the nearest official was about two days away on the other side of the Rockies. By the time he got there and back with a posse, Burn-hand would be long gone. If he tried to arrest the man himself, he'd probably get shot by the overly-friendly crowd Burn-hand was playing cards with. Not a respectable prospect for bringing in his man. And that still didn't account for Skinny.

"Damn!" Hud muttered under his breath. His grand plan suddenly disintegrated when confronted with the real situation.

"You want a refill?" the bartender asked.

Hud shook his head. Mary Alice was playing another game of faro with the gambler, who was looking slightly harassed. She must be winning, he thought.

He cleared his throat. "Jimmy, I'm ready to move on."

"Jimmy" raised her eyebrows. "But we were just chatting a mite here—"

"You'd talk the ears off the man if you could," Hud interrupted, forcing himself to play along. "If we're going to make Idaho this spring we got to get moving." He raised his eyebrows meaningfully.

Mary Alice frowned. Clearly, she didn't understand, but sensed some kind of urgency on his part. He wanted to shout at her to get out of there so he could figure out what to do.

"I suppose we ought to," she said slowly. "But

we got to finish out the turn to the hoc. Please?"

She used just the right tone to plead with him. Hud had to admit she knew her craft. He nodded reluctantly. "This turn's the end. Sorry, mister."

"Can't say as I'm disappointed since I'm losing to the boy," the man conceded with a wry grin.

Mary Alice made her bets and Hud waited impatiently. Somehow, she managed to allow the man to win back most of his money by the time he pulled the last card, the hoc which paid nothing, out of the faro box.

"Thanks, mister." She collected her slim winnings and walked out of the tent. Hud nodded to the others and followed behind her.

"What's wrong?" she demanded, once they were outside the tent.

"Burn-hand's in there playing cards," Hud replied, noting that Brown and the buckskin were still tied to the tri-post. The camp was more honest than he'd feared.

"Then let's get him," she said.

"I've got no evidence."

Her mouth gaped open in astonishment. "Are you serious?"

"I'm serious." He set his jaw. "Get on the horse and let's get out of here so I can think. And so you can yell at me."

As they rode, Hud found he couldn't think straight, not beyond the shock of coming upon Burn-hand with no Skinny and Mean and no guns. Clearly, though, they were heading straight into Ute country, just as he'd guessed. First the remnants of Cheyenne and Arapahos on one side of the Rockies and now the Utes on the other. What the hell was going on?

They were a mile out of the camps and surrounding mines and well into the forest when Mary Alice pulled up short. She snapped, "What do you mean you have no evidence? What have we been chasing this . . . this . . . outlaw for if you *can't* arrest him?"

"I'm trying to catch a couple of gunrunners!" he snapped back, glaring at her. "But I've got to find the guns and his partner. I just can't go up to a person and say, "You're under arrest because I've been told you're selling guns to the Indians."

"You did it with me!"

"I had half the territory as witnesses," he reminded her. "That was evidence and plenty of it."

"Well . . ." She sniffed. "What are you going to do?"

"I don't know," he admitted.

She slumped in the saddle. "This is just wonderful. I think you've been drinking too much of that Taos Lightning. That's the only thing that explains why you put me in jail, break me out of jail, and drag me across God knows where to arrest someone you can't arrest!"

"I'm not crazy," he muttered.

"You're not in your right mind, either."

"I just didn't expect to come on them this way. Or one of them," he said, disgusted with her. "We'll have to watch Burn-hand and wait for Skinny to show up, then find them with the guns."

"That means going back and sitting in that

saloon until the other one shows up." She smiled sweetly. "That's going to be real suspicious for two brothers who are supposed to be heading for Idaho. I'll bet Burn-hand isn't the only one with something to hide. We'll make them all nervous."

"Do you have a better idea?"

"I don't have to have a better idea," she said. "But I could probably think of several that don't entail playing faro day after day with that sorry excuse for a gambler. I'm surprised nobody's shot him yet. He's a terrible cheater—"

"What!" he practically shouted, ready to strangle her. "What are these *better ideas?*"

He turned away, positive he would kill her with his bare hands if he looked at her any longer. She could make him crazy faster than bad whiskey. "There's a pattern to this. I just can't see it. Why supply all these Indians, and why take your time about it? What's the purpose? I feel as if I ought to know. If only I could see it, then I would have all the answers."

"Maybe there isn't any reason except greed," she offered. "Greed makes people do things that make no sense."

"You're the expert." A desperate thought occurred, and he turned back to her. "You know, Countess, we can't go after the gold until we get these gunrunners. That's the bargain. Now if you want to wait for me to think of something, that's just fine. Just so you understand we'll be delayed a bit while I figure this out."

"Sit outside town and wait for them to come out and follow them," she said promptly. "They'll lead you to the stuff. You've just got to hope they come out the way you expect. Or you could do something to force them out . . ."

Hud tried to keep his facial expression bland, but he could feel the smile attempting to break through. He was learning with her.

"I know!" she exclaimed, grinning. "Go into the gunrunning business yourself."

"Are you crazy?" That bad whiskey had damaged her brain.

"Nothing forces action faster than a little competition," she said. "Think about that."

It had a certain logic to it. "But how? I can't just go in there and announce I've got guns for sale to the highest bidder. I'd be lynched. These miners don't want the Indians coming down on them."

"I didn't mean that!" She shook her head, clearly indicating she thought he had a brain the size of a pea. "But you could say something to Burn-hand, something he'd recognize. He'll go right for his buyers to beat you out or come after you to kill you. You'll have your evidence either way, right?"

He snorted. "I'm sure you're thrilled with the latter thought."

Her face became a mask of stone. "I'm not quite that stupid. I've got to keep you alive to get me out of here."

At her words, he had the urge to kiss her. "Glad I'm useful for something."

"Of course," she continued, "you've made a hash of us going back in there without arousing attention. They think we're heading out for Idaho."

He'd forgotten about that. "Damn!"

She grinned. "Unless, of course, your brother takes ill, and you have to return and wait for me to recover."

Hud grinned back. "Get you some doctoring—"

A look of horror came over her face. "You *are* insane! Whatever's here in this camp saying he's a doctor is no doctor. Even the so-called authentic ones are idiots half the time. I've even seen some of them still use leeches, for God's sake! I know! I'll have taken a fall and addled my brains for a day or two. Everyone knows there's nothing to do for that except let the patient alone until he comes around."

"Okay." He turned Brown back. "Let's go back and get started—"

"Really, Hud. Have a little sense. Some drama goes a long way. Besides, there isn't a place I can fall around here without looking like a complete greenhorn. And that's not going to be convincing for your role."

"True." He turned Brown back around, sweeping his hand in a motion of gallantry. "Shall we go find a place for you to fall off the world, Countess?"

She inclined her head, her young-man disguise notwithstanding. "Thank you, kind sir. But if anyone tries doctoring me, I'm going to have a miracle cure!"

Chuckling, Hud tapped Brown's side, sending the horse on their latest mission.

* * *

"We're here."

I know that, Mary Alice thought to herself as she hung unceremoniously over her horse. She could hear the mining camp routine going on around her, and could even see walking legs, both human and equine, if she opened her eyes slightly. The odor alone would have told her where she was without Hud's whispered words.

Her arms, tied to her feet by a rope under the horse's belly, had been dangling for the better part of an hour as she played unconscious, and it felt like all the blood had rushed to them. And her head. It ached, and her nose kept bumping the edge of the saddle seat. She'd have a bruise by nightfall. If this were real, she'd be dead by now. Certainly, her brains would be addled for eternity after being dumped over a horse like this.

"Is he dead?" someone asked.

"No," Hud replied. "But he fell bad. I thought we'd better come back."

"There's a man up on the north ridge that does doctoring—"

Mary Alice groaned loudly.

"I think he's coming around some," Hud said. "He's been groaning for a while. Is there a hotel or boarding tent? Somewhere he can rest?"

"The saloon lets people have spots in front of the stove for twenty dollars a night."

Mary Alice groaned again—at the price. Stagecoach robbers weren't as greedy.

"Thanks," Hud said.

The buckskin stopped, Mary Alice sensed, because Brown had. She heard Hud dismount, then felt his presence near her head. He bent down to untie her hands.

"We're not paying twenty dollars," she muttered in a bare breath.

"Shut up. You're supposed to be half-dead."

He slowly dragged her from the saddle, hefting her over his shoulder. She let herself go limp, completely dead weight. Hud grunted and shifted her weight, holding her arm against his chest for balance. His other hand gripped her high on the back of her thighs to keep her body in place. Mary Alice could feel the imprint burning through her skin and wanted to scream against it. Her forehead banged against his back, yet she couldn't move without giving the show away. Patience, her mind chanted. Patience, patience.

A commotion started the moment Hud entered the tent with his burden. Her stomach skittered with anticipation and dread. It always did the first few minutes until people accepted the deception.

Hud spilled her almost gently onto a gaming table. Her head thumped against the rough wood. She groaned meaningfully.

"Jimmy lost the horse going over a ridge and hit the ground hard," Hud explained to those in the room. Mary Alice could feel people bending over her and resisted the urge to pop up her eyelids and scare them to death. She prayed no one looked too closely under the dirt.

"He's still breathing," a voice with terrible breath said right into her face. It was all Mary Alice could do not to gag. The voice added, "He'll come around after his brains calm. 'Taint nothing a body can do until then, 'cept let him rest."

If this were the camp doctor, he had more sense than most, she acknowledged.

"He can't rest in here." She recognized Fred the bartender's voice. "Unless you pay."

"How much?" Hud asked.

No, she thought, knowing whose money would be used. Worse, they'd be the target of any thieves if they could afford to spend twenty dollars to rest. She groaned loudly.

"Twenty dollars," Fred said, confirming the earlier words of the passerby.

"Twenty!" Hud exclaimed, the perfect note of shock in his voice. "It's more'n the two of us have!"

"Can't help that," Fred said. "If I gave space to every shitty-tail greenhorn that came through here, I wouldn't have no room for my business. We'd all starve and where'd that get any of us? For all you're crying so poor, you two had money for whiskey and faro before. If ya didn't waste your money for that, ya could've paid for a place for your brother."

"Five dollars," Hud offered.

"Twenty," Fred said. "If ya don't have it, then get him outta here."

"Come on, Fred. The boy wasn't a bad sort, and he's not bleeding all over the place, making a mess. Besides, he's already groaning. That usually means they're coming around. How mean are you gonna be?" She didn't recognize the voice, but it had a needling quality to it despite the words. Whoever it was could care less about her; he only wanted to irritate the bartender. A shiver of uneasiness went up her spine, and she had a feeling she knew who it was.

"Can't pay, can't stay," the bartender said. "That's the rule."

"Your customers might not want to know you're so un-Christian, Fred. That could be bad for business, too."

A chorus of voices and guffaws joined the speaker. The men were getting a charge out of twisting up the bartender.

"All right!" Fred shouted over the din. "Ten dollars! That's final."

It was still too darn much as far as Mary Alice was concerned. Hud made a pretense of protest, but eventually paid out the ten.

People dispersed from around her now that the excitement was over. Hud set her dangling feet onto a chair. She flopped them over slightly, letting them turn from lack of control. He whispered, "Here goes nothing."

That's what she was afraid of. He'd better not make a hash of this, too, or she wouldn't give a fig for their lives, Mary Alice thought. Unfortunately, it was all up to an amateur.

She forced herself to lie still and wait.

Hud maneuvered himself next to Burn-hand as interest in the prone figure faded and the men drifted away. He had no idea what he'd do or say, but he had to pull off something.

Burn-hand moseyed over to the bar. Hud

moseyed with him.

"Thanks," he said.

Burn-hand grinned smugly. "I like to see Fred get kicked in the backside. He gets meaner every time I come here."

Fred muttered several vindictives while glaring at Burn-hand. "You buying a drink or wasting my time?"

"Buying." Burn-hand plunked down a dollar.

"You're not mining here?" Hud asked.

"Not me." The grin widened. "I'm too smart for that."

Hud allowed himself a knowing smile. "Me, too."

The man's eyebrows shot up in disbelief.

Hud shrugged. "Playing the fool has its advantages, especially with what I'm selling. But this sets us back some."

"What're you selling?"

"Things. Things people don't like, especially the government." Hud curled his lip in a sneer.

"Things people don't like, eh?" Burn-hand's expression was unconvinced. "That's whiskey or meat."

"It's more than that."

Burn-hand curled his lip in a superior sneer. "And who're you selling to?"

Hud took a deep breath. "People most folks don't like."

"You're real free with your talk, friend," Burn-hand said. "I could be the marshal."

Hud grinned. "I don't think so. You look too smart for that."

The man laughed. Hud resisted the urge to punch him in the mouth.

"Maybe you're not so dumb as you seem," Burn-hand acknowledged. "Why're you telling me this?"

Hud shrugged. "I heard some things. Let's just say you and I are covering the same territory now."

Burn-hand frowned. The bartender laughed. "And you got me to charge him just ten."

"No hard feelings?" Hud said, smiling at the bartender. "My cash is tied up in my . . . stock."

"Maybe I'll take some of that stock in exchange."

"Sorry," Hud said. "One of them's worth more than half a night's payment."

Burn-hand shrugged and walked away. Hud had a feeling he was far more interested than he wanted to let on.

As time passed, it became clear Burn-hand was interested. He kept glancing over at Hud, who had taken a seat next to his "unconscious brother." Hud ignored him and waited, letting Burn-hand think on what he'd hinted at.

While he waited, his mind drifted. He could still feel Mary Alice against him when he'd carried her in. She was no brother. His hand had itched to caress those thighs as he'd held her over his shoulder. Knowing that she was forbidden to him only seemed to enhance her charms. Knowing what he'd tasted only made him want to taste again. Even now, when he ought to be concentrating on his quarry, he still found himself distracted by her.

Eventually, however, he noticed that Burn-hand's concentration wasn't on the game, evidenced by his steadily losing. Hud wanted to continue to hammer home the points, say something even more blatant, but he sensed that it was better to let the information stew.

When the break finally came, it came from an unexpected source. A man strode into the tent, a skinny man with a sour expression. He went straight to Burn-hand. Excitement ran along Hud's veins.

"Where the hell have you been?" Skinny demanded, knocking the cards from the other's fingers.

Burn-hand eyed him. The entire saloon was silent. "Waiting for you. Where the hell have *you* been?"

"Walker ought to shoot you," Skinny said. "I ought to do it for him."

Although the man's fingers never moved toward his holster, Hud had the distinct impression that it would take nothing to change those fingers' minds.

"Walker knows what he's doing," Burn-hand said.

The fingers twitched. "I don't think so."

Burn-hand grinned. "Now come on, Bill. Why are you getting yourself all worked up because I was playing a bit of cards while waiting for you? You'd be playing if you had to wait on me, right?"

Skinny stiffened. Hud thought all hell was about to pop, and he wondered how to get Mary Alice out of there without both of them getting in the line of fire.

"Bastard," Skinny spat. But he just spun on his heel and stormed out of the tent.

There was a relieved sigh from everyone. Hud relaxed.

"Game's over for me," Burn-hand said, rising from the table.

Hud immediately wondered what to do. Mary Alice ought to be having that miracle cure about now. Maybe she didn't realize who was leaving the tent saloon. But how was he supposed to tell her?

It occurred to him that a better plan was to see where the men were going and pick up their trail outside of camp later, where it would be easy to follow. But that meant leaving Mary Alice by herself with a bunch of men in a ne'er-do-well saloon. He didn't like that idea one bit.

Burn-hand paid up and left the saloon.

Hud silently counted to ten, then muttered, "I'll be back."

Mary Alice groaned in acknowledgement.

He strolled out of the tent, looking for all intents and purposes like a man heading for the nearest outhouse. Once on the planks outside, he glanced up and down the street, his stomach churning when he didn't spot the two at first. Then he saw them further up the temporary sidewalk. He followed behind casually.

The cloudy afternoon sky was darkening with evening, and the miners were coming in from their claims. Hud lost track of the two momentarily at times in the throngs and was occasionally bumped into the muddy street, the ooze grasping at his boots and releasing them with a wet pop.

Steadily, the men were making their way to the north side of the camp, turning corners and going deeper into where the miners were actually housed. Hud came around the end of a tent on the outskirts of the camp and nearly plowed into them as they were paused in front of a wagon. A tired-looking Indian sat on top of the bench. Fortunately, Burn-hand didn't notice him, although Skinny gave him a look just before he turned around. Playing the innocent, he frowned as if he'd simply made a misdirection.

Not caring to take a further risk and ruin everything, he hurried back to the tent saloon.

Miners were milling around outside, and there was a commotion inside. Hud bullied his way through to find the game players arguing with Fred the bartender.

"Here!" Fred said, spotting him. "Your brother's got to be moved. He's taking up table space I need."

"Can't move him," one of the players broke in. "The man paid fair and square. Maybe we'll pull up our game and take it elsewhere. Maybe others'll take their drinking elsewhere, too!"

"Now you just shut up!" Fred snapped.

"It's okay," Hud said, striding over to the prone figure. He had no idea how she managed to keep so still amid all the ruckus. He leaned forward, right over Mary Alice's face. "Miracle cure now."

She groaned loudly, and slowly her eyelids fluttered open.

"See?" Fred exclaimed, pointing to her. "He's all better."

"He still shouldn't be moved," one said. "He ain't right all the way through."

"Well, he can't lay on my table no longer!"

"How about if I just move him outside?" Hud suggested. He slipped his arm under her shoulders. "Think you can move now?"

"I'll try." She slowly sat up, holding her head. The men cheered. They weren't a bad bunch, Hud decided.

He helped his "little brother" out the tent flap.

"What now?" she asked, keeping to her gruff voice.

"We take a ride."

Chapter Twelve

"They came up this way. See the wagon ruts?"

Mary Alice leaned over the buckskin's withers and peered down at the soft ground. Two parallel grooves were cut into a large patch of moss before they disappeared farther along on the stone. They were about two miles out of the camp and the trail was becoming fainter as the gunrunners began cutting across the mountain slopes.

She straightened. "I see them. But how do they expect to get the wagon over the Medicine Bows?"

"I don't know, but that wagon's carrying something heavy," he said, staring down at the tracks. "If it wasn't warming with spring, the ground would be too hard to leave anything. Once I know for sure what's in the wagon, then I can arrest them."

"Maybe they're just setting up a claim," she suggested. "That would explain why they're cutting cross-country with a wagonload of something."

"I don't think so." Excitement was an undercurrent in his voice.

Now that they were actually closing in, the disadvantages were rapidly becoming clearer. She said, "Hud, how are you going to catch them by yourself? There are two of them—"

"Three," he interrupted, grinning cheerfully at her. "They've got an Indian with them. Skinny brought him."

"Three!" She gaped at him, then shuddered. "This is ridiculous. Let's go get help."

"From that mining camp?" he asked with a snort. "Burn-hand and Skinny are regular customers there, remember? Hell, they'd probably string us up. And the nearest help is two days back."

"Then how do you ever enforce the law?" she asked, disgusted.

"It's a miracle sometimes." He chuckled. "Keep your voice down—God knows how close we are. Those wheel ruts aren't that old. And the Indian may be some kind of lookout or scout for them."

Stricken, she stared at him wide-eyed. The truth was, Indians terrified her.

Hud grinned at her. "Cheer up, Countess. I've got a plan."

"I hope it's not like the last one," she muttered.

He didn't seem to hear her. "I figure to take them by surprise and then take a look at what's in that wagon."

"And where am I in all this?" she asked, eyeing him sourly.

"Behind some bushes, out of trouble for once."

His return gaze was stern.

She smiled happily. "Just so I know my place."

They rode forward slowly, Hud watching the ground for any further sign of their quarry.

"Why are they selling guns up here?" he muttered, swinging his horse slightly to the right, following the tracks.

Mary Alice followed, careful to stay behind him and out of the trail left by the wheels. "The Indians have got to eat, so they need to kill buffalo."

"The herds don't migrate up here."

She shrugged. "I don't know then. Maybe the miners have been raiding their villages?"

"I haven't heard of any trouble lately. They tend to keep away from each other."

"Well," Mary Alice began, thinking. "Maybe you should ask the other side of the question. What do the gunrunners get from the Indians that's profitable enough to make them break the law?"

Hud pulled Brown up and straightened. He swiveled in the saddle to face her, staring intently. "That's a good question, Countess. What do they have for payment that's so attractive?"

"Furs?"

"They aren't more plentiful here than in other areas of the country," Hud answered. "Probably less."

"Gold?"

"Maybe. The Utes aren't known for their wealth, though. And the other side of the mountains is grasslands. There's no gold on the high plains, yet they've been selling to the bands of

Cheyenne and Arapaho still hanging around there. But if you want something they have, why arm them with the means to kill you just to get it?"

"They're stupid?" She made a face. "Even I don't believe that one."

"Those guns are for more than hunting food," Hud said. "The sooner we find out, the sooner I can stop it."

"And in the meantime, you and I are the perfect targets." She looked around nervously, feeling as if eyes were suddenly peering through the scrub pines and conifers. "I thought you didn't want us talking."

"Not you screeching at me, as usual." He swung back in the saddle and nudged Brown to moving again before she could make a retort. "Makes me wonder how you laid there back at that camp and never even flinched, let alone kept your mouth shut. Actually, that was a real pleasure."

"Never turn your back on your enemy when you're insulting them, Marshal," she advised, resisting the urge to take out her gun and aim it at the broad-shouldered bull's-eye. She'd probably do it, too, if the shot wouldn't be heard by anybody within a one-mile circle. No one infuriated her more in so many ways than Hud.

He chuckled. "If you shot me, who would get you out of here?"

"You're aiming to get us both killed anyway, so that's not something I'm worried about."

"True. Still, the coldcocked brother was your best performance by far. By the way, did you hear anything of interest while you were lying on that table?"

"No," she admitted. The conversation had been boring, except at the end when the bartender was all for throwing her out after Hud had disappeared. She had wondered how to handle that. Fortunately, she hadn't had to. "Mostly, they were baiting each other and talking about a . . . well, things. Burn-hand was very friendly, I thought."

"Skinny's not. I think he's a hired gun." He veered further off the track. "They went this way."

Mary Alice peered down at the ground. The only sign of a change was a part of a hoof print and a few inches of deep groove before rock took over.

They rode along, walking the horses as he watched the trails and she watched for someone watching them. She had decided that she was being a fool for some shiny yellow metal, when Hud suddenly backed Brown up into the buckskin. Mary Alice swung the horse's head to avoid a complete collision.

"Get down!" he practically hissed, scrambling off his bay.

Mary Alice had no idea what had happened, but she wasn't stopping to ask. She swung off her horse and followed Hud as he pulled Brown into a deep copse of trees. The noise they made sounded louder than gunshots to her.

"They're just over that slope," Hud whispered, nodding off into the distance. "I glimpsed a fire and heard voices. Can you smell the smoke?"

She sniffed the air. Burned wood was easily discernible. She couldn't hear voices, however.

"A few more yards and we would have been joining them for supper," he added.

"Shouldn't we be hiding better than this?"

"I don't know that there's anything better." He patted her arm. "Don't worry. We're pretty safe here."

"I bet Lee said that before Gettysburg," she muttered, peering through the trees.

"No. He said it was a lost cause before he started."

She turned to face him, open-mouthed at his words. Hud smiled sadly. "Anybody who was with Pickett that third day knows we doomed ourselves."

"Were you with Pickett?"

"Yes." He turned away.

It was obvious he didn't wish to continue the conversation. She wasn't about to press him, anyway. Neither of them needed any further distractions this close to trouble.

They waited, Mary Alice impatient with each long, dragging minute. Her legs began to ache from standing, and her back from bending slightly to see if she could see the men. She couldn't. The horses eventually began to paw restlessly at the ground, having exhausted any edibles within their reach. Only Hud seemed unperturbed by the lack of any action. He peered through the bushes, one hand absently stroking Brown to keep him quiet.

The sun had long dipped behind the horizon when he finally held out Brown's reins to her and whispered, "I'm moving closer."

She stared at him, her stomach twisting in

apprehension. "Are you insane?"

"I want to try to see what they're doing." He looked up at the clouds moving across the sky. "It feels like rain coming. I won't be long. You'll be all right here."

"No," she said, in unison with every leaping nerve in her body.

He grabbed her arm and shook her. "Yes, damn you. For once will you listen and stay put where I don't have to worry about you?"

"Hud," she began.

His mouth came down on hers in a fiery kiss. Without thought, she plastered herself against him, wrapped her arms around his neck and kissed him back with everything she had. His tongue mated and swirled with hers, spinning her into that dark cocoon she'd craved. She could feel every inch of him on every inch of her.

Suddenly, he pulled her arms from around his neck, breaking the kiss. "Don't move. If I'm not back, just head back east and keep the sun on your right shoulder and you'll get to the camp. Do you understand?"

She nodded.

He kissed her again—quick, sharp, assured. "I'll be back. Don't worry. I'm your bad penny, Countess, and you're mine."

He shoved the reins in her hands, slipped through the trees, and vanished.

"You son of a . . ." She trailed off the whispered curse, too furious to even speak.

She couldn't believe he'd left her behind like this. She peered through the bushes, trying to see him, but he was already gone from sight. The silence slowly closed in on her, and she became aware of exactly how quiet it was. And exactly how alone she was. Pinpricks of uneasiness skittered along her nerve-endings, raising goosebumps on her arms and the back of her neck. Blackness, unrelieved by stars or moon, was rapidly closing in around her. She felt blind to whatever might be nearby, rather than safe from any prying eyes. In the far distance, a faint rumble of thunder rolled across the sky.

Time passed . . . and passed. Fear raked her spine as she tried to calculate the minutes and realized it was so long since Hud had left that it had to be hours. Something happened, she was positive of it. His voice came strong into her mind, firmly telling her to stay put, get out, go back. She knew he was right. She never listened to him before. But it was what he wanted her to do. He didn't want to worry about her. For all that had happened between them, she didn't want him to worry, either. He wasn't a bad man, or uncaring. And now he only asked one thing of her. It ought to be the easiest instruction in the world to follow.

A breeze kicked up, rustling the trees in chilly sweeps. The air wafted across her skin, causing the goosebumps to turn into mountains. Like a premonition, she thought.

She tied the reins of both horses to a sapling. Carefully, she slipped through the bushes, heading straight for the flickering light barely visible in the far distance.

* * *

Hud crept as close as he dared to the small clearing and the three men inhabiting it. The fire was big enough to attract the attention of everybody within twenty miles, the smell of woodsmoke very strong. The wagon was directly in front of his hiding place in the underbrush. Only a few yards separated him from the proof he needed. His fingers itched to reach out and pull away the canvas, but he refrained. The clearing was too damn open.

"Don't see why Walker doesn't get up here and sell this stuff himself," Skinny said, poking at the fire with a stick. "He sits in that sporting house day after day back in Denver and lets us take all the risks."

"You're just jealous," Burn-hand said, eating a *frijole*. "He pays us very well to take the risks. Quit complaining."

The Indian was sitting on a rock, a blanket wrapped around him, staring off westward. He didn't seem interested in the conversation.

"I'm not complaining and I'm not jealous of a bunch of whores, no matter how fancy they dress 'em." Skinny spat on the ground as if to emphasize his point, then added, "All women are whores."

The hairs on the back of Hud's neck rose as he thought of Mary Alice. Please, God, he thought, make her stay put for once in her life. Skinny didn't sound like a man who put women on a pedestal. He dreaded thinking what the man would do with one who was dressed like a man.

He wished now he had never brought her this far—especially after that kiss. She felt something for him. No woman sent a man off into danger that way if she didn't.

Burn-hand just laughed. "You never did forgive that little gal in Waco who threw you over for that Mex gambler, did ya?"

"Shut up!" Skinny shouted, rising to his feet.

The two of them would probably kill each other any second, Hud thought. It did have the advantage of solving his problem and stopping their illegal activities. Except for this Walker, whoever he was. And Hud was beginning to burn with curiosity.

"Now, Bill," Burn-hand said in a placating tone. "You know I draw faster than you do. Besides, that railroad's coming through this way next year. What good's it going to do us to shoot each other and lose all that money?"

Skinny grumbled but settled down. The Indian didn't move during the entire exchange.

Things were quiet after that. Hud stared at the back of the wagon, willing himself to see through the buckboard to what was hidden underneath. Unfortunately, no amount of will power could penetrate. As time passed he knew he wasn't getting anywhere fast, and worse, Mary Alice would be getting impatient. If the Lord was managing to keep her corralled, even that wouldn't last much longer. Nothing was worse than Mary Alice when she was impatient. Besides, it was thundering in the distance. That rain would be coming on soon. He wanted to be gone by then.

He was about to turn away and creep back to Mary Alice when several riders suddenly appeared into the light of the clearing. Utes, he thought, the hairs prickling on the back of his neck. Their horses made very little noise on the mountain floor, several of them without riders but dragging travois slings behind them. The men themselves were painted with war colors, an immediate sign that they were not only expecting trouble—they intended to create it. They each carried shields, several with bows, the others with clubs. One held a rifle, the stock braced against his thigh.

The Indian rose from his rock and turned away from the Ute warriors, who spit in his general direction before he faded into the trees. Nothing like an amiable greeting, Hud decided. His body was tense with anticipation. He had a feeling he was about to be his own best witness. His brain screamed a warning back to Mary Alice to stay where she was. He'd kill her himself if she moved now.

Greetings were exchanged, with Burn-hand smiling. He and Skinny walked over to the wagon and let down the buckboard. Hud watched as they took out a long, narrow, wooden box. Skinny jimmied up the nails on one of the slats, reached in among the straw padding, and pulled out a gleaming army-issue rifle.

Got you, Hud thought with a grin.

"Now, boys, these here ought to do you fine," Burn-hand said. Skinny looked no more disgusted than usual. "There's a hundred rounds of bullets to go with them. All we want is to have the land of the farmers and miners, just where we told you the iron horse is going to go."

"No iron horse," one snapped.

"No guns," Burn-hand countered.

They conferred among themselves. Hud had the distinct impression they were discussing how to say yes and break the covenant afterward. Sheridan and his flunky Custer had taught their lessons too well, Hud acknowledged. He wondered if the Utes knew how ineffective they'd be against the railroad once it came.

Suddenly, everything clicked in his head. He knew the parts to this puzzle now. Whoever was backing the gunrunners knew where the railroads planned their future branches and was using the Indians to create "incidents" and clear out the land so they could buy it up cheap. That poker game Mary Alice spawned weeks back had been much more full of help than he'd known.

This Walker they had mentioned must be the boss, that was clear enough. Walker would replace these gunrunners with others. None of this would stop until he found the man. And how would he find Walker if Skinny and Burn-hand decided not to talk?

But he had a more immediate problem. The Utes would be using those guns tonight, if he were reading all the signs right. And he was. Innocent people in the form of new settlers, foolish greenhorns, and adventurous miners were about to be killed in a wave of raids this side of the Rockies. And they would go on for a long, long time until the army wiped out the Indians in retaliation. Somehow he had to stop them before they started . . .

Cold steel pressed against his throat, forcing his chin up from the sharp blade of the knife. Hud froze, his brain numb and yet waiting for the sudden slice of death. The dry, malodorous scents of unwashed body and wet wool hung over the air suddenly and he realized the Indian had come in downwind of him. No hand removed the gun from his holster, the weapons still too new to the tribes for any member to recognize the dangerous potential. Hud cursed under his breath, knowing this one probably didn't have to. One move on his part and that knife would do its work long before he could turn and fire.

The Indian nudged him into the clearing. Hud stepped carefully, painfully aware of what one slip could do. He willed the message to Mary Alice to run and run now.

Everybody turned as one when he broke through the last of the bushes, their surprised expressions turning hard and cold. Skinny looked more menacing than the Utes.

"You!" Burn-hand glared at him.

"You know him?" Skinny asked.

"He was trying to cut in on our business here back at that mining camp before you came," Burn-hand replied. "Looks like he was still trying when Young Otter caught him."

"I listen better," Young Otter said in a sneer from behind Hud. "Utes couldn't hear their mothers give birth."

The Utes howled and shook their fists. "The

Cheyenne eat their mothers."

"Shut up!" Skinny snapped, pulling his gun. He waved it in everyone's direction at once. He was cool and calm in his movements, ready to shoot anyone who moved in a way he didn't like—and shoot to kill.

Hud felt he had a better understanding of the expression "Out of the frying pan and into the fire." Unfortunately, he preferred to remain ignorant of the meaning.

The Indian suddenly pushed him into the dirt, nearly on top of the fire. Intense heat flamed his face for an instant before Hud scrambled back, away from it.

Burn-hand reached down and pulled Hud's gun out of its holster. He was careful not to get too close in the process. "And where's that little brother of yours?"

"Dead," Hud said, hoping they'd believe it.

He laughed. "It was probably Fred's bad whiskey. So what's your price for your goods? He can't beat ours, can he, Bill? We're givin' 'em for free."

"That's a good price," Hud said. It was time for the mask to come off. He'd never been comfortable with this play-acting. "Real good. But I'm not looking for a cut of your goods. I'm a marshal."

Skinny yelled and jumped, furious. He pulled back the hammer on the pistol and pointed the gun right in Hud's face. "Say hello to the Devil, you—"

Burn-hand knocked the gun from Skinny's hand. It went off, the retort a loud boom, even as the bullet spun harmlessly into the air. The horses pranced and whinnied, trying to break their restraints. The Utes brought theirs under control, looking on with interest.

Hud's heart was right in his mouth, knowing Mary Alice must have heard the shot. He prayed she wasn't so foolish as to come investigate. Run, he shouted mentally. *Run*.

"Don't be more of a jackass than you are," Burn-hand said.

Skinny pulled a knife from his boot and slashed the air in front of Burn-hand. "I'll cut your liver out. You're the jackass for letting him live!"

"I didn't say we'd let him live," Burn-hand said, grinning. "But we'd be fools to kill a marshal. You don't know when something like that'll come back to haunt you."

"So if we ain't killin' him then how's he gonna die?" Skinny asked.

Hud was wondering the same thing.

"We give him to the Utes. Let them have the fun." Burn-hand winked. "And anything else that comes with it."

Hud decided he didn't like the answer. Skinny did, however. He grinned from ear to ear.

Burn-hand gestured to the Utes. "A gift for you."

They grinned evilly. Hud wasn't surprised. The tribes west of the Rockies from Idaho to Utah were known for their brutality, even among the other tribes of the West. The fire crackling around him was growing with each second. He decided he was better off provoking Skinny into killing him outright. Regret washed over him at the thought of never seeing Mary Alice again. There were so many things he wanted to say, wanted to explore. But he didn't mind that so much if only he knew she would be safe.

Another body was suddenly shoved into the firelight as the Cheyenne Young Otter walked into the clearing. "Another one those sons of dogs didn't hear."

Burn-hand punched Young Otter right in the face. "That's enough. We have guests."

The Utes grinned at the Cheyenne's humiliation. Hud's heart sank at his first glimpse of Mary Alice.

"Sorry," she muttered, not looking at him. Scrambling up to a sitting position, she wrapped her arms around her legs and wisely kept her head down. Hud's stomach churned at the thought of what these men would do if they discovered she was a woman.

"Looks like little brother's alive and well," Burn-hand continued. "What is he? A deputy?"

Hud said nothing and hated himself for it. If he said "yes" they would turn Mary Alice over to the torture of the Indians. "No" meant a cleaner disposal of the witness . . . but one he couldn't force himself to condemn her to. Even though things looked bleak, he couldn't help feeling they might have a chance to escape if he waited. Common sense told him it was impossible, and he knew he was foolish not to listen.

"Looks like you boys get something extra tonight," Burn-hand said. "Bill, you and Young

Otter unload those guns and we'll be on our way."

The Utes got down from their horses, their leader signalling to one to watch over their latest prizes. Hud sat sullenly, waiting for an opening and seeing none. The boxes were unloaded quickly despite their weight. The Utes checked the sights on the barrels and the breech-loaders of several to ensure all was in working order. They spoke to each other for several minutes, then began to laugh.

"We will honor the woman from the Cheyenne with the Sun Dance for these whites," the leader said.

Hud's body jolted with fear, thinking they had discovered Mary Alice's secret. But Young Otter snatched his knife from his belt, while the Utes laughed at him. Hud realized they had been referring to the other Indian. Skinny stood by, grinning with meanness.

"That's enough," Burn-hand said to his outraged companion.

Young Otter spat. "They are fools! The Creator will kill them for this."

The Utes laughed. "Woman! We don't fear your Gods."

"You shall!"

"Let's go," Burn-hand snapped, pushing Young Otter toward the wagon.

"I don't trust them," Skinny muttered. As he passed by Hud, he kicked him in the thigh. His muscle quivered with pain, but Hud forced himself to show no reaction.

The three got on the wagon. Young Otter

slapped the reins, then spat one last time at the Utes as the vehicle lurched forward and headed out of the clearing. Hud watched as Burn-hand and Skinny grinned at them, Skinny sighting him along his pistol's barrel and pretending to get off a few shots. With each flick, Hud was sure he'd hear the retort and feel the sudden thump of lead in his chest. The wagon rolled out of the clearing.

The Ute leader signalled to two of his men, who silently melted into the trees behind the wagon.

Then he turned his attention to his "gifts."

Chapter Thirteen

For once in her life, she should have listened to Hud.

Out of the corner of her eye, Mary Alice watched the Indian come closer. Hud was tense—she could feel him ready to break free the moment the opportunity presented itself. Their chances of getting away were nil, however.

She would never forget the sudden feel of cold, sharp steel against her throat as she was edging closer to the clearing, or the guttural tone of the Indian's orders in her ear. Her stomach had dropped all the way to Hell in a second and her mouth had filled with the sour taste of bile, she had been so terrified. All her worst nightmares had become reality. Hud had looked livid when she'd stumbled into the clearing. He still did. She wanted desperately to apologize. She didn't want him going out of this world mad at her. For once, she wanted peace.

"He's just a boy," Hud said, nodding in her

direction and taking advantage of her masculine dress. "Let him go."

The Ute just grinned.

It wasn't an answer she cared for, Mary Alice admitted. But somehow, she hadn't liked the question either. The last thing she wanted was Hud taking some kind of double punishment on her behalf. At least the Indians hadn't found out she was a woman. Maybe, if she were incredibly lucky, they never would.

The distant sky glowed with a spring storm. Moments later, gunshots rang out in the night, sharp and clear, followed by screams and whoops. The Utes murmured approvingly among themselves, nodding and laughing.

"Fools," the Ute scoffed. "They will not take our land."

"Killing them didn't stop it," Hud began.

The Indian hit him. The others piled in, fists and feet swinging.

"Stop it!" Mary Alice shouted, scrambling toward the mass of flailing bodies. She was knocked flat by a roundhouse punch that came from nowhere. Pain flooded her cheek, even as her head banged against the iron-hard ground. Groggy, she pressed her hand against her throbbing cheek and tried to sit up. The world spun for an instant, then righted itself.

"Shut up!" Hud shouted from under the melee.

Somebody yelled something and the Indians stopped as one. They pulled Hud upright and one slammed his rifle butt against the side of Hud's head, knocking him cold. Mary Alice screamed and immediately found herself grabbed upright by rough, unkind hands. The Ute leader yanked Hud's jacket from him, then ripped his shirt off. What happened next was so fast, she still couldn't believe she was seeing it.

They had attached two rawhide ropes to Hud's chest with some kind of skewers. Blood trickled from the wounds. Her insides chilled. She didn't know what they intended to do with him, but the ropes were ominous. Her stomach turned over and bile rose to the back of her throat again. She had argued with him every inch of the way, fought him and fought with him, but never for all her anger had she ever wanted to see him like this.

"Hud, no," she whispered. He never stirred, although his chest rose and fell visibly with his breathing. That gave her hope and yet she didn't know for what. *Think, damn you,* she cursed to herself. She hadn't stayed alive this long for the two of them to come to an end here.

Before she could think further, the Indians gathered around her. She struggled against the hands that ripped her jacket and shirt from her upper torso.

Everything went quiet.

The Indians stared at her chest, her femininity obvious under the union suit she was wearing. "A woman!"

The leader reached out and squeezed one of her breasts. Mary Alice flinched and struggled away from his hand. The men laughed. She swallowed back her fear and touched the heavy belt hidden at her waist. "Please. I have gold. In here. Take it."

They laughed again. "We have guns. And now we have a woman. We do not need gold."

"Everyone needs gold," Mary Alice said, thinking desperately. "You could buy many things for your tribe—"

"Can we buy our land and our lives back?" one asked. "No gold can buy them. But we will kill for them."

The two who had slipped out of camp after the gunrunners returned, waving their bows and whooping. They pulled the horses from the gunrunners' wagon with them. Mary Alice realized the three who had ridden out were now dead. Hud would never resolve this case. He wouldn't like that, she thought. If he would ever know.

The Ute leader snapped a question at the two, whose good cheer after killing their fellow man immediately faded. They scuffed at the ground and looked like children caught out of school. One said something, and the leader began to shout angrily at them. He pointed to Hud and then to the nearest tree. He began to circle the clearing, chanting and shaking a bag hanging around his neck.

A fetish, Mary Alice thought, realizing he was trying to warn something away. Indians wore fetishes as charms against evil. She knew they were highly superstitious. Something not good had happened out there with the gunrunners.

"I curse you back, Cheyenne dog-woman," the Ute suddenly shouted in English. Then he began to laugh until he howled with amusement. "Your

Sun God is weak. He will not come! We will hand the white pig to call him down, and still he will not come!"

Mary Alice wondered if the Cheyenne Indian had gotten away during the attack, not that it would do her or Hud any good. The Ute turned around and signalled the others. They grabbed Hud and took him over to a tree, then threw the ropes attached to him over a thick lower branch. She screamed and tried to run to him, but an Indian held her back. She fought her captor, kicking and scratching, but he slapped her. Her ears rang with the force of it.

Horrified, she watched as the Indians pulled the ropes up until Hud was no longer touching the ground. One of the men pulled a feather from his hair and stuck it in Hud's mouth. The men roared with laughter, shaking their fists at all their enemies embodied by the man hanging from the tree in the blasphemous Sun Dance ritual.

"NO!" she screeched, feeling all the pain Hud, in his unconscious state, couldn't feel. Her chest throbbed with an agony that felt all too genuine. It was real for Hud.

She had to stop this. Had to, had to, her brain chanted, images tumbling through it. The Ute's chanting, his superstitions and the rivalry between the Cheyenne and this group coalesced along with all that she knew about people's weaknesses, in turn giving birth to an idea.

"Stop!" Mary Alice shouted, instinctively deepening her voice. "I have come, and I curse you unto death!"

The Utes turned in unison, their mouths gaping open.

"I am the Sun God!" she announced. "Cut the man down or I will bring sickness and death to each of you."

Lightning blazed white across the sky and thunder rolled in punctuation, as if the Sun God were ready to breathe fire.

Mary Alice smiled triumphantly.

Hud slowly surfaced from the grey nothingness, disoriented. Horrible fire pulled at his chest as if trying to rip out his lungs, something that tasted like hard worms was in his mouth, and he had the sensation that he was hanging. His head felt weighted back somehow, too. He lifted it. The pain didn't go away. Instead, the fire deepened to white-hot stabs as he spun slightly to the right. He spit the thing out of his mouth, then tried to move his hands to his chest to remove the pain, but they wouldn't respond. Wondering what had happened, he opened his eyes . . . and stared.

Ropes were running straight out of his chest. Appalled, he tried to swipe at them. He whirled like a marionette on a string, rivets of agony at once shooting through him. He realized his feet were off the ground by a good foot or more, his back arched at a sharp angle. He wondered how he'd gotten like this. It didn't seem like something one would voluntarily do. Slowly, he became aware of a voice shouting words.

". . . You are not Cheyenne, You blaspheme . . .

you lie to me! I will punish you with all my powers. Death comes unto you now!"

The voice was familiar. It sounded like Mary Alice with a bad cold. He forced himself to look. It *was* Mary Alice. Her shirt was torn away and she was facing down five Indians. The events of the last hour came rushing back to Hud's hazy brain. He had to help her. But first he had to get free.

One man stepped toward her. "You are a woman—"

She waved her hands, driving him back, and screamed, "I come in her body because you insult me with this white. Your tribe shall be punished. Your fathers and sons, your mothers and daughters. I curse you all!"

The screaming became gibberish, causing the Indians to mutter to each other and back away as one from the maddened woman.

Light flashed and a great noise boomed across the mountains. How, Hud wondered dimly, had she managed lightning? Boy, she was even better than he'd thought. They'd need it to get out of this. He tried to reach for the pain in his chest again to ease it, but the moment his hand jerked against something solid, the pain crescendoed to an ungodly intensity. He heard a scream from far away. Then he realized it was his own voice.

The lightning flashed again nearly on top of them.

"Get him down!" the other voice screeched. "No! No! Don't run! Get him down!"

He heard her sobbing and then hands came around his knees, trying to lift him. The pressure in his chest eased slightly, but his balance wobbled with nothing for him to steady himself upon. His back arched dangerously and every bone and muscle in his body felt stretched beyond its sockets. He moaned, as the pain came back fourfold. The sobs below him became wails.

"Get away! Don't hurt him! No! No! Don't kill us, please don't kill us!"

Hud was swung back and forth, pain shooting through him like cannons at Shiloh.

"No kill! I come back to help." Suddenly, he felt two quick jolts on the ropes and he plummeted to the ground. His back crashed into the hard earth, knocking the air out of him. He gasped, fighting the void inside his body.

"Hud! Hud!"

The air slowly re-entered his lungs in tiny, tiny bits. Hud gasped even more until the twin pains in his chest finally eased. He opened his eyes to find two faces swimming before him. Mary Alice. And an Indian. The Cheyenne who had been with the gunrunners. Hud knew he couldn't match the man now.

"Run," he whispered.

Mary Alice ignored him, still staring down at his face.

"They are too deep," Young Otter said, picking up the trailing ropes. "They are supposed to pull out as you make your sacrifice to the Sun. He has spoken through you. I saw."

Hud didn't understand what the man was trying to say, but he realized the Indian had helped him. Wet dripped on his face and he glanced around to find tears falling from Mary Alice's eyes.

"You bastard," she said. "I thought you were dead."

"Bad . . . penny . . . Countess."

"I know. You always come back." She smiled and lifted his head onto her lap, her thighs cradling him. The wet dripped even more on his face.

"Stop that," he said, feeling tired, very, very tired. "You don't cry."

"It's the rain. Just what we need."

"The Thunderer comes to make his anger known. We must go."

"Can you move, Hud? We have to get out of here before those Utes come back."

He tried to move, but his body refused to cooperate. He groaned, feeling only pain burning up his chest and radiating to every part of his torso.

"They won't come," Young Otter said. "You have cursed them now. They will not return, women that they are. I would have staked myself to a wolf skin to fight their Gods, not run as they have from mine."

The rain began to come down in heavy sheets. It soaked his skin in a second, chilling him. He shivered, feeling hot and cold, even as goosebumps rose on his skin. Mary Alice shrieked curse words Hud didn't know she even knew. "Hud, you've got to move. We've got to find the horses and get back to that camp."

"Horses are gone," the Cheyenne said.

"Noooo!" Mary Alice wailed.

"I'm getting up," Hud said, trying to lift his

head off her lap. He got as far as his chin to his chest, when he collapsed, panting for breath. The wind blew in a freezing blast like a train out of the mountaintop. The sheet of water pouring out of the skies turned to little cold needle-stabs pinching everywhere. His teeth began to chatter. "Cold."

Mary Alice cried and pulled her jacket over him. It was as wet and cold as he, and smelly besides. Hud tried to push it away, but his hands flapped uselessly.

"There is a white man's placc," Young Otter said. "How you say . . . cabin. Not far."

"Thank God. Will you help me?" Mary Alice asked.

Hud thought about it for a moment and decided he just wasn't up to helping her. He couldn't even help himself at the moment. To his surprise, he found himself being pulled upright by strong hands, and he realized she wasn't talking to him. Pain shot everywhere, duller now, blunted by the chill on his skin. The Indian hefted a shoulder under Hud's armpit for support and began walking. Mary Alice closed the gap on the other side.

Hud staggered between them, trying to concentrate on getting one foot in front of the other. Somehow his feet weren't willing to cooperate. He did notice the boxes of rifles piled on the ground.

"Don't lose them," he told Mary Alice. "Evidence."

"He's delirious already!" she told the Indian.

Hud didn't care, feeling colder and colder. Their bodies, rather than giving warmth, only seemed like wintry marble against his side. Each step was torture, far worse somehow than what he'd just suffered through. All he wanted to do was lie down and go to sleep. Sleep forever.

"Let me go," he pleaded.

"Stop being an ass, Hud," Mary Alice said.

He smiled. "You're a good woman."

And then he fainted.

"I'll kill him," Mary Alice muttered as she helped the Indian drag an unconscious Hud along to the cabin. Leave it to the stubborn marshal to pass out. He weighed a ton, and her body ached from carrying the dead weight. She had no idea where she was. So far, she'd followed the Indian blindly. Maybe he was leading her into a trap.

"There!" Young Otter pointed ahead as lightning illuminated the sky. The outline of a squat cabin was visible for one bright second.

"Come on." Mary Alice tightened her grip on Hud and started to trot toward the cabin.

They managed to get through the door, which was half-hanging off its leather hinges, and let Hud down as easy as they could on the floor. Inside, the cabin was dark and cold, but the rain only dripped in from several narrow gaps in the roof. It was better than being outside for the moment, Mary Alice decided, listening to the pounding on the wood above them. She hopped up and down, rubbing her arms to get the heat and circulation back. She knew Hud needed it more, but if she didn't get life back in her first, then how could she get it back in him?

"He needs a fire to warm him," the Indian said. He wasn't much more than a shadow in the darkness.

"Why are you helping me?" she asked. "You nearly killed us earlier."

"Because the Creator came to you. He came even though the Sun Dance was a joke of the Utes. You cursed them. I got away from two fools the Utes sent and I came back to kill you all, but I saw. I knew then I had to save the man. And help you now."

Mary Alice didn't know what to say. She had only intended to play on the Indians' superstition in an attempt to save Hud. If she told this one the truth, he'd kill the two of them in the wink of an eye.

"He has to have the ropes cut away," Young Otter said. "I will find dry wood for a fire."

"In this?" Mary Alice asked, pointing out the cabin door.

"It can be done." First, the Indian explored the small cabin, finding some burnable things left behind. He piled them together near Hud and took out two pieces of flint, striking them until they sparked on some old crumbling leaves. Carefully, he blew on the trickle of flame, nurturing it into a small fire.

The cabin, now slightly more visible, revealed rough-hewn chairs and table. At least the remnants of them were recognizable among the heap of wood in the center of the one room. A pan, the bottom mesh, was overturned on the packed dirt floor, clearly indicating this had been a miner's cabin. A stream must be nearby. But the room's disarray made it all too clear the claim hadn't been abandoned. Cobwebs hung everywhere.

"Utes," Young Otter said.

Mary Alice shivered and wiped her running nose with the back of her hand. She knelt down next to Hud, reaching out blindly to rub his arms. His skin felt like ice, the muscles underneath limp. She massaged his arm, trying to put the warmth back into it. Fear crawled along her spine at his waxen complexion. She'd be damned before he left her in the middle of nowhere with an Indian whom she wasn't sure wanted to worship her or sacrifice her. By God, she'd fly right up to Heaven and drag Hud back if she had to before he pulled a stunt like that on her.

Young Otter shifted through the pile of wood for some dry pieces, it being directly under a leak. He set the decent wood on the fire, building it up until it was burning merrily. He stood up, walked over to the door, and pulled it shut.

Mary Alice froze.

He settled down next to her. "Now the warmth will stay in and help the man."

Mary Alice relaxed, then froze again when he took out his knife.

Young Otter laughed at her wariness, the broad planes of his face easing with his amusement. He wasn't old in spite of the weathered lines from constant exposure to the sun. In his late twenties or early thirties, she estimated. He said, "You whites have no honor and so you trust no one. I will not hurt him, but we must free the ropes. His wounds will turn bad unless we get them out."

"You were the one riding with the gunrunners," she reminded him. "And you were ready to slit my throat fast enough. How can you expect me to trust you?"

He shrugged. "I left my tribe with dishonor. To get guns to the tribes to kill the whites who take their lands would give back my honor. But to give the guns to the Utes? That is madness. The tribes on this side of the mountains kill for pleasure. They are animals."

His disgust was evident, and Mary Alice had the impression that their troubles might have only started—not a reassuring thought. He held the knife over the flame, waiting and watching as the blade slowly turned red. Mary Alice swallowed as he lifted the knife finally from the fire.

"It makes the blade clean," he said. She nodded.

Hud groaned once but didn't wake up as Young Otter took out the ropes.

"He will need medicine," Young Otter said, rising to his feet. "And food and water."

He disappeared out the door.

Mary Alice glanced down at Hud's chest. The wounds looked nasty, the flesh torn, but better without the ropes hanging obscenely from them. She reached out and traced around the wounds, feeling the muscles underneath. Bits of rawhide were left behind and she removed them as best she could, relieved to find his skin warming. So many emotions washed through her, confusing emotions. And they were all centered on this man. She couldn't define them but somehow she felt changed.

"What have you done to me?" she whispered, touching his cheek to trace the angle of his jaw. "What have you done?"

Young Otter returned nearly at dawn, waking Mary Alice from a fitful doze. The fire was almost ashes.

"Where have you been?" she asked, setting a chair leg on the crumbling white charcoal. The wood immediately crackled.

"I went hunting and I went to the wagon." He had a bundle in his arms. "I brought clothes—"

"Hud's not wearing any gunrunner's clothes," Mary Alice said, trying to find her mental equilibrium.

"That is evil!" Young Otter exclaimed. "Besides, even they should not be ashamed when they return to their Creator."

She felt woozy, her mouth tasted of smoke, and she had a memory of strange dreams with Hud flitting in and out on wings. She shook her head, trying to clear it

"I have brought some blankets. They are not too wet. And I have brought this for you." He handed over a white deerskin shift, fringed at the neck and sleeves and beaded with blue and red beads.

She looked at it longingly. Her pants and shirt had dried hard and were chafing her skin. What they looked like must be even worse, she admitted. But she shook her head. "I couldn't."

"Yes." He thrust them out to her, his expression hard.

Mary Alice took the dress from him gingerly. The suede was incredibly soft, smooth like butter against her hand. She looked up. "This is so beautiful."

"It was my mother's."

"I thought it was evil to wear the clothes of a dead person."

"Only those who have bad hearts." He smiled. "You do not have a bad heart. My mother did not. I have no woman to give it to, and it would bring me honor if you wear it."

She nodded.

Hud groaned in his sleep catching her attention.

Mary Alice smiled over at him . . . then noticed how flushed his skin was. Her smile faded and she reached out and touched him.

He was burning up.

Chapter Fourteen

"No," she whispered, feeling his cheeks and his chest. They felt even hotter than his head. "This can't be. He was fine last night."

Young Otter brushed her hands away and felt. He nodded. "It is the fever. From the wounds."

He pointed to Hud's chest. The area around the wounds was an angry red, indicating infection. No deadly streaks ran out from the site . . . not yet.

"What do we do?" she asked, frantically looking around the cabin for help. They had no medicine and no way of getting it. Her hands shook and she pressed them together tightly to stop the trembling. She hadn't even imagined that Hud could become ill.

He frowned. "He needs medicine."

"We need water," Mary Alice said, his comment triggering her own knowledge of cures. All those times she sold phony medicines and now she needed the real thing desperately. How ironic. "We've got to bathe him and bring the fever down.

And make a tea. He'll dry out from the fevers."

Young Otter nodded, rose abruptly, and left her.

Her stomach growled and she sat back on her heels, muttering, "Breakfast would be nice, too."

She cursed the selfish thought as soon as she'd uttered it and, instead, stroked Hud's forehead to comfort him. He murmured words she couldn't quite make out and then he seemed to settle down. But his skin felt too dry. He coughed, the sound of it ominously matching the feel of his skin.

She wished there was something she could do to help him, but she had to wait for Young Otter to come back with water. It hurt more than she cared to admit to see him like this. She looked down at the dress in her lap. She realized belatedly they probably should have taken his clothes off last night, but there had been nothing else to put on him then. Having him naked would have done him no good in the chill air—nor her, especially after what had happened and with Young Otter present. One humilation she might have managed, but not two at once.

Still, he needed better clothes if he were to survive. She knew she was being stiff-necked about his wearing things that had belonged to the gunrunners. Maybe too stiff-necked. As long as they were arrow-free, what did it matter? A lot, probably, to Hud's health. First, she would change her clothes and then change his.

Pushing the door shut against Young Otter's reappearance and glancing at Hud to make sure he was still unconscious, she stripped off the last of her clothes. The dress slipped on over her head and slid down her body like heavy silk. She ran her hands over the material, marveling at the workmanship. The shift was loose and very comfortable, unlike the wasp-waists and bustles currently in fashion. The deerskin had been pounded thin, bringing it to its utmost flexibility and softness. How, she wondered, had it ever been bleached so white? The long fringe tickled her upper arms, in sharp contrast to the quill trim interwoven with the beads across the breasts. Truly, it was beautiful, she thought, and made her actually feel like someone a God had spoken through. She chuckled, wondering how she could add her latest portrayal to her repertoire.

She sorted through the blankets Young Otter had brought. They were actually dry in big patches, their only advantage. She knelt before Hud. He moaned restlessly as she strugged with his boots.

"Shut up," she muttered under her breath, finally yanking the boots free. One sock had a hole in the toe. She grinned and stripped them off his feet. Men had such ugly feet, she decided, staring at Hud's. All bony, with long, waggly-looking toes and tufts of hair. Shrugging, she moved up to his waist.

Mary Alice moaned in humiliation, knowing what she had to do next. What had happened between them came rushing back to her. He was her enemy, and yet she'd been intimate with him in her kisses, if not her body. He'd said terrible things about her father. She hated him and yet here she was, trying to save his life. She didn't understand herself any longer. But she couldn't leave him to his illness. Her conscience wouldn't allow it.

"I'm getting soft," she muttered, then took a deep breath and undid his belt. Turning her head away, she unbuttoned his pants very carefully. Her fingers touched a soft mound. She pulled them back as if burned.

She pushed the pants down off his hips. Underneath, she could feel the dampness still in his clothes. She'd made the right decision, she thought, even as she cursed it again. The undergarment would have to go, too, for the same reason the pants did.

Her face heated and she managed to keep her eyes averted as she finished tugging the pants off his legs. As she did, she chanted, "Please don't wake up."

She tried not to look as she pulled down the underdrawers in movements that seemed to take forever. But her gaze caught a glimpse of his nakedness. She stared at his man's flesh. How could something so soft-looking have caused pain? It looked innocent enough. In fact, it looked rather ugly in a fascinating sort of way. Women were made prettier in more than face, she decided . . .

Realizing what she was thinking, she groaned in horror and turned her face away, skinning off the undergarment with rough hands.

Hud moaned. His eyelids fluttered open.

"Hud," Mary Alice whispered, tossing the pants up over his naked hips to cover them. Her heart leaped with joy that he was awake, even as the rest of her died with embarrassment.

Hud stared at the vision before him. An Indian Goddess—there was no other word for it—dressed all in white. It must be Indian Heaven. That made sense, he thought. He'd been killed by Indians. Pain still burned his chest as a reminder. Several other things didn't make sense, though. The Goddess had Mary Alice's face and he had a vague half-memory of her taking off his clothes. That couldn't be right, he thought dimly. Angels didn't do those things. Did they? He knew Mary Alice wouldn't. There was a cold breeze in Heaven, too, oddly heating his skin, especially his legs. It must be the cloud he was on. He stared at the face before him. The countenance didn't change. "Did they . . . kill you, too, Countess?"

It was more of an effort to speak than he'd thought. Hud stared at her for another moment, then closed his eyes. He was so hot. His backside felt as if he were lying in dirt. Heaven was rapidly turning into something else.

Mary Alice moaned in relief. He was lucid—sort of. Still, it was a good sign. "No. You're not dead, either."

"I'm not?" He licked his lips. "Thirsty."

"We're getting water."

He glanced around. "Guns . . ."

"Safe," she said. "You sure don't forget your job, do you?"

"Can't. Chest . . . hurts."

"You . . . you had a little run-in with some Indians."

"Hanging. I remember. One helped."

"The Cheyenne. Young Otter."

"Skinny . . . Burn-hand." He struggled with the words, his voice as tired as the rest of him.

"Dead." She stroked his forehead. "Rest now."

He wanted to, but his mind was filled with too many questions. "Where am I?"

"In an abandoned cabin, not far from that clearing. Hud—"

"We have . . . get out . . . be back." He tried to rise, but his body refused, his head spinning with the effort.

Mary Alice pushed him flat again. "You can't go anywhere, except to sleep. You get better and then we'll go."

"Feel fine." He gasped, finding no air in his lungs. He concentrated on her until he could breathe again. She looked beautiful in the white dress, like an Indian maiden going to her wedding. "Those clothes . . ."

"Young Otter gave it to me."

"Figures," he muttered, thinking how he was half-dead through Indian torture and she came out smelling like a rose. "Must go. You'll . . . get into trouble."

Her laugh was shaky. "I'll behave. I promise."

"Heard it before." He sighed and closed his eyes. "I'll just have . . . to get you out."

"You do that," she whispered.

He opened his eyes at the funny catch in her voice. Her eyes looked like they were filled with tears. He must be dreaming, he thought, then closed his eyes again.

He seemed to fall back to sleep. Mary Alice's heart flipped over, half with pity for his condition and half with stronger, much more confusing emotions. Finally, she let out her breath. At least, he hadn't noticed his state of undress. She'd squeaked through that one. Carefully, she removed the water-stiff pants from over his hips.

At that moment, the door to the cabin swung open. Young Otter stared at her, then at Hud. She immediately dropped the pants on Hud again.

"I was changing his clothes!" she said defensively, her face suffusing with the heat of embarrassment. "He's sick, and he needs dry garments."

The Cheyenne said nothing. He held, of all things, a canteen in his hands. Mary Alice focused on that. It was Hud's. "Where did you find this?"

"With the brown horse. And the Indian pony."

She gaped at him. "Brown and the buckskin? I thought you said they were gone."

"The wagon horses. The Utes took them. I meant those." He grinned, rather like a smug child. "I find these two on the mountain. They are yours, yes?"

"Yes." Mary Alice grinned in return. "Well, break out the packs on their saddles. We've a pot you can make tea in, and Hud won't have to wear gunrunners' dirty clothes after all. We can use his own. That ought to cheer him up."

Young Otter went out for the packs. Mary Alice relaxed. Deciding to get to work, she poured some water on the tail of her shirt, pressing the cool wetness against Hud's face. He flinched and tried to slap her hands away.

"Stop that," Mary Alice coaxed, pushing his hands down to his sides. "It'll cool you off."

"Wet."

"It's water." She bathed his chest, careful around the wounds.

Hud shuddered when she accidentally touched one. She murmured, "I'm sorry."

Young Otter came back in with the packs, including the one with the beef jerky. She grabbed up a strip and shoved it in her mouth, then unrolled the blanket from its oilskin, grateful to find it dryer than the ones they were using. So were Hud's clothes inside. She immediately handed them to Young Otter. "Put them on him, please. He needs the warmth."

Young Otter frowned, but she turned her back on him and busied herself with making up a bed. When she sensed the Indian had finished the task, she turned around. Hud was dressed from the waist down.

She pointed to the reddened wounds. "They're infected. Poisoned."

Young Otter nodded. "First I will scrape them clean, and then I will make a poultice to draw it out."

"Good." Otis had told her Indians sometimes had better cures for people. "Let's move him onto the blanket."

Together, they got Hud settled onto the makeshift bed. Young Otter built up the fire again, and laid his knife on it. Mary Alice poured some water into the pot for tea from the bark the Indian had brought.

"I will go find the . . . roots for the poultice," Young Otter said, frowning at the words he'd chosen. She smiled, acknowledging she understood what he meant. He went on, "And I will put evil charms around this cabin against the Utes. They will not cross them."

"Can you bring up those guns?" she asked, knowing Hud would worry about them.

Young Otter nodded. "And I will take care of the horses. You will need them."

Mary Alice began to skin-bathe Hud. "I'll keep him cool."

The Indian left the cabin and she had to admit both of them would have died by now without Young Otter. Funny, all the stories about the Indians were so terrifying, and the ones she'd seen before in some of the towns and forts had been silent and unsmiling, with faces always seeming to carry a look that was on the edge of violence. But Young Otter had shown her another side of the people who inhabited this land before hers came to it. Maybe there was more to the Indian Wars than what was in the penny dreadfuls. She wondered how she would feel if people came and uprooted her, willy-nilly. She'd probably be a lot less generous than Young Otter was.

She turned to Hud, working on him, keeping his face and arms moist, dribbling liquid around his mouth, then repeating the process over again and again.

Young Otter returned and made his poultice, a foul-smelling mass. He took the knife out of the fire and let it cool slightly, then with gentle, almost delicate movements, he pulled the edge of the knife against the wounds, shaving away some of Hud's chest hair and bits of rawhide in the process. Mary Alice held Hud down as he flinched from the contact, keeping her gaze focused on his face, rather than on what Young Otter was doing. Finally, he pressed the poultice against Hud's chest.

Mary Alice wrinkled her nose at the odor, saying, "Wonderful. I think I'm going to be sick next."

The Indian chuckled and held his nose. "Bad smell, yes. But it makes better."

"It had better make better," Mary Alice announced. "Otherwise, it'll be the Woman's Regulator next." Young Otter frowned, and she chuckled. "Never mind. Let's get some tea into him."

The minutes stretched into long, arduous hours that blurred together in a mix of bathing and forcing tea into the patient. The heat of the fire made the room a smoky blast furnace. Young Otter left her to the task of caring for Hud, while he gathered wood, tended the horses, and brought up the guns. He came in and out of the cabin, changing the poultice from time to time. The wounds didn't look any better, but at least they didn't look any worse. Mary Alice labored over Hud, fretting with his every restless movement and dry, hacking cough, continually keeping up the baths until her arms ached. And still the fever didn't break. She knew in her heart of hearts what it was.

Pneumonia.

*   *   *

The demons chased him around and around a tree as wide as a building, flailing at him with rawhide ropes. Faces bent over him, some sad and worried, others chortling and grinning evilly. He tried to run away from them all, to find the darkness that beckoned, but he couldn't move his arms and legs.

A huge rock pressed his lungs in an ever-squeezing vise, forcing him to gasp for each breath. It burned him like a red hot iron, searing his flesh. He tried to push the thing off, but it wouldn't budge. He faded in and out of consciousness. The faces leaned over him almost constantly, like two opposite mirror images.

The kindly one cursed him heartily. "Damn you, don't you dare die on me, Hud Jackson, you bastard."

He wanted to answer but he was in an oven that was slowly baking him to death. Someone poured cool water on his skin and forced him to drink an awful-tasting liquid that burned his throat. He coughed and gagged against it.

Mary Alice floated by him, slowly stripping her clothes away. Her arms were soft and white and beckoning, forgiving him for what had happened in Longville. He swam after her, trying to catch her. He wanted her like this so badly. For him . . . just for him . . .

His brother stepped between them, and Mary Alice disappeared into the mist. He tried to push his brother aside to get to her, but she was gone.

Two men—one dead, one alive—drifted toward his brother. He couldn't make out the faces of either as they caught his brother and pulled him away, back into the past.

"Damn it, open your mouth," a voice demanded. "Hold him, Young Otter."

He was lifted into the air, his arms pinned back by an Indian with a compassionate expression on his face. Mary Alice loomed over him, suddenly sharp and clear. She pried open his lips and poured warm liquid into his mouth. He gagged on the sour, bitter taste, like bad cabbage. His stomach heaved sickeningly once. More was forced in until he had to swallow it. Somehow it went down.

"You die on me, and I swear I'll come to haunt you," Mary Alice whispered. She was crying again.

He hated to see her cry and tried to tell her he was sorry, but he was pulled back down into the inferno. Faces roared around him, horses screamed in agony, gunshots boomed as one. Grey line charged blue and broke against it among the hills of Pennsylvania. Hud rode and rode and yet he never reached his goal. He wasn't sure what the goal was anymore, he just knew he had to get there to survive.

More faces floated up until Mary Alice's finally appeared. She was beckoning again, driving back all the horrors, challenging him to come to her. She wasn't soothing. She would never be soothing. But she would always be exciting.

Suddenly she was sitting in a rocker, staring

vacantly at the wall. She seemed older and her face wasn't quite the same. He called to her, trying to get the frightening expression off her face. But she never turned around, never heard him. It was as if she weren't inside her body. Nothing he had ever seen on the battlefield was as horrifying as this. Not Mary Alice, he thought, frantically clawing toward her. Nuns, their black veils flowing around their faces, gathered in front of her, blocking his way. They were all shaking their heads sadly.

"You did this," they said as one.

"No," he said. "I didn't mean to hurt her."

They were silent, staring accusingly.

"I'm sorry, Mary Alice," he called out, trying to break through the physical and mental barrier. "I love you."

"Oh, God, he's sick in the mind now," she said from somewhere above him. Cool water washed against his skin, and the bitter tea was poured down his throat again.

Eventually, he opened his eyes. Mary Alice was bent over him, a worried look in her gaze. Lines pulled at her mouth and her skin was a funny sickly pale color as if she were very weary.

"You're alive," he said. His voice cracked and his throat was raw.

She smiled. It was a beautiful smile. "Barely. When are you going to get well?"

He frowned in puzzlement. "I'm sick?"

"For three days."

"Oh." He thought about it for a moment, trying to assess what she'd told him. His body ached everywhere, as if he'd been in a fight with a bear and lost. His chest still hurt but not nearly as bad as he remembered it. And he was wet with sweat.

An Indian suddenly towered over her. In panic, Hud tried to jump up and get away, then he realized it was the Cheyenne who'd been with the gunrunners. Disjointed memories raced through him like the strange dreams he'd had and he had a vague picture of the Indian helping her with him.

"The fever breaks," the Indian said, his expression stolid. "Good."

"Very good," Mary Alice agreed. She grinned.

He became aware of her dress. The white buckskin was a sharp contrast to her dark hair. Conversations went in and out of his head. "You're an Indian Goddess."

She chuckled. "Hardly. It's just a gift from Young Otter here."

Somehow he didn't like the sound of that. Suddenly, he felt exhausted, too exhausted to pursue the matter. He'd save her from this new scheme of hers later, he decided. "I'm sick and you're dressed like an Indian. I told you you'd get in trouble. I want to sleep now."

"Go to sleep," she repeated, stroking his forehead.

Her fingers were soothing and gentle. Surprising coming from her, he thought, and yet he revelled in it. She'd nursed him during this illness he couldn't quite remember. That was a surprise, too. A big one. And she hadn't run out on him when she'd had the chance. God knows, he hadn't been in a position to stop her. And now she was soft and kind. At each turn, he discovered a new facet of her that only made her more intriguing. Her heritage didn't matter when she was like this with him. Who her father was hadn't seemed to matter for a long time now.

Her hands still soothing him, he went to sleep.

"They look good," Mary Alice acknowledged to herself, critically surveying the wounds on Hud's chest. Whatever was in the poultice Young Otter made had worked very well. The angry red swelling was gone, and the flesh was healing. Hud would have scars for the rest of his life, but she doubted they would bother him. In fact, they'd probably be a point of pride.

He slept on contentedly, not disturbed by her or the Indian's examination. His fever had broken at last, and he'd come out of the ravings and convulsions. Young Otter had had to hold him down at one point, when he'd kept calling her name . . . and other things.

It was the sickness of the mind, she told herself firmly. He didn't mean anything he'd said, just the rantings of a brain-fevered man.

So why had her heart leaped with joy at his silly words? Foolish, she decided, hardening her heart. She'd seen people do stranger things than declare undying love for someone they hated when in the grip of illness.

She'd brought him through this, and she couldn't help feeling that evened up the score between them. But while the fever was gone, the worst wasn't over yet. Sometimes people were weakened for the rest of their lives after lung fever—even young and healthy men like Hud. They would just have to wait and see.

She set her jaw against the sudden jump of fear in her own chest. Hud would be fine. She had to believe that.

"He'd better be, after what he put me through," she said out loud.

Hud stirred slightly, as if in acknowledgment.

She sighed and sat back on the dirt floor. Her shoulders ached from tension and from her constant bent-over position. Every bone in her body screamed with weariness, and she doubted she'd had one full night's sleep in three. She'd dozed off and on when he'd been quiet. Those times had been rare enough. Her eyes burned, half with grit and half from the small, smoky fire they'd had to keep going. Her own lungs hurt from breathing it in.

Three days she had fought for him. She wondered what her father would have said.

Young Otter came into the cabin. While she'd cared for Hud, the Cheyenne had cared for her. She never would have made it without him. If he had wanted a way to regain his honor, he had done it here. He was carrying food. He'd taken to cooking outside and guarding the cabin and the horses. So far as she knew, no one had bothered them. Maybe his fetishes and charms were working. Maybe her new reputation preceded her. She smiled to herself at the thought.

She realized she hadn't thought once about the

gold while Hud was sick. Not once. She couldn't believe something that had consumed her for so long had become insignificant in the fact of illness. She looked over at Hud, sleeping unconcerned.

Somehow, he'd managed to do that, too.

Chapter Fifteen

Being alive had its drawbacks, Hud decided, as he shifted back against the wall of the little cabin. His lungs hurt like hell, compromised by the sharp pangs in his bruised chest muscles. At least he wasn't lying in the fire any longer.

Jesus, but it hurt to breathe, he thought, cautiously letting air in and out of his lungs. He'd drifted in and out of sleep over the last four days since his fever broke, taking care of bodily functions with the help of the Indian. He was wide awake, and he didn't want to hurt anymore or sleep again, either. It had been important for him to move, to know he could do it. He'd seen too many men weaken from being bedridden. He'd suffered great agony to get to the wall, but he'd done it.

Mary Alice, still dressed in the white deerskin, was on the other side of the small fire. He had no idea where the Indian was, and he didn't want to ask.

She looked so beautiful, he thought, watching her movements. And she looked so tired. His fever had taken its toll on her. He wanted to walk over and put his arms around her and just hold her, give her comfort. He doubted he could even stand upright at the moment, let alone walk. She'd probably throw him off anyway.

He remembered images and words of . . . love. He'd really been sick, he thought. Yet as he looked at Mary Alice, a funny sensation sent shivers up his spine. He pushed the sensation away.

"What did you do to my chest?" he asked, catching a whiff of a strong, noxious odor.

Mary Alice paused from rooting through one of their saddle bags. "Young Otter made a poultice for the wounds to draw out the poison."

"Did he have to make it smell so bad?"

She grinned. "Why, Mr. Jackson, you never smelled sweeter."

"Thank God," he said, shifting slightly. "I wouldn't want to ruin my reputation."

"It's intact . . . as long as the women stay fifty feet away."

He grimaced at her.

"Make that one hundred." She tapped a tooth with a fingernail in contemplation. "Maybe a mile. Fortunately for you, I'm the only one who can smell you right now. And I don't smell much better."

"God's looking out for us then. But I think I need a bath." Just the idea of it was exhausting, and he leaned his head back against the wall and closed his eyes.

"Put it out of your mind, Hud," she said. "You're too weak yet."

"I'm too something." He sighed, feeling tired again. It had come over him like a wave. But he wanted to say something. He opened his eyes and looked at her. "Thank you. For what you did."

She shrugged and turned back to the pack.

He was determined to say it all. "After all that happened, I wouldn't have expected you to."

"Me, neither."

"So why did you do it?"

She shrugged again, not looking at him.

The silence grew. He knew he ought to leave it alone and just be grateful that she had helped him. Besides, this could all just be temporary for both of them if any scoundrels or Indians found the cabin. Safety was a relative thing. Still, something inside him drove him to press on. "Countess, why did you take care of me?"

"I don't know!" she snapped. "To even up the stakes between us. They're even now, right?"

"They're even." The answer was so unsatisfactory. What had he been wishing for anyway? She would never change. "What happened with the guns?"

"Young Otter brought them up," she said, her voice terse.

"They're here?" He looked around the near-empty cabin. "Where?"

"Outside." She finally found what she was looking for, holding up her hairbrush. She began to brush her hair, working out the knots.

Hud looked on, fascinated with the gentle, even

strokes as she pulled the brush through her dark strands. He wanted to watch her do this every night . . . The thought brought back reality, and he set his jaw for a moment before going on, "Now I'll never know who this Walker is, or where he is."

"But at least the guns won't be going to the Utes." She paused in her brushing. "I have a feeling they wouldn't be as nice as they were to you and me."

"Probably." He smiled wryly. "But it could all start up again because I can't find Walker now and stop him."

"Well, he's got to be staying around here. That wagon didn't come from too far."

"True." He tried to imagine from where, but his brain felt dead. "Maybe from Fort Vasquez?"

"Or Denver, I suppose."

"Denver." He nodded. It felt right. "The fort would miss those guns real fast, but not in Denver. Too many people. Walker could easily blend in. Hell! How do I find someone who's blended in?"

Mary Alice frowned. "I don't know. Apply for the job?"

"Apply for the job!" He stared at her as if she'd grown two heads. "How would I apply for the job?"

"Same way you did in that camp. Just let it be known you're willing to do it, and he'll find you." She smiled smugly. "Can you think of a better idea?"

"No," he grumbled. "By the time I can move he'll have hired about ten more, anyway."

"Maybe not," Mary Alice said. "After all, no one knows about those two being dead but us. And I don't expect the Utes will ride into Denver demanding their missing guns."

She had a point, he thought. As usual. "At least I know it's about the railroad, and I can have it stopped on that end. That might bring Walker out."

"What do you mean *it's about the railroad?*" she asked.

He sighed, wishing he didn't have to say it. She would be smug for weeks now. "You were right the first time about the two things being related. They're having the Indians cause trouble for farmers and ranchers along where the railroad line's supposed to go, and then they come in afterward and buy the people out cheap."

"Brilliant," she commented in a dreamy voice.

"Countess!"

She flinched. "I'm sorry. I was just admiring the cleverness of it, not the method. Anyone who has to kill to fool people is no master at his craft. Otis Wainwright said that a long time ago."

"And who's he?" His voice was too sarcastic, and too revealing.

"The man who found my sister and me on the trail and took us in," she replied, frowning at him in puzzlement. "He taught me everything I know. He was like a father to both of us."

Hud wasn't sure whether to be grateful or not to this Otis.

Young Otter came into the cabin, drawing their attention. Distrust rose to the surface, but Hud suppressed the urge. The man had had plenty of opportunities to kill him and Mary Alice, yet he hadn't. In fact, he'd saved Hud's life.

The Indian had a haunch of cooked rabbit on a plate. He set the plate next to Mary Alice. "You must eat now. For strength."

"Thank you." She smiled at him.

To Hud's surprise, the Indian smiled back. He glanced over at Hud, the smile immediately disappearing into a grim line. Then he left the cabin again.

"That was cozy," Hud couldn't resist saying.

Mary Alice frowned. "What?"

"Him bringing you food like that."

"Oh, that." She grinned. "He thinks his God spoke through me that night with the others."

"He thinks . . ." Hud shook his head. "Damn it, I told you to stay out of trouble!"

She gaped at him. "What trouble? You're lucky to be alive from that 'trouble.'"

He gritted his teeth, counted to ten for patience, and said, "Don't you see? You're some kind of religious being to him now. Did you ever think there might be a ritual he'll do? A sacrifice that might include you?"

"Me?" She waved her hands. "Don't be ridiculous, Hud. He's just been nice."

"No one is just nice. And you ought to know that."

"Since when did you get so cynical?" she demanded, tucking her hair back behind her ear.

"Since you stopped," he replied. "Forget it. Just watch yourself."

"Right." She broke off a piece of the rabbit and came around the fire. "Here."

"I'm not hungry," he snapped. His stomach made a liar out of him by growling. Angry with her and with himself, he took the meat out of her fingers and plopped it in his mouth. It tasted delicious.

"More?" she asked.

"No."

She smiled sweetly. "Hud, don't be a crabbier patient than you already are."

"I'm not being crabby," he muttered. "I just don't want that Indian hanging me from some tree again because I ate the food of his talking God."

"But I'm sharing, so it's okay," she replied. She went and got the plate. After she brought it back, she sat down next to him. She was careful to keep a foot of space between them, but it still felt good to have her beside him. He grinned to himself, deciding he was soft in the head, too. She took some meat for herself, then handed it over to him.

Hud wanted to resist the food, but he couldn't. Not when all he'd had were broths and tea over the last few days. He took another piece of the meat. It melted in his mouth, all smoky and sweet from being staked over a fire.

"Were you ever in love?"

Hud choked in the middle of his swallow. "Wha . . . ?"

"Have you ever had a girl?" she repeated. "Do you have one in Denver? Or back home in . . . where was home?"

"Virginia." He shrugged. "I was engaged once."

"You were?" She turned away.

"Until she married a Yankee. She didn't want to lose her creature comforts." He clamped his jaw together, and then was surprised that it still rankled a bit. He recognized it for what it was. "I think it hurt my pride more than anything else. My brother did warn me not to get involved with her. But I hadn't listened. I don't think you do when you're twenty. Why do you ask?"

"Just curious."

"Why? What made you curious?" The question burned at him. What was she bringing this up for? What did it mean?

"Nothing made me curious," she said, starting to get up.

He grabbed her arm, keeping her in place. "Something, Countess. And I want to know what it is!"

"Just friendliness!" She stared at him. "We've been together . . . around each other for awhile now. You mumbled some things when you were sick, and that made me curious."

"What things?" he demanded, panic running through him as he remembered the weirdest dream of all.

She tried to pull her arm free, but he gripped her more tightly. She gave up the struggle. "I don't know, Hud. Just . . . things about women in general. Names and all."

"What names?" He couldn't have, he thought desperately. Granted it was a dream, but he couldn't have said what he was terrified he'd said about her.

"I don't remember!" She glared at him. "I was too damn busy keeping you alive!"

He glared back. "Don't swear. It's not ladylike."

"I'm no lady as you're happy to prove whenever possible."

He dropped her arm like it was a hot iron. "How many times do I have to apologize for that?"

"Forever. That was my pride you took that day."

"No wonder you're so empty inside," he muttered, closing his eyes.

He sensed her rising to her feet, but didn't bother to open his eyes. She said, "I saved your damn life, Hud. That wasn't so empty. Or maybe it was."

She went to the other side of the cabin, back to her work. The tension in the small space grew until it was almost tangible. Hud wanted to say something, but he was damned if he would apologize. She was empty inside. Just greedy, without a soft spot in her heart.

A voice reminded him of all they'd been through, of the way she'd held to her promise to stay with him. She'd nursed him back to health such as it was at the moment. He hadn't expected that, either. And he hadn't meant to be ungrateful that she'd saved his life twice from torture and illness. He was grateful to her, but that didn't mean he felt anything else.

And what did it matter if he'd actually said something stupid while he was sick? He had no control over it, and it certainly didn't mean it was true. He wanted her. She was a woman and he was a man, but that didn't mean there was more to it.

The voice inside him began a different discourse. Hud told it, in firm internal tones, to shut up.

"I should have let him rot on that tree," Mary Alice muttered, taking down the sun-dried pants from a bush just outside the cabin. She folded them over, then rubbed her bare arms against the slight chill in the breeze. The dress might be comfortable, but it left her limbs exposed to the cold. She knew she couldn't stay out long, and yet she didn't want to go back inside because of Hud.

She couldn't believe how he had pounced on her with those questions. Clearly, he was still in love with his fiancée, and the idea of it hurt, somehow. She wished she'd never asked those stupid questions in the first place. She should have known the words weren't meant for her.

"Snow is coming."

She jumped at the voice behind her and whirled around. Young Otter stared at her. Hud's words of warning came back, and she tried to push them aside. But he'd planted a seed of mistrust now, and she couldn't help responding to it.

She shivered, both at his words and at her thoughts. Just what they needed, snow. She could just imagine being cooped up in that cabin with Hud during a snowstorm. There was no doubt one of them would finish off the job the Utes started. "Will there be much?"

He glanced up at the blue sky with its fluffy white clouds. There were a lot of them. "No."

The horses were tethered in front of the cabin,

both grazing contentedly on the new spring grass. She pointed to them and asked, "Will they be okay?"

He nodded. "There is a shelter on the side of the cabin for them. I will hunt. We will need the food."

"Thank you," she murmured, wondering how she could ever repay him. It didn't feel right just to take from the man when he thought her some kind of miracle. She preferred a more honest cheating. "What happened with you and your tribe?"

The young man turned away. "I loved the chief's daughter, but I had no ponies to offer for her. Another did. He was killed on a hunt. Some said by me."

"Was he?" she asked gently.

He shook his head. "But no one would listen. He was a rich man, with many ponies and two wives already, and he was a good hunter for the tribe. He fought well against the whites. The people . . . they do not see me now, even if I am there."

They shunned him, she thought. "You have done nothing wrong."

He looked up in surprise, then smiled and nodded. She felt as if he'd thought his God were speaking through her again and decided not to disabuse him of the notion. Young Otter deserved a little peace and dignity in this small way.

She returned to the cabin reluctantly after the Indian went off to hunt their next few meals. Hud was asleep in his sitting position against the wall. Relieved, she set the clothes down.

"What were you and the Indian talking about?"

She jumped and whirled around, her heart thumping a panic rhythm in her chest. Both men were making it a practice to scare the wits out of her. "I thought you were asleep."

"I'm tired of sleeping. So what were you two talking about?"

"Snow. He says it will snow before the day is out."

"Just what we need."

She shivered. It had nothing to do with the cold. "He's gone hunting. What does it matter what we talked about? And how did you know we talked?"

Hud stared at her for one long moment. Finally, he said, "Because I dragged myself to the cabin door and saw you."

"I think that was a brain fever you had," she said, shaking her head. It was the only explanation for his strange attitude.

"Must have been," he muttered barely loud enough for her to hear him.

"Hud, the sooner you're rested up, the sooner we can get out of here . . ." She paused. "Where are we going?"

"I don't know. Back to Denver, I guess. I have to take those guns back as evidence."

"But you broke me out of jail in Denver, remember?" Apprehension shot through her. "Are you going to put me back in?"

"No. We have a deal. But you're going to have to stay out of sight until I get this settled." He glared at her. "And no damn interviews for the paper. Do you understand?"

She nodded. "I'll be a little mouse."

He pressed his head back against the wall and closed his eyes. "Woman, you wouldn't even know how."

She wanted to be indignant, but admitted he was probably right. If she knew how to be a mouse, she'd be on some sod farm in the middle of Kansas taking care of her sister, rather than holed up in the mountains as a fugitive and Harriet with the kindly nuns. Things were a lot quieter when she had been the Countess.

He was silent after his comment. She busied herself with things in the cabin, whatever she could find to do. There wasn't much, since this was only a temporary accommodation. Slowly, she became aware of a tension building within the room. Each time she glanced at Hud, he wasn't looking at her, and yet she could feel his gaze on her when she was turned away. The tension became tangible, almost visible in fact, and she could feel it pulling her toward him. She checked to be sure she hadn't actually moved. If Hud had twitched even a muscle she would have been surprised. He just sat, motionless, patient as a snake waiting for its next victim to come into striking distance.

She wanted to go outside, escape the pressure building within the cabin, but without Young Otter close by, the mountain seemed more ominous. Her brain kept bringing back the way his skin had felt as she'd bathed his arms and chest to bring the fever down. She had been too busy at the time to notice things about him, but now that the fever was over, she couldn't seem to forget. She could still feel the way the dark hair on his chest contrasted with his lighter skin. It had leisurely tickled her hands as she'd stroked his chest. The hair ran across the upper broadness, then tapered to his waist, almost as if in invitation to his . . .

She shoved the thoughts away, horrified at where they'd been heading. Cautiously, she glanced over at Hud, worried that he could read her thoughts. He was staring back at her, his eyes intense and unfathomable. She gaped at him, then, mortified with her reaction, glanced away again—and then realized what a giveaway that was to her emotions.

"I think I'll get some air," she said, rising to her feet.

"You better stay inside," he told her. "It's not safe. The Utes can come back at any time."

"Well, we wouldn't know it being cooped up in here," she reminded him tartly, pulling a blanket around her shoulders. "Besides, after our performance that night, I would think they'd be long gone."

"They might come back for the guns. Or there could be other bands of Indians or ragtags from the camps. You're better off in here. And we haven't even gotten to the wild animals yet."

"I'll be right outside the door," she said. "I just want to feel the sunshine on my face."

"You were just out there a little while ago with Young Otter." He glared as he said the Cheyenne's name.

She walked out the cabin door without answering.

"Damn him," she muttered, stamping around the clearing. The horses, sensing her foul mood, danced away from her as far as their tethers would allow.

But the fading sun did nothing to temper her. Instead, the tension seemed to have followed her outside, surrounding her. She couldn't get away from it.

She heard a faint noise behind her and whirled around again, all of Hud's warnings racing through her.

Hud stood in the cabin doorway. Rather, he leaned heavily against it, his face pale with the exertion.

"Hud, you idiot!" she snapped, racing toward him. Without a thought, she grabbed up his arm and put a shoulder under it, taking on his weight.

"Thought I might get some sunshine, too," he murmured, his face a mask of concentration. "I feel like a baby."

"And you're acting like one," she said firmly, but she helped him along the front of the cabin and settled him back against the wall. She tried to ignore the way her hand was pressed against his ribs, bracing him. The muscles were firm, and sensations seemed to spin around inside her. "All right. Probably sitting outside will do you some good, get rid of some of the cabin fever."

He shivered slightly, despite being bundled in his coat. She could only imagine the effort it had taken for him to get it and put it on. Her heart was cheered by his determination, even as she worried he'd have a relapse. This caring about people was scary, she acknowledged, and wondered why she was even doing it. Except for her sister and Otis, she'd never cared.

"The Cheyenne's right. We are going to have snow," Hud said, looking up at the greying sky. Crisp dampness permeated the air, deadening it to other sounds.

"I just hope we can get you back inside before it starts," she commented, letting go of his arm.

When she would have stood, he reached up and tucked a finger in the front of the dress. He pulled her back down to him and kissed her gently but soundly on the mouth, then let her go.

Speechless, she straightened, her lips buzzing with his touch.

He shrugged. "You look pretty in the sunlight."

She swallowed back several different emotions. "Oh."

"Brown looks good," he said, staring at his horse. "Both horses do."

"Yes. Young Otter's been taking care of them. They were out all night that night."

"We were lucky some bear or mountain lion didn't get them," he replied, letting out a deep breath. His lungs sounded clear to her sensitive ears.

"Or the Utes before." She realized she was standing inanely next to him. The conversation wasn't much better. Unfortunately, she had nothing to do outside here, either.

She wanted to run away from him, but she had a feeling that no matter how far she ran she would never get away from her heart.

* * *

Richard Walker paced and cursed. "Damn them! Damn them! Where the hell are they?"

The set of hairbrushes on top of the bureau caught his attention. He glared at them, then swept them up and threw them against the wall. They smashed into the flowery striped wallpaper, leaving brushmarks indented in the wood. The woman sitting on the bed winced and tried to make herself smaller. Even she didn't provide the relief he needed anymore.

Everything was collapsing, Richard thought. First, that notice in the personals column and now his two men vanish without a trace and with several hundred dollars worth of guns. The western edge of the territory was quiet these last weeks, when the papers should have been filled with news of Indian raids on camps and settlements.

He cursed again, knowing the railroad would be coming through within the year, buying up land for future spurs. Land *he* should have by then, but because of two incompetents he wouldn't. His grand scheme that had taken years to build was in danger. Getting other men to do the dirty work seemed almost impossible. Those two had taken a long time to cultivate and trust—as much as he could trust anyone.

Panic was welling up inside him. He forced it away, trying to stay in control. He reminded himself about his last meeting with the pair. They had been arrogant. He'd known then that their dealings were numbered. The situation had just changed sooner than he'd thought.

He would take care of both problems, and he would be in control again.

The woman on his bed shifted. He stared at her. "Spread your legs."

He picked up a hairbrush and moved toward her.

Chapter Sixteen

Young Otter stared off into the woods. He hadn't moved from his stance, a hunkered-down position against the outside cabin wall, all day.

As he exercised Brown and the buckskin around the clearing, Hud watched him, marvelling at the man's stoicism and wondering at the same time how he could sit so still for so long a time. He'd been there since early morning. Young Otter had barely spoken, either, since he'd returned from hunting several days ago. Not even to Mary Alice. The antelope buck he'd brought down would feed all three of them for a month, though. Unfortunately, the moutain wasn't overflowing with beans, flour, and coffee. Those items were dwindling fast. The meat was packed in the snow for safekeeping.

Young Otter had been right about the snow. It had come on fast, but had only left a few inches. Unfortunately, all of them, including the horses, had been cooped up in the cabin during the storm.

Maybe the man was determined to have fresh air after that. Hud couldn't blame him if he did. He took a deep breath himself, his lungs twinging only slightly from the icy sharp air. He turned up his collar against the cold trying to seep down under his coat. The Indian didn't seem at all bothered by it, having wrapped himself only in a horse blanket.

"You are better?" Young Otter suddenly asked, coming to life. "Your strength is coming back?"

Hud nodded. "Yes, thanks to the meat you brought in." They had sliced up steaks and cooked them rare, Mary Alice insisting that would bring back his blood. In fact, she had assessed him in a dispassionate way that reminded him of the doctors during the War. It was as if he really were her patient. He supposed he was, since she nursed him through his illness. But he preferred a far more personal manner with her . . .

"I will go now."

"What?" Hud asked unconsciously, looking up as the Indian stood.

"I will go now. To the Cheyenne in the North. You will leave here soon, too."

Hud paused, staring at him. Mary Alice came out of the cabin at that moment. She was dressed in the pants and shirt again, wearing her heavy coat against the chill. The Indian dress was getting an airing. She carried a pan full of water from her washing up, then tossed the water out onto a bush; the liquid turned into a glistening shell over the branches.

"I will go now," Young Otter said to her. "To

my people. I will take some meat. You will leave soon also. You will be safe from the Utes until then."

She gaped at him. "Go? What do you mean? That you'll go back? You said they don't 'see' you."

"I will go north to the others of Cheyenne where they still live free." He glanced up at the sky. "Many went there after Yellow-Hair killed our great chief, Black Kettle."

"The Sand Creek Massacre," Hud said, knowing Young Otter was referring to that event. "Even many whites thought Custer was a bastard. And Chivington. People were sorry it happened. I was one of them." He pointed to the piles of gun boxes. "Was that what these were to the Indians? A new war against the whites in the territories after you did what the gunrunners wanted?"

Young Otter shrugged affirmatively. Then he turned to Mary Alice. "They will always come now, won't they?"

"The whites?" shc asked. "Yes, they will come."

The Indian nodded again. "I will go north then, to join my people. Maybe they will accept me now."

He began to gather up his things, the few items he had. Mary Alice turned to Hud, a stricken expression on her face. "Just like this?"

"I guess so," Hud said, his mind scrambling with the knowledge that he and Mary Alice would now be alone again. One thing he knew was that he wasn't physically able to make the trip back to Denver yet. In another day or two, but not yet.

Thank God. He tried not to appear too eager. Things had been stilted between Mary Alice and him with Young Otter present.

"Hud! Stop him!" she demanded. "He can't just go like this. And north! It may be spring, but there's still bad weather."

"I will go now," Young Otter said matter-of-factly. It was clear there was no dissuading him.

"Take my horse," Mary Alice said in a complete about-face.

Hud gaped at her.

"He can't walk all the way," she added, glaring back. "And you owe him your life."

"I wasn't saying 'No,' goddam it!" Hud snapped. He'd intended to use the bucksin as a pack horse to carry the guns back to Denver.

Young Otter was wide-eyed. He exclaimed to Mary Alice, "You *are* the Creator! You give me the horse, just as you gave them to the people that first time from the sky."

"Sweet Jesus, help me," Hud muttered to himself. The damned idiot thought she was a Goddess again. Still, he walked the horse over to the Indian and handed him the reins. "Go in peace."

"I'll get some of the meat for you," Mary Alice said. "And other food."

Hud came to a decision after she disappeared into the cabin. He went over to the wooden box that had been broken open on that fateful night and took out a gun. He gave it to Young Otter, along with some ammunition. "The horse is Mary Alice's gift. This is my gift to you for my life. You may need more than a bow and arrows on the trail."

Young Otter stared at the weapon in his hand.

"Oh, hell," Hud muttered, and took out a second rifle and more ammunition. "This is a gift for your chief. Maybe it'll get you out of trouble with them. I must be crazy."

"I will tell him that all whites are not bad," Young Otter said.

"And I will tell my chiefs that the Cheyenne have honor," Hud replied.

Mary Alice came forward. From her smile, Hud realized she'd witnessed the exchange. She set packed saddlebags around the buckskin's withers. "I wish you wouldn't go."

"I must." Young Otter smiled briefly, then effortlessly swung himself up on the horse. Waving only once, he set off, allowing the animal to pick its way along the trail.

Mary Alice watched him leave. Hud watched her.

"Well," he said to Brown. "It looks like it's just the three of us again."

Mary Alice shivered as Hud shut the door of the cabin for the night.

She wished she'd ridden out with Young Otter. The Indian had kept her safe in more than one way, she admitted. They'd brought Brown in tonight because of possible natural predators in the area. The horse was bedded down along the far wall of the cabin. Its presence hardly took the place of Young Otter. The cabin would smell interesting in the morning, she admitted. But that was the least of her problems right now.

"I'll stoke up the fire," he said, taking a seat on his blanket. Only a few feet separated them. She'd spent nights with him before, but always in wide-open spaces. With the closing of the door had come the closing of a trap.

She nodded in acknowledgement and began to fiddle with her blanket. She wished he'd sat on the other side of the fire as he usually did, but his blanket hadn't been there. The silence grew awkward. It seemed to be doing that every time they were alone. She could feel the tension thrumming through her, pulling all her senses taut like a bowstring. The walls of the cabin were stifling, closing in inch by inch.

Once the fire was going again, Hud filled the coffee pot with water from an old bucket they'd found unbroken and set it up on the heated stones surrounding the small flames. "We'll need more coffee and staples if we don't get back to Denver soon."

"How're you feeling?" she asked.

"Better. You were crazy to give him the horse. Now how'll we get those rifles back to town?"

"I wasn't crazy," she said, bristling. "He can't walk all the way north. Besides, who gave him those two guns? Evidence, I'll remind you."

"Don't bother," he muttered, then snapped, "Hell, what else could I do? He needed it. I guess Brown'll have to drag the rest of the boxes on a travois."

She smiled sweetly. "I'll be happy to accept your apology anytime you're ready."

He made a face. "I should know better than to argue with you."

"Yes, you should."

"Don't start, Countess."

Mary Alice lapsed into silence, preserving her dignity. She set out the meat to cook, wishing they had a wire holder rather than having to hang it over the fire. Without saying a word, Hud began to help her skewer the meat on sticks. His fingers touched hers in the process. Both pulled away, burned by the invisible current passing between them. The meat dropped directly into the fire.

"Hell," she muttered, fishing it out while trying not to get burned for real this time. She couldn't look at Hud.

"You seem nervous," he said finally.

She glanced up to find his gaze intense on her. Looking away, she began, "Ah . . . well, I was wondering if we really are as safe here as Young Otter said."

He chuckled. "Your legend is probably all over the territory by now."

"Yes, but which one?" she asked, grinning.

He laughed. "I think we're all right tonight."

The amusement gave way to the terse silence again, as she was reminded they were alone in the cabin together. Brown was no chaperon after all. She knew she didn't have the conventions of most females, either. Her life hadn't allowed for much of that, although she aped them as the Countess. But this was different from her earlier travels with him. She could sense it, she could almost see it in the very air.

She didn't understand herself—or him. One minute, they were angry, and the next they were like awkward school children, and the next easy with each other. It made no sense. And something else that didn't make any sense was her domesticity. She had nursed and cooked and washed for a man. And not just any man, either. Hud Jackson. Those silly, crazy words he'd uttered in the throes of a fever had turned her world upside down.

"Mary Alice."

She looked up. "Yes?"

"Nothing." He poked unnecessarily at the fire. "We'll leave tomorrow."

She nodded again, wondering what would happen when they got to Denver. A shiver of premonition ran down her spine, chilling her for a moment. She forced it away. Hud wouldn't turn her in once they got there. They had an agreement. Of all the things she was never sure of, his honoring that wasn't one of them. And she intended to stay well-hidden when they returned. Denver was more than big enough to hide in.

"You're not taking me back to jail, are you?" She cursed as the question she'd already mentally answered popped out of her mouth.

His lips narrowed in annoyance. "No. I said before I wasn't. You don't trust me, though, do you?"

"Yesss." She heard the indecision in the drawing out of the word.

So did he. "The real question is whether you'll honor our agreement, isn't it?"

"I have so far!" she exclaimed. "And damned near got . . . damaged goods for it. I did get damaged goods."

His jaw worked. She had no idea what he would say, but she mentally braced herself.

"I can't make up for that," he said. "And I can't say I'm sorry enough for it, either. What the hell else do you want from me?"

"Nothing," she said. "Just to be left alone."

He didn't say anything for a while. "I guess you're right about you holding up your end. You did stay with me until we found the gunrunners. Now it's my turn to stay with you until we find the gold. Unless you don't want me to."

"No. You need it as much as I do," she replied. Somehow the gold seemed so distant, unreal. The desire for it had cooled. So much else overshadowed it.

This time the silence drew out through their meal. An odd apprehension grew inside her as she drank the last of her coffee and then cleaned up. There wasn't much to do, unfortunately. She prepared her makeshift sleeping pallet, bundled herself in her coat, more to shield her body than for warmth, and lay down on her blankets. The hard earthen floor felt chilled despite the fire and the body heat building up in the cabin.

"You turning in already?" he asked.

"I'm tired." She kept the words blunt and dismissive.

He said nothing, just banked the fire for the

night. He took up his pallet between her and the door. His head was inches from her feet. He set his gun and a rifle next to his hand. Mary Alice resisted the urge to shift around and not because of fear of the weapons. She wanted to give no signal of restlessness that would betray her inner turmoil. She stared into the embers, watching the red glow and trying to clear her mind of all thoughts of sleep.

Hours passed in agonizing slowness. She was aware of his breathing gradually becoming deeper as he drifted off to sleep. She relaxed now that she knew nothing would happen, and yet an odd disappointment ran through her at the same time. Truly, she didn't want him to approach her intimately again. She wouldn't want that. She closed her eyes and tried to get to sleep.

She didn't know when the images began but once they did she couldn't stop them. She could see nothing wrong but the visions were horrifying. Her mother was crying, and her sister, Harriet, seemed to be yelling at her, but Mary Alice couldn't hear the words. Otis shook his head and a herd of horses walked behind Young Otter. She watched them spin around and around, nothing making sense.

"Mary Alice."

She blinked her eyes open at her name and immediately felt disoriented. Hud's face hovered above her, actually looking concerned.

"What?" she asked.

"You were dreaming, I think."

She realized she'd actually been asleep for some

time. The fire was nearly out. He reached out and touched her face with gentle fingers, wiping something away, even as she felt a wetness on her cheeks.

"Don't cry," he said, and leaned down. His lips touched hers.

The kiss was soft and meant for comfort. He lifted his head and stared down at her. Something broke inside her. Suddenly his mouth covered hers, hungrier this time. Mary Alice drank it in like a woman in a desert too long. She couldn't stop it any more than she could stop breathing. His arms lifted her up into his embrace until she was nestled against his chest. His tongue swept hers in a mating, rubbing against each other, heightening the pleasure seeping through her veins. This was so nice, she thought, wrapping her arms around his shoulders. Why couldn't the rest of it be as nice as this?

The kiss went on for endless minutes, pulling her into its vortex. The satisfaction was overshadowed by a growing restless ache inside her. His words in his fevered dreams came back to her, luring her with their promise. No one had ever said that before. No one had even ever dreamed it.

"Mary Alice," he whispered, when he broke the kiss. "Stop me. I can't stop myself."

She had been afraid of this the moment Young Otter left, and she had been waiting for it, knowing it would happen. Her emotions coalesced inside her. A part of her was flattered that he had a need only she could satisfy. This time it didn't seem sinful. Too much had already passed between them for that. She couldn't find the words inside herself to deny him, even knowing there would be pain. Instead, she wanted to brand him, make him remember her forever. She leaned up and kissed him in acquiescence.

"It won't hurt this time," he said. "And there won't be a baby."

She wanted to ask him how he knew that, but his mouth covered hers again, sweeping her back into a hungry kiss. His arms were strong around her, holding all the world at bay outside the cabin. His hands caressed her back, creating sensations that left her craving more. She matched him kiss for kiss as he slowly eased her back down on her pallet.

His hands were careful, almost tentative as he unbuttoned her coat. His fingers slipped inside. His touch was so light against her heart she almost didn't feel it. His finger traced the very outer curve of the mound of her breast, leaving a trail of sensual shivers in its wake. She had the oddest urge for more of his touch, the aching started by his kisses growing stronger. She dug her fingers into his shoulders, trying to convey a need she couldn't describe. He seemed to understand as his hand covered her breast completely. Her nipple throbbed against his palm. She couldn't help the moan that escaped into his throat, the sensation catching her by surprise.

He kissed her harder. She pressed herself into him, her fingers threading through his thick hair. He pushed aside her shirt and undervest, baring her skin to his gaze. She lowered her lids, half-shy and half-bold at the pleasure in his face.

"I've dreamed of this," he whispered, then lowered his head and took a nipple in his mouth. Sensations rocked through her, shocking and delightful. The yearning swept along her veins in a sensuous onslaught that was unstoppable. Her flesh was taut, crying out of its own accord now. She gripped his hair and pulled him impossibly closer, wanting the feelings to go on and on.

He lifted himself away from her for a brief minute and took off his shirt, the movement exciting her and yet leaving her bereft of his touch. The hair on his chest was silky-looking, arrowing down below his belt. The wounds from the Sun Dance had healed over. Mary Alice reached out and touched them gingerly, tracing them with her forefinger, feeling the slight ridging left from the injuries.

"Do they hurt still?" she asked, noticing the odd delectable tickling of his chest hair against the pad of her finger.

"No." He grasped her wrist and pulled her errant hand up, planting a kiss on her palm. His mouth was soft on her skin, sending shivers up her arms and across her bosom. Her nipples puckered taut and ached with yearning.

He lowered himself to her, her breasts pressing against the hard wall of his chest, taking his weight. Mary Alice gasped at the sensation of flesh to flesh. Never had anything felt so right. Hud's lips came down on hers, taking the breath into his own mouth, as if taking life from her. His tongue mated with hers over and over. Her body throbbed everywhere, but especially in the most intimate of places. She wouldn't stop it, and she didn't want to try. She wanted . . . more. She clung to him as if he were an anchor in the storm building up inside her. Never before had it been like this. How, she wondered, could something this good be so wrong? It wasn't, she realized. It couldn't be. Yet if feeling this made her a wanton, then she would live with the slur gladly. Never to have experienced this was the real sin.

Whatever pain she would suffer during the actual intimacy would be far overshadowed by this pleasure. And Hud was being kind and gentle . . . and caring. Her memory didn't go back far enough to remember if her parents had shown a tenderness before the war. But this was different, so different. It was as if they were alone in the world tonight and tomorrow would never come.

Hud's mind reeled at the feel of Mary Alice, pliant in his arms. He didn't know what had made her agree, but he would never give her cause to regret it. He reminded himself to be gentle, to make this a true first time, to make up for what had happened before. It meant his own needs—the need to take her wildly, to have her match him, to pour himself into her—would have to be suppressed. But he wanted her to know that all men were not the same, that he was very different. He needed to know she would never forget him.

He kissed her everywhere, drinking in the incredible unique taste of her. He circled the nipple of one breast and then the other. He took one into his mouth and shuddered in satisfaction when she moaned and twisted beneath him. There was no mistaking her movements this time. She wanted him, even if she didn't understand it. Carefully, keeping his kisses soft and gentle, he unbuttoned her pants. She tensed slightly, almost indiscernibly, but he felt it nevertheless.

"It'll be okay," he chanted over and over against her flesh.

She relaxed, trusting him. He vowed he wouldn't betray that trust. He eased the men's pants from her. They should have seemed strange on a woman but they hadn't on her from the first. Her hands began to cover herself. He pulled them away from her thighs.

"No," he said, smiling. "You're beautiful there."

Her face turned pink. He bent and kissed her at the junction of her long, slim legs. She gasped again at his shocking move, and he chuckled. He planted kisses high on her thighs and low on her abdomen, and her shock turned more restless, her flesh relaxing, opening. He kissed the inside of her thigh, deliberately not kissing her more intimately. Her hips bucked, meeting his kisses with a fervor. He pressed his hand to her, coaxed her into accepting his caresses, stroked her, watching with hooded eyes as her facial expressions changed from shock to wonder. Her female's flesh was moist and hot.

Her hands gripped his back as he slowly rose up over her body, trailing kisses, conscious of any hint of resistance. There was none. He shucked off his pants. Her eyes widened for one swift second, but he kissed her long and hard until her arms were wrapped around his shoulders, her fingers kneading his skin.

He eased his hips to hers, pressing her legs apart, then slowly, forcing his own passion under control, he eased himself into her. She gasped as she enclosed him tightly. He drew in a sharp breath and willed himself to wait, to allow her to adjust to his intrusion—and to allow himself the pleasure of feeling at one with her. His mind reeled at the sensation. His heart told him there was no other woman in the world like Mary Alice. There would never be.

Slowly, carefully, he began to move. Her flesh rippling around his was nearly his undoing. He'd never wanted anyone so badly as he had wanted her. Now he would make her his.

"Oh, Hud," Mary Alice whispered in astonishment. The sensations were so different from before.

Hud smiled to himself. Nothing had ever sounded so good as her saying his name like that. She began to move with him, finding the rhythms of a man and woman together. He kissed her, catching little moans she made, his tongue encircling hers in rhythm with their bodies. He had heard of women having the same response as men, but he'd always been suspicious of a whore's nearly instantaneous thrashing. It had never mattered before, but it mattered very much now. He wanted Mary Alice to feel exactly as he did.

And then it happened. She jerked slightly, a cry of astonished pleasure escaping her lips. Her body shuddered—then Hud could feel himself being pulled into the vortex with her, everything inside rushing to meet her in the silken void. With a groan of pleasure and pain, he withdrew before he could spill his seed inside her. But that didn't stop him from joining her in mutual joy.

All too soon, he resurfaced to reality. His face was buried in her hair. He drank in the feel of her, sated and in his arms. He could barely move; his limbs felt like dead weights. Yet he knew he was crushing her. With monumental effort, he turned his head and kissed her at the curve of her shoulder. She snuggled closer. He sucked in his breath at the sudden shot of desire that went through his body. He wouldn't have thought that would happen. But then, Mary Alice turned everything else in his life upside down—why shouldn't she do this?

Happily pushing the thought away, he kissed her again. "Did I keep my promise, Countess?"

"Mmmm." She wrapped her arms around him. "You didn't tell me I would be cold."

He laughed. Lifting himself, he reached behind them and pulled his blanket over both of them. "Better?"

"Oh, yes." She was like a contented kitten. Hud was fascinated by the change.

"I hope the Utes aren't at the door," he murmured. "It'd be a heck of a thing if they caught us like this."

"Think of the town of Boulder."

He laughed, her chuckles mingling with his amusement. "We'd be strung up for sure."

They were quiet for a long time, just taking

pleasure in each other's arms.

He had kept his promise that their lovemaking would be better this time, but he had made another promise: he would let her go after they found the gold.

He knew now that that was a promise he couldn't keep.

Chapter Seventeen

"Am I . . . does this make me a whore now, Hud?"

No sooner had she said it than Mary Alice wished she hadn't. But all the things she'd ever heard from preachers and others made sex out to be a duty, not a pleasure, and a wife's burden, not a woman's joy. She had experienced the latter in both cases. But a whore was the last thing she wanted to be, especially in Hud's eyes.

His head snapped up, the shock clearly mirrored in his expression. Relief washed through her immediately.

"No!" he said. "Being with me like this would never make you that. A whore is someone who has sex for money . . ."

Hud's voice faded as he thought about the "soiled doves" he'd seen. Some had been boisterous, some bitter, some blank, some scared. It didn't seem right to put such a word to any of them now. In fact, the only person it seemed to fit was his former fiancée, who had used him for her own ends.

"I am one now, aren't I?" she said more than asked, turning her face away. "It was my one pride, that I hadn't turned to that . . ."

"No." He pulled her tighter to him, his body hard and strong and warm on hers. "Mary Alice, you're a lot of things, but you're no whore."

She wrapped her arms around him and began to cry. She couldn't stop the tears and was horrified at her loss of control over her emotions. She almost *never* cried, and certainly not like this. Yet she'd never felt so wrung out before, either, as if all the tension in a huge spring had suddenly unwound.

He just held her helplessly, patting her on the shoulder. "Why are you crying?"

"I don't know," she gulped out, burying her face in his already-wet chest.

"Was I that bad *again?*"

She gave a watery laugh. "No. Oh, God, no, Hud."

"I would have hung up my manhood if you had said yes." He grinned at her, then asked, "When was the last time you had a good cry?"

"Like this? I don't know. Forever, I think." She swiped at her tears, but they still rolled helplessly down her cheeks.

"Then you're probably overdue for one." He grew serious. "If you're worrying about you and me and . . . this. I'll take care of you, Mary Alice, for as long as you want to be with me."

The words weren't quite as reassuring as she would have liked, and yet she couldn't place where they were wrong, either. She knew how she felt about him, but she was also more confused than ever. She had obligations and responsibilities that would take her away from him eventually, and he had been her enemy for so long. How could he become a gentle lover forever?

She nodded, though, accepting what he offered for now. He kissed her, tenderly at first and then hotter and wetter, until their mouths were fanning their passions once more.

Mary Alice surrendered to them, gladly, happily, snatching what she could for herself, for her memories.

Just as she always had.

Hud put the finishing touches on his travois of young saplings and settled the arch over Brown's rump. The horse looked back at it.

"Sorry, boy," Hud said, shrugging. He hated to use the animal as a pack horse.

"Are you talking to the horse?" Mary Alice asked, emerging from the cabin as Brown returned to grazing on the last of the grasses.

"Somebody's got to apologize because he's hauling the guns all the way to Denver," Hud said, snatching her to him. She looked beautiful in the morning sun, her man's travelling clothes not detracting from her loveliness. They never would. He kissed her, then said, "You gave away the buckskin, after all."

She grinned at him. "I should have left you hanging from that tree."

He leaned over and whispered in her ear, "Think of what you would have missed if you had."

She swatted him on the arm and danced out of his embrace. "Are we going back to Denver today or are you going to talk?"

"We're going to Denver."

She had no regrets, he thought, watching her tie up their bedrolls. Whatever had caused the crying jag last night, it wasn't there this morning in her intimate smile and bewitching gaze. Hell, he was ready to carry her back in the cabin and make love all over again. He wished they could, but they'd been in one place too long now. He picked up one crate of guns and set it on the travois.

"Have you figured out where you're going to hide me in Denver?" she asked, taking an end of another and helping him load it.

"In a respectable boardinghouse as far from the jail and the newspaper as I can get."

She laughed. "I said I'd be a little mouse, Hud."

"That'll be the day." But he grinned at her. "I'll be staying at the boardinghouse with you."

She paused. "You will?"

"I will. And I won't be your damn brother, Mary Alice."

She didn't ask him what he would be. He didn't tell her. But the word "husband" lay between them like a visible curtain.

"What about your sister-in-law? Isn't she there, where you live?"

"She is. So I don't even have a bed anymore." Hud wondered what Missy would do if she met

Mary Alice. She knew what the name Macaffee meant as well as he did.

"I don't see how we can put any of these other crates on the travois," she said, changing the subject entirely.

He frowned as she pointed to several more boxes haphazardly stacked against the cabin. "I don't think Brown could carry them, either. Not all, anyway. But I don't want to leave them out here for someone to stumble across them."

"Maybe that wagon is still out there," Mary Alice said. But the look on her face told him all too clearly how she felt about using it.

He admitted he had no desire to go looking, especially with the condition of its contents. "I think if it were usable, Young Otter would have hauled it back here. Anyway, I don't know if Brown could haul it. I doubt it."

"That leaves only two possible things to do," she said. "Burn them or bury them."

He raised his eyebrows. She looked straight back at him. "We can't burn them," he said. "That's near impossible without a huge fire. And we can't afford to attract attention to us here. We've been lucky Young Otter's death warnings have worked for this long." He had come upon one of the corpses, feathers and beads hanging from it, in a tree. He made sure Mary Alice never went in that direction afterwards.

"Then we bury the rifles," she said, drawing him out of his macabre thoughts. She frowned. "We don't have a shovel."

"And I'm damned before I dig with my bare

hands." Hud grinned. "However, we can do something."

He knelt down at a box, took out his knife, and proceeded to snap off the sights of the rifles they couldn't carry with them.

"At least they won't be usable," he told her.

"Well, maybe you couldn't hit the broad side of a barn with one, but you can use them." Mary Alice stared at one, picked it up, and examined it. "If we took out the trigger, then they'd be unusable."

"I have always liked the way you think," Hud complimented her. "But I don't think we could get the panels off with just a knife. Let's bend them."

Hours later, Hud was sweating and cursing as he forced the last trigger out of position. The sweating and cursing had begun with the first and hadn't let up since; the idea of bending them was a whole lot easier than actually doing the deed. He flung the rifle down on the ground with one last oath. "Damn it! What kind of metal did they use?"

"The hardest kind," Mary Alice said, picking up the weapon and eyeing his handiwork. "At least it's done. I think it would be helpful if we move the crates into the bushes, rather than leave them out in the open."

"Right."

They lugged them deep into the brush, eliminating their tracks as best they could. Within a few days nature would take care of any other human traces.

Back at the cabin, they packed up the last of their things. Hud took up Brown's reins and walked the horse forward. The travois jerked over the ground, leaving twin trails. Nothing could be done about them, unfortunately, until nature grew them over, too.

Mary Alice turned once and looked at the little cabin. She turned back and jammed her hat over her eyes.

They left the quiet clearing behind them.

Richard Walker looked over the men in the saloon. Cowpokes, local businessmen, and gamblers all. None of them were good candidates for the job. And none he would trust. They were too stupid, too dishonest, or too honest.

He had yet to hear from his "associates." Or even a rumor about them. They'd been up in the northwest corner of the territory, as his source had indicated that area as the next target of the railroad's branch line expansion. Not only hadn't he heard from the two men, but he hadn't heard of any raids on the mining camps. Obviously the Utes didn't care for the deal he'd offered or the men had completely bungled the job. The latter seemed more plausible. But to try and recruit others to take over in time would be impossible. Walker cursed at the lost opportunity.

The city was becoming too civilized. There was a time, just after the war, when men were more . . . haunted. Men with a modicum of honor still left in them, but who had gone too far down the road of shame to turn back. Men like himself. The territories were good places for a man to turn over a new page or take the final descent into Hell. But Denver was far too settled now, with its respectable families, neighborhoods, and schools. Walker realized his own time here was over. Nameless and faceless he had wanted to be; unwanted he couldn't be.

He gulped his whiskey down, hoping to wash away the feeling of despair. It never happened, no matter how much he drank. He had paid for what he did, and he was still paying. Macaffee had gone home only to find ruin and a horrible death on the trail. It had been Roger Ward, though, who had panicked and brought the Indians down on the company. And he who had forced Macaffee to leave Jackson behind.

He pushed away thoughts of that time, and of his real name. He'd never gone back for the gold. He never thought he could find it by himself, for one thing, not without the rest of the pieces of the map. And he could never face the ghosts of the past.

No one had ever answered his letter to that notice in the personals column. God willing, no one ever would.

"Mister, would you like to dance?"

Walker glanced over at the girl looking up so hopefully. She was new and fresh, with fear and humiliation in her eyes. Her dress was scarlet, with a low neckline and short skirt, and her boots were big and clumsy-looking, marking her instantly as a dance girl. She had probably lost her family somewhere and was alone in the city and forced to take a job in order to keep from starving. If she were careful, she wouldn't fall into prostitution.

But she wasn't careful. She had picked him.

"Sure," he said, fishing out a coin. He tossed it to her and sealed her fate.

"You need a dress."

Hud glanced critically at Mary Alice's pants as they stood once more on the outskirts of Denver.

She chuckled. "Last time I needed a dress, I was going to jail."

"You're not going to jail," he said firmly. "But you can't traipse into the city in those pants. You'll cause another stir."

"I can wear the dress Young Otter gave me . . ."

"God help us, no!" He glared at her. "I said discreet, did I not? Although I don't suppose you know what that is."

Mary Alice made a face at him. "I can be very discreet. I have that dress from before, in the jail. One of the donations to the Countess in her time of trouble—"

Hud snorted.

"But," she continued innocently, "I suppose I could be recognized. You'll have to buy me a new one."

He looked heavenward, and she burst into laughter. He was wonderful to tease. The trip back to the city had been uneventful, even idyllic. And the nights . . . the nights had been gentle and frenzied.

Groaning, he said, "I should have known you'd try to swindle me out of another dress. You've got one in your saddlebags."

"But it's old, Hud." She shrugged. "I've got to have a new one, in the latest fashion. It was your suggestion."

"I didn't mean to buy it. The latest fashion is the one in your bags. Trust me. Now go get in some bushes and get changed."

Trust me. Mary Alice thought about those words a short time later, after she'd changed into her "sister" clothes and they were walking through the outskirts of Denver. People stared at them, this time because of the cargo Brown carried. At least she hoped so. She'd added a bandanna around her face to hide her features. But apprehension crawled along her spine, chilling her despite the warm, sunny day. With each step, she felt as if she were walking to her doom. The notion was one she'd suppressed over the last few days, but now it was more real than the first time, when he had arrested her. Her brain kept telling her to run, not to trust Hud. Her heart somehow held her in place next to him.

He took them into a different part of the city, away from the center. The neighborhood was a little more run-down, but fairly respectable. He stopped next to a boardinghouse. The sign hanging from the porch post read "MOTHER WILKINS.'"

"I've heard this is a clean house," he said in reassurance.

Mary Alice just looked up at the curtains. They were pulled aside, making each window a half-smirking wink. Inside, the floors, walls, and furniture of the front hall and parlor were scrubbed scrupulously clean and nearly worn through, as if dirt were a mortal sin against the Lord. Mother Wilkins didn't inspire any confidence either, with her small, stiff build and sharp, bird-like features. She scrutinized Mary Alice from head to foot with a disapproving frown. Mary Alice never felt so immoral in her life, as Hud told Mother Wilkins a song-and-dance about them being new to the city. It wasn't a good feeling, either.

"Your . . . wife doesn't wear a wedding band," Mother said.

Mary Alice resisted the urge to cover her left hand with her right. Hud said, "I can't afford one yet."

Mother nodded. "Two dollars a week for each, provided your wife works in the house and you in the stables."

Mary Alice glanced around the room in a panic, having a wild vision of boarders like busy ants scrubbing and rescrubbing the floor, day in and day out. "How much if you don't work?"

Mother's iron-grey eyebrows almost shot off her forehead. Evidently it wasn't a question that was ever asked.

"We'll pay five a week for the both of us," Hud said. "Plus meals."

"You greenhorns will be broke before the month's out." But the eyebrows settled back down into their normal stern arch. Mother nodded. "The Bible says I am my brother's keeper, but I'll be darned before I waste my time with that. First door on the right. It's clean."

"The key?" Mary Alice asked softly as the woman began to march toward the back of the house.

"Key?" Mother sniffed. "This is no hotel. You want a key, you go to one of those filthy places."

Mary Alice had no doubt the woman was talking about more than dirty floors. When they were up in the small room with its iron bedstead, single chest, oil lantern, and door shut but not locked, Mary Alice said, "I don't want to be here, Hud."

"It's just for a few days," he reminded her, "until we can get supplies. I think you're safer here than in a hotel. People are in and out all the time, so there's more chance of you being recognized."

She went to the window and stood. "I don't like her. And she doesn't like me."

"Charm her. You know you can." He chuckled. "Hell, Countess, it ought to be dead easy."

She shivered. She'd always avoided people like Mother Wilkins with that ability to look right through a person and see the truth. At least Mother left that impression. The thought of her being anybody's parent horrified.

Hud came up behind her and put his hands on her shoulders. The warmth in them didn't penetrate her skin, leaving her oddly colder.

"Look, I'll arrange for the guns to get to the sheriff's office," he said. "Then I'll check in on my brother's family. I'll be back before dark. We'll be out of town again before the end of the week. I promise."

"Are you sure you won't be blamed for my escape?" she asked. "Maybe they'll arrest you."

"I'll be careful." He laughed. "This town would probably line up in droves with pies if they knew you were here."

She smiled ruefully. "They'd probably lynch me."

He kissed her shoulder, then just under her ear. He covered her hands with his, bringing her back into his embrace. "Mary Alice, I *will* be back. You'll be fine. Just stay put."

The moment the unlockable door closed, dread shot through her. The sensation of being caged overwhelmed her senses. She tried to force her way up through the panic, but the vortex sucked her back down. Where was her inner strength? When had she lost it? When she'd become dependent on a man?

Shaking, she sat down on the bed's edge, the springs squeaking loudly under her weight, and gripped the thin iron columns on the headboard.

She couldn't stay here, she thought, with that beady-eyed old woman downstairs taking one look and knowing exactly who and what she was. If this was what love created, then she knew now why she'd always so deftly avoided it.

The urge to leave grew even stronger.

Hud stared at his sister-in-law.

Missy lifted her chin defiantly. "I'm working at the mercantile store down the block. I have to work. Your money ran out a week ago. Besides, you didn't leave much."

"I didn't have much to leave," he muttered.

"You were in an all-fired hurry," Missy reminded him.

He thrust out his chin. "I had urgent business. For the law. I told you that when you came."

He had contacted Mike and explained all he'd found and what he'd done with the rifles. Mike was taking the information back to the office. Hud discovered he just couldn't face going in there himself. It was hypocritical, after what he'd done with Mary Alice. Mike had told him that all the protests against him had immediately died out, once she'd "escaped." He'd at least retrieved his reputation. Unfortunately, it was at the same moment that he'd lost his honor.

"Did you know that Countess you brought in just disappeared?" Missy said, giving him a spasm with her mind-reading. "Everyone was talking about it."

"I heard," he mumbled, looking over at the cheap dresser in Mrs. Jerome's parlor. It hadn't changed a bit in all the years he'd boarded with the old lady.

"The story in the paper was that a knight in shining armor came to release her from the injustice," Missy added.

It figured she'd come out smelling like a rose, Hud thought. At least the sheriff's office wasn't blaming him any longer, although it explained why they weren't actively looking for her. Why turn a lynch mob on themselves?

"She was a nine-day wonder in this town."

Missy shrugged. Hud didn't bother to tell her different.

"I don't like you working in the store like that," he said, changing the subject. "It doesn't seem . . . proper."

"And starving is?" Exasperated, she waved a hand in the air. "I ran that farm for years, sinking with each season, but you didn't seem to mind then."

He glared at her. "I *did* mind. And I sent you every dime I had. You know that."

His sister-in-law slumped, the starch going out of her. "I know you did. You did your best for us, Hud. I don't mean to sound like you didn't. And I did *my* best. I don't think even your brother John could have kept that farm going. We stayed at it far too long, to honor him. But I have to make a life for myself now. And I have to do what I need to for my children. Mr. Hansen at the store is very nice to me, and the customers are polite. He pays me well and is grateful for my help since his wife passed on."

"I suppose," he said dubiously. But he still felt inadequate as a provider. He could only hope she was right, that not even his brother could have made a go of the farm.

"Jeannie and Jeff are in school." She paused, then added, "Young John is going into the army."

"But that's Union!" Hud blurted out.

"It's U.S.," Missy corrected. "The war's been over for eight years. What would you have him do? Starve to death? I certainly don't want him going to the camps. And he doesn't want to be a cowhand on a ranch. He's sixteen. He has to make a life for himself, Hud."

"Can't he clerk? Or work at the feedstore or something?" Hud asked, reeling from this latest piece of news.

Missy smiled bitterly. "He has too much of you and his father in him to sit still for that."

Hud staggered over to Mrs. Jerome's shredding horsehair chair and sat in it. The stiff padding rubbed his backside as always, but he was less aware of it than usual. He had come here to try and settle his brother's family in and everything had been settled without him. He couldn't very well object to Missy working at the mercantile as he had no income to support them right now.

Women, he thought. They just took things right out of a man's hands when he wasn't looking. He hadn't been in control of anything since Mary Alice had come into his life. Especially his emotions. What, he wondered, was she doing now? Sitting in that boardinghouse room like the little mouse she promised to be. Suddenly, the reluctance to be away from her turned into an urgency to return.

He stood up. "All right, Missy. You work at the mercantile. I can't stop you. But stop John, however you can, from joining up. I'll have some better opportunities for him, if he'll just be patient. Tell him that. He's sixteen, not a man yet, and don't mistake that. I'll leave some money with Mrs. Jerome and be back shortly."

He turned on his heel before his sister-in-law could reply and left the room. After paying out some more of Mary Alice's stake to Mrs. Jerome, he left his first boardinghouse and headed straight for his second. Every step brought a feeling, stronger and stronger, that he never should have left it.

He went up the stairs two at a time and through the first door on the right. Inside, the little room, with the iron bedstead, oil lantern, and single dresser, was empty.

Mary Alice was gone.

Chapter Eighteen

Mary Alice shivered in the cool evening air. She ought to be used to the mountains by now, she thought, but the wind seemed to find its way up her skirts as she walked through the twilight. Pants had been a definite advantage. She gathered up the grey woolen shawl closer around her face to hide her features from the passersby and kept her gaze toward the sidewalk planks as an added precaution.

Somehow the streets didn't feel any freer than that stifling little room at Mother Wilkins' boardinghouse. Denver was more of a jail than the first time she'd been here. So what was keeping her in the city when she ought to be running?

Not the gold this time, she acknowledged. The gold would solve all her problems, but somehow the yellow magnet had lost its attraction. Not entirely. She was no fool. But gold wasn't first any longer. It was her word.

And the man.

The notion of caring scared her half to death, no matter how wonderful the lovemaking. Almost wonderful, she corrected, remembering the way he always withdrew from her at the last moment. Each time left her feeling a vague sense of emptiness. How she wished . . .

But the cabin in the woods seemed like a lifetime ago. Now they were back in the real world and nothing had changed. He was still her father's accuser and she was still Macaffee's daughter. And a kept woman. Doubts crept in, had been creeping in all day while he'd been out arranging and checking. Why hadn't it occurred to her that turning her into a soiled dove could have been his revenge all along? What trust could there ever be between them? She'd lost a lot of her protective armor since meeting Hud Jackson. It was time to put it back on again.

Mary Alice sighed, thinking of this latest escapade. But she hadn't been able to stand being in the room a second longer and had bolted, preferring to come back and find he'd never returned than to sit there waiting and waiting. She'd also preferred walking, rather than berating herself for never getting the maps from him when he'd been incapacitated. The thought made her lift her chin in pride. At least she hadn't done that evil deed. She still had some honor left.

And she also had the letter from Roger Ward.

She clutched the sealed paper, her grip nearly crumpling it. She'd remembered the personals message she'd arranged before they'd escaped from Denver. It hadn't been easy to slip inside the post office and ask for it, but the clerk never looked twice at her.

She couldn't believe someone had actually replied. Roger Ward, she reminded herself. Who else would have? Ward would know what really happened with Hud's brother. He could clear her father's name. Even now, in spite of what Hud said, she was sure her father had not abandoned the man. They must have thought he was dead. That was the only explanation.

She ignored the perverse little voice inside that wondered otherwise and focused on the hope the letter brought. She decided not to tell Hud about it. He would just kill the man outright in revenge. Better to get the information from Ward, then gradually give it to Hud.

She no sooner entered the boardinghouse when Mother Wilkins was practically stepping on her toes. Her face was a mask of disapproving reprimand.

"Where have you been?" she demanded.

Mary Alice stared at the little woman, who stood directly in front of her like a ruffled prairie chicken. Something inside her snapped together, puffing up her self-worth. Why she had ever thought this prim, self-righteous woman's opinion mattered was beyond her. She took her time, lifting the shawl from her head and settling it back around her shoulders. "I was out."

"I want to know where my people go," Mother Wilkins snapped. "I don't want any funny business in my house!"

"I can't imagine anyone finding anything

funny here," Mary Alice said. "Now if you'll excuse me . . ."

"You haven't answered my question, *Missus.*" The emphasis on the last word was delivered in a sneering tone.

"Mrs. Wilkins . . ." Mary Alice began.

"Mother," Mother Wilkins interrupted. "My boarders call me Mother. I insist."

She drew herself up to her full height. "I do not insist. You are *not* my mother, and I accord that title only to her memory. Let us come to an understanding, madam. I come and go as I please, and it is not your business. If you do not like this arrangement, we'll be happy to take our business elsewhere and you will lose more money than you take in from all your other boarders in a week and you know it."

Mother Wilkins gaped at her, clearly stunned by the unaccustomed insubordination.

"Thank you for the use of the shawl," Mary Alice added, and dropped the woolen triangle on the hall table. She pulled back her skirt and walked around the woman without another word. The Countess still came in handy upon occasion. She was actually halfway up the stairs, when the voice came.

"Your husband was looking for you earlier."

Mary Alice turned around and stared at the triumphantly nasty expression on Mother Wilkin's face.

"You're not going to be so uppity when he gets back."

Mary Alice began to climb the stairs again,

murmuring, "Nosey old bag."

She grinned.

"That uppity wife of yours is back," Mother Wilkins declared as Hud passed by the parlor on his way to his room.

He froze in mid-step. "She's here?"

"Sashayed in like she owned the place. And she took my shawl!" Several of the other boarders, a meek-looking man and a young, mouse-like woman, were sitting in the parlor with their landlady. They nodded vigorously at the woman's next words. "You ought to beat that sassy tongue of hers right out of her head, otherwise you'll be henpecked."

Not a bad notion, he admitted, heading up the wooden stairs.

"I don't want trouble!" Mother called after him.

At the top of the stairs he turned right and swung the door open. Mary Alice looked around from her stance at the window. The oil lamp gave off a smoky illumination.

"Where the hell were you?" he demanded, slamming the door shut behind him.

"Good evening, Hud," she said, smiling politely. "I was out for an evening stroll. Did you enjoy yours?"

A fireball of anger shot through him like an erupting volcano. He stalked toward her. "Don't play your goddamn games with me, Countess. We're way beyond that now."

She pressed back against the wall. "I took a

walk, Hud. You can't expect me to be cooped up here all the time."

"You promised to be a little mouse!"

"Not with that witch down there."

He was forced to admit she had a point. Mother Wilkins was hardly a saint. "That's no excuse for disobeying me. Damn it, Mary Alice, you can't afford to be arrested again. You have to be extremely careful—"

"I was careful. You ought to know I'm capable of disguising myself."

He looked heavenward. "Who the hell were you? President Grant? And what's this about taking Mother's shawl?"

"I wasn't Grant. Just an immigrant woman, so I needed a shawl over my head and I borrowed *Mrs.* Wilkins'. And we will not call her 'Mother.'" She pushed back a nonexistent strand of hair. "No one saw me."

He tried to calm down, knowing that dealing with Mary Alice in a red haze of anger was foolish. She could tie a person into a million knots in less than a minute. "I don't care that no one saw you. It was dangerous. I'll make sure Mrs. Wilkins doesn't bother you. All right?"

She stared at him for a moment, then finally nodded. "All right. But I don't want that busybody around. I wouldn't be surprised if she were listening at the door right now."

Wanting to show her how wrong she was, Hud whipped it open. "See—?"

Mother Wilkins straightened up from her crouched position in front of their door, a look of horror on her face.

"I . . . I was picking up a piece of lint on the carpet," she stammered.

"There's no lint in front of our door," Hud said, setting his jaw tight to keep from pouncing on the woman in anger. "Ever."

She nodded and scampered away like a scared rabbit.

Hud turned back to find Mary Alice grinning.

"That was a change," she said.

He shut the door. "I'm more concerned with what she might have overheard."

Her amusement immediately faded. "Oh."

"Yes. *Oh.*" He frowned, trying to remember exactly what was said and wondering exactly how much Mother Wilkins overheard, if she could overhear anything at all, and what she made of it.

"We need to move to another place then," Mary Alice said in a hopeful tone.

Hud smiled wryly. "The problem is where. This place is at the far end of town, for one thing. Others are closer and more frequented—the same problem with hotels. I won't put you in a poor part of the city—that wouldn't be safe in its own way." He made a decision. "I don't think she heard enough to give her more than suspicions of you and me. I'll get our gear together and get us out of here in a few days."

"I'll be sweet," she promised.

He chuckled and moved closer. "You don't know how."

"All right, I'll be sarcastic." She made a face at him.

"Just don't antagonize her any more than you have to." He reached out and touched her hair, wanting their fighting to be over. The gentleness that had grown between them had become an addiction for him. He added, "We ought to give her something to burn her ears."

To his surprise, she moved away from his touch. "She can hear—"

"The hell she can!" Hud snapped. He stared at her. "What's wrong?"

"Nothing." She shrugged and didn't quite look him in the eye. "I just don't think it's a good idea to . . . with everyone here. These walls are very thin, and obviously people don't mind their own business."

"I don't believe it," he said flatly.

"I'm sorry," she replied. Her voice was cool, too cool, and it scared him,

"Don't turn from me now, Mary Alice."

Her eyes widened at his words and she turned a shade paler, giving way to her own vulnerability.

He moved quickly to her and and put his hands on her arms. "Please. I can't . . ."

He couldn't say more, couldn't find the words, so he leaned forward and kissed her gently on the lips, a plea and a question.

Her mouth was soft in answer, as if whatever her words, they were not her will. He gathered her to him, deepening the kiss, drinking her into his already-captivated senses. By the time he eased his mouth away from hers, she was sagging against him.

"Don't leave me, Countess," he whispered,

kissing her hair. "Whatever you do, don't do that."

"I can't, damn you," she murmured, tightening her fingers around his shirtfront.

"Be mad as hell, just as long as you're here."

He kissed her again.

"They don't look like much of anything," Mary Alice said, staring at the two worn and crinkled pieces of paper Hud was holding against each other.

They were lying together in the cramped little bed, he completely naked and she in just her shift. Every inch of him was warm, almost hot, as she leaned against his side, their heads touching as they looked at the chunks of the map. She wondered just how much noise had penetrated the wooden walls earlier and decided that squeaking springs had given *Madam* Wilkins and her boarders more than an earful. It would probably be counted as yet another black mark against her, Mary Alice acknowledged, then dismissed the thought.

She hadn't been able to find a shred of resistance within herself when Hud took her into his embrace. She'd wanted him, wanted what they created, so badly. She couldn't do without him—no matter what it made her in other people's eyes. She didn't need to hear the words "I love you," even though she wanted them badly, too. But with her background, she knew that would never be. She had broken, and was still breaking, all her personal rules, for him—rules that didn't seem to matter. She would pay for this, she knew, and she was willing to endure it when the time came. But the here and now was an endless stretch in front of her, and she was taking the road for as long as she was allowed.

"I can't figure out where in the territory this is supposed to be," he said, trying the pieces in a different combination. "And what are those lines with dots along them and cross-hatchings?"

Mary Alice shrugged. This was hardly the time to tell him that she'd been . . . imagining the territory, not that she knew for sure as she'd implied. "I've never seen anything like them. Maybe stones and a railroad crossing?"

"Maybe. The rest . . ." He snorted. "Hell, this stream marking and such could be anywhere."

Mary Alice knew she ought to say something about what had been waiting for her at the post office—the letter from Ward and the man's willingness to meet as the letter had indicated. But she was afraid of what Hud would do. Look at what he'd done with her, just because she was her father's daughter. She had no doubt Hud would kill Ward on the spot. And then where would they be? She'd used a lot of her money to finance the chase for the gunrunners—money desperately needed for her sister . . . and half the residents of the nuns' home, she reminded herself. Now Hud had his brother's family here to take care of, another burden. Dammit, they both needed that gold, but they wouldn't find it without Ward's knowledge and his part of the map. That was why she needed to go and talk to Ward first. She only hoped Hud would forgive her in the end for not telling him.

Hud groaned, capturing her attention. "I had been wondering if the men had come along the old Santa Fe Trail, although my brother didn't say. It would be the most sensible—"

Fear and fury shot through Mary Alice. "You didn't tell me about this idea. When were you going to?"

He glanced over at her, raising his eyebrows. "Don't get riled, Countess. It was an idea I'd been having *now*, as we were looking at the map pieces. We've got a bargain which I intend to keep. All right?"

She eyed him for a long moment, and he grinned. Finally she said, "All right. Just tell me these notions as you get them, please."

The irony of her request didn't escape her. But her problem *was* different because Hud's reaction would be different. Very different.

"As long as you do the same." He looked back at the map ends, then dropped them on his lap in disgust. "Even if this area is somewhere along the old trail, the damn thing is hundreds of miles long through the worst country—mountains, desert. We wouldn't know where to even begin looking. And how can we go until we do?"

"We'll find it," Mary Alice said optimistically. "We'll ask around about a place with a railroad and streams and a lot of rocks in the south of the territory."

"And probably get told of a million places that fit the description," he said. He gathered up the map pieces and set them aside on the little table next to the bed, then turned to her. The mattress springs squawked in protest.

Mary Alice grinned at the noise.

So did Hud. He moved again. The bed squawked again.

Silent laughter shook her . . . and the bed. The squeaking had an oddly familiar rhythm. Both of them burst into outright amusement, the bed "laughing" with them.

"I did say give them an earful," Hud commented.

"It won't be the marshal Mrs. Wilkins calls," Mary Alice said, smiling. "It'll be a preacher to drive out the evil from this room. But the music of the bed will strike, and they'll succumb to the temptation, sinning in squeaking song . . ."

They both started laughing again at the idea.

Eventually, they grew serious and the atmosphere in the room changed to something more intimately charged. Hud slowly ran his hand along her bare arm. Her flesh tingled. His chest was exposed from the folded-down cover, and she could see the scars from the hanging by the Utes. He would be marked for life, she thought. And by her. Every time he looked at them, he would have to remember all that had happened. Everything. Satisfaction warmed her veins.

"Have I told you," he said, his voice hoarse, "how pretty you are?"

"No." She tried to keep her voice from betraying the emotions inside her, emotions she still wasn't used to.

"You are." He moved closer, his body aligning with hers. The bed squeaked again. "This bed's too damn noisy."

She chuckled. "I know."

"So does everyone else."

"I thought that's what you wanted," she replied, reminding him of his earlier words.

"It's nobody's damn business what we do," he said, kissing the corner of her mouth. The lightest touch of his lips sent shivers down her spine.

"And when will you introduce me to your family?" she asked, frantic to keep the conversation going.

He paused. Her heart sank.

"I see," she said, the intimate spell between them snapping. She turned away, not caring about the loud creaking under her weight.

"Mary Alice," he began, sliding his arm around her.

She flipped it off.

"Be sensible," he said, frowning. "Missy would know who you are in an instant. Besides, she's been through enough upheaval lately, with the farm and all that. She wouldn't be ready. Look at how I reacted to you. It's better to wait. You know that, Mary Alice."

What could she say? She wished she could believe what he said was the real reason for his hesitation. But she couldn't. What did she want from him anyway? Marriage? Children? She had always looked upon them as a noose. Now they held an odd appeal. She had never been close to anyone before and never like this. She had a deep hunger inside her for quiet and peace and intimacy. But Hud wouldn't be the one to give them to her. He wasn't the kind of man to choose her kind of woman for life.

You made your choice back there in that cabin, she thought. Now she was living with it. He had asked her not to leave and that had to be enough. For always.

She forced herself to turn around and face him. His eyes were soft brown with concern. She touched his cheek, feeling the hard bones of his features and the bristling of hair along his jaw. She loved the texture of his skin. "I do know."

"You'll meet," he promised. "And she'll come around."

"It doesn't matter."

He raised an eyebrow. "You scare me when you're agreeable like this. The world usually falls apart right after you do."

She laughed. "Hud, it does not. Besides, we were on opposite sides then."

"You make life interesting even when you're on the same side." He kissed her. "Damn interesting."

He kissed her again and took her into the realm she craved, a place of soft light and softer shadows.

And love.

It wasn't that he didn't trust her.

But he didn't trust her.

Hud hurried with his order at the mercantile where Missy was employed. It was far beyond the shebangs of the small towns. The store was a true place of business with everything under the sun including building plans for nearly any structure imaginable.

Peter Hansen was a tall, stooped man, very thin, whose gaze followed Missy Jackson wherever she went among the stacked nooks and crannies off the main aisles. Hud frowned as he watched, not sure whether to interfere or if there was anything to interfere about. He was a brother-in-law by deceased husband, and not a very good one at that. Besides, the man didn't look capable of resisting a strong wind, let alone plotting the downfall of a good woman with three children. He supposed Missy was attractive, although he'd never thought of her as anything other than John's wife. Her features were more careworn than he'd remembered from their youth and her figure not as slender as it was before three children. Four, he corrected, remembering a baby that had died years ago between young John and Jeannie. Hansen had three children, too, he'd discovered. He wondered if Missy knew and supposed she did.

He reminded himself he had better get back to Mary Alice. Leaving her alone for long was dangerous, especially with Mother Wilkins. The old biddy had frowned fiercely at him when he'd told her his wife wasn't to be disturbed. She didn't protest, and Hud wasn't sure whether that was a good sign or a bad one.

"Here you go, Hud," Missy said, piling several blankets on top of his purchases. "Fine-woven. They ought to do you well."

"Thanks."

"There's still the coffee, beans, and hardtack." She frowned in thought. "Are you sure you don't want fresh meat? Peter . . . Mr. Hansen has some hanging in the back."

"No." Hud didn't comment about her familiarity with her employer's first name. He set one of Mary Alice's golden eagles down on the counter. Missy didn't comment on his having money, and he wondered if she wondered where he'd gotten it. "I want you to hold this until I'm ready to move out."

Hansen nodded.

"Are you . . ." Missy swallowed visible. "Are you leaving us?"

"Just for a time," he replied. "I have some business to attend to in another part of the territory."

Missy smiled, her relief obvious. "I didn't know."

"I'll . . . I'll look after Missy and her children while you're gone, marshal," Hansen offered, his voice cracking nervously.

Hud eyed him for a long moment.

"Thank you, Peter," Missy said, staring at Hud meaningfully.

Hud realized why his brother had married her. She was a strong woman in her own right. Recently, he'd come to appreciate how much appeal that could hold for a man, having tangled with the strongest woman this side of the Mississippi.

"Thanks," Hud said to the man, who nearly

passed out in relief. It probably wouldn't hurt Hansen to be around Missy. She'd most likely give him some spine.

As he left the store, he wondered what he would find when he came back. He wondered what Missy would do if he could actually hand over a pile of gold to her. Both notions were intriguing.

But first he had to figure out the map.

Chapter Nineteen

Mary Alice tiptoed into the boardinghouse hallway, grateful to hear voices in the back. She might have taken a stand with the Wilkins woman but she had no desire to run the gauntlet a second time. The big question was whether Mrs. Wilkins' greed would hold out over her need to cause trouble before she and Hud escaped town.

Besides, she didn't want Hud to know that she had gone out again, this time to reply to Roger Ward's letter and arrange a meeting with the man. She'd worry about how to explain that one when the time came.

The post office wasn't too far and she'd only been gone less than an hour. Few people were on the streets in the late afternoon, for which she'd been grateful. She'd taken advantage of her trip to mail a letter to her sister. She knew the nuns would read it to Harriet. She also knew Harriet was incapable of listening, but that didn't matter.

With a sigh of relief for having made it back

unnoticed, she twisted the knob to their room, positive she'd gotten in and out without anyone knowing.

The door was abruptly yanked from her hands. Hud stood on the threshold, glaring. "Where the hell have you been?"

His face was red with suppressed anger. Mary Alice resisted the urge to run for her life. She stepped into the room, forcing him back from the threshold, and closed the door behind her. "I don't think you need to shout it from the rooftops, Hud."

"I'm not shouting it from the rooftops!" he shouted. Immediately, he shook himself and lowered his voice. "Dammit! I just got done telling you how dangerous it was to show yourself. And you agreed. *Again!* Then you turn around and disobey me all over *again*. What is it? The moment I say the world is green, you have to say it's red?"

"No," she said, her brain scrambling for a legitimate answer. "Actually, do you realize how suspicious it is for the people here if I never come out of my room? And if that old bat downstairs isn't already suspicious, my hibernating will certainly set her off. I wouldn't put it past her to run to the law. Ironic when you consider that you are now—"

"Countess!"

"People run errands, Hud," she added hastily at his half-bellow. "It's the most natural thing. Not to do so is most unnatural. Think about it."

He paused in his tirade, glaring at her. Mary

Alice knew she had to press her point. "Hud, I have to act like a wife. At least if we want to ensure that people don't scrutinize us any more deeply than they already have."

He stared at her for so long that she wanted to scream at him to say something. Finally, he muttered, "I hate it when you're right."

A chuckle nearly escaped her before she could suppress it. She had a feeling he wouldn't appreciate the joke.

"I shouldn't have brought you back to Denver," he added. "But the chances of your being recognized would have been greater in a small place."

As he finished speaking, he whipped open the door. No one was bending over at keyhole level or even in the hallway or stairs. He shut the door, took her arm, and walked them both to the opposite wall.

He suddenly swung her around, startling her. "If you're just being a wife getting ready for us to travel across the country, where the hell are your purchases?"

"Ahh . . ." She gulped in air and decided to tell the truth—with a few essentials left out. That was always better than an elaborate lie. "I didn't make any purchases. I went to the post office—"

"The post office!" he exclaimed, then immediately lowered his voice. "With your likeness plastered all over it!"

"It was a terrible drawing," she lied. She'd been too fearful to look at the *WANTED* posters to see if any were of her.

He swore a stream of curses that hurt her ears.

"Don't tell me, let me guess. You sent money to the nuns. Do you have any idea how much attention that drew? I bet the clerk goggled like a schoolboy."

"I didn't send money. I'm not that stupid." She glared back at him, furious he would think her so. "I mailed a letter to my sister."

The tension in him dropped slightly, very slightly. "Just a letter?"

She nodded.

He relaxed a little more. "I suppose just a letter is all right. But I don't like you going out."

"I'll be more careful," she promised.

He laughed bitterly. "Why do I think that's a hollow vow."

She set her jaw against an immediate reply. If she opened her mouth, she'd be a hypocrite and she knew it. Lies came too easily for her; after a lifetime of telling them they were as natural as breathing. For once they were for a good cause, and for once she wished with all her heart she didn't have to. Instead of answering, she turned and went over to the bed. The iron stead squeaked loudly under her bottom.

Hud's jaw was set, a sure sign he wasn't about to apologize. She couldn't blame him, even when she wanted to smack the righteousness off his face.

"You've gone on about me being out," she said, mostly to break the silence. "Where were you?"

"Making real purchases at the mercantile store," he replied. He leaned against the wall, as there were no chairs in the small room. Obviously, he preferred to keep his distance, rather than sit on the bed with her.

She raised her eyebrows. "Well, where are they?"

"I left them there to hold until we're ready to leave. We couldn't have them here—this room can barely fit us."

"I see." She smiled innocently. "No purchases for you, either."

He bristled. "I bought things. Hell, I damn near bought everything in that stupid store just to see—"

He bit off the last words, but Mary Alice didn't need that to know he was hiding something of his own. She almost asked what, then stopped herself.

"I suppose you're right," she said. "We really don't have room here, and you couldn't keep them out in the stable with Brown. They might be stolen or that Wilkins witch might decide they were hers."

He nodded. "I think I'll go check on him. He might need exercise."

She refrained from reminding him that he'd ridden Brown out earlier. Instead, she said, "You know, Hud, that could solve my problem. If I had a horse, I mean. I would need to ride it daily, and I could ride outside the city."

He pursed his lips thoughtfully. "You'll need one eventually. I wasn't thinking of that, although I know we'll need pack mules, but they're not the same thing. Of course, I'll ride with you."

That wasn't quite what she had in mind, but she couldn't voice a protest. Not without arousing even more suspicions.

"I'll see to Brown, then come back for dinner."

"Thrilling," she muttered, wondering if she could face another meal. Wilkins was as good a cook as she was a gentlewoman, which was to say she wasn't at all. Given her scrutiny and the mousy boarders she dominated, meals were an uncomfortable affair.

"It won't be long," he promised.

But late that night, "long" defined itself as intolerable. Hud didn't turn to her. He settled into the little bed on his side, facing the wall away from her. Mary Alice stared at his back. She hoped it was only remnants of his anger with her for leaving the room that day. But her senses told her it was more than that.

He was pulling himself back in, turning away physically as a precursor to his turning away emotionally. Emotion had been such a fragile thing between them that she couldn't imagine how it would survive a slow withdrawal.

Pain shot through her like bullets from a six-shooter. She'd expected this to begin in the far distant future, not in the here and now. Her gaze drank in the hard lines of his form visible in the soft moonlight. All that had happened played across her mind far too quickly to savor.

Get this last quest over with, she told herself. Then get out.

Hud watched Mary Alice guide the roan around the hills outside Denver, giving the horse its head over the flats—whatever flats could be found.

Woman and horse were moving along quickly. Mary Alice concerned him. She hadn't uttered a murmur of protest when he'd come home and told her he'd found a horse for her and now it needed to be paid for. Her money for her sister was dwindling quickly. He never considered it actually Mary Alice's, the coins being ill-gotten, but he couldn't help wondering how much of her sister's care was being drained off. And the others the nuns took in. The notion gave him an immediate perspective into Mary Alice's drive to gain enough because "enough" could never be had.

But he knew what the real problem was. He had turned away. He hadn't meant to, hadn't thought about it. But that first night after she'd disappeared for the second time, he just couldn't turn to her. He knew, *knew*, she was hiding something from him. He didn't know what it was, but he could sense it with every bone in his being. Getting past that was impossible.

She rode up to him, her horse's sides heaving with exertion, air blowing from its flared nostrils. Mary Alice's cheeks were rosy and her brown eyes sparkled with vitality. He realized that she had been caged in that room, like a prisoner again.

She had changed into pants for the freedom of riding, and Hud swallowed, his eye drawn to the long line of her leg. Her thighs gripped the horse's sides naturally, reminding him of the way they had gripped his own hips and pulled him into her moist velvet warmth. Her belly was taut and her spine erect. With her shoulders back, her breasts thrust out under the shirt, the curves familiar and enticing. His hands curled around Brown's reins in the urge to reach out and take her here in the meadow with the first of the spring wildflowers blooming around them. He wanted her everywhere, every waking hour of the day and in his dreams at night.

"She's a good horse," Mary Alice said, patting the animal's neck.

He nodded, willing his body to cool. "I thought you'd like her."

"I do. Is the Wilkins witch charging for her, too?"

He grinned wryly. "Does a bird sing?"

"There ought to be a law against that woman instead of me," Mary Alice muttered. "She's running a slave empire, not a boardinghouse. Did you hear that young woman crying this morning? She was slapped. Guess by who."

He sensed she was looking for conversation to ease the tension between them, but he could feel her riling up. "Let it go, Countess. She's not worth the effort. Besides, when did you turn into a crusader for the downtrodden?"

She made a face. "I don't know. But that woman ought to be taught a lesson."

"I have a feeling that if I forbid you, you'll march right in and hang her by her thumbs," he muttered.

She grinned. "Probably."

"You can't afford to attract attention to yourself. We're taking a big risk." He made up his mind. "I think it's time to move on, out of Denver."

Her eyes widened, panic easily readable in their depths. "But . . . but we don't know where yet. I'll put up with Mrs. Wilkins for a few more days if I have to."

If ever he needed a clincher to tell him she was up to something, that was it. *What?* he wanted to shout at her. Somehow he held himself back. It was time to be as shrewd as Mary Alice. The notion was daunting.

"I'm glad you can manage for a few more days," he said smoothly. "I'm sure we'll figure out the pieces of the map soon. Are you ready to go back?"

She nodded, relief evident in her smile. She turned the roan toward the city again and he followed behind her.

At Mother Wilkins's, he opened the door to their room, allowing her to pass through ahead of him. As he closed the door behind her, he said, "I'm going out. I think if I ask around about a place like the one on the map, I might find someone who can tell us where it is."

She nodded. "That's a good idea."

He smiled and went back out the door. The moment it closed behind his backside, he wiped the smile off his face.

"Are you and that wife of yours going to bother to come down to dinner tonight?" Mother Wilkins asked, materializing from nowhere.

Startled, Hud blinked.

"I don't make meals for absent people," she went on. She was hissing like a stepped-on rattlesnake, and her voice held about as much venom. "And I'm not your servant to serve them, either. I won't tolerate this from my boarders. I expect you—"

"We're paying you extra for the service," Hud said. "And we *expect* to receive what we pay for."

"You're not using my house for a hideout!" the woman snapped. "I don't want trouble—"

"And you won't have it as long as you mind your own business. If you don't, you'll have to contend with me."

Hud stalked away before he did something he might not regret—like shooting the woman.

In the stables, he fussed over the horses and fumed over women in general, one in particular. Afterwards, he settled in a position that allowed him to see the front sidewalks on either end of the house.

He waited.

It wasn't long. About half the hour had passed when he spotted a woman, her head covered by a shawl, hurrying away from the house. He hadn't seen her scurrying toward the house from the other side. He didn't need to note that the woman was too tall for Mother Wilkins and had too much vigor for the mousy young boarder, to know exactly who it was. If Mary Alice breathed within a mile of him, he could sense her presence.

It looked like Mother Wilkins's shawl was taking a walk again.

He got up and sauntered along behind, keeping her just visible in the distance. She looked exactly like any other woman, with her head bowed and her features hidden in the shadows of the shawl. It was amazing how much she resembled a shy immigrant who knew no English and wanted no problems because of it. No one looked twice—except for him. He couldn't keep his gaze from her.

She made several turns purposefully, going closer each time to the center of the city. And each time Hud's stomach flipped over sickeningly at the chances she took. He breathed a sigh of relief when she slipped into the post office. And then he breathed a second when it occurred to him that she really was mailing letters to her sister. Then he realized that her sister was in no condition to read them. The nuns would read them to her, he told himself. It made sense.

From his position across the street, he frowned when she emerged with something in her hands. From the scrap of white visible, he knew it was a letter. A reply so soon from St. Louis? He supposed it was possible, with the railroads . . .

He noticed a man emerge from the post office and turn in her direction. He was older, dressed in brown trousers, cream knee-length jacket, satin vest, and flat-brimmed town hat. He was heavier with the years, yet whipcord lean in his movements, with sandy-colored hair and a matching mustache that drooped around his mouth. Hud had never seen him before, but something about the way the man strolled along behind Mary Alice held his attention. He never glanced to the side as he stepped around people moving in the opposite direction. And he never quite kept to the natural pace with those going in the same direction as he. Instead, his stroll always maintained an equal distance between him and his quarry ahead.

His muscles tight with tension, and his stomach crawling with apprehension, Hud crossed the street and fell in behind the stranger.

The man followed Mary Alice until the last street turn, then he walked on. Confused, Hud followed him as he continued to stroll along, leaving Mary Alice to go her own way on the short route left to the boardinghouse. Hud wondered why the man followed so far and didn't follow farther. Maybe he wasn't following Mary Alice on purpose. Maybe he just happened to be going in the same direction, all this way. Then why had he followed so seemingly deliberately behind her like that? It didn't make any sense. Maybe the man was just following a pretty face and figure for a bit. A half a mile was more than a bit, he reminded himself. Maybe it was a man from Mary Alice's past, someone who had a grudge. He prayed not.

Eventually the man swung toward the part of the city that wasn't quite so respectable. This wasn't the way to the law offices, if the man were intending to turn Mary Alice in to the sheriff. Houses were fewer and shabbier here, and further along the streets they were replaced by transient dwellings and saloon fronts. The man disappeared into one of them. Someone banged loudly on the piano, pounding out a song rather than playing it in order to be heard above the hum of boisterous voices. Haze drifted along the well-lit room and bodies moved back and forth across the front door opening. Hud debated whether to go inside, afraid he might be recognized by someone he had once arrested. Lawmen were usually marked for life.

Coming to a decision, he jammed his hat low on his forehead and plunged into the smoky interior.

He took a spot at the corner of a long bar that must have been imported from back East. His position ensured that he was out of the hub of activity and his back was protected at the same time. No one seemed to notice him in the crowded room, and he didn't see anyone who had been his handcuff "partner" in the past.

A long painting of a sprawling nude woman, her hand coyly covering the junction of her legs, graced the wall behind the bar, with oily-haired barmen walking her length underneath. Poker players sat like spokes in wheels of concentration. Bar girls worked the patrons for drinks and dances, the house's take increasing with each purchase. Smoke hung in the air in miniature clouds around coal oil lanterns, the acrid odor stinging the nose and blurring the eyes.

Disdaining the pickled egg jar at his elbow, Hud ordered a beer and flipped a coin to the barman, who, in turn, slid him a glass. He picked it up and sipped the warm brew as he eyed the stranger who'd follwed Mary Alice.

The man was lounging a little farther down the bar, drinking whiskey and watching the men dancing with some of the house girls. Hud turned enough so he could still keep him in sight, yet seem to be watching the dancers. He winced as several of them got too enthusiastic and swung their female companions right into each other. With much laughter, the dancers retrieved their partners and the dancing picked right up where it left off until the music died.

One of the girls made her way directly to the man.

Hud watched out of the corner of his eye as the girl leaned against the man and caressed his vest-front possessively. The man smiled a smile that chilled rather than warmed. He whispered some words to the girl, who frowned, then smiled up adoringly.

Hud set the beer down. It looked to him as if the man had followed one female for sheer pleasure before meeting another. Odd as those actions seemed, no other explanation made sense either.

Satisfied, Hud left the saloon.

"But I don't want to dance with them anymore. They're clumsy and they've broken my toes, I think."

"You're still standing." Disgusted, Walker tossed off his whiskey and shook off Clara's hand. She had become a clinging vine all too quickly. "Get out there and dance. It's what you're paid to do."

Tears filled her eyes. "Please, I can't—"

Walker never flinched. Growling, he repeated, "Get out there. I don't want you hanging on me."

Another cowboy came up and claimed her, forestalling any more protests. Or tears. The young man swung her around, stepping on her toes in the process. Walker smiled to himself in satisfaction. The girl just wanted an easy ride from him, something he refused to tolerate. He was in no mood for her, as it was.

Someone had come for his letter.

His heart had stopped when he'd finally received that reply. He'd been so sure the whole thing was a joke. Now he knew it wasn't. The reply suggested a meeting. He'd hung around the post office waiting for someone to show up again, determined to see who it was. And to see what he was tangling with.

It had been a woman, a young immigrant woman from her look. He admitted he hadn't quite known what to make of that. He still didn't. What would an immigrant woman know about Jackson or Macaffee—or the gold? He'd followed, and in the course of doing so had begun to wonder if she were only a paid messenger.

Until the hackles had risen on the back of his neck.

He still had no idea what had caused the reaction, but he stopped trailing the woman immediately. He'd had that reaction many times in the war, and it had saved his life. He'd learned to follow it the moment it appeared. He still hadn't shaken the strong feeling of danger. Yet as his gaze swept the saloon, he couldn't see anyone or anything out of place, just rough cowboys and cool gamblers.

Maybe he was coming out of his skin, losing his edge—beyond losing it, had gone over it. He cursed the idea, knowing it wasn't a good one . . . if it were a wrong one. And he'd lost the woman because of it. He'd never had more than a glimpse of her face. She kept that damn shawl so tight around her, it put her features in perpetual shadow. At least he knew what part of town she was from.

And he knew where to meet her next. He'd suggested it in his reply.

There wouldn't be a third meeting. He would make sure of that.

Chapter Twenty

"You were out late."

From her position on the ledge of the window sill, Mary Alice watched Hud shrug his answer. He sat down on the bed in their little room. With his overpowering presence, it became more cramped than a prison cell. A torture chamber, she thought, as she found her gaze assessing the physical attributes she knew so well. He was fascinating to watch, with his grace of movement and whipcord tension always only a heartbeat from exploding in anger . . . or in passion.

"I had some business to wrap up," he said, setting his hat on the bureau.

"With your family?" she asked. The small rectangle of paper burned a hole in her skirt pocket. She wondered how she would get out of the boarding house unseen by Hud to meet Roger Ward tomorrow night, as this new letter requested. Absolutely nothing came to mind.

Hud stretched and pushed off his boots, clearly

settling in for the night. Finally, he said, "Yes. Why are you asking?"

"Bored." She shrugged. If he settled in tomorrow night like this, the meeting was a goner.

"I'll get you a book." His words weren't said unsympathetically.

She smiled at the gesture. "I'd like that." She paused, then added, "When can we go, Hud?"

"Soon. As soon as we figure out where."

"I've been thinking about that."

He groaned. "That's trouble."

She glared at him. But his tone was more teasing than sarcastic. He seemed to be relaxing with her again. She still didn't know what had upset him, but something had. Hurt and guilt mixed all inside her, creating confusion.

"All right." He sighed. "What were you thinking?"

"Oh." She pulled herself back to her thoughts. "Why don't we just follow railroad tracks to wherever they go? We're bound to see something that looks like those boulders and the stream."

"Do you know how many railroad tracks there are in the territory?"

"Well . . . no." She raised her eyebrows. "But there can't be all that many."

"There are spurs being built every day all over the place. Colorado is expanding—"

She smiled sweetly and interrupted. "But, Hud, we just have to find out what railroads were in the territory during the war when the map was made."

"But . . ." His eyes widened. "Sweet Jesus, I didn't think of that!"

"Then maybe it's a good thing I'm thinking, isn't it?" she asked in a very smug tone.

"Yeah, well . . ." His gaze narrowed suspiciously. "You're thinking so well, Countess, did you think that there were no railroads in the territory until '70?"

She gaped for a moment. "Well . . . I didn't know . . . I remember now. I guess. I didn't think about that."

He grinned slyly. "See. All that thinking. I knew better."

She straightened from the sill and came over to the bed to stand in front of him. "Oh, you knew better. Then tell me this. If those marks aren't railroad tracks, what in heaven's name are they?"

He flopped back on the bed, the mattress creaking ominously. "Only God knows, Countess, 'cause I sure as hell don't."

She groaned. "I think we're back to the beginning again."

To her surprise, he reached out and pulled her down on top of him. The bed groaned in protest. Hud chuckled and settled her against him. Through her skirts, she could feel the outline of his thighs and the thrust of his hip bones.

"What are you doing?" she asked.

He ran his hand along the indent of her spine down to the curve of her derriere. "What do you think?"

"You haven't seemed interested," she reminded him, still smarting from his neglect.

"Oh, I've been interested." His mouth sought hers. She stiffened at first, but the warm feel of his lips flooded her senses. She softened, and his tongue slipped inside, tasting her, coaxing her into an intimate duel. Her body slid into the velvet greyness of pure response. She curved her hands up and cupped his face, delighting in the roughness of his cheeks and the silky threads of his hair. His breath deepened at her touch. She had missed the sound of that over the last days. His hand worked under her, finding her breast and teasing the nipple to aching life through her clothes with his palm. Desire wound hot and sharp through her thighs and belly.

When she finally surfaced from the devastating kiss, she murmured, "Dinner."

"The hell with dinner."

His lips captured hers again, pulling her into the silken whirlpool. His hands were like fire all over her, freeing her from the encumbering outer clothing. Her petticoat was stripped away finally, and as her legs tangled with his, Hud sighed. The bed sighed with him. Mary Alice smiled at the twin sounds.

"I've missed you," he whispered.

"Who's fault is that?"

"Mine. All mine."

A brace of pure feminine power shot through her. "Just so you know."

She teased open the buttons of his shirt, running her fingers through the exposed chest hair. The hard bone underneath was a solid contrast. Leaning forward, she spread little butterfly kisses along his flesh. His hand tightened around her. She looked up to find his face flushed with passion, passion she created. Passion he could not ignore. Whatever had bothered him for the last few days was gone. She wanted only to take for herself what he was offering and hold it close for later.

Guilt rammed through her senses, reminding her of what she was keeping from him. She forced it away, telling herself it was for *his* good that she hid her news. That she was only temporarily delaying telling him about finding Roger Ward. That she would tell him tomorrow night, after the meeting.

She opened his shirt the rest of the way, her kisses dipping lower with each loosened button. He sucked in his breath with her last touch, his stomach muscles tight and hard. He pulled her up, flipping down the straps of her plain cotton chemise. He pushed the material past her breasts and captured one in his mouth. His tongue swirled around her nipple, causing the already intense ache to nearly explode inside her. She clutched at him, threading her fingers through his hair, gripping the strands as his mouth worked its magic. Pressing herself into the hard bar of his flesh between them, she moaned in pleasure.

His mouth went from breast to breast, laving, nipping, sucking, until she was a wild thing, almost clawing at him in need. The wanting was like silken ties drawing them closer together, binding them in ways she'd never conceived of.

His hands practically shredded her bloomers off her lower limbs, leaving her in just the chemise and rolled stockings. His pants were coarse against her already too-sensitive skin. She helped him push his pants and underdrawers away. His mouth was hot and savage against hers as the passion flamed high at the touch of flesh to flesh. His fingers found her moistness, stroking her into a frenzy. Her hips bucked against his hand. She couldn't stop the wanton movement. She didn't even want to try.

But he stopped, right before she'd gone over the edge. She tried to move against him, seeking relief from the intense pressure inside her. "Hud, please. You can't . . ."

"I won't."

He poised her over him and she slowly took him inside herself. The sensation of stretching to accept him made her cry out at the shock of it. They held together to a long, endless moment, letting nothing and everything swirl around themselves. Finally, she rocked over him, dying a little with each movement and then dying again. Through slitted eyes, she watched his face, watched the way his jaw was set to keep him from crying out his pleasure, watched the vulnerability heighten in his dull-red features. If this was wicked, she thought dimly, then she gladly accepted it. The tension spun so high she thought it would never burst, leaving her desperate. And when it did finally, it drowned her in wave after wave of release shuddering through her body, meeting and matching the waves beginning to shudder through his.

And then he pulled her up and away from his release.

Mary Alice cried at the sudden jolt of emptiness.

Her body's climax continued, even as she cried his name in anger and sadness. He held her tightly, his own separate release diminishing.

Slowly their breathing returned to normal, but the emptiness continued unabated. Mary Alice lay against him, wanting to scream and hit him in rage and knowing she could do neither. At first, she had been pleased by this protection he offered. Her monthly time had come on the trail back to Denver, relieving both of them. She knew he was right to do this. But that last moment of intense joy was denied to both of them. Now, with each time, she hated that more and more. She felt as if another layer of resentment and desperation was coming between them in the aftermath.

"Damn you," she murmured, tears welling in her eyes.

"I have to," he said. "You know that."

"Then hate it as much as I do," she whispered.

His arms tightened around her in answer.

Someone pounded on the door. Mary Alice jolted, startled by the sudden noise. Hud bit off a curse, "Watch the knee!"

She realized her knee had come dangerously close to his more vulnerable body parts. Chuckling, she eased the limb away. The unexpected humor helped to relieve the pain of his withdrawal.

"What is it?" Hud called out as the pounding began on the door again.

"Dinner," Mother's voice snapped through the wood. "And I'm receiving complaints about . . . about. I'm receiving complaints!"

Hud got up and strolled over to the door.

"About what?"

Mary Alice clamped a hand over her mouth to stifle the giggles. Hud was completely naked, and she couldn't help envisioning Mother's reaction if she swung open that door. She bet the woman's eyes would pop right out of her head.

"About . . . about the noise," Mother said finally, the question clearly leaving her nonplussed.

"Noise? What noise?" Hud asked, grinning at Mary Alice. She pressed her hands into her face. The giggles shot right out the sides of her mouth.

"Noise!" Mother's voice was a screech of desperation. "I won't tolerate that kind of . . . noise in my establishment. My boarders are quiet people, with decent lives."

"So that's what's wrong with them," Hud whispered to Mary Alice.

"I won't have it here. Do you understand!"

"Thanks for the dinner, Mother," Hud said. "You might want to move away from the door. I'm not exactly dressed—"

A gasp erupted, following by a clatter of feet down the staircase.

Mary Alice let go of her giggles. "She's a nasty old woman."

Hud came over to the bed and retrieved his pants. "No doubt. Notice she didn't ask us to leave."

"I noticed. But she's trouble."

"And not a fool, either." Once his pants were on, he got their dinner tray from the hallway. Closing the door, he said, "Not a Mother in sight. Or anyone else."

Mary Alice had the covers pulled up around her chin, hiding her nudity. She wasn't quite as comfortable with Hud as he was with her. Maybe that was just a man thing. She didn't care.

He frowned at the covers, but set the tray on her legs. "Soup again."

"Doesn't the woman know how to make anything else?" Mary Alice muttered.

Hud grinned. "She can stretch a half-dollar until it snaps."

"And cheat her boarders in the process."

"Eat your soup, Countess," Hud admonished, handing her a spoon.

Mary Alice smiled at his teasing and at him. The only thing that mattered was that he was pleased with her again. And she had never thought having a man pleased with her—especially this one—would matter so much.

"Don't you need to go check on your sister-in-law?" Mary Alice asked.

Hud paused in polishing his gun, years of taking care of his weapons ingrained in his brain like breathing. The question she asked was natural, innocent, but the underlying desperation in her voice wasn't. And if anyone knew Mary Alice's nuances, it was him.

"I just saw them the other day," he said, beginning to rub the bit of flannel over the butt again. "Everything was fine. I told you that."

That should have been it, but it wasn't.

"I really think you should talk to your nephew at least," she persisted. "Him going into the Union army! They'll eat him alive. I really think you need to tell him that."

He cursed under his breath, furious with her and with himself. She was trying to get rid of him this evening, that was obvious. And after last night . . . after he had been so positive she was only posting letters to her sister and not wanting him to know. He'd been angry about that risk, true, but not as suspicious as when he'd seen that man following her. But he'd forgiven her for any major misconduct. Again. And again, she'd made a fool of him. He'd opened himself, opened his heart, and she'd abused it without a blink of an eye. When would he learn with her? Never, a voice inside said. *Never.*

He was about to say he wasn't going anywhere when he stopped himself. Setting the gun aside, he said, "You're right. I think I will go see them and talk to young John. He needs some sense hammered into him. It might take all evening. Will you be all right here?"

She nodded. "Except for that busybody Wilkins, yes. But I can handle her."

"I'm sure you can," he muttered, picking up his gun and shoving it into his holster. He wrapped the wide strap around his middle and buckled it at his waist, then tied the rawhide string that kept the holster itself snug along his outer thigh. "I'll be back later."

He didn't kiss her before he left, but she didn't seem to notice. She was already distracted with her plans, he was sure. He went down the stairs and out the front doors, slamming them shut with a rattle of window panes. Striding down the street in the evening dusk, he picked out a spot between two buildings.

He faded into it and waited.

It was a long while later, the sun gone completely from the sky, but she didn't disappoint him. And that she didn't disappoint him, disappointed him terribly as the door to Mother's boardinghouse opened and a figure slipped out. A woman. She closed the wood and glass panel and immediately moved along the streets with quick, light steps. Hud allowed her to get quite a bit ahead, then fell in behind her.

She went into the part of town where he'd gone that night he'd followed the older man. Tension crawled along the edges of his stomach, and the hairs rose on the back of his neck. He'd catch her red-handed with her lies this time, and they would have it out. And he would stop making an ass of himself with her once and for all.

The twists and turns of the streets she took led her near the saloon where the man had been. Hud clenched his jaw as she began to pause and look around. He knew she was close to her destination. He never thought . . . never conceived that she would have an assignation with another man. Well, he did in sheer jealousy, but he didn't honestly believe her capable of being that deceptive. A voice reminded him that she'd been a virgin. Her suddenly taking a second lover seemed a boldness beyond even her. Could the man be a "business" partner? She never said she had one . . . except Otis. But he'd died in an accident; she'd told him that herself one night when they'd talked on the trail.

Maybe he really hadn't, Hud thought. Maybe she was meeting him now. But why keep that secret?

His questions became wilder as she hunted for her final destination. So self-absorbed had he become that he was only about twenty feet from her when he realized she'd stopped completely in front of a narrow alleyway. Hud cursed, knowing if she walked down that alleyway precious seconds would be lost before he could reach it. He cursed again, knowing she was standing completely exposed to anything or anyone at the other end of the alley. The street was too dark, the shops closed for the evening. It was exceptionally dark where Mary Alice was. He could just see the outline of her figure in the gloom. A knot of warning sank into his gut. This place had all the makings of a trap.

She stood, obviously undecided, until several men strode along the boards, coming toward her. She made up her mind—and plunged out of sight into the alley.

"Shit," Hud muttered, racing across the walking planks, his ears straining to hear a scream or worse, and praying not to.

The men passed by where she'd been, glancing at him curiously, but he rounded the street corner of the alleyway, just in time to see her at the end. Upright and moving. Relief shot through him. At the end of the alley was a small building—a house, by the looks of it. A candle burned in the window, giving off a low light in the open space in front of the home.

Hud crept down the alley, keeping his back pressed to the clapboard of the tall building on his left. His gaze never left Mary Alice as she knocked on the front door of the little house.

"Mr. Ward?" she called out softly when no one answered.

The hair on Hud's neck rose at the name.

He raced to the back end of the alley, ready to demand to know what the hell she was doing with a bastard named Ward. Instead, an ominous glint of light on metal to his left caught his eye.

"Down!" he shouted, whipping out his gun and firing directly at the glint. Two shots rang out almost simultaneously.

Mary Alice fell to the ground.

Hud fired again as he ran right out into the open space. Boots pounded out of the deep shadows at the edge of one of the buildings as the gunman escaped. A whiff of cordite stung the air before being blown away.

Hud knelt down next to the prone figure and slowly rolled her onto her back. His hands shook violently. *Don't be dead. Please don't be dead.* The words echoed through his brain in a desperate litany.

"Mary Alice," he whispered, even as her eyelids fluttered open. His hands felt all over her body, dreading the anticipated warm, sticky connection.

"I'm all right," she said, sitting up. Her voice

quavered with fear. "I think he missed. And I think I fainted."

His fingers confirmed her words and relief washed through him, leaving him drained of emotion.

And then what she had done hit him like a poleax to the gut.

"How did you get here?" she asked, the fear even more tangible in her voice.

He was too furious to answer. He had the distinct impression she was more terrified of him than of what had just happened. She ought to be, he thought.

Footsteps clattered down the alley.

"What's going on?" someone asked.

"The lady had a mishap," Hud said, helping Mary Alice to her feet. He looked around at the small crowd. None of the men was the man from the saloon. Satisfied, he added, "It's all right now. I'm a marshal. You folks can go on home."

People milled for a second or two, gazing curiously at Mary Alice one last time before dispersing toward the street.

"Oh, folks," Hud said, a thought occurring. "Does anyone know who lives in this house?"

"No one lately," a man said. "A Chinaman tailor used to live there until business ran out on him."

"Thanks," Hud said.

They followed the people up the alley and into the street, Hud keeping his hand tight around Mary Alice's arm.

They hadn't gone three feet when she said,

"Don't say it. Don't say it."

"Ward?" he asked, in a growl. *"Roger Ward!"*

She shivered. "I was stupid."

"What were you doing?" he demanded, delayed pain and shock running through him like twin bludgeons. He walked faster, muttering, "You destroy my trust. Each time you destroy my trust."

"I . . . I'm sorry," she whispered. "I'm sorry. But I had this letter from him, asking to meet. I thought he could help us find the gold, sell us the last piece of the map. I wanted to tell you. Honest, Hud, I did. But I was terrified you would kill him the moment you found out about him."

"Damn right I would have," he snapped.

"See? The way you treated me . . . and I was only a daughter. We need that gold, Hud. It can do good for once. For my sister. The nuns. For your brother's family. They're the innocents who have suffered. Don't they deserve to inherit it?"

"You talk damn good," he said. "You always have. But it doesn't change what you did. You put yourself in danger of being discovered. What if the newspaper had been there? Or someone from the marshal's office? That's bad enough. But you betrayed me, Countess. You always have and you always will."

"I kept you from making a mistake, from breaking the law you're always so ready to uphold. I thought it would be better to meet with him first, then tell you." She raised her chin. "I still think so."

He spun her around to face him, oblivious of anybody watching. "Really? Then think this:

someone tried to kill you tonight. How brilliant was that?"

She turned away, clearly not wanting to answer.

He yanked her forward again, and the two of them walked in silence to the boardinghouse. Once inside, Mother Wilkins came flying out of her parlor, as if on a broomstick, took one look at Hud's face, and disappeared back into the safety of her worn furnishings.

Mary Alice had been desperate to find the right words to head off the explosion that was coming. He was right. She had betrayed him. But she was right, too. He wouldn't have listened, he just would have taken his revenge.

And she'd also been a fool. Roger Ward tried to kill her tonight. If Hud hadn't been there . . .

When they were alone inside the room with the door closed, Mary Alice braced herself for the eruption. It never came.

"Hud," she began, trying to find the most logical and gentle words to explain her actions.

"Don't bother," he said wearily. "There's nothing you could say to make up for what you did."

"Hud, I had a message put in the personals column while I was in jail, long before you and I . . ." She swallowed. "I didn't betray you. I didn't want to deceive you even a little. But you never would have listened to reason first."

"I'll be in the barn," he said, then opened the door and left.

Mary Alice stared at the blank wood for the longest time.

Then she burst into tears.

Chapter Twenty-one

Hud strode unerringly through the city of Denver until he reached the saloon. He went right through the doors and gazed around at the men until he found his quarry.

He would kill Ward.

It *was* Ward, he thought, searching the room frantically. The right Roger Ward. The age was right, and the cowardly deception was right. Shooting a woman was the same behavior as leaving a man in the wilderness to die.

Roger Ward, however, wasn't in the saloon tonight.

Hud smiled grimly at this bigger indictment against the man. He spotted the girl who'd been talking with him that night and stalked over. He took her arm and spun her away from her partner.

"Hey!" the girl yelped, stumbling. Hud caught her upright.

"Lookit here, mister," the cowboy with her began.

Hud rounded on him, glaring. The man seemed to shrink in size.

"Mind if I talk with the lady a moment?" Hud asked in the softest of voices. "It's important."

"Well . . . ahhh . . ." The young man was wall-eyed with anxiety. "I did pay for the whole dance."

"I'll see you get a second one free." Having said that, Hud pulled the girl away from the dance floor.

"Mister, I don't know who you are," she said, her voice shaking, "but I got me a protector you have to see first if you want anything more than a dance—"

The memory of the way his quarry had watched the woman before clicked into his mind, and he made an educated guess about who her "protector" was. Hud stopped walking. "I have a message for him."

"For Richard?" The girl's mouth was an "O" of astonishment. The innocent surprise wiped away the harder edges she'd acquired in her profession. Hud realized how, through sheer tenacity, Mary Alice had avoided that edge.

"No. Roger," Hud corrected, frowning. "Roger Ward."

The girl gasped. "But I don't know any Roger Ward!"

"That man you were with the other night when I was in here." Hud set his jaw against the thought that he was making a horrible mistake. "The fancy-dressed one."

"That's Richard Walker." She glared at him. "What's going on here?"

"Nothing," Hud muttered. The twin initials hit him. Roger Ward. Richard Walker. They had to be one and the same. "Tell 'Richard Walker' that Hudson Jackson said he'd kill him if he touches the Count . . . the Macaffee woman again."

"Woman!" The girl's eyes narrowed. "That son of a—"

"Just see he gets the message." Hud let her go.

He left the saloon, eating up the planked sidewalk in long, angry strides. Fury and fear rode him like the two devils they were, until he reached Mother's boardinghouse and the stables behind it. The horses shifted restlessly as he grabbed up a pitchfork and dumped more hay in their already-filled mangers. He shoved some more into a makeshift pallet for himself and plopped down onto it. Both horses eyed him warily, picking up easily on his mood.

He couldn't believe it. She had been writing to Ward all this time. She confessed it! Of all the things she had ever done, this one stood out as the winner, he decided, grabbing up a handful of hay and throwing it at Brown in complete frustration. The horse whinnied in protest and shied away from the harmless threat.

"Well, hell, you liked her," he muttered.

Brown flicked his tail as if to say in answer, "You more than liked her, friend." The mare was noncommittal in her judgment.

Brown was right, he thought. He'd more than liked her. He'd fallen in love with her.

It explained a lot. And Mary Alice had proved herself, like his former fiancée, a traitor. This time it was worse. This time it wasn't a woman everyone, including himself, had expected him to marry. This time it was despite all the barriers.

He could trust her with his life, but he couldn't trust her with his heart.

He lay back in the straw, feeling sick to his stomach. Half because he'd fallen in love with Mary Alice, and half because she'd nearly been killed tonight. He'd wanted neither to happen.

There would be no cure this time, he acknowledged. Mary Alice was unforgettable. Bonds lay between them that would never be snapped.

He tried to turn his thoughts away from her, but they swam around inside his head—Ward, the gold, her sister, his brother's family. Mary Alice.

Was her motive really only to insure he wouldn't take revenge without thought? Would he have?

His heart beat strongly at the notion. He wouldn't have thought twice, and he knew it. Ward wasn't like Mary Alice, innocent of her relative's actions. She was guilty of a lot of things but she was innocent of that at least. His thoughts jumbled around again over her.

And all through the night.

Roger Ward stared at the boardinghouse that looked like any other. The man he'd seen coming out of the saloon like the devil out of Hell had seemed vaguely familiar. Then it had come together in his mind. He'd caught a glimpse of the fellow before he'd deserted that back alley by Fong

Lim's old tailor shop. He was the reason his own shot had gone wide in surprise and fear.

When he'd finally felt it safe enough to make his way to the saloon, he saw the same man leaving and followed him at a discreet distance. Again, he'd found himself in the same part of town, respectable but verging on seedy, as when he followed the immigrant woman. On the same streets, too. The man had disappeared to the back of this boardinghouse, Mother Wilkins's, according to the sign swinging from a porch post.

Had he stopped here? Or had he cut through to another street? Roger had no answers to the desperate questions and no desire to walk down between the buildings to find out. He knew all too well what could be lurking at the other end.

He cursed softly at losing the man—and at the entire evening. It had been a disaster from the beginning, just as it had been with the gold. Bringing it overland had been the most foolish of ideas. The amount they could carry was a pittance to what was needed and what a ship could bring. But the blockades had tightened considerably, and the government had become desperate for a way to get the gold waiting in California to Richmond so the war could continue.

He had been just as desperate to eliminate his past, so desperate he'd been ready to kill a woman tonight. He'd known he'd lost any vestige of honor, but tonight was proof positive of how far he'd go. All he knew was that the woman and the man were tied to Jackson and Macaffee.

And they were out there, waiting for him.

* * *

The porridge was cold and Mary Alice disdained it, preferring to confront Hud on an empty stomach rather than with Mrs. Wilkins's witch-glue lying like a rock in her gullet.

The bottom of the sun was just touching the horizon as she slipped out the back door, leaving the witch to berate her other boarders about their morning slowness, and went around to the stables.

The horses shifted in their stalls, recognizing her. She patted Brown's nose, then the roan's. She really ought to give her a name, Mary Alice thought, then she caught sight of a pair of boots, toes up, sticking out beyond the edge of the stalls. Getting closer, she discovered Hud, fully dressed, sleeping in a mound of hay. He looked almost vulnerable, and she wondered if he had been up most of the night as she had.

She reached out with her foot and shoved at his boot-tip. "Hud."

He jolted up, his eyes wide and confused. "What!"

"We need to talk."

He glanced around, clearly trying to orient himself to his surroundings. His gaze finally focused on her and his expression turned sour. "Couldn't it wait?"

"No." She drew in a deep breath. "You know, you and I have been going round and round about what's on the map pieces. But Roger Ward has the last part to the puzzle. You may want to kill him, Hud, but can I suggest you wait until *after* we find the gold? That's if you're ready to talk sense."

He scowled. "That last remark just guaranteed I'm not. Even if I were."

She snorted. "So we stop here? Forget it and just go on with our lives? What's left of them?"

He rubbed his hands across his face and sighed. "Hell, I don't know. It's too damn early for this—"

"No, it's not." He glared up at her in warning, but she ignored it. "Damn you, Hud Jackson. I hated deceiving you, but I had to get that gold for my sister. And clear my father's name if I could. And for your family, too."

"Sure," he said with a cynical laugh.

She waved a hand. "Think what you like. You will anyway. I cried my eyes out last night over you, until I realized that. All that horrible guilt I felt—"

"You cried?"

She ignored the question, still hell-bent on venting her feelings. "I shouldn't have worried about your understanding. You never would have. I shouldn't have worried, either, about you killing a man and hanging for it. The same laws don't apply to you, do they? But you made me a bargain. I see now your intent to honor it only goes so far—"

"What the hell does that mean?" he demanded, getting to his feet.

He towered over her, all snorting male anger. She lifted her chin and faced him down, saying, "It means that as long as the bargain doesn't get in your way, you honor it. If it does, your honor means nothing."

"Who the hell are you to tell me what my honor means?"

"I'm someone you've dishonored, so I ought to know," she answered, then turned away.

It had taken her nearly all night to figure out she wasn't the only one to blame in all this. He had to shoulder his fair share. But she couldn't face him anymore at the moment. It hurt too much. She wondered how she would ever raise the money her sister needed, with the Countess gone from her repertoire. She had no repertoire, she realized, now that she was notorious in the territory. Despair pressed down on her shoulders and her stomach felt queasy.

"All right!" he snapped. She whirled around. His lip almost curled in derision as he said, "I'll keep the damn bargain, every bit of it. But the moment it's over, I kill the son of a bitch. You understand?"

She nodded.

He reached down and picked up his hat, whacking it a few times against his thigh to shake out the hay dust. "No more of these . . . discussions first thing in the morning, Countess. I can't take it."

She smiled, but wisely didn't give vent to the smart remark on the tip of her tongue.

"And when we're done with this, we're through," he said. "You and me."

The smart remark dissolved into an unuttered cry of anguish. Tears pushed at her eyes and she closed them against the pain. Finally, when she got her emotions under control, she said, "Hud—"

"No. I can't trust you again. I've done it too

many times and been kicked in the teeth for it." By the time he finished speaking, his jaw was set in determination.

Mary Alice said nothing.

"What's the Wilkins witch got for breakfast?" he finally asked in a near-growl.

"Porridge."

He uttered a curse that was hardly appropriate when one was contemplating eating. "Hell, that stuff'll kill you."

"That's why I didn't eat it."

Without another word, he turned his back on her and made his way to the outhouse on the other side of the stables. Mary Alice walked in the opposite direction, toward the house.

"Miss?"

The timid voice startled her. Mary Alice stared at the shy woman boarder who was standing near the woodpile holding an armful of logs. The woman smiled tremulously.

"I . . . I'm sorry you and your mister are having a tiff," she said.

Mary Alice winced at the words, knowing everyone within three blocks probably knew it by now. Heat flamed her cheeks.

"I . . . I admire you," the woman added quickly, seeing her dismay. She shifted her load. "You . . . you say what you believe."

"So can you," Mary Alice said softly, realizing the woman was talking about the time she'd stood up to the Wilkins witch.

The woman shook her head. "No . . . I . . . I couldn't. I need my home here."

"There are other boardinghouses. You don't need to put up with what this Wilkins woman is doing to you." Mary Alice didn't know why she was talking to the woman. She had nothing in common with this frightened mouse of a person, and her entire world had collapsed around her.

"No. I couldn't. Mr. Hoffman . . ." The woman swallowed visibly. She looked around the yard, then said in a low tone, "I . . . I also wanted to tell you to be careful about . . ."

"I know." Mary Alice glanced at the house.

The woman nodded. "Well, I wanted to tell you. I'm sure you and the mister will make up. You two are so much in love."

Mary Alice choked at the words. The woman didn't seem to hear them. She sighed at her imagined romantic notions.

"Well, I better get inside," she finally said. "Mother will miss me and that won't do."

She bustled away with the wood precariously perched in her arms.

Mary Alice watched her go, then looked heavenward for salvation for the poor thing. How she could think Hud was in love with her, Mary Alice, was a mystery beyond anything she'd ever heard. And she'd heard plenty.

Mary Alice walked slowly toward the house, her mind behind her still in the stables with Hud. He hated her now. He'd made that plain enough. She'd gotten what she'd wanted from him, a promise to keep him from killing Ward outright.

But at a price she'd never contemplated having to pay.

*   *   *

Hud sat down on the bed that he'd vowed only last night he would never touch again.

He couldn't believe the things she'd said to him that morning. *She'd cried her eyes out all night.* The words swirled around in his head and he glanced at the pillows. They didn't look tear-stained, but he wondered how much of a stain tears would actually leave behind. Mary Alice's eyes were red-rimmed . . .

"What the hell does it matter if she cried about me?" he mumbled to himself.

But it did.

The door opened. Mary Alice stood poised on the threshold, her eyes widening at the sight of him, the doorknob frozen in her hand. He stared at her for a long second. Then his gaze lowered, absorbing the curve of her breasts against her grey dress. His denial of her ate at him now, showing him exactly how foolish pride and honor could be. Trust was another matter entirely, however. And he had none for her.

She walked forward and shut the door behind her, breaking the spell. She asked, "Have you come to tell me you've changed your mind?"

"No." Insolently, he lolled back on the bed. It creaked under him, evoking immediate memories of how it had creaked under the both of them.

Her face grew rosy.

"I'm here," he drawled, "because I'm honoring our bargain. Since Mr. Ward has decided to turn the game in a dangerous direction and then vanish, we've got to lure him back into play—and safely."

It was a fair imitation of her as the Countess, he decided. Barely fair.

"And how do you propose to do that?"

"We're going to pay him a visit," he said.

She laughed. "Pay him a visit! No one lives at that little place I was sent to. You heard those people say that."

"You don't know everything," he said. "Ward doesn't live there. He does spend a great deal of time at a particular saloon."

Her eyes blazed with suspicion. "And how do you know that?"

"Because I followed him there the last time you went to the post office."

"The last time . . ." Her voice trailed away and her eyes widened in shock. "You followed me!"

He raised an eyebrow at her indignant tone. "What made you think I'd believe that nonsense about you out wandering around looking like you're getting your greenhorn family ready to move on? Do I look that stupid? Hell, I must, for you to hand me that cock-and-bull story."

"But you . . . you . . ."

"What?" he scoffed. "Treated you exactly the same way you treated me?"

"I didn't treat you like a criminal," she said, sitting down on the window ledge. "I didn't want you killing Ward. For a lot of reasons!" she added, clearly comprehending the look of disbelief on his face.

Hud ground his teeth together, furious with her

and with himself. But he hadn't come back to their room to squabble. He had come to get their damned bargain over with as soon as possible, a refrain he'd kept up weeks ago. This time he'd follow it through to the end.

When he had his temper sufficiently under control, he said, "Are you interested in how I've come to know about him?"

He could see her set her jaw, obviously in an attempt to control her own anger. "Yes."

"When you left the post office a man followed you out. Did you notice him? Blond mustache, in his forties, dressed more like a businessman than a gambler?"

"No . . ." She shook her head. "I wasn't paying attention, either."

"I could see that." He frowned. "You were reading a letter from him, weren't you?"

She said nothing, which gave him her answer.

"He followed you, and I followed him. He got as far as the end of the street, but continued on. I don't know why. He ended up at a saloon not too far from your little rendevous last night."

She blanched. "He . . . he followed me this far? Why didn't you tell me?"

"Because I thought it was perfectly innocent," he said in disgust. "Because you were 'writing to your sister and the nuns,' remember? Why should I think he had any other interest in you except that you were headed in the same direction as he was, and you were more enjoyable to admire from afar than some cowboy a month from his last bath?"

"Why didn't you tell me this last night?" She

wrapped her arms around her waist and bent forward, rocking slightly.

Not able to stand watching her fear, yet not able to comfort her either, Hud got up off the bed and began to pace the room. "Because I was too damned mad to even think about it. But now I have. All day today. He won't stop trying to kill you. Or me, now that he knows there are two. We threaten him in some way."

"Or he just wants the gold all to himself," Mary Alice whispered. "Hud, I wanted the stuff so bad, look at what *I* did."

The heartfelt confession nearly broke him. He grabbed hold of his emotions, reminding himself that she might feel regret but it didn't change how often she'd betrayed his trust. "Whatever he wants, we need to ensure he doesn't get it over our dead bodies. I think a little visit to the saloon is in order."

Mary Alice laughed bitterly. "He's probably halfway through Wyoming by now. I would be."

"Maybe," Hud conceded. "Maybe he's just holed up in a room somewhere in the city, lying low because of last night. He was with a woman the night I saw him. She might just know where that room is."

Mary Alice shivered. "He tried to kill me. Next time you'll be a target, too. And next time he may not miss."

"Then he won't get the gold." Hud smiled coldly at her. "Come on. She ought to be there by now. The dancing started at dusk. It's time Mother Wilkins's shawl took another walk."

He opened the door to their room. Mary Alice sat on the window ledge for a long moment. Finally she got up and walked past him. The scent of lavender teased his senses, and the air seemed to ripple along his nerve-endings. He forced himself to push aside the torment she caused just by moving. He followed her out into the hallway and down the stairs.

He had better pay attention to their business tonight—if he wanted to keep them both alive.

Chapter Twenty-two

The saloon was as brightly lit and noisy as any entertainment establishment west of the Mississippi, yet Mary Alice felt a foreboding chill, as though she were walking alone in a forest filled with wolves.

She had no idea what Hud intended to do; she only knew what he'd said he wouldn't do. Whether he would keep his promise once he faced Ward was another matter. She knew him well enough to know he'd hate himself afterward if he took justice into his own hands.

People passed by the open doorway of the saloon, and she stared at them, trying to see if anyone fit the description of the man who had followed her . . . and tried to kill her. There were a lot of men in their forties, and a lot of men with blond mustaches. She swallowed back a lump of fear, knowing that any of them could be the one.

Hud nudged her to get her frozen feet moving. They entered the saloon. Mary Alice almost choked on the smoky haze. The sour odor of sweat combined with the mustiness of beer yeast bludgeoned her senses, sending her back to the time when she worked in the dance hall and further back to when she'd sit and kick her heels while waiting for Otis to finish playing cards with the locals.

"The man's either more of a fool than I thought or much cooler than I want him to be," Hud said, bringing her back to the present.

He steered her to a table on the far side of the room. Mary Alice was aware of people staring at her as they passed, but she kept her gaze riveted on the table's single occupant. He played solitaire, a bottle of whiskey and a glass next to his hand. He looked up as they approached. His eyes widened at the sight of them.

Hud pulled out a chair for Mary Alice. She folded her hands on her lap, her fingers gripping her skin almost painfully in order to keep her composure. She braced herself for the sound of Hud's gun killing the man or the man's gun killing her. Neither came. Instead, Hud calmly took the chair opposite Ward, leaving her between the two of them.

Mary Alice forced herself to look at her nemesis just as calmly. He didn't seem any different from any other man, and he showed no recognition, no fright at their presence. Yet he had to be hiding something so deep he was willing to kill to keep it secret.

Fear chilled her spine as the two men faced each other. Hud's expression held a kind of hatred she'd never seen in another human being. She had deprived him of revenge and satisfaction and left him with this instead. Would it pass eventually? It had to, or Hud would never be a man true to himself again.

"Who are you people?" Ward began. He looked coolly at Hud.

Hud cut him off. "We're not here to play your games. We're here to make you a proposition—one you might have heard last night, if you hadn't been so hasty."

Mary Alice had no idea what Hud planned to do, but common sense told her to follow his lead. She decided to listen to her common sense for once.

"I don't know what you're talking about—"

"Save it," Hud snapped. "I don't expect the truth from a man who'd leave another to die in Indian country. Or try to kill a woman in a back alley."

Ward's body went completely still. It was a dead giveaway, Mary Alice realized. The man relaxed again, but it was too late.

"I don't know who you are or what you're talking about," the man said dully. "Now get out."

"I don't think so," Hud said, fishing out the two pieces of paper from his shirt pocket.

"I believe these introduce us," Hud said.

"Who the hell *are* you?" Ward whispered.

Hud didn't answer. He just crooked his eyebrows and held up the two crumpled yellow papers in his hand.

"That's the man I told you about, Richie. Who

is he? And who's this woman?"

The unexpected female voice broke through the thick tension at the table. They all looked up, startled. The young dance hall girl stared back at the three of them, her gaze going from Hud to Mary Alice to Ward, then back to Mary Alice. Her eyes narrowed in suspicion. Mary Alice didn't need an introduction to know this was the girl Hud had come to see tonight about Ward and instead found his quarry.

"They're . . . friends," Ward said. "Go away and dance."

"But I'm tired—"

Ward rounded on her. "Get out, damn you! I've had enough of your whining. Find someone who'll put up with it, if you can, whore."

The girl's face crumpled in shock and hurt. She ran from the saloon. Mary Alice felt sorry for her for being humiliated in front of others. The sudden urge shot through her to get a gun and shoot Ward herself. She controlled it. That wouldn't do, after the lecture she'd given Hud.

Hud glanced at her in warning, as if he expected her to shoot Ward anyway. She merely raised her eyebrows. She wished he'd told her what he intended to do at this meeting, but it was too late now to ask.

With a steady hand, Ward poured himself a glass of whiskey and swallowed it. "Is there some point to all this?"

"One or two." Hud fished a box of matches from his pocket. "My brother didn't die out there, Ward. Not then. It took weeks from the gangrene that set in. But before he died screaming like a woman, he left me his part of the map, just as Mary Alice's father left her his. There's a lot of gold out there, waiting for someone to find it. So far, you haven't. We'd like to."

"I haven't looked!" Ward snapped. It was another confession if Mary Alice ever heard one.

"But you'd like to," Hud said. "Maybe now you can . . . maybe now you need to. Maybe your gunrunning scheme just ran out of steam, 'Walker.' The Utes killed Skinny and Burn-hand, by the way. Did you know? They didn't care for your proposition."

Mary Alice glanced at Hud, surprised by the connection he'd made and positive he was stretching it. It was too much coincidence, surely, that this man was his man. His man's name was Walker . . .

Ward's eyes never left Hud's, but his jaw tightened.

"Maybe you need that gold," Hud said softly, holding the map pieces in a way that Ward could actually see what was on them. Mary Alice wanted to snatch the papers away, but Hud folded them, adding, "Maybe you always wanted to go back and get it. But you needed *all* the map pieces, didn't you? Well, we're willing to work with a bastard like you to get it. That's our proposition. We go get the gold together."

"How do I know you won't kill me and take my part of the map?" Walker asked. "If I had such a thing."

"You've got it," Hud said. "We'd like to live, too,

Mary Alice and I. But you have a point about our killing you. It's what you'd do, isn't it? It's what you *will* do once we're on the trail. So Mary Alice and I took out a little insurance to prevent that from happening."

Hud struck the match. It flamed into a small, bright yellow-tipped light at the end of the little wooden stick. All around them the music and voices played on, but at a distance. Mary Alice watched in fascination and horror as Hud set the match to the papers. The two pieces caught and burned in little more than a blink of the eye. She wanted to cry out and stop him, but it was already too late. The damage was done.

Ward gasped and smacked his hand over the burning pieces as Hud dropped them onto the table. He put the smoldering flames out, but the papers were a mass of ashes; only the little tips where Hud's fingers had held them were still intact. Ward seemed to shake as he gazed at them.

"We've got our pieces memorized," Hud said. "She her half, and me mine. Kill us and you're no farther than you ever were. Kill one of us and you still won't find it. I suggest you memorize yours . . . just so you can sleep nights, too."

Ward sat there and stared at them. Mary Alice kept her face carefully blank even as her brain screamed "Fool!" over what Hud had done. She *didn't* know what was on her part of the map. She'd only seen the damnable thing a few times!

"You're not like your brother," Ward said finally.

Hud's mouth turned bitter. "Not even close."

Ward glanced at her. "You look like Cullen."

She could have been invisible before, for all the man looked at her during Hud's little show. But now he never blinked, his gaze never wavered. Hud had offered him his wildest dream and then backed him into a corner to get it, yet here he was, already attempting a rapport with her. She knew he would try to divide her and Hud from each other and then conquer them before they reached the gold. Philosophy straight from Machiavelli's *The Prince.* Otis's horde of books had contained one or two about political philosophers.

Ward was an extremely cool customer, she thought, setting aside her panic for the moment. To sit here in this saloon like a complete innocent had taken nerves of steel, especially knowing Hud had been here once for the man. Yet it was smart. What looked more innocent—and what could Hud do in front of a roomful of people? Unfortunately for Ward, he didn't know Hud.

"Yes," she said at last, taking on the game. "I look like Cullen."

Ward surveyed her again. This time his stare held a sensual glint. Mary Alice kept her gaze coolly on his face, giving no outward indication of what she thought. She'd practiced controlling her expressions for far too long not to know when the muscles weren't in the right place.

"Do we have a deal?" Hud asked, breaking in.

Mary Alice felt the "clank" of a misstep immediately.

Ward glanced at him, his mouth turning down at the interruption. "I don't think so."

Hud's jaw dropped in astonishment. Mary Alice rose to her feet to cover her "partner's" surprise, mentally cursing at his giveaway.

"You're all out of ace cards, mister," she said. "We're leaving in two days, with or without you. Don't think we can't find it without you. We found *you*. You can join us, or you can face the law over your little railroad ventures. I'm sure you remember how to get in touch."

Mary Alice turned and walked away. She heard a chair scrape back behind her and in a few more steps Hud was beside her. He took her elbow and escorted her out of the saloon.

Several people stared. Several more speculated. No one followed.

Outside, the night air hit her face in a cool rush of a breeze. They walked in silence along the streets, not fast, just putting distance between themselves and the saloon. Mary Alice strained her ears to hear any unusual sounds from behind them. The spot exactly in the middle of her shoulder blades twitched in anticipation of invasion and sudden, searing pain. She wondered if Hud was listening and feeling the same. His face in the lamplight didn't indicate a thing.

When she decided it was safe enough, she demanded, "Why in God's name did you burn my part of the map? I don't know what's on it!"

He chuckled. "Fortunately, I do."

"So how do I know I won't take a bullet in *my* sleep?" she asked. "I don't have any protection, thanks to you."

"I'm the only one who knows that. You'll have

to trust me." He snorted. "At least I won't betray *your* trust."

"You'll never forgive me, will you?" she said in a low voice, sighing. "No matter how often I apologize. And no matter that I'm right."

He said nothing. She had a feeling his jaw was clenched tighter than a rusted cap on an old Mason jar. She shouldn't have added the bit about being right, but the words had been stuck in her craw long enough.

"I pushed him too hard at the end, didn't I?" he said, changing the subject. She wondered if it was a concession to her in some way.

"A little," she agreed.

"Well, you put him right back up against the wall again," Hud said, adding slyly, "You're the expert in this."

"You were doing just fine." She actually laughed in true amusement. They were on friendly ground, exulting a little over their victory. Maybe this could bring them closer again. Maybe.

"I thought about what you would do and that's what I did." He paused. "I damn near killed him when I first sat down. John's face just swam before me . . . and Missy and the kids. God knows I wanted to so bad. But they need the money—if we can get it."

She nodded in understanding, admiring him. Somehow, admiring his principles hurt worse than having fallen in love with him.

"Do you think he'll come?" Hud asked.

"Yes," she replied. "Fear and greed are twin devils most of us can't fight. Otis said that. He said that's why his business did so well wherever he went. I think our Mr. Ward is full of fear and greed. But why did you think he's your gunrunner? There have got to be a lot of Walkers in Denver."

"Just a guess," he said. "All of sudden it seemed right, like the old saying about all roads pointing in the same direction. It's just one more thing to hang him for."

She glanced over at him, seeing very little of him in the shadows. "And when do you intend to do that?"

"When I bring him back in for the crimes he committed," Hud said. "*After* he helps us get the gold."

Mary Alice groaned. "Oh, Lordy, here we go again." And then she grinned. "At least you're talking like the Hud Jackson I know."

"They're up there, Sheriff. Now you arrest them and get them out of my house! I . . . I think they're bank robbers!"

The sound of Mother Wilkins's shrill voice carried up the stairs and through the door like a locomotive with its steam up. Hud's eyes widened in disbelief at the woman's audacity. He whipped around to Mary Alice even as heavy tramping sounded on the stairwell. To his shock, she was dropping her petticoat to the floor.

"Wha—"

"Damn that woman!" Mary Alice cursed, lifting her skirts up around her thighs. She put one foot out the window, saying, "Hide that thing, Hud, and don't look so surprised. I leave a lot of towns this way."

She was through the window and running along the porch roof toward the back of the house before he could utter a word.

"Damn!" he snapped, grabbing up the clothing and shoving it under the mattress. Today was the deadline they'd given Ward to reply, but he hadn't taken the bait. Now this. Nothing had ever gone right in this whole fiasco, he muttered to himself.

The door flew open and Mike, his old adversary at the marshal's office, stood on the threshold. The moment he spotted Hud, his mouth opened in astonishment.

Mother Wilkins hopped up and down behind him. "See? He's a criminal—"

"Hud Jackson!" Mike exclaimed, then rounded on the jumping jack box behind him. "That's no bank robber, lady. He's Hud Jackson, a U.S. marshal. At least he used to be before he resigned last month."

It was Mother Wilkins's turn to gape. Her mouth looked like a trout he'd once seen taking its last breath.

"Howdy, Mike. How's things at the office?" Hud asked, sitting down on the edge of the bed. He deliberately lounged back, relaxed. His mind, however, whirled frantically, wondering where Mary Alice was, where she would hide, and how he'd get in touch with her.

"All right," Mike said. "Sorry for the disturbance, but this woman insisted she had a couple of bank robbers living here."

Hud forced a chuckle. "Me? That's a good one, Mike."

"Where's the woman?" Mother asked, suddenly snapping to life again. "That fancy woman of yours with the sharp tongue."

Mike frowned. Hud could actually see the wheels turning in the man's mind, but whether they'd hit the mark was a long shot, knowing Mike. Still, he wasn't taking chances.

"You mean my wife?" Hud asked. "She's—"

"Wife!" Mike gaped again. "Since when did you get married?"

"A few weeks ago," Hud said, finding the lie an easy one. "After I left town. Met a wonderful woman and just couldn't walk away. You know how it is, Mike."

"Sure," Mike said dubiously. Hud knew the man stayed as far away from the marrying kind of woman as he could get.

"But . . . but . . ." the Wilkins woman sputtered. Finally, she found her voice. "He told me they were passing through town, going to Oregon. He said they were strangers—they sure *acted* strange. Didn't take meals with the others and kept to their room—"

Hud chuckled. "It's our honeymoon, Mike. We wanted to be alone."

Mother blushed bright red. Mike just grinned. "Sounds normal to me. But I thought you was livin' over at that other place . . ."

"My sister-in-law came to town with her kids. I gave up my room to them," Hud explained. The conversation seemed endless and he cursed under his breath, knowing the least show of anxiety on his part would rouse Mike's suspicions. The man wasn't entirely stupid; he just seemed that way. "I wish you could meet my wife, but she's gone out for some supplies. Last minute gewgaws, I expect."

"I didn't see her go out!" Mother snapped.

"Can't help your eyesight, lady," Hud replied.

Mike laughed.

"He threatened me!" Mother added, seeing her grand arrest slipping away. Actually, it was bounding away like a rampaging herd of buffalo, Hud thought. Now all he had to do was keep it up.

"She's a nosy woman," Hud said. "It's my honeymoon, Mike, and I had no interest in there being three of us."

Mike guffawed while Mother turned blood red. Hud waited for her to pop like a bloated tick.

Mother stamped out of the room in ruffled indignation. Mike shut the door behind him and leaned on it. Hud cursed again at the delay.

"Hell, I'm sorry, Hud," Mike said. "She's been coming down to the office three, four times a day. Finally, the boss said go and take a look, just to shut her up."

Hud swallowed at the thought of how close they'd come to being caught over the last days. Mary Alice had been right about Mother. He should have known. She was a shrewd judge of character . . .

The thought made him wonder about himself.

"You really going to Oregon?" Mike asked.

"Possibility," Hud said, deciding to stick as

close to his story as he could. "We just said that because the woman was so damned nosy."

"Picked a heck of a spot for a honeymoon," Mike said. "Surprised you didn't go to a hotel—"

"Thought this would be more quiet," Hud said to divert him. Mike was thinking again. He rose from the bed. "It's been nice talking to you, Mike."

"Good talking to you, but I better go," he said, taking the hint. "A dance girl turned up dead this morning. It looks like suicide and I gotta make the arrangements."

Hud felt certain that the girl was the one from last night, the one who had been with Walker. All roads leading, he thought.

"We . . . well, you probably could get your job back easy if you want to," Mike added, opening the door. "Oh, by the way, don't you want to know about them gunrunners of yours?"

Hud froze. He knew about *one* of them. "What?"

"Couldn't come up with anything, although Rollie went up to that place to bring those guns back. Ought to be here in a day or so."

Hud nodded. "Thanks."

Mike headed out the door. The moment it shut behind him, Hud strode to the window and stuck his head out. The porch roof was deserted, just bright sunshine on the shingles.

He left the room and went down the stairs and out the door, heading for the back stable. Maybe she'd hidden herself in there. Knowing she might have been caught if Mike had decided to search the place, he muttered, "Fool woman."

The stable was empty, more than empty. The roan mare was gone.

Hud spun around, helplessly staring at the four walls as if they'd tell him where Mary Alice had gone. Brown just stared back. If only the animal could talk. His stomach roiled at her escaping like this without a word.

"Mister."

Startled, Hud whipped toward the sound of the voice. The timid woman boarder stood just inside the doorway. She smiled tremulously, but looked as if she expected him to take her head right from her shoulders any second. She was holding a bag in her hands.

"I . . . your wife gave me a message for you—"

"What?" Hud snapped. The woman jumped at his tone. Hud forced himself to calm down. "What?"

"She said . . . she said she'd meet you at the place where you ride. But first you're to go to the post office to get a message or leave one." The woman frowned slightly in puzzlement.

"I know where and what she means," Hud said.

Her face brightened. She glanced back outside, further explanation obviously unimportant to her. "I have to go before Mother misses me, but your wife explained that her father was trying to get her back and break up your marriage. That you'd been in love since you were children and finally decided to make your own life." She sighed. "It's just so romantic."

Hud managed to keep his face straight. He should have known Mary Alice would ensure her ally's trust. This one was a doozy.

She held out the burlap bag. "Here's your things. From your room. I didn't think you'd want to go back in there, so I got them for you."

Hud took them from her, gazing at her in amazement. "Yes . . . well . . . thank you for your help."

The woman nodded. "I'm real happy to. Tell your wife . . . tell her Mr. Hoffman and I, we're going to try to strike out on our own, too."

Hud grinned. He ought to be telling these two mice not to budge from their unhappy home into a world they weren't equipped to deal with, but he couldn't. At least they were thinking for themselves for once, rather than letting Mother do the thinking for them. He threw a saddle over Brown and cinched it tight in record time, then slung the bridle over the horse's ears. "Good luck to you. And thanks. Oh, and if Mother should ask, I've gone for a ride."

The woman grinned. Hud flung himself up on Brown and guided the big horse on a flat run out of the stable.

Jerusha Tobin watched the romantic drama take its final turn out of her grey life, admiring the couple's courage to dare all for love.

She swallowed back a rush of fear and stiffened her shoulders. Maybe she could be like that if she just let herself. Maybe Mr. Hoffman could, too. And if they could, then she'd find a preacher and finally start living up to her name, which meant "one who is married." Mr. Hoffman might just make a fine husband.

She went back inside Mother Wilkins's boardinghouse to slay her own dragons.

She heard the horse's hoofbeats before she saw the animal.

Mary Alice smiled in relief as Hud and Brown rode into view on the other side of the meadow where they took their daily rides.

"Glad to see you didn't get arrested," she commented, taking hold of Brown's reins when the horse got close.

"Be a helluva thing." He grinned. "You missed a reunion with your friend Mike."

Mary Alice chuckled. "Somehow I don't think he'd appreciate it as much as I would have."

"I expect not." Hud handed down a burlap bag slung over the saddle horn, then dismounted. He gave the horse a light slap and sent him into the meadow to graze with the roan. Pointing to the bag, he added, "Courtesy of your accomplice. She said to tell you she and Mr. Hoffman were going to strike out on their own."

Mary Alice laughed. "Wouldn't that be a shock to Mother."

"And she's had plenty today." Hud started roaring with mirth. "You should have seen her face, Countess, when Mike told her I was a former marshal. I thought her eyes would pop."

"I'm sorry I missed it." She smiled mischievously. "By the way, when was the last time you paid Mother?"

Hud burst into laughter again. "I just did—

for the week."

Mary Alice made a face. "Too bad. I was hoping we'd stiffed her."

"She'd have Mike after us, with good cause this time." He grinned.

"I suppose. What else happened?"

"Nothing after that. I just told Mike that my wife was out shopping."

She chuckled. "Right across the rooftops!"

Hud pulled her to him, suddenly very sober. "You scared me to death with that stunt. Don't do it again."

She gazed up at him, all the amusement gone, rapidly replaced by something much more intimate. "I didn't know you cared."

"I care." His voice was a low growl.

His lips came down on hers. Mary Alice clung to him as she swirled with him into the dark velvet depths. All the veneer was stripped away, leaving only honest emotion and need. No matter what he did, he could always cut through her control and bring her to this point. She didn't even try to hide it, just gave herself up to the kiss.

He finally lifted his head. "Damn you, Mary Alice Macaffee."

"Damn me for what, Hud Jackson?" she whispered.

"For this." He lifted her into his arms and carried her to the edge of the meadow where the grass was soft and the trees could hide two lovers who could no longer wait.

His mood was half-gentle and half-angry and she matched it with her own. But his hands were untainted with the blood of revenge and his cries of pleasure more honest than before. Mary Alice clung to him and clung to the knowledge that she'd kept him from harm and he'd forgiven her. Even if he didn't know it yet, she knew.

And that was all that mattered.

Chapter Twenty-three

Ward came.

Hud watched the man ride in to the meadow a little after sunup. While the man guided his big white horse unerringly toward him, Hud loaded up the last of the food on the pack horse, a small sturdy Indian pony with sure feet and a gentle nature. He'd left a message at the post office and gotten both pack horse and supplies from Hansen's store the previous night, though he was positive the man wouldn't come. Mary Alice had been positive he would and had prevailed in the "discussion" beforehand.

Hud marveled at the man's willingness to face the place of his cowardice again. Hud knew if he had ever left a man to die—and he never would—he wouldn't go back for all the gold in the world.

"Can I say I told you so?" Mary Alice asked in a low voice, even as she sidled toward him as if for protection.

"Then I get to spill all the I-told-you-so's *I've*

been saving." He straightened and admitted he liked the idea of the two of them presenting a united front. The sooner Ward got that through his head, the better things would be. Hud vowed to protect her unconditionally.

Mary Alice shielded her eyes from the sun with her hand. She was wearing her travelling pants. Hud wished she wouldn't but the skirt would be too cumbersome and just as revealing once she got into the saddle. At least the pants had the advantage of giving her freedom of movement in case there was trouble. Unfortunately, the pants had the ability to create trouble in the first place.

His stomach crawled sickeningly at the notion. He wanted to ask her not to go so he wouldn't have to worry about her. Yet he couldn't do it. He knew she was capable of taking care of herself on the trail, and she was the driving force behind this expedition. And the funding and the supplies were courtesy of the Countess's "earnings." He had told her about her third part of the map so she had the knowledge for herself. If anyone had a right to be here, it was Mary Alice.

The right thing never felt so wrong in his life.

"Mr. Ward," Mary Alice said, by way of greeting.

"Miss Macaffee." The man's voice was deep and flat, devoid of emotion. "Jackson."

Hud nodded. He noticed Ward came with his pistol, rifle, bedroll, and little else. Obviously, the man took them up on their invitation at the last minute. Mary Alice's prediction about fear and greed had won out. Hud wondered where the twin devils would take them now.

Satisfied with the pack horse's burden, Hud grabbed up the roan's reins and held the horse still while Mary Alice slung herself into the saddle. He flipped her the reins, tied the rope to the pack horse onto Brown's saddle horn, then mounted up.

He turned to Ward. "Where are we headed?"

"The old Santa Fe Trail."

Hud didn't blink. "We thought so."

Ward's eyes narrowed. "You wouldn't have gotten far."

"I expect not," Mary Alice said smoothly, cutting the tension. She smiled and continued. "It was an educated guess, Mr. Ward, that the company would have come that way."

"Roger. And you're only barely right."

"Mr. Ward," Mary Alice repeated. "And I said it was a guess."

Hud smiled. "If you're ready, Ward . . ."

Ward stared at him for a moment, then swung his horse south. They slowly headed away from Denver.

Hud kept himself between Mary Alice and Ward as the three rode side by side. No one wanted to ride out in front. No one talked, either. Talking meant trust, and neither he nor Mary Alice trusted Ward to talk to him or overhear their own conversations. Hud rode with his hand low by his hip, ready to reach for his gun if necessary. He realized he'd never ridden this cautiously with Mary Alice—and not because she was a woman. For all their problems, he trusted her on a far more basic level then he'd ever trust a man.

She glanced at him and smiled knowingly as if she heard his thoughts. Hud grinned back. He hadn't meant to make love with her yesterday, but he couldn't stop himself the moment he saw she was safe. He felt as if this trip promised more than gold at the end, as if it would make stronger or break what was between them. He hadn't forgiven her for keeping her contact with Ward from him, but he could almost understand her. Almost.

He turned his attention to Ward, knowing that was where it would have to stay. Every instinct told him the trip out would be dangerous, but that wasn't where the real danger lay. It would be the moment they found the gold. *If* they found the gold.

The day passed without a word, but it put them nearer to the edge of the Front Range of the Rockies. When they encamped for the evening, Hud made sure Mary Alice's bedroll was next to his, across the fire from Ward.

Ward sat nonchalant in front of the flames, stirring the small pot of beans. Hud hadn't wanted to trust the man with the job, positive they'd be fed rat poison, but Ward had begun the task of cooking before anyone could stop him. Hud kept an eye on him as they settled in for the night. He also kept his gun at his side.

"I'm surprised you're coming on this trek, Miss Macaffee," Ward said, finally breaking the silence. "It's dangerous, especially for a woman. And your reputation will suffer."

Hud clamped his jaw against the outburst on

his lips. It would make him vulnerable to reveal his emotional state.

Mary Alive said coolly, "You'll find I'm not a namby-pamby, Mr. Ward. I can take care of myself, and my reputation is my own to handle as I see fit."

Ward laughed mirthlessly. "Your father called you his hellion. Did you know that?"

Hud felt her tense immediately. He stepped in to make light of them. "Her father wasn't off the mark."

Ward ignored him. "You have an older sister, I believe. Where is she? Why isn't she with you?"

"She's half-dead," Mary Alice said flatly.

That effectively cut off the conversation, and Hud smothered a sympathetic smile. Ward stirred the beans up, then divvied them onto the tin plates. They ate in more silence, cleaned off the plates, banked the fire for the night, and settled in.

Hud wanted to put his arm around Mary Alice and pull her into his embrace, away from Ward. But he knew he couldn't reveal the full extent of their relationship to the man. He'd use it against them. Better to keep Ward guessing, he realized.

Ward gazed at them, clearly guessing more accurately than Hud had hoped.

"You two been together long?" Ward asked.

Not to answer was as much a giveaway as saying "yes." Mary Alice replied before Hud could.

"Mr. Jackson and I are here for the same reason as you."

She said no more. Ward just looked at her speculatively, but didn't ask again. He pulled his blanket up over his shoulders and closed his eyes.

Hud hadn't wanted him asking questions, but this dismissal wasn't satisfying either. Mary Alice glanced up at him questioningly. Hud just shrugged his shoulders. She sighed and pulled up her own blanket.

Hud leaned back on his saddle, taking the first watch by general consensus. They were going pretty far south in the territory. Hud had been down that way a time or two as a sheriff, but he couldn't conceive of any place that resembled the streams and hash marks of the maps.

The rest of the first night passed. Hud kept his focus mostly on the danger that was just on the other side of the fire rather than what was beyond.

Roger Ward cursed his fate. He hadn't wanted to come, but he'd been forced to do so by their knowledge of his activities. How they had found out, he didn't know, but they could shred his life with a word. He could run, but never far enough. He couldn't kill them, much as he wanted to, because they possessed the elusive secrets in their heads.

And he wanted the gold. That damn gold he'd sold his soul for, all those years ago, only to come away with nothing but an inability to face himself in the mirror each day. Maybe if he finally got it, he would have peace.

As he rode abreast with his odd companions, he glanced over at them. The man, Hud Jackson, didn't look like John, but reminded him vividly of the companion he'd left to die all those years ago. He had the same steely will as his older brother and the same way of discerning what was inside a man. But this one was far more bold.

The woman was an enigma. He couldn't figure out what she was doing in all this. No woman would be on the trail with two men unless she was a whore. Cullen's daughter didn't act like one. She had a dignified, reserved manner, even if she wore men's clothing. She resembled Cullen, with the same dark hair and eyes, bringing back more memories to haunt him. But Cullen's emotions had always been easy to read. They used to kid him about being a lousy poker player because everyone knew when he had a good hand just by looking at him. His daughter, however, kept her feelings hidden. He hadn't given much thought to her at the saloon, as his focus was on Jackson and those precious map pieces. Yet she had been the one to play the trump card and put him on the brink of disaster.

Both of them had left him no choice but to join them.

He didn't know the nature of their relationship; they were politely at ease with each other. And they presented a solid front. For now. But he would find the chink in the armor. And he would break the chink.

Maybe then he would have the gold. And peace at last.

As the days passed, they slowly made their way

along the foothills of the Rockies. Pike's Peak thrust upward like a mighty pyramid in the sky, visible for miles and miles. They avoided the few towns and ranches, keeping to themselves.

Ward did nothing.

Mary Alice was amazed by the man's lack of interest in them as he directed them southward. Her senses screamed at the precarious tightrope she was walking. Going after the gold had been an obsession for weeks and weeks, and she still couldn't quite believe they were actually on their way. But she'd never imagined this. She felt as if she were in a dream in which she was on a trip to Hell with the devil's own.

"Maybe I need more sleep," she muttered, guiding her horse through a stand of piñon pines. The small, sharp needles pricked at her flesh to remind her it was no dream. Lack of sleep was a reality, too. She'd only dozed off and on during the nights—and uneasy dozes at that. Every time she awoke, she found Hud was awake. Each day she was grateful they had made a tentative peace between them. Her gaze strayed to him often, sometimes in lust but most times in love. She wanted to be held by him, to feel safe, but he didn't touch her. Ward was watching them. Just as they watched him.

The land changed eventually, flattening out into empty, dry plains. Hud began to sleep, and Ward began to dream.

Mary Alice was taking her turn on the unspoken watch agreement between her and Hud, when it happened. Ward twitched and muttered, at one point crying out almost painfully.

She put her hand over Hud's mouth. He came instantly awake with a start. She put her fingers to her lips for silence, then pointed to Ward.

Hud sat up and watched as Ward twisted and turned, moaning in a voice filled with despair.

"What do you suppose he's seeing?" she whispered.

"The gates of Hell," Hud replied. "No one deserves to see them more."

Ward quieted, falling back into a more natural sleep. Mary Alice released her breath and turned away. Hud was staring at her. She gazed back, knowing all her emotions were in her eyes. He reached across the short space and touched her cheek.

"Hud, please," she whispered, even as she curled into his hand. Her skin was so hungry for his touch, but she said the words she knew had to be said. "We can't."

He exhaled and pulled his hand away, then his fingers came back stronger and pulled her to him. "The hell with it. I miss touching you."

His mouth came down on hers, soft and gentle and aching. She fed from the kiss stolen in the night, her hands sliding along the sides of his face, almost clutching in an attempt to anchor herself and keep him with her.

But the kiss was far too short when he let her go. "No more temptation. We have a long haul ahead."

Tucking up her blanket to her chin in a fatherly gesture, he glanced over at the sleeping man. Ward was mumbling again.

"He'll be facing those ghosts soon," Hud muttered.

Mary Alice shook her head. "They're already here."

The journey was like the eye of a hurricane, quiet and peaceful, yet one knew the force of destruction was closing in upon them. They kept to their own thoughts, holding conversation only about making camp at night or breaking camp in the morning. Her brain idle, long suppressed questions about her father began to eat at Mary Alice again.

She wondered what had really happened with her father and Hud's brother, but to ask was to open doors better left closed—even if she got truthful answers. Ward's dreams, however, were getting stronger and stronger each day as they moved farther south. What was in those dreams? She couldn't resist pondering the answers.

The day came when they passed the tail-end of the Rockies, with hardly a break in the mountains. The peaks to the south were surprisingly white, in spite of the simmering heat.

Ward wiped the sweat from his forehead. "We didn't come up to Santa Fe from California. Too dangerous with what we were carrying. People were all over it then, especially Union calvary. We thought it was safer to come east through the Sangre de Cristo Mountains there . . ." He pointed to the southern peaks. ". . . Then ride south of the trail but parallel to it, dropping around Comanche country and right into Texas where we'd be safe."

"It was a fool's mission," Hud said. "You might have brought back enough gold to make several men wealthy, but not enough to save a country."

"We weren't the only ones to go out," Ward said. "There were others. All that gold waiting for the South in California and no way to get it by sea with the blockades. A country with its back broken suddenly sees the impossible as attainable. But it just took away men who could have fought on for the cause, and done more good there. It took the best of us."

Ward kicked his horse forward.

Mary Alice stared after the man. He'd opened up one door to the past. And he'd given her a drop of hope about her father in the process.

Hud's expression was thoughtful. Then he snapped, "The man would like to put himself with the best *now.*"

Mary Alice looked heavenward. "Maybe he was then, Hud. Tragedy changes humans, sometimes for better, sometimes for worse. Maybe leaving your brother weighs heavy on him."

"It should. But regrets come too late." Hud spurred his horse forward, effectively ending the discussion.

That night Mary Alice stirred in her sleep, uneasiness seeping through her veins along with awareness. More than her bones protested the hard-packed ground under her thin bedroll. She blinked her eyes a few times, staring up at stars like brilliant white points in a black velvet sky. She glanced to the dying fire, and across it she saw Ward staring back. She knew his gaze had awakened her.

His eyes never looked away once, and she couldn't tell what he was thinking. She wasn't sure she wanted to. Ward's gaze shifted beyond her for a second, then he turned and settled back down in his bedroll. She looked to see what had caught Ward's attention behind her and found Hud leaning up on an elbow, watching their unwelcome companion. Clearly, he'd been awakened, too, by the man's perusal.

Hud turned his gaze to her. He smiled and she smiled back, feeling relieved and protected. She'd never had another person to lean on emotionally like this, and it felt good. Better than good. Deeply satisfying. Was this the bond that held the passions of love together? No wonder people married, Mary Alice thought, her smile widening.

A silent message passed between them, and she knew Hud would keep watch for the rest of the night.

Even so, she could feel the tension building within herself and within the men. The truce between them was far too uneasy. And she reminded herself of how dangerous Ward really was. When Hud arrested him for his crimes, the truce would explode.

What, she wondered as she tried to relax back in the bedding, was in those agitated dreams he had? Were they really about the past as she and Hud surmised? Or were they about the present and what he would do when he got the gold?

Her own dreams were oddly quiet, something she never would have expected under the circumstances. Or they were about her and Hud. She only hoped she didn't express them visibly as Ward did.

Over the next days, they followed the line of the mountains, skirting the old town of Trinidad and heading across country through the Stonewall Valley. The Santa Fe Trail veered south from Trinidad into New Mexico. They were completely bypassing it. In fact, they'd barely touched the old trail, just as Ward had predicted. Now they were entering the back country of the territory.

As they passed through the valley, Mary Alice stared in wonder at the great stone wall hundreds of feet high seeming to block their path. The valley itself was a contrast of fertile green meadows and jaunty conifers. A host of colors vied for the eye—the vivid greens of the trees, the azure blue of the sky, the pristine white clouds, the solid grey of the valley walls. Spring wildflowers were blooming, and Mary Alice wanted to stop and pick dandelions for a salad to break the monotony of the three Bs of the trail—beans, bacon, and bread.

A small ranch had established itself at one end of the valley. They managed to avoid contact with its inhabitants, although straying cattle were occasionally seen. Wagon ruts were slashed deeply into the land, a testimony to those who had come through this pass looking for a better life.

"It doesn't look like you can even get to the other side," Mary Alice commented as the stone wall towered over them with no break in sight.

"There's a gap," Ward explained. "We came up through here, your father and I."

The mention of only two coming through brought the tension in the group nearly as high as the valley walls. Hud just clenched his jaw, but rode on. Mary Alice wanted to put her arms around him for comfort. He was probably hating her at the moment, too.

"Your father wanted to settle here," Ward went on, regaining her attention.

"I didn't know that," Mary Alice said, staring around the valley again with a new perspective.

Ward nodded. "He thought it was the prettiest place on God's earth, and he often said he wanted to bring his family here."

"I remember him talking about that 'prettiest' place." She smiled wistfully.

"Cullen was a fine man," Ward said. "One you could trust to the ends of the earth."

"My brother might dispute that," Hud broke in. His voice was cold with anger.

"No, he wouldn't," Ward said, then slapped the reins against his horses's withers.

Mary Alice glared at Hud for cutting Ward off from talking about the past the way he had, but a gap in the valley suddenly appeared. They slipped through the small opening, into the other side of the mountains.

Mary Alice turned and looked back to the place that would have been her home, looked at the fertile land and the beautiful rising of the wall as if they were enclosing paradise. Her father had never reached it.

How different would her life have been if he had?

The other side of the Sangre de Cristo Mountains brought change.

The land was dry and brown, with thin scrub pines competing for places to grow among the sand dunes and plateaus. After the verdant mountain valleys it was a disturbing difference in scenery. Man had not arrived here to settle yet, just passed through on a rare occasion.

Hud didn't like the absolute silence. Neither did he like the way Ward was just talking, as if to pass the time of day. Mary Alice was paying far too much attention, and she was letting down her barriers in the process. The man talked about her father a lot, making him out to be practically a saint, and Mary Alice hung onto every word. Hud could feel the division growing between them each time Ward talked. Maybe things would have been different if he hadn't been so angry about her writing to the man secretly. Yes, it had been wrong of her, but now, despite their reconciliation before leaving on this harebrained goose chase, the bonds between them hadn't mended enough. In the meantime, Ward was like a snake, slowly infiltrating while the bird, who did know better, paid it less and less attention because it didn't attack it right away.

Matters weren't helped, either, as they headed farther and farther into Southern Ute country. Hud's chest twinged as a reminder of his last encounter with them. And the Utes, mindful of the way Chivington and Custer had cleaned out most of the Cheyenne on the eastern side of the territory in '68, were less than hospitable ever since then when the whites showed up on the western side. He hadn't seen any traces of Indians yet, but that didn't mean they weren't out there.

Another set of mountains, the San Juan, bordered them on the right as they moved northwesterly, leaving them boxed in on both sides by tall peaks. Nothing looked like the parts of the map he'd had, and that lack of knowledge only made them completely dependent on Ward. The only good thing he could say was that the weather was holding.

But he wasn't liking the rest of it a bit.

"I think we're being led into a trap," Hud commented quietly to Mary Alice as they watered their horses at a small river Ward claimed was part of the Rio Grande. Ward was farther down with his horse, away from her for once.

"I don't know," she said, looking around the river. "Why would he do that? He wouldn't get the map pieces out of us and he knows it."

"I'm wondering," was all Hud would say. "Watch yourself, Countess. Remember, he was ready to put a bullet in you once."

"I haven't forgotten."

Her tone was tight with annoyance, and Hud wisely held his tongue. Instead, he said, "I miss holding you at night."

Her expression softened in a way he found utterly captivating. Mary Alice was such a strong woman that he was always amazed at her gentler moments. "I . . . Hud, we have to be careful—"

"I know," he interrupted in disgust. He had no wish for her to make that statement. At least she knew it and heeded it. He hoped. "I didn't mean anything back there about your father. It was just—"

"I know," she said, interrupting him this time. She smiled sympathetically.

". . . We're coming to it," he finished, and wondered if facing the past would cost them their future. Could he forgive what happened with his brother? Every time he looked at her, he felt he could, and every time he looked at Ward, he knew he couldn't. But she had been right about one thing: he wouldn't have been better than Ward if he'd killed him outright.

Being right all the time was really becoming an annoying habit of hers, he decided, still grinning at her.

"I found a place to cross," Ward called out.

Mary Alice smiled at the man to Hud's consternation, then pulled the roan back from the river bed and mounted up. Hud followed her, Brown protesting at yet another trek. As they crossed the river without mishap, he felt his nerves tighten to the breaking point.

That he didn't like most of all.

The first trace of the Indians came in the form of a burntout fire several days old.

Hud examined the area closely, but it was too

sandy and rocky at the same time. Feet and hooves either sunk in too deep or didn't sink at all in order to leave good traces. He straightened and said, "About the only good thing I can say is that they were in front of us maybe three days ago, so they're on their own business, not making us theirs. If they were, they wouldn't be so open about a fire."

Mary Alice cleared her throat. "Let's hope they had a good hunt and are long gone home by now."

"We're going into country they don't like," Ward said, seated atop his horse. He looked around the abandoned campsite. "It's between here and there that worries me."

Hud swung himself up on Brown's back. "Then the sooner we get there, the better off we are."

"Is this where they got . . ." Mary Alice paused. "Were you attacked around here?"

"Not that far," Ward admitted. "But it's hard to say. We were running for our lives."

Just two got their lives, Hud thought, knowing not all who ran survived. But he had to agree with Ward—between here and their destination was a whole lot of trouble waiting for them.

Mary Alice looked at him, her eyes wide with dismay. He wanted to say something in comfort, put his arms around her, and take her right out of this. But he knew she wouldn't go back because of her sister. In his mind's eye, he could still see the disturbingly vacant features of the older Macaffee daughter. Mary Alice, he knew, had seen what had caused her sister's mind to snap, and it had shaped her own attitude. Maybe he ought to remember that more often when she exasperated him.

He smiled at her and patted her arm, then swung up into the saddle. Ward looked at him with speculation. Hud stared back steadily. Maybe it was time to let the man know he couldn't trespass with Mary Alice, even if Ward didn't know the nature of his own relationship with her. He still had his precious memory of the map pieces to keep threats at bay for now—and Mary Alice safe.

He had to be honest with himself and admit that they never would have gotten this far without Ward's guidance. But he wasn't forgiving the man, and he wasn't trusting him, either.

Especially when it came to Mary Alice.

Chapter Twenty-four

They were nearly over the San Juan Mountains, leaving the Rio Grande behind, when Ward halted the small party.

He pulled his gun and cocked it, aiming it squarely at Hud's chest.

Mary Alice bit back a scream. Hud didn't move.

Ward said, "My part of the map runs out here in these damn mesas. Now which one of you has it?"

"We wouldn't be telling you," Hud said.

"You're going to have to if you want to get there," Ward replied. "But I'm damned if either of you'll shoot me dead now that I'm through. Mary Alice, take a rope and tie Jackson up."

"No," she said, shocking even herself. She'd just put Hud's life in more jeopardy. Ward looked at her in amazement, but she persisted, "We had an agreement, Mr. Ward. We'll honor our part."

He glared at her. "You maybe, but not him."

Mary Alice laughed. She couldn't help it. "Hud's far more honorable than I am, believe me.

I expect it's from being a U.S. Marshal."

"Marshal!" Ward's eyes narrowed. "Damn you, what the hell is this?"

"A private matter between you, me, and Mary Alice that's got nothing to do with my job," Hud said, not bothering to add details about the exact status of his employment. His gaze was steely, and Mary Alice could feel the waves of anger emanating from him. "Put down the gun, Ward, or we won't go any farther."

Ward's hand never moved. Mary Alice swallowed a lump of fear in her throat, knowing neither man would back down. Nothing killed a man faster out here than showing weakness. She realized Hud was more important than anything, and she'd never told him. Fear of another kind was driving Ward at the moment, revealing his unstable emotional state.

"I can't trust you," Ward said, an edge of panic in his tone.

Her heart beating right out of her chest, Mary Alice said, "Yes, you can. And as Hud is so fond of telling me, Mr. Ward, you've got no choice."

"How do I know you won't shoot me now?" he demanded.

Hud snorted. "Don't tar us with your own brush. And don't waste our time here unless you want the Utes to find us."

Suddenly a vision of the two map pieces as Hud had held them that night at Mother's boardinghouse came full into Mary Alice's head, as if her brain had opened a locked door leading to vivid sunlight. She could see the details on each one, could see the zigzag lines of one mountain interspersed by one higher with two peaks on either end . . . and could see that same formation on the mountain peaks running directly on the right.

Mary Alice blinked and looked again. The mountains still followed the pattern. She knew exactly where they were. And all the rest of the map patterns were imprinted in her mind. Within those peaks somewhere was a crossing they had to take.

She could open her mouth right now and eliminate Hud from the race to get the gold. She could ensure that he'd never send her back to jail. She could ensure her cut of the gold was even more than a third. She and Harriet would be secure for life.

Mary Alice didn't consider the questions. She kicked the roan between the men, putting herself in the path of the bullet. Half her brain screamed at her that she was insane, and the other half was overjoyed she was taking action to protect her man.

"Gentlemen," she began, keeping the quaver of terror out of her voice. She wasn't brave, just desperate. "You can fool around here until Doomsday or when the Utes find you, but I'm going to get the gold. I suggest you don't shoot Hud, Mr. Ward. He has the last part of the map, so I think keeping him in one piece will serve you better."

"Mary Alice, get out of the damn way!" Hud snapped.

She flashed him a grin. "I don't think so. The

mountains over southwest of us are the next step . . ."

Hud stiffened, not enough for Ward to notice but Mary Alice wondered what surprised him like that. Maybe he didn't expect her to give away any part of their map.

Ignoring him, Mary Alice continued, ". . . We're going. If you're that afraid of what we'll do, Mr. Ward, then don't come with us. But why bring us this far if you don't want the gold?"

"Damn you!" Ward burst out angrily. "I ought to kill you both."

"But you won't," Mary Alice said, playing a hunch. "It'd be like killing John again—and Cullen this time, too. You've become a lot of things, but you haven't gone that far."

Ward's gun never moved. "How the hell do *you* know what I am?"

"I only know what you were," she said softly. "Otherwise my father never would have ridden with you."

Myriad emotions crossed Ward's face. Finally, he seemed to shake the worst off and Mary Alice could see the danger level lower.

He said,"My gun stays out."

"Then it stays out," Hud said, tapping Brown forward. "Just make sure it doesn't go off."

Mary Alice sent the roan at a steady pace next to Hud. Ward hovered for a second, then joined them. His gun hand rested on the saddle horn, but the gun itself had had the hammer eased back into the safety position. She wanted to slump in the saddle with relief, but didn't dare. At least she'd kept Hud safe for a time.

Later, much later, as they settled into camp in the lee of a small mesa, Hud murmured to her, "You saved my life. Thank you. And don't ever do anything so stupid again."

A little genuine gratitude without the lecture would have been nice, she thought, spreading out her blanket. But she realized he was angry because she'd endangered herself for him. "You're welcome. I think."

"How the hell did you know?"

"Know what?" she asked, watching Ward seated far from them on the other side of the clearing. Cooking fires hadn't been made since they crossed the Sangre De Cristos. The man gnawed on some stale bread, his gun openly at his side. She continued, "That he didn't want to shoot—?"

"No. The mountains, that little pass we went through," Hud said.

"Oh. I remembered my map piece."

"That mountain pass was John's map piece, from his watch, not your father's." His expression was a combination of disbelief and confusion. "You know what was on both pieces, don't you?"

She nodded, wanting to confess. "I remembered suddenly how you held them that night at Mother's, and I could see all the markings again."

"You don't need me for the rest of this now," he said. He clenched his jaw so hard it looked ready to shatter.

"No more than you ever needed me in the first place," she replied. She took a deep breath. "I love you, Hud, and I want you to know you can trust me."

Hud cursed, startling her. Her heart lurched with grief.

"You picked a helluva time to tell me," he said, suddenly grinning at her.

"Are you . . . happy about it?" she asked, unsure of his reaction.

"I'm not sure being in love with you will be peaceful," he said. "That would be a miracle. But I know damn well when I'm licked."

Mary Alice didn't know whether to throw her arms around him or strangle him. Finally, she muttered, "It's nice to know you feel the same way. Maybe."

Chuckling, Hud flicked his blanket not far from hers, within arm's reach as always. "You put me through Hell, Countess. Anyway, I'm not one to stand on my head and shout it from the rooftops."

"It'd be nice," she told him. But she sighed, admitting to herself that he was as unexpected for her as she obviously was for him. "I suppose this isn't the place for that, either.

"Don't think so." Hud glanced over at Ward, then back. His gaze practically raked over her, as if he were stripping off her clothes piece by piece. She was hot, tired, and dirty, yet all of that fell away with his lambent look.

"I'd kill the man just to be alone with you," he murmured. "This is sheer torture."

"I know." She found herself watching his hands as they did the ordinary tasks of putting his bedroll in order. She wanted them desperately on her body, turning it into a living flame that took her to the brink and beyond. Never had she thought he would say he cared for her, let alone that he loved her. What would come after this, she didn't know, but she'd cherish what he said.

"Do you think we'll get out of this alive?" she asked.

"Good question. I don't know who I'm more worried about." Hud lifted his chin. "Indians, or our friend there. He's getting nervous."

Mary Alice was more worried about what would happen if they got out.

When they got out.

The dreams were no longer dreams.

Roger Ward lurched in the saddle as the landscape suddenly swam before his eyes. He was already so tired, he thought, and now he had to guard himself even more carefully from the other two. His gun was ready at all times during the day. At night it was next to his side.

He'd thought the dreams had been bad when this journey had begun. Now . . . now they were haunting him continually. John's face and Cullen's would appear before him from nowhere, bringing back in vivid detail the run they'd made through this godforsaken place. All flat-topped mesas and stunted pine, with land brown and unforgiving. Unforgiving just like John. Just like Cullen had become. If only he could remember the route they'd taken those years ago. He would think he did, but then the girl would turn in another direction and he'd realize hers was the true way, not the one his faulty memory produced.

He kept Jackson and Mary Alice almost literally in his sights. And he couldn't sleep. He had to watch that they didn't kill him during the night. He had to be ready. Damn Cullen's daughter, he thought. She'd known he couldn't kill one of them without losing that part of the map. She kept a cool head that day to save the man. They worked as a team, those two. And they could kill him and keep all the gold.

He didn't believe the nonsense about being able to trust them. He just didn't believe it . . .

A movement to his right caught his eye and he jerked in that direction. A figure seemed to materialize by a piñon pine. Tall and pale, the figure seemed to be missing a leg. Ward stared at it, wanting to shout to the other two, but his voice was paralyzed. No sound emerged. The face of the figure was accusing. A second form slowly coalesced, this one two-footed but emaciated. Disappointment filled this one's features.

John and Cullen were back, in broad daylight. Ward wanted them to get away from him, go away forever back to the hell where they belonged.

Kill them, he thought, but his hand never stirred.

The figures wavered finally and were gone. His companions rode casually, their attention forward along the canyon floor between the mesas. Obviously, they hadn't seen what he'd seen.

He hated them for it.

* * *

They travelled three days through some of the worst country in the territory.

Hud kept himself between Mary Alice and Ward. He didn't know how much longer it would be before the man cracked. His eyes were blood red and glazed from lack of sleep. At times he swayed in the saddle with exhaustion, his hands shaking dangerously. He seemed to stare off in the distance, and a wild look would come over him. His devils were riding him high and hard—Hud didn't know when they would overtake Ward and their own time would run out.

He ought to kill the man, just to keep them safe. Yet he couldn't do it. He pitied Ward . . . and he didn't want to stoop to that level. He couldn't arrest him yet, either. He'd made a bargain with Mary Alice about that, and he would keep it, although he had a feeling he might regret it. Besides, Ward wouldn't leave them now, and that meant Hud only had to fight him on the way out. If they got out.

And then there was Mary Alice. His mind still reeled at the way she'd put herself directly in the path of Ward's gun to save his life. He wanted to kill her himself for doing such a foolish thing . . . and he loved her beyond words for it. Then she told him she loved him. She gained absolutely nothing by saying it, just as she gained nothing by trying to save him. For all the times he couldn't trust what she said, she'd made up for it spectacularly.

When they were done with this, if they ever got themselves out of it alive, he and she had some serious settling to do.

Eventually the party rounded several mesas, following a natural pathway along the canyon floors. The land got quieter. Hud couldn't explain it, but it was as if the birds had been abruptly choked off. Even the breeze had stopped. The silence was eerie. The canyon walls narrowed, bringing three streams to converge as one, and he realized where they were. At the last piece of the map. Mary Alice had brought them straight to the end.

He kicked his horse forward, unmindful of the sudden clatter of rocks and dirt he left behind. Mary Alice recognized the place at almost the same moment, spurring the roan after him. Ward gave a yelp of surprise as he awakened from his trance and forced his horse to catch up.

They squeezed through the last canyon and the vista immediately opened out on a line of cliffs rimming the far end. Everyone pulled up their horses.

The cliffs were riddled with hundreds of openings, terraces and brick buildings built right onto the stone as if at one time a city had been cut into the sheer rockfaces. Stairs carved in the cliffs ran every which way, joining together the various dwellings. No creature stirred, human or animal.

Mary Alice gasped. Hud stared in amazement. Ward murmured, "Here. We're here!"

"Do people still live here?" Mary Alice asked, craning to look at the top of the cliffs.

"No," Ward said. "It's haunted. Sacred ground now to the Indians."

Hud muttered a curse, having a bad feeling about the cliff houses. The last thing he wanted to do was trespass on any peoples' hallowed ground. "The Utes won't appreciate this."

"They didn't the last time," Ward said. He sounded almost civil.

Mary Alice shook her head. "I'm not sure I like this."

"It's where the gold is," Ward reminded her. "We brought the wagons in here for safety, because you can defend the opening with just a few men. We nearly trapped ourselves, though. We hid the gold up there." He pointed to the cliff dwellings. "Somewhere."

Hud knew where. The hash markings he and Mary Alice had thought were railroad tracks were actually the stairs, or a set of stairs to one of the dwellings. He gazed along the cliff face while dredging up the map piece in his mind. Then he spotted the distinctive circle of stones the map piece indicated high up to the far right.

"Over there!" Hud said, urging Brown forward.

Mary Alice and Ward breasted him as they all raced for the bottom of the stairs.

"What do we do with the horses?" she asked, even as they halted at the beginning of the cliffs. They weren't quite sheer, but the slope was extremely steep.

"Take them up as far as we can," Ward shouted, dismounting. True to his word, he began the ascent, dragging his hesitant horse behind him.

Hud looked at Mary Alice. The expression in her eyes was half-excited and half-wary.

"I can't believe we're here," she said.

Hud grinned slowly. "I can't believe there is a 'here.'"

"Do you think it's safe to go up with the horses?"

Hud glanced at Ward, now more than halfway up the stairway. "It looks like it'll accommodate a horse single file at least a part of the way. No worse than a narrow ledge, and no better, unfortunately. But it seems it's been done before."

They dismounted and coaxed their horses up the stairs, Hud going first just in case Ward was thinking of ambushing them at the top. He left the packhorse behind, knowing he couldn't control two animals at once on the steps. He'd come back for it if he needed it.

Halfway up to the top, the stairs leveled out into a terrace. Ward's horse stood near the cliff face, nibbling on some spindly bushes. Ward was nowhere to be seen.

They left Brown and the roan with the other horse and made their way into the first opening. Hud took Mary Alice's hand in his, squeezing her fingers in reassurance.

"Where is he?" she whispered, gazing around the large room.

"I don't know." Hud drew his gun. He turned to her. "Can I persuade you to stay and watch the horses?"

She shook her head. "Are you kidding?"

"Hoping." He sighed, knowing he could no more order her to stay than order the man in the moon to stop coming out at night. He held up his firearm. "Got yours?"

"Yes." She nodded and patted her jacket pocket.

"Good. According to the map piece, this room led back into a series of rooms with inner stairs, like a mansion."

"Let's hope your memory isn't failing," she commented.

He grinned at her. "I remember the way you moan very well."

She made a face at him. "That was you who did the moaning."

"That was both of us. Come on, before you start a fight neither of us can win."

They made their way cautiously through the rooms, the joking vanquishing their anxiety only for a moment. Sunlight filtered through the door-like opening, providing a little illumination which was then reduced by the low ceilings. Natural debris swept along the corners and a faint musky animal scent, like nesting foxes or skunks, was noticeable. The whole place was ghostly silent, and Hud wondered about the people who had built these cliff dwellings. Who were they, and why weren't they here? But as they climbed the inner stairs, his heart began to pound with more than wariness.

"Do you think the gold's really here?" Mary Alice asked eagerly, voicing his own overriding question.

"It'd better be, otherwise we've taken a helluva ride for nothing."

They entered the upper rooms slowly, Hud taking good long looks before they ventured into the place. Noises came from one of the forward rooms. They followed them.

Ward was kneeling in front of several piles of burlap against a wall. More debris was scattered around the pile, as if torn away in haste. He was laughing and stuffing his pockets with chunks of dullish rock.

"It's still here!" he said gleefully, holding up a gold chunk. "I can't believe after all these years it's still here. Look at this, Mary Alice."

Mary Alice moved forward to the pile. She picked up a piece of gold and held it up. "It looks like a rock."

"It's gold," Ward said, grinning. "Unpolished, but real. But only some of it's raw. The rest is bullion and coin. We hauled it up here—took forever."

Ward was relaxed with no weapon in sight and nothing from the past seeming to haunt him. It was as if he'd made it through the worst and was normal again—as normal as a man like him could get, Hud opined. He holstered his gun, still ready to draw if he needed to.

He said, "But the Indians . . . weren't they attacking you when you got here—?"

"They had before, several miles out," Ward answered, opening his shirt and stuffing more nuggets inside. "When we saw they were on our trail again, we hid the gold here. They didn't venture beyond the valley opening. They weren't crossing their forbidden ground. We threw some dirt and leaves over the bags to hide them. Looks like it worked. No one's been here since. But getting out of the valley wasn't as easy." Ward stood, staggering under the added weight as he did so. "We need to get this loaded up."

Hud stared at the pile, tried to calculate its weight. "The horses can't carry all this."

"Yes, they can!" Ward snapped. "They have to. I'm not leaving any of it again."

He picked up a smallish bag and left the room, heading for the stairs.

Hud watched Ward go, deciding to fight the battle over what could be carried later. He turned back to the gold. Mary Alice had found a coin bag and was letting the glittering pieces slide through her fingers. Time had barely tarnished them. He joined her, amused by her actions. Digging his own hand into the bag, he felt the hard metal coldly caress his skin.

"Feels wonderful," Mary Alice murmured.

"Not as wonderful as you," Hud said, smiling. He leaned over and kissed her, the warmth of her lips sending him spinning far more than any precious metal could ever do.

She sighed when he lifted his head. "You're right."

He chuckled. "You sound almost disappointed."

She kissed him again, longer and more intimately until he was ready to take her then and there. She finally eased away, murmuring, "Never."

Hud sat back on his haunches to allow his equilibrium to return to normal. He stared at the pile of gold. Wealth beyond any he'd ever dreamed of was before him. Amazing, he thought in wonderment. "It really is here."

Mary Alice grinned at Hud as she hefted as much as she could of the small rotting bags. "I agree with Ward. We have to try to take it all back, you know. How can we leave it? Look at it, Hud. Enough to help my sister and your brother's family . . ."

Coins spilled out from a sudden hole in the bag, and she pressed her hand over the spot before it split some more.

Hud grinned at her. "Talk about leaving a trail. Here, wait for me."

He got a bigger bag, the weight of it sagging in his arms, and rose to his feet. As they left the room, they passed Ward coming back in. He was rubbing his hands together in anticipation. Ever mindful of the man's betrayals, Hud couldn't help grinning at the sight.

The three of them passed up and down the stairs, carrying the gold out to the horses. Hud was careful to stay with Mary Alice. Ward was cheerful, but Hud still didn't trust him. Anyway, Ward wouldn't be happy when he was arrested for his railroad crimes—something just about to happen. The pile grew on the small terrace until it was obvious that the four animals could never carry the load. Mary Alice brought down the last of the bags, coins trailing unheeded behind her.

Hud's legs felt wobbly from all the climbing and Mary Alice was flushed and perspiring, but she grinned at him. Hud opened his mouth to voice his opinion about how much could be carried by the horses. But he never got the words out.

Cheerful Roger Ward was glaring murderously

at him, his gun already drawn. It had been the ominous click of the hammer being pulled back that had captured Hud's attention. Gold fever had finally overtaken the man's mind.

"Mr. Ward, what are you doing?" Mary Alice began in overly soothing tones.

Motioning with the gun, Ward said, "Get over there with him."

"What is this?" Hud demanded as a stall while his brain scrambled to assess the situation. He cursed himself for letting his guard down even slightly.

"I'm afraid you're joining your brother, and you, your father," Ward replied. His eyes were wild with emotion. "You'll kill me now—"

"No, we won't," Mary Alice said. "We made a promise—"

"Lies!" Ward screeched. "All lies! You'll kill me for my gold. *My* gold! I hid it here, not you! I lost everything for this, everything, not you! It's mine, I tell you. I deserve it, not you!"

Hud's heart thumped painfully in his chest. Not for himself, but fear for Mary Alice. He didn't want her to die, not ever. Not like this, over gold. It was nothing compared to her. Somehow, he had to stop Ward.

"We'll give you the gold," Mary Alice said. "You do deserve it, more than we do."

Ward gaped at her. So did Hud.

"I wanted it for my sister," she went on. "Harriet's mind snapped. She's with nuns in St. Louis, but her care is costly. And Hud wanted it for his brother's family, who have been evicted from their farm. But it's obvious you do deserve it more." Mary Alice smiled warmly. Hud held his breath, waiting to see if Ward would accept it and put away his gun. His own brain came up with absolutely nothing to alter the situation.

Ward rubbed his temple as if his head ached unbearably. "You're lying. You're both liars. You'll kill me, I know it. You have to because of . . . of before."

"No," Hud said, willing himself to speak. "You are just . . . upset. We understand." He hated to say the words, wanted to kill Ward now, but the man had to be defused first to protect Mary Alice. His gun was out, and Hud's wasn't.

"Not then!" Ward screamed. "Before . . . *I* left your brother. I told Cullen he was dead! I thought he was—he wasn't answering me. Cullen didn't know, and he didn't look. The Indians were right on us. We had to ride out hell for leather—"

Something whizzed between them on near-silent wings, then thunked into the terrace floor beyond, turning into an arrow as it skittered along the stones. It came to rest against the far wall.

All three of them stared at it in complete astonishment. Another shot right past Hud's left ear, just missing it and missing Ward by less than a foot.

"Duck!" Hud shouted, throwing Mary Alice down behind the safety of the gold pile. Ward was already crouched and peering over the terrace ledge when Hud joined him. Both had their guns drawn.

"There's a group of 'em around the foot of the

stairs," Ward said, keeping his gaze focused downward. "Maybe twenty, maybe more. They didn't dare come into the valley last time, too respectful of their dead. That's what we figured."

"Looks like they're not so respectful this time," Hud said, then he realized how all of them had reacted without thought to the common threat. Ward could have easily killed him in those first seconds, yet he hadn't. And he hadn't now.

Ward suddenly fired his gun. Down on the valley floor, someone screamed. A hail of arrows rained over the terrace edge. Hud shouted again for Mary Alice to keep low, even as he and Ward lay flat for cover. The arrows overshot them harmlessly. The horses whinnied in fright, their hooves clattering on the stones as they danced away from the menace.

"You all right?" Hud called back to Mary Alice.

Mary Alice tried to answer and found her voice could only croak incoherently. Her entire body was frozen in a scream that just wouldn't emerge.

"Mary Alice!"

Finally, she took a deep breath, forced the terror racing through her to slow down, and managed a shaky "Yes."

Hud smiled encouragingly and turned back to this latest threat. He looked so calm, she thought in amazement. How could he be so calm? She wanted to throw herself into his arms and hold him forever. But if she had to die with anyone, at least it was with him.

She asked the question uppermost in her mind. "Got any suggestions on how we get out of this?"

"Not really, love," Hud replied, inching toward the edge of the terrace again so he could see where the Indians were. He fired off a few shots. Another barrage of arrows followed without injury to anyone. Mary Alice hugged the gold pile tighter, deciding the arrows had been too close for comfort, most of them falling along the back wall of the terrace. The horses shied away from the few that had come their way.

The cat and mouse game with the Utes continued, with several more forays being halted. It was obvious that the terrace was easily defended by two, with no chance of being surprised or overwhelmed. Of course, that was until the bullets ran out.

Mary Alice realized that she was hiding again, just like the time her mother had locked her away in the barn when the Union soldiers had come. She did nothing then while people died protecting her. She couldn't allow it a second time, she decided, pulling together all the courage she had. She loved Hud, and she needed him. And he needed her right now. At least she'd be fighting this time.

She crept forward, knees and hands scraping on the uneven paving, until she reached the men. Hud glanced at her, his face immediately turning livid.

"Dammit! Get back!" he snapped.

"No." Her jaw was set and she gathered all the defiance she had into her gaze. "I can at least shoot enough to scare the bejesus out of them."

"It's safer back there," Hud said, even as he turned back to his vigil.

"Safer!" She snorted in disgust while drawing her gun. "That's where all the arrows land! I'm not staying back there to get killed. And you may be grateful for my help in the end."

What a welcome, she thought. If they ever got out of this, she'd teach Hud a few manners. Her heart pounded with terror, and she wondered if she'd just made the worst mistake of what was left of her short life.

"Last time, we went right up the stairs to the top of the cliffs," Ward said, interrupting them. He pointed behind and up. He also sounded sane and sensible again, as was his expression, the gold madness seemingly gone with this new threat. He continued, "There's a way down on the other side that takes you around the valley. If you go northeast, you'll hit the Rio Grande again."

Mary Alice glanced back at the upper stairwell. It was steeper and narrower than the lower one.

"Someone's got to stay behind," Ward suddenly said. "To keep them busy for as long as he can, so you can get away."

A funny kind of look came into his eyes that to her seemed determined and regretful all at once. Hud said nothing, just assessed the man.

"Somebody's got to stay," Ward repeated. "I . . . I see them all the time, you know. John and Cullen . . . and the others. They haunt me like the Utes believe this place is haunted. If I kill you, they'll make me go mad. I know that now. I owe this, and if I stay maybe they'll stop."

Mary Alice knew he meant his own ghosts.

"Now you need to trust me," Ward said, even as

he condemned himself to a horrible death. "Take your horses and go. Leave mine, in case I can get out. Go now or you may never get another chance. Go!"

Mary Alice didn't know what impulse prompted Hud to trust Ward, but she found herself being dragged away from the edge. Ward never once looked at them as they left him.

When they were far enough away from the edge of the terrace, Hud grabbed her upright and ran for the horses.

"But the gold!" she protested, glancing back.

"Forget it!" Hud snapped. "There's no time."

And then she saw the strangest thing. Wispy shapes moved forward along the terrace toward Roger Ward. She gaped as they took an almost solid form on either side of the living man. Ward never looked at them, yet his shoulders seemed to swell with a pride long lost.

"Hud," she whispered, knowing who the figures were, knowing she was seeing her father for one last time. Tears misted over her gaze.

"Sweet Jesus," he murmured, his hand tightening on her arm.

They stood and stared at the sight of three men, two in grey, one older, defending their final mission together, all honor redeemed.

Suddenly, Hud yanked the reins from the bush they were tied to and thrust the roan's into her hands. "Move, come on. Now!"

He slapped the roan on the rump, sending her into a startled trot. Shots rang out behind them. Mary Alice ran for the upper stairs, the roan with her. Hud followed with Brown.

The horses balked at the steps. Hud slapped the roan so hard she whinnied and bolted, nearly knocking Mary Alice off the stairs completely in her haste to get away from the pain. Mary Alice felt her feet slip out from under her as the roan crowded against her. She pushed away from the rim of the steps and struggled up to the top, the roan on her heels.

She no sooner got on level ground when Hud nearly leaped over the steps with Brown.

"Mount up!" he shouted, swinging onto his horse.

Mary Alice flung herself onto the roan, sending the animal on a run across the cliff top. They broke into the cover of a thick copse of firs and shrubs, finding the pathways through to the other side instinctively.

Getting off the mesa was easier than getting on, just as Ward had said. They guided the horses down the gentler descent to the valley floor and ran straight northeast. By some miracle the Indians hadn't posted anyone there, or hadn't known to, as no one stopped them.

Shots were heard reverberating off the valley walls, fainter and fainter over the rhythmic clatter of the horses' hooves. Clearly, Ward was keeping the Utes busy while they made their escape.

They rode hard for as long as they could, skirting valleys and mesas, not caring who might see them, until the horses were dangerously winded. Even though they didn't feel safe, they slowed to a walk to cool the animals.

"Do you think we got away?" Mary Alice asked, looking behind them.

"Hard to say," Hud allowed. "From them, I think. But there's a whole lot of others out here. This is their country. Come here."

He pulled her half out of the saddle and kissed her, his mouth roving over her lips with hot fire and gratitude. She returned the kiss with her heart and soul, giving all her love to him. The horses walked along, their movements leaving the humans clinging to each other.

He eased his mouth away and whispered, "I love you. Thank God you're all right."

She sighed contentedly. If the Utes found them right now, she'd die a happy woman. "I love you, Hud. I think I have for a long time."

He kissed her again, longer and softer this time before finally letting her go. "If I don't pay attention, the Utes'll be putting marks in my chest again."

"Think I ought to get out my dress from Young Otter?" she asked.

"Somehow, I don't think that'll work twice."

"Do you think we saw what we saw?" she asked, needing to know.

Hud nodded, smiling slightly. "I think they've forgiven Ward."

She didn't ask if he thought the man would escape, too. Both knew the answer. Roger Ward had joined his companions for all time.

She groaned at one thought. "All that gold, Hud, and I didn't even put a nugget in my pocket!"

"I'm glad one of us had some brains," he said, reaching behind him and flipping open the flap of his near saddlebag. Coin sacks crammed the bag nearly to the brim.

Mary Alice gasped in astonishment.

Hud chuckled. "It's nice to see you speechless. Those occasions are few and far between. By the way, the other saddlebag is just like this one."

"When did you do that?"

"When you were bringing down that last load. I stuck them in, thinking why should we waste the time putting them on the pile only to pick them up and load them on the horses anyway."

Mary Alice began to laugh. "You, of all people!"

He grinned crookedly. "It was innocent, honest. I suppose the packhorse is an exchange of sorts."

"I think I'd better marry you," Mary Alice announced. "Just to keep you out of trouble."

"I think you'd better, too," Hud replied in the most angelic of voices. "Lord knows what kind of trouble I'll cause if I'm let loose on the world."

"Who knows," she murmured, then leaned over, grabbed up a handful of his shirt, and pulled him close to meet her kiss. "A marshal's wife. God help me—who would've thought?"

Hud just laughed.

Days later, they made it to the Stonewall Valley, and they never left it again, having found their hearts' content.

Epilogue

1876

"Look at this!"

Mary Alice tapped the page of the weeks-old newspaper in disgust. Lying next to her in their bed, Hud glanced over his wife's bare shoulder to read that silver had been discovered at Leadville in the Sawach Mountains, a huge mother lode worth millions.

"You're retired, and the Countess doesn't exist anymore," he said firmly.

"I know," she muttered, giving him a pointed look.

He kissed her thoroughly. The kiss began as a reminder of their new life, but it turned quickly into something more intimate. When he finally lifted his mouth from hers, he murmured, "I can't be spending all my time in bed with you. Somebody's got to run this ranch."

She chuckled. "Who got lazy and wanted to

sleep late?"

He whipped the covers back and pressed his naked body to hers, the touch of flesh to flesh igniting his senses. "Who says we'll sleep?"

She smiled lazily and wrapped her arms around his neck, the newspaper falling from her fingers. It was all the invitation he needed.

When they finally rose to start the day, Mary Alice was the epitome of decorum in her gingham apron. She was happy. He knew it from the smile she gave him in the morning to the mischievous grin at night—every night.

He grabbed up a couple of slices of day-old bread, slathered them with apple butter, and stepped out onto the porch. The Stonewall valley had grown some since that first small ranch, theirs joining it. He marshalled here in the southern end of Colorado, too, upholding the law when necessary. Mary Alice was fond of pointing out she was in a self-made prison, so he didn't have to worry about her. Life was pretty quiet, though, just the way he liked it—just blizzards, floods, and predators. Statehood had been applied for and was expected to be approved by Congress. Hud wasn't quite sure how he felt about joining the Union, but the war was long over.

His son romped across to the paddocks to watch his nephew John break a mustang. Young Michael was nearly three and a handful for his nurse, Rosita, who was hurrying after him.

"Not too close!" Hud called out, grinning. They ignored him, but Michael didn't duck under the fence poles. The makings of a hellion, he acknowledged ruefully—with love.

Missy had married her storekeeper, but John had come with them to the valley instead of joining the army. He was going to college back east next year—if he could stop making moon eyes at Rosita. Mary Alice's sister was well cared for in St. Louis. They had thought of bringing her to live with them but the upheaval would have done more damage to her. The nuns had practically elevated Mary Alice to sainthood when they'd given them the rest of the money.

In the fall of the year they had found the gold, the Cheyenne and Arapaho chiefs had gone to Washington to see President Grant, feeling they had been ousted from their lands while the government held that they'd ceded them away. They'd held firm for three years, until it had culminated with Custer at Little Big Horn. Hud wondered if Young Otter had participated and admitted the whole affair was right and just.

"You going to let Luke do all the work today?" the saint asked, emerging from the house.

"Maybe." He put his arm around her when she came up next to him. He loved the feel of her next to his heart.

She sighed. "All that silver in the hands of idiots. Hud, you don't suppose . . ."

"No, I don't suppose, Countess." But he laughed.

"A marshal's wife and now a rancher's wife," she commented. "Who'd have thought?"

"Just you and just me," he said.

And kissed her.